"You're going to hold this book so tight you'll leave thumbprints on the page." —Mark Leggatt, author of *The London Cage*

"A superb political as well as military thriller, *The Red Line* stitches an all-too-plausible doomsday scenario that pulls no punches in scoring a literary knockout. Terrifyingly prescient in its premise and scarily spot-on in its execution, Walt Gragg's debut novel channels both Tom Clancy and W.E.B. Griffin."

—Jon Land, *USA Today* bestselling author of *Strong Cold Dead*

"[An] impeccably researched, riveting first novel . . . Must reading for any military action fan. Nearly every page reeks of the smoke of battle and the stench of death." —*Publishers Weekly* (starred review)

THE RUSSIANS HAD MADE THEIR MOVE.

Jensen lunged toward the radio. He had to get Brown and his men away from the border. It was their only chance. If they were going to inflict maximum damage on the enemy and hope to somehow live to see another sunrise, he had to get his overmatched soldiers into the protective cover of the welcoming tangle of German forest. And he had to do it now.

The lieutenant's Humvee chose that exact moment to burst from the woods. His hand already positioned to key his headset, he beat Jensen to the punch.

"Open fire!" Powers screamed. "Open fire!"

He squeezed the trigger of his machine gun, firing wild bursts toward the border.

"No-o-o!" Jensen shrieked into the platoon radio. "Fall back! Fall back! Brownie, get everyone into the trees and set up defensive positions!"

Jensen was, however, too late. None of them heard him over the battle erupting in every direction.

W9-BZJ-538

DISCARD

THE RED LINE

WALT GRAGG

BERKLEY

NEW YORK

PUBLIC LIBRARY
EAST ORANGE PUBLIC LIBRARY

Gragg

BERKLEY
An imprint of Penguin Random House LLC
375 Hudson Street, New York, New York 10014

Copyright © 2017 by Walter Gragg
Penguin Random House supports copyright. Copyright fuels creativity, encourages
diverse voices, promotes free speech, and creates a vibrant culture. Thank you for buying
an authorized edition of this book and for complying with copyright laws by not
reproducing, scanning, or distributing any part of it in any form without permission.
You are supporting writers and allowing Penguin Random House to continue to
publish books for every reader.

BERKLEY is a registered trademark and the B colophon is a trademark of
Penguin Random House LLC.

Library of Congress Cataloging-in-Publication Data

Names: Gragg, Walt, author.
Title: The red line / Walt Gragg.
Description: New York, New York : Berkley, 2017.
Identifiers: LCCN 2016041996 (print) | LCCN 2016054963 (ebook) |
ISBN 9780425283455 (paperback) | ISBN 9780698409842 (ebook) |
Subjects: LCSH: World War III—Fiction. | Imaginary wars and battles—Fiction. |
Russia—Fiction. | Germany—Fiction. | United States—Fiction. | BISAC:
FICTION / Suspense. | FICTION / War & Military. | FICTION / Action & Adventure. |
GSAFD: War stories. | Suspense fiction.
Classification: LCC PS3607.R3326 R43 2017 (print) | LCC PS3607.R3326 (ebook) |
DDC 813/.6—dc23
LC record available at https://lccn.loc.gov/2016041996

First Edition: May 2017

Printed in the United States of America
1   3   5   7   9   10   8   6   4   2

Cover art: Tank on dirt road © 508 collection / Alamy Stock Photo;
Abrams Main Battle Tank platoons © 615 collection / Alamy Stock Photo
Cover design by Pete Garceau
Book design by Kelly Lipovich
Map by Kelly Lipovich

This is a work of fiction. Names, characters, places, and incidents either are the product
of the author's imagination or are used fictitiously, and any resemblance to actual persons,
living or dead, business establishments, events, or locales is entirely coincidental.

To my wife, Jeri. My friend, my love, my life.
Without you, it wouldn't have been possible.
Without you, it would have no meaning.

ACKNOWLEDGMENTS

Few writers have the opportunity to work with the editor and agent of their choosing. I am surely one of the lucky ones. No one could ever collaborate with an editor more incredible than Tom Colgan or an agent as tremendous as Liza Fleissig. My dream of partnering with both came true. I also wish to thank my friend and former boss, Lannette Bailey. Without her encouragement and insistence, this dream might not have reached its end. Last, but certainly not least, I want to thank the wonderful folks at ThrillerFest. Without your unbelievable conference, this would have never happened.

Many of the places depicted in this novel are entirely fictional. Others, however, are actual cities, towns, highways, and locations of United States and Allied military units and installations within Germany, Great Britain, and the United States. Even where real locations and military units were used, license was taken in describing those places and units in order to conform to the flow of the story. Occasionally, license was also taken when describing the capabilities of military weapons, armaments, and command and control systems. The intent of The Red Line *was not to write a military technical or field manual but to create a story that would be enjoyed by a wide variety of readers. To do so, where the technical aspects and the story line were in conflict, the story prevailed.*

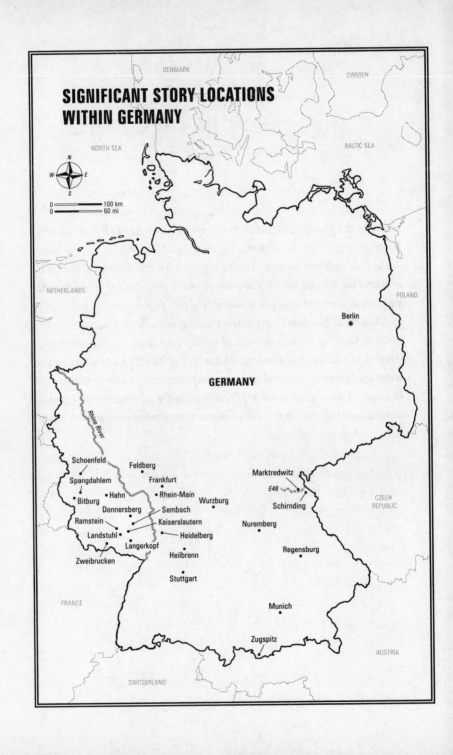

SIGNIFICANT STORY LOCATIONS WITHIN GERMANY

CHAPTER 1

*As with all wars, there were a million good reasons
to go to war, and there were no good reasons at all.*

January 28—10:27 p.m.
2nd Platoon, Delta Troop, 1st Squadron, 4th Cavalry
The German-Czech Border

Beneath the bleak border-guard tower, a solitary figure stood in the drifting snows. Deep within him, the soldier sensed something was wrong. It was a sensation he hadn't felt in a very long time. It was the same helpless feeling he'd first experienced moments before his initial firefight so many years ago.

The blizzard pelted him. The windswept snows tore at the exposed cheeks of his aging face. For the moment, however, he had no choice but to endure the intolerable conditions. Sergeant First Class Robert Jensen raised his night-vision goggles. When the heavy goggles masked his eyes, his world turned from one of darkness and swirling snow to a surreal shade of green.

Two hundred yards away, across the open landscape, stood the stark cement-and-barbed-wire fence that separated East and West. When Jensen scanned the area beyond the border, the images confirmed what he already knew. On the other side of the wire, less than a mile from his position, hundreds of armored vehicles were on the move.

On a small hilltop, a Russian main battle tank's crew watched the lone American with mounting interest.

"Josef, are you ready?" the tank's commander asked.

"Nearly, Comrade Commander," the tank's driver said. "The engine doesn't want to start in the bitter cold."

"Well, hurry it up. We need to begin our attack. The American will soon get into his Humvee and leave, and he won't return for over an hour."

"But, Comrade Commander, how can you be so sure he won't be back before then?"

"Because the American hasn't varied his routine in the two weeks we've been watching. Every two hours he rotates the soldiers in the three towers. He's changed the guards in the towers to the north. Now he's satisfying his curiosity about our division's activities while he waits for the final pair of soldiers to ascend this third tower and relieve those inside. Once that's done, he'll get into his vehicle and return to his headquarters hidden in the woods. He won't come to the border again until nearly midnight, when he'll begin replacing the soldiers in the towers once more."

The T-90's engine struggled to life. The driver revved the engine again and again as it rebelled against his efforts.

"Okay, Josef, whenever you're ready, you can start your run at the American position," the tank's commander said. "Attack at full speed; hold nothing back."

"But, Comrade Commander, what about the three Bradley Fighting Vehicles the Americans moved forward this morning and placed between the towers? Shouldn't we concern ourselves with them?"

"You just worry about getting to the wire as quickly as you can. Dmetri and I will watch the Americans, won't we, Dmetri?"

"Yes, Comrade Commander," the tank's gunner said.

Jensen was growing more miserable by the minute. Exposed to the elements, there was nothing he could do to make his predicament any better. He'd been out in the blizzard for the forty minutes it had taken to rotate the shifts in the three widespread towers. And it was beginning to take its toll.

Although squadron intelligence had reported that the unrelenting storm would end well before morning, it had yet to release its paralyzing grip. It was officially the worst blizzard to strike Europe in over thirty years. For seventy-two endless hours, the storm had been unceasing, slamming the center of the continent with gale-force winds and waist-deep snows.

For the forty-five hundred men of the American 4th Cavalry Regiment, their month guarding the southern half of the German border was nearly over. In three days, the relief regiment would arrive. It would be none too soon for the exhausted cavalrymen.

Jensen surveyed the distant landscape as the mock battles of the Russian war games continued. On a far ridge, a company-level encounter of BMP armored personnel carriers and T-80 tanks caught his eye. While he waited for Sergeant Foster and Specialist Four Marconi to start down from the forty-foot-high tower, he focused his attention on the armored attack.

Inside his parka, a brief smile came to Jensen's lips. The enemy movements were exactly what the veteran platoon sergeant had anticipated. The struggle was predictable. There was nothing subtle in the Russian approach. Forget finesse. His adversary only knew one way to play the deadly game—straight ahead with brute force. What they lacked in cunning and guile, they made up for with a willingness to sacrifice men and equipment to overwhelm their opponent.

Having briefed Privates Ramirez and Steele, Foster and Marconi began climbing down the tower's ladder.

"Christ, Michael, watch your step," Foster called out. "Every inch of this thing's covered with ice."

Jensen dropped the heavy goggles from his eyes and turned toward the sound of Foster's voice. A second fleeting smile found its way to his face. His exposure to the elements would soon be over. Even in this weather, five minutes from now, the trio would be safely within the warmth of the platoon building. After that, there would only be four guard rotations to accomplish before the relief platoon and the rising winter sun arrived at eight tomorrow morning.

Jensen turned back toward the border and raised the goggles to his eyes.

Slicing through the blizzard like a runaway snowplow from the depths of hell, the Russian tank was roaring straight for him. The T-90 was three hundred yards away and closing fast. At the last possible instant, the tank dug its broad treads into the deep snow and clawed at the frozen earth below. Fifty-one tons of deadly steel screeched to a halt inches from the wire.

"Excellent, Josef, excellent," the tank's commander said. "Another superb job by the best tank driver in all of Central Army."

"Thank you, Comrade Commander."

"What do we do now?" Dmetri asked.

"Bring your main gun forward and aim it at the American."

"Yes, Comrade Commander."

The tank's turret swung slowly around until Jensen was squarely within the sights of its massive cannon. From two hundred yards away, the Russians wouldn't miss.

"I'm ready to fire upon your order, Comrade Commander."

"Patience, Dmetri."

Jensen stood rock steady. Not a muscle flinched. If the enemy's bold move had unnerved him, he didn't show it. Instead, he turned and scanned the area to his left with his night-vision equipment, searching the American side of the border. A half mile away, he located Staff Sergeant Brown's Bradley Fighting Vehicle sitting in the ever-mounting snows.

Jensen spoke into his communication headset. "Delta-Two-One, this is Delta-Two-Five."

"Yeah, Sarge," Brown said.

"Brownie, I've got a T-90 in front of me that appears to be aiming his cannon right at my head."

"We know, Sarge. We spotted him the instant he began his run at the fence."

"I don't think he's going to fire. But just in case I'm wrong, why don't you have your gunner lock onto this guy."

"We already have. That Russian son of a bitch is sitting in the cross-hairs of a TOW missile. Give the word, and we'll blow him away."

"If the time comes for you to destroy him, it'll be because I'm already dead. Don't do anything rash. But if he fires on my position, don't wait for me to give the order. Send him straight to hell, then get all three Bradleys and the teams in the towers out of here as fast as you can. Your only chance will be to slip into the deepest part of the woods before the Russians get organized and set up your defenses there."

"Okay, Sarge, you can count on me."

"Brownie, notice anything unusual about this guy?"

"Unusual?"

"Take a good look. Tell me if you see what I see."

Brown peered through his Bradley's sophisticated thermal night-vision system at the idling Russian tank. It didn't take long for him to locate what Jensen was alluding to.

"Jesus, Sarge, look at all those pennants flying from his radio antenna."

"That's right, Brownie. What you've got in your sights is the division commander himself."

"A goddamn Russian general," Brown said. "The guy must be insane, rushing the wire like that. He's got to know we could blow him away at any time."

"He's probably thinking the exact same thing about us at the moment."

"Well, this certainly confirms what squadron told us at this morning's briefing."

"No doubt at all, is there, Brownie."

"None at all, Sarge," Brown said.

"On our platoon's three miles of border, we're face-to-face with an entire Russian armored division. More than eight thousand men, three hundred BMPs, and three hundred tanks. And we've got forty-three men, eight Bradleys, and the two Humvees."

"Doesn't seem like much of a fair fight, does it," Brown said.

"Yeah, the Russians won't stand a chance if they're crazy enough to take on 2nd Platoon, will they."

"No chance at all, Sarge."

"All right, Brownie, Foster and Marconi are climbing down as we speak. Doesn't look like the T-90's going to do anything but sit there for a while. Even so, don't let your guard down. Keep your TOW trained on him until he decides he's had enough of this foolishness and moves away from the wire. I'm going back to wrap these frozen fingers around a hot cup of coffee. The Russians are in your capable hands."

"Don't worry, Sarge. I'll watch our little friends real close while you're gone."

Sergeant Foster dropped the final six feet to the waiting snows. The instant his boots touched, he grabbed the night-vision goggles dangling from his neck.

"Christ, Sarge. I was halfway down the ladder before I realized that bastard was headed straight for the wire. I damn near fainted, then I damn near fell. What the hell's going on?"

Marconi reached the ground and joined the pair.

"Hell if I know," Jensen said. "For the past two weeks, we've been watching Comrade and his crazy winter war games. Every shift's been reporting that the Russians are getting bolder by the hour. But nothing's come close to this. A division commander taking this kind of chance is nuts. Something's wrong here, I can feel it."

"Do you think the Russians might be considering an attack?" Marconi said.

"Up until two days ago, Michael, I would have said no way, no way at all. But when they evacuated all American dependents living within one hundred miles of the border and ordered us to move three of the Bradleys up to reinforce the towers, I began to have my doubts. Now a Russian general has charged the wire. I don't know what to think anymore."

"Look at him sitting there checking us out," Foster said. "Just like he owns the place."

"At the moment, with six hundred armored vehicles to back him up, I'm afraid he does."

"But, Sarge, if the Russians were thinking about an attack, wouldn't we be on full alert?" Marconi said.

"You'd certainly hope so . . . Look, I know it's impossible to do when you're staring into the muzzle of a T-90's main gun, but you two need to take a deep breath and relax. I suspect this is nothing more than some kind of sick Russian joke. Nothing to worry about. Nothing at all. Even the Russians aren't stupid enough to risk a war. This general's just getting his kicks at our expense."

"You're probably right, Sarge," Foster said. "But even so, are you certain you want to leave Ramirez and Steele alone in this tower for the next two hours?"

"I never want to leave those two alone anywhere. Every time I bring them out here, I'm convinced that given a couple of hours to work on it, one of them's bound to accidentally shoot the other before I get back. Even so, Lieutenant Powers thinks it's good for morale to let you guys pick who you go up in the towers with."

"But, Sarge, there weren't Russian tanks everywhere you looked when the lieutenant made that decision."

"Well, I've got a solution. You two could stay here and take their places. Ready to climb back up that ladder?"

"Not me," Marconi said. "Another couple of hours out here freezing my ass off, and I might go up to the wire and beg that Russian tank to do me a favor and shoot me."

"And I'd probably go with him," Foster said. "I suspect Becky would never forgive you if you let that happen."

"Then it's settled," Jensen said. "Let's head back to the platoon building and get warmed up."

"I'm all for that, but what about them?" Foster said. He motioned toward the Russian tank.

"Leave 'em there," Jensen said. "Brown's got a TOW aimed at them. If they do anything halfway threatening, I guarantee you there'll be one less T-90 to worry about."

The trio climbed into the cab of the platoon sergeant's Humvee. Jensen pulled away from the tower and headed west across the two hundred yards of barren ground that would take them to the edge of a thick forest.

"There he goes, Comrade Commander."

"Yes, Dmetri, I see."

The Russian tank crew watched as the small vehicle churned through the snows toward the narrow trail that would return the cavalry soldiers to their home.

"Crushing the token enemy border force is going to be so easy," the tank's gunner said.

"I wish I had your confidence, Dmetri. But I'm not so sure. Did you see the American when we made our charge? It didn't affect him at all. There can be little doubt about that one's courage. And there's no doubt he knows what he's doing. Do not underestimate our opponent. I assure you that before this is over, he'll have proven himself to be an able adversary."

"Comrade Commander, what I assure you is the next time you see the American, his bloody body will be lying in the snows. And we'll be on our way to conquering Germany."

"We shall see, Dmetri. We shall see."

Upon locating the opening to the constricted trail, the Humvee disappeared into the dense woods.

"Okay, Josef, I've seen what I needed to see. Back up slowly and get us out of here."

"Yes, Comrade Commander," the tank's driver said.

CHAPTER 2

All around the Humvee, the relentless snowfall caused the forest's mantle to droop. While the cavalry soldiers traveled down the twisting pathway, the snow-covered evergreen branches a few feet overhead closed in tightly, blocking out the winter's night sky.

Usually, the familiar mile drive back to the cinder-block platoon building would go quickly. In the darkness and snow, however, Jensen carefully felt his way home.

"Has there been any further word on our families?" Foster asked.

"Nothing more than what they told us this morning. The wives and kids arrived at Rhein-Main last night and were being put on flights to the States."

"All headed to the States . . . When we get back to Regensburg in three days, it's sure going to feel different with our families gone. Everybody's going to be awfully lonely."

"Everybody except Ramirez," Jensen said. "He's never lonely. How many *Frauleins* is he presently engaged to?"

"It changes from day to day," Marconi said. "Last count I heard was six, give or take one or two."

"Yep, Ramirez won't be lonely," Foster said. "If there's an attractive woman within five hundred miles, Ramirez will find her."

"No doubt about it, our little Ramirez is destined to be killed by an irate husband someday," Jensen said.

"If he doesn't fall out of one of the towers first. That would sure disappoint the *Frauleins* in Regensburg," Marconi added.

"You know, I'll bet our wives are back in the States right now, warm and cozy by the fire while the grandparents spoil the kids," Foster said. "I'm sure my folks were waiting at the airport in Des Moines when Becky and the kids arrived. This'll be the first time they've seen the baby."

The short journey reached its end. A few feet from the low-lying building, the platoon sergeant's Humvee eased to a stop between Lieutenant Powers's Humvee and the platoon's five remaining Bradley Fighting Vehicles. The armored vehicles sat in the darkness beneath a foot of newly fallen powder.

To the uninitiated, the platoon's fighting vehicles could have been mistaken for tanks. Although they tipped the scales at nearly twenty-five tons, that was only half a tank's weight. Nevertheless, with the Bradleys' thick steel treads, tanklike shape, and full body armor, such a misidentification could easily occur. Yet the one recognizable feature that distinguished a Bradley Fighting Vehicle from a tank was the size and shape of its main gun. While the American primary battle tank, the M-1 Abrams, had a huge 120mm cannon, the Bradley's was significantly smaller.

The 25mm Bushmaster chain gun was extremely thin. Even so, with its armor-piercing Bushmaster and array of TOW missiles, the Americans' Bradley Fighting Vehicles had proven capable in more than one war of standing up to even the most menacing enemy tank.

The trio shook the snow from about their heads and headed toward the ancient building. A wave of moist heat greeted them as they entered the smaller of a pair of rooms. The drafty building was dank and gave off a distinctive odor from the thousands of cavalry soldiers who'd called it their temporary home over the years. A chorus of animated voices resounded from deeper within the old structure.

Foster and Marconi passed through the anteroom that served as the platoon's operations center. Jensen paused.

Gregory Powers sat at a tired metal desk in the far corner. The blond-haired, blue-eyed second lieutenant was fiddling with the pipe he'd adopted when he took command of the platoon eight weeks earlier. The pipe was an attempt to give himself an air of authority. He seldom smoked the ordinary-looking pipe, but he played with it constantly. Powers, having finished the easier task of changing the shifts in the three Bradleys, had been sitting at the desk for the past twenty minutes.

Against the wall nearest the door, the platoon radio operator, Specialist Four Aaron Jelewski, sat reading a comic book. On the table in front of Jelewski was a pair of military radios. The first was tuned to the squadron frequency. The other's dials were set to connect the platoon command post with the Bradleys, Humvees, and guard towers.

Jelewski looked up as Jensen entered.

"Anything going on?" Jensen asked.

"Not much. Lots of talk on the squadron net about how busy Comrade is tonight. But nothing compared to what I heard you and Brownie discussing a few minutes ago."

"Yeah, when a Russian general's willing to chance rushing the wire like that, something's definitely up. One thing's certain—you've got to have a death wish playing division-level war games in the middle of a blizzard."

"You've got that right, Sarge. Except, squadron says it's not just the division in front of us that's involved. Apparently, across the fifty-mile 1st Squadron area, there are ten Russian divisions racing around like madmen in the snow. And over the 150 miles of the American sector, there are twice that many. The British up north are reporting the same kind of activity."

"Squadron have any further information on what the Russians are up to?"

"Nothing more than what they've been telling us for the past two weeks. This is still officially a war game the Russians are conducting to test their ability to defend Eastern Europe during winter. We're to stay alert but avoid confrontation with them at all costs."

"Someone needs to tell that to that general who had his cannon pointed at my head."

"Maybe somebody did, Sarge," Jelewski said.

"Yeah, maybe they did. I'll be back in a couple of minutes. Holler if you need me."

Stripping off his gear as he went, the platoon sergeant entered the larger living area. When he pulled the heavy parka from his head, he revealed his closely cropped hair, which was every bit as gray as the old soldier's eyes.

Inside the noisy room, the never-ceasing card games continued.

When Jensen entered, a few members of the platoon lounged on double-decked bunks along the walls. But the majority of the cavalry soldiers were crowded around the three tables, playing in the games or hovering to pounce upon the slightest mistake by those involved.

With a newly poured cup of strong coffee, Jensen wandered over to the farthest table. There, the three squad leaders not at the border, Staff Sergeants Cruz and Austin and Sergeant Renoir, along with his assistant squad leader, Sergeant Richmond, were involved in a furious game of pinochle.

"Want to take on winners, Sarge?" Specialist Four Winston, standing next to Jensen, asked.

"Wait a minute, Winston," Cruz said. "I'm not giving up this seat for at least another hour. And Brown told me that when I relieve him, he wants my spot."

"Thanks for asking, Winnie," Jensen said. "But I can't right now. Got to go back in the other room and watch the lieutenant so he doesn't hurt himself with that pipe."

Jensen's comment met with laughter all around. It saved him from having to explain that the real reason he wasn't interested in the game was his concern over what was happening on the other side of the snow-choked border.

Cruz tossed a card on the table and looked up with a broad grin on his face. "You just don't want to get your butt kicked again, Bob, that's all."

"Fat chance. When's the last time you two amateurs were able to beat me?" Jensen said.

"I think it was what? About three thirty this afternoon, wouldn't you say, Hector?" Austin said.

"Sounds about right to me, Seth."

"You guys got lucky, and you know it."

When Cruz and Austin ignored his comment, Jensen wandered back into the operations center. He slumped into a cold metal chair next to Jelewski, glanced at his watch, and noted it was 10:40. Just over an hour before he would bundle himself in his wet winter gear once more and return to the blowing snows.

It turned out to be an uneventful hour. Jelewski made communication checks with squadron headquarters at 10:45 and with the towers and Bradleys at 11:00. The Russians continued to rumble through the furious snowstorm all along the Czech and Polish borders with Germany. Cruz and Austin humiliated their younger opponents. And the lieutenant played with his pipe.

Late in the hour, Jensen removed three computer-generated cards from his shirt pocket. Printed on the cards were the names of his wife, Linda, and the couple's teenage daughters. The cards had arrived yesterday. They were official notice that his family had left Regensburg. If all went well, in the next few days he would receive three additional cards for each of them as they cleared the hurdles on their way home to Texas.

And in a short time, he knew he'd be clearing those same hurdles. In five weeks, Robert Jensen was scheduled to join his family in the small East Texas town that held such fond memories of his boyhood days. There he'd begin a long-overdue retirement.

11:40. Time to prepare the next shift to go forward to the border. Jensen shoved the cards into his shirt pocket and headed into the platoon living area.

"All right, next shift get ready to move out." He took his parka and gear off the bunk where he'd hung them earlier. "First groups for the towers and Bradleys in five minutes."

This was met with the usual pleas for "just one more hand" and some rather unkind comments about the veteran soldier's parentage, which, with a smile on his weathered face, Jensen ignored.

He grabbed his M-4 assault rifle and loaded a thirty-round clip of ammunition. Ready to return to the blizzard, Jensen stood in the middle of the living area, waiting for the pair of troopers scheduled for the northernmost tower.

In the other room, the lieutenant got up and started to prepare himself to sally forth once more with a trio of soldiers for the farthest Bradley.

Up and down the 150 miles of border under American control, scores of 4th Cavalry platoons were doing the same.

The platoon's routine was suddenly broken.

"Hey, Sarge! I think you'd better get in here!" Jelewski called out. "There's something odd happening at the border."

The urgency in the radio operator's voice was unmistakable.

CHAPTER 3

"What's wrong?" Jensen asked the moment he entered the room.

"Listen," Jelewski said.

". . . can't tell for sure, Brownie. So many coming toward the wire that I can't count 'em all," Sergeant Kelly, commanding the northern Bradley, said. There was no mistaking the fear dripping from each of Kelly's anxious words.

In the platoon's operations center, Jelewski, Jensen, and Powers froze the instant they heard the compelling tone in the young soldier's voice. Just then, the three replacements for Kelly's Bradley, Specialists Winston and Johnson and Sergeant Reed entered the small room.

"It's the same here, Kelly," Brown said. "There are a dozen tanks at the wire in front of me. Got BMPs in support, with infantry dismounting from most of them."

"What do you want us to do?"

"Wait one, Delta-Two-Two," Brown said. "Delta-Two-Three, are you there?"

"Roger, Brownie, we're here," came the excited reply from third squad's Bradley, a mile south of Brown's position. "Lots of them moving our way, too."

"Okay, Two-Three . . ." Brown said, pausing just long enough to make a final assessment of the utterly unanticipated situation. "All of you listen to me. Nobody panic. At this point, we've no idea what the Russians are up to. More than likely, it's just another one of their stupid stunts. After two weeks of staring across the border at us, that crazy general must've gone snow-blind. By now, the sorry bastard's probably bored out of his skull. So he's decided to have some fun at our expense. I know things look pretty grim at the moment. But we're going to be just fine as long as we stay calm. Everybody take a deep breath and hold your ground. Keep your heads down and don't do anything foolish until I find out what platoon wants us to do . . . Delta-Two, Delta-Two, this is Delta-Two-One."

"Go ahead, Two-One," Jelewski said.

"Jewels, is Jensen there?" Brown said, ignoring the likely presence of the lieutenant in the room.

Jensen took the handset from Jelewski. "Roger, Brownie, go ahead."

"Sarge, we've got some really strange goings-on up here. The Russians have obviously lost their minds."

"How so, Brownie?"

"I've got to tell you, I don't know what to make of any of it. Things seemed perfectly normal until about three minutes ago. The Russians were playing their little war games just like they'd been doing all day. Their tanks and BMPs were racing around in the snows, making their mock attacks on each other. I was just sitting here halfheartedly watching their antics and counting the minutes until this shift was up. That's when it happened."

"When what happened, Brownie?"

"All hell broke loose, Sarge. Without warning, the Russian armor turned and raced at top speed across the snows straight for us. They came from every direction. And they didn't stop until they'd reached the wire. But that's not the worst of it. There are dismounted infantry in full battle dress pouring from the BMPs. I still can't believe what I'm seeing. Everywhere I look, an endless stream of Russian armor's moving toward the border. The other positions are reporting the same. What do you want us to do?"

"Are the tanks making any attempt to cross the wire?"

"Negative. For the moment, they're just sitting there."

For the briefest of instants, Jensen's mind begged him to believe it was nothing more than another Russian ploy to test their American adversaries. Just that brazen general trying to see how his foe would react this time.

But the veteran platoon sergeant knew otherwise. Tanks and BMPs at the wire might be a test of wills. Moving dismounted infantry into position to support the armor, however, could mean only one thing. As much as he fought against it, there was just one conclusion he could reach—the Russians were preparing to attack.

Jensen's mind was racing. Still, he forced himself to sound completely calm. "Roger, Two-One. Wait one."

Jensen turned to the lieutenant. Searching looks passed over their faces, each knowing what they needed to do but wanting the reassurance of the other. When Powers made no move to take charge, Jensen issued the order for the platoon's fifteen men at the border to prepare for war.

"Second Platoon, lock and load."

In the towers, each soldier chambered a round into the barrel of his M-4, released the safety, and selected a target from the Russian infantry. In the three Bradleys, the vehicle commander reached for his machine-gun controls and went through the identical procedure. Each then did the same with his 25mm armor-piercing Bushmaster. The soldier in the "gunner" position armed his pair of upgraded TOW missiles. They all knew the powerful missile, tested in a dozen nasty little wars, would slice through the thickest Russian armor with ease. The Bradley drivers started their engines and revved them against the cold.

In all, it took less than ten seconds for the platoon's border force to be ready for battle.

"Jewels, let squadron know what's going on up here," Jensen said.

Without waiting for a response, Jensen pushed past the three replacements and into the platoon living area.

As he stood in the middle of the room and made the fateful pronouncement, the platoon sergeant's voice was almost casual in its tone and belied the terror welling in his soul. "Let's go, 2nd Platoon. We've got bad guys at the wire. And they appear to mean business."

At the tables, cards flew. Confused soldiers in various states of dress scrambled to ready themselves for whatever lay ahead.

With Jensen busy in the living area, Powers decided the moment was ripe for him to exercise his newly acquired leadership skills.

"Come on, men!" Powers said. He motioned for Winston, Johnson, and Reed to follow.

Rushing out the door, with the three cavalry soldiers close on his heels, the fresh-faced lieutenant ran to his Humvee. With trembling fingers, he removed the thick canvas tarp covering the Humvee's machine gun.

"You drive," Powers said, pointing to Johnson.

The soldiers scrambled into the Humvee. Powers climbed into the rear and positioned himself behind the machine gun.

"All right, men, there's no time to waste. Let's get up to the border!" Powers yelled.

In one motion, Johnson started the engine and slammed the accelerator to the floor. The tires spun wildly, spraying snow in every direction. The small combat vehicle careened its way onto the twisting trail. The border was a mile away. Reaching forty miles per hour as they roared through the blackness of the narrow roadway, the soldiers were in for the ride of their lives. In the rear of the Humvee, the lieutenant held on with all his might.

Satisfied that Cruz and Austin could finish organizing the platoon's remaining twenty-two men, Jensen returned to the operations room.

"Where the hell's the lieutenant?" he asked.

"Took off in his Hummer," Jelewski said.

"When'd he do that?"

"A couple of minutes ago. Right after you went into the living area, he took Reed's team and left for the border."

A mixture of anger and frustration flashed in the platoon sergeant's eyes. But before Jensen could utter the endless stream of expletives forming on his lips, Brown was screaming into the radio, "Delta-Two,

I've got tanks through the wire! Jesus Christ, they're everywhere! Say again, I've got tanks through the wire! Request immediate instructions! Request immediate instructions!"

The Russians had made their move.

Jensen lunged toward the radio. He had to get Brown and his men away from the border. It was their only chance. If they were going to inflict maximum damage on the enemy and hope to somehow live to see another sunrise, he had to get his overmatched soldiers into the protective cover of the welcoming tangle of German forest. And he had to do it now.

The lieutenant's Humvee chose that exact moment to burst from the woods. His hand already positioned to key his headset, he beat Jensen to the punch.

"Open fire!" Powers screamed. "Open fire!"

He squeezed the trigger of his machine gun, firing wild bursts toward the border.

"No-o-o!" Jensen shrieked into the platoon radio. "Fall back! Fall back! Brownie, get everyone into the trees and set up defensive positions!"

Jensen was, however, too late. None of them heard him over the battle erupting in every direction.

Targets were everywhere in Brown's night-vision sights. With his Bushmaster chain gun, the squad leader tore into a BMP2 that had stopped to discharge its seven infantrymen. Under Brown's relentless assault, smoke poured from the BMP. Flames licked at the enemy armored vehicle's sides. As Russian infantry emerged from the rear of the crippled personnel carrier, Brown switched to his machine gun. With two quick bursts, he cut down four white-clad figures and watched them crumple to the snow.

Brown's gunner had a T-80 in his sights. He fired the first of his TOW missiles. The missile screamed through the night, ramming headlong into its massive target. The ground beneath them trembled. A fearful explosion threw huge pieces of the dying tank high into the winter sky. The resulting fireball was visible for miles around. The blizzard-swept battlefield turned as bright as the brightest day.

A half mile to Brown's left, the pair of Americans in the center guard tower opened fire on a squad of Russian infantry caught by the false daylight of the burning tank. Struck repeatedly, the advancing infantry went down. The firing from the tower attracted the attention of the T-80s the infantry squad had been attempting to support. The lead tank methodically raised the elevation on its 125mm cannon, located the M-4 muzzle flashes, and fired from close range. In less than a heartbeat, the massive shell slammed into the frozen tower, obliterating it and the cavalry soldiers within. America had suffered its first losses of the new war.

Powers's Humvee headed north across the open ground that separated it from Brown's position. While the battle intensified, the Humvee ripped through the blizzard with guns blazing. A BMP's machine gun returned the Humvee's fire. Lethal streams of tracer fire soared in both directions.

The deadly duel of men and machines would, however, be shortlived. The Humvee was overmatched. Its armored opponent was far too powerful. The Russian fire homed in, coming ever closer to the speeding Americans. The BMP's gunner focused on the figure behind the enemy machine gun. The inviting target of the standing Powers was struck by a pair of armor-piercing bullets that found their way through the machine gun's protective plating and the lieutenant's body armor. The first found his right arm, tearing a huge gash in a well-developed biceps. The other smashed into the lieutenant's broad chest and dug for the fragile life hidden within. The impacting bullets forever silenced the Humvee's machine gun.

A second burst of machine-gun fire caught Johnson in the shoulder and neck. The shorter Winston, sitting next to him in the front passenger seat, was struck just above his left cheekbone by the withering Russian assault. Winston died instantly, as a substantial portion of his face and head disappeared.

The searing pain of Johnson's wounds soared deep into his brain, overwhelming all conscious thought. He instinctively jerked the steering wheel sharply to the left, away from the BMP's fire. The extreme actions of its driver were too much for the Humvee to overcome. It tumbled over and over in the treacherous snows, finally skidding to a stop beneath a heavy drift. In the rear seat, Sergeant Reed was pinned beneath the twisted wreckage. His neck was broken.

The crash threw the severely injured Powers from the vehicle. The lieutenant slammed to the bitter ground. His motionless form lay in the snow, barely alive. His broken pipe, torn from his shirt pocket, lay next to him.

The Humvee's crash also broke Johnson's left arm and crushed his rib cage. He tried to scream out, but the enemy bullet that had ripped through his neck had destroyed his larynx. In barely a minute, as his freely flowing blood mixed with the snow, his pain was over.

The rest of 2nd Platoon's border force was faring little better. On the far right of the platoon's position, 3rd Squad's Bradley never got off a shot. Shortly after the battle began, a duo of T-80s fired their main guns at nearly the same instant, destroying the smaller American armored vehicle and its crew of three.

On the far left, the soldiers in the platoon's northern guard tower met with the same fate as had befallen those in the middle tower. A single shell from a Russian main battle tank quickly ended their lives.

Sergeant Kelly's crew fired both its online TOWs. The first destroyed a BMP and the ten souls within the false protection of its metal walls. The second missed its target, a T-80 flying full speed across the snows.

Kelly's gunner began the tedious process of refilling the empty missile tubes. It would take at least two minutes, an eternity on a battlefield of such intensity, to reload the TOWs. Kelly pounded away at the enemy with his Bushmaster cannon while he waited for his gunner to finish the task. The Bradley's gunner had the first missile in place and was reaching for a second when a Russian tank fired from point-blank range. Another death-filled cannon shell ripped through the night to seek and destroy. In a fiery display of the tank's impressive power, Kelly's Bradley was added to the crimson field's mounting infernos. The false light was growing ever stronger.

Three tanks moved toward the final American tower.

"Let's get the hell out of here!" Ramirez screamed, the terror visible in his dark eyes.

Steele threw open the trapdoor. Both began furiously descending the icy ladder. Steele's feet had just met the snow, with Ramirez ten feet above him, when the lead tank fired. The shattered tower disappeared. A plummeting piece of jagged cement struck Ramirez on the top of his head, opening a large gash. The stunned private lost his grip on the rungs. He fell the final ten feet to the snow, landing on his tower mate.

The pair lay motionless on the cold ground, with the bloody Ramirez on top of Steele. Both were conscious, but neither could catch the fleeting breath the collision had stolen from them. The moment their senses cleared and the air returned to their lungs, they scrambled to their feet. Each started running as fast as his wobbly legs would carry him through the deep snows. While he ran, the panic-stricken Ramirez didn't notice the blood pouring down the side of his face and clotting in his thin mustache.

A pair of M-4s lay forgotten in the snows beneath the destroyed tower.

While the battle raged around them, Brown switched back to his Bushmaster cannon. Once more, an outgunned BMP fell. With exacting accuracy, his gunner fired a second TOW. The missile ruptured a T-80, setting it ablaze. Another fireball rose to meet the snow-filled heavens.

Brown's missile tubes were now empty. But the combat-experienced squad leader wasn't going to make the fatal mistake Kelly had made seconds earlier.

"Whiting, get us out of here now!"

Without hesitation, the Bradley's driver responded to Brown's command. Its broad treads churning through the deep snows, the Bradley raced away from the battlefield.

To survive, they'd need some luck. The woods were a long ways off. A half mile of open ground had to be crossed before Brown's crew would reach the safety of the trail. And scores of Russian armored vehicles were right on their tail.

As it was, poor marksmanship from a T-80 gunner gave the Bradley crew a chance for survival. The Russian tank's gunner had the Bradley squarely in his sights. In the excitement of his first combat, however, the gunner rushed his shot by the thinnest of margins. The roaring shell passed inches in front of the American armored vehicle and exploded in the woods.

Even so, the cavalry soldiers weren't safe yet.

Brown's Bradley closed to within fifty yards of the opening to the trail. A BMP's gunner took aim and fired. Three 30mm shells pierced the Bradley's thinner rear armor, entering the back compartment where two Americans would have been sitting had the vehicle been carrying its normal load of five. A few feet forward, however, the three crewmen in the separate command compartment were unharmed. The fighting vehicle scurried into the woods and raced for home.

One hundred yards into the trees, the twenty-five-ton Bradley nearly ran down Steele and Ramirez. Reduced to an exhausted trot, the pair was jogging down the middle of the narrow path. With the Bradley rushing headlong down the trail, Brown's driver didn't spot them until the last possible instant. The fighting vehicle slid to a stop inches from the panicked figures. Brown flung open the commander's hatch.

"Jesus Christ! What the hell do you two idiots think you're doing running down the middle of the trail like that? You damn near got yourselves run over." Neither Ramirez nor Steele, their heads bowed, answered. "Shit! I've no more time to waste on the likes of you. Hurry up! Get in before you get us all killed. The Russians are right behind us."

The rear hatch lowered, and the frightened privates scrambled inside.

For a few minutes, the lieutenant lay on the frozen battlefield. The snow beneath him slowly turned a bright shade of red. When his eyes painfully opened, he found himself staring into the muzzle of a Kalashnikov AK-47. Second Lieutenant Greg Powers had become the first prisoner of Europe's third great war. In another thirty minutes, he would also become one of its initial fatalities. For without the quick medical attention he desperately needed, he'd soon bleed to death from his wounds.

CHAPTER 4

The first fight of the new war had taken little more than a handful of minutes. At its end, fourteen of 2nd Platoon's soldiers lay dead or dying in the deepening drifts of the border. It had been a foolish struggle, one that shouldn't have been fought. Outmanned and outgunned, Jensen understood their only chance was to battle the vastly superior enemy on 2nd Platoon's terms and on 2nd Platoon's terrain.

And Jensen's plan to do just that was already under way.

Despite its outcome, Powers's ill-advised attack had accomplished one positive thing for the platoon. It had given Jensen five full minutes to organize the remainder of the unit's men.

The battle-tested platoon sergeant didn't waste a single second of it.

After making a final desperate attempt to get the platoon to fall back, Jensen turned to Jelewski.

"Contact squadron and let them know what's going on up here," Jensen said in a voice that reflected strength and a growing confidence.

"Roger." Jelewski picked up the radio handset for the squadron net. "Sierra-Six, Sierra-Six, this is Delta-Two."

"Roger, Delta-Two, this is Sierra-Six, go ahead."

Specialist Four Aaron Jelewski was about to make history. In the next moment, he would say the words a stunned world would repeat over and over again in the days to come.

"Sierra-Six, the Russians have crossed the border with Germany and are attacking in force. I say again, the Russians have crossed the border with Germany and are attacking in force."

"Roger, Delta-Two, we copy. Russians are crossing the border and attacking in force."

While the soldiers hurried about the living area, preparing themselves to battle for their lives, Jensen took Cruz and Austin aside and started laying out his plan.

Their job, Jensen knew, was not to defeat the powerful Russian armor. That would be an impossible task for the lightly armed cavalry. Their job was to slow the enemy down long enough to counter the Russians' surprise attack. At the border, the cavalry regiment's purpose was a simple one—buy as much time as they possibly could. Jensen understood there was only one way for the soldiers of the 4th Cavalry Regiment to accomplish such a mission.

They'd pay for each precious minute with their lives.

He was certain his platoon's location had been the first one breached because of its close proximity to the sole north–south highway within fifteen miles of the border. He knew his tiny force had no chance of defeating the six hundred armored vehicles they faced. Still, he hoped his plan might slow them down. In the dark, the Russians had only one way to get through the impassable woods. If they were going to seize the north–south road, the enemy armor would have to come down the platoon's narrow, twisting trail.

And they'd have to come down it one tank at a time.

Jensen had selected the perfect ambush spot during his very first month at the border nearly two years earlier. Halfway up the trail, it made an elongated right-hand turn in the deep woods. The trail widened a few feet as it made the sweeping turn. He would hide three Bradleys at the curve and wait. The protection of the woods would be adequate. And the fighting vehicles would have a clear shot at the first four or five tanks as they made their way around a narrower turn from the left. From curve to curve, it couldn't be more than 250 yards. The Bradleys' missiles and Bushmasters wouldn't miss at that range. If he could stop the leading tanks, he could possibly block the Russian column's advance, buying valuable time for them all.

"Here's what we're going to do, Seth," Jensen said, looking at Austin and speaking loudly to be heard over the ever-growing noise of the ferocious little battles springing up all along the entire length of the border. "You and Foster stay here with your Bradleys. I'll leave you eight men. Take Jelewski and the ones who aren't ready yet. I'll take the others and the final three Bradleys. We'll set up an ambush at that wide curve about halfway to the border and wait for the Russians. If we can't stop them, or the Russians beat us to the curve, it'll be up to you to slow them down. If we succeed, I'll need you back here to cover our retreat. Set up about a hundred yards back down the trail toward the highway. There's a decent spot for an ambush there. Any questions?"

"No, Bob, I've got it."

Jensen then quickly explained the details of his plan. When he was finished, he calmly asked both what they thought.

"What have we got to lose? Let's get up there," Cruz said.

When Jensen turned to Austin, Seth furrowed his brow and nodded in agreement.

While the five-minute battle raged at the border, what was left of 2nd Platoon was beginning to move into position. Jensen's force ran through the blizzard to the three Bradleys, and four soldiers entered each. Jensen and Marconi leaped into the platoon sergeant's Humvee. The cavalry soldiers charged up the trail toward the border. They held their breath and prayed they would beat the Russians to the ambush spot. Each knew if the enemy caught them out in the open on the tiny roadway, there would be no chance of escape. All their lives would be over in an instant.

As it was, Brown's Bradley roared around the left-hand curve just as Jensen's force reached its objective. The initially unidentified armored vehicle's sudden appearance on the curve above them brought terror stabbing deep within each American heart.

Brown's Bradley screamed to a stop at the ambush position, and the commander's hatch popped open.

"Where's the rest of the platoon?" Jensen asked.

"I don't know, Sarge. I guess they're probably dead. All hell broke loose up there. To tell you the truth, I don't even know how we survived. I've got my crew and Ramirez and Steele. That's it. I didn't see anyone else. Except for the enemy, that is. I saw plenty of them."

"Any idea where the Russians are now?"

"Right on my tail, last time I looked."

"Brownie, we're going to wait for the Russians here. Austin and Foster are setting up a secondary position about a hundred yards past the platoon building. Get down there and give 'em a hand."

"All right, Sarge, I'm on my way."

Brown pulled the commander's hatch shut. The Bradley roared down the trail toward the highway.

To the north and south of Jensen's position, the war's intensity was growing by the second. The Russian invasion was fully under way. In front of Jensen, however, the noise of 2nd Platoon's battle had stopped completely.

When the vicious skirmish with the Americans ended, the Russian general needed a few minutes to get his division organized before initiating the next phase of the assault.

It was just enough time for Jensen to spin his deadly web.

Renoir's Bradley took up a firing position inside the trees to the right of the trail. Sergeant Richmond directed his Bradley into the woods on the left. Cruz's Bradley waited to the rear of Richmond's. It would move out to fire from the trail the moment the engagement began. The platoon sergeant pulled his Humvee into the heavy woods on the right. Jensen would command the platoon from the Humvee's position.

The remaining four soldiers split up. With their M-4s, two disappeared into the shadowy evergreens on the left. The two on the right did the same. The four were to protect the platoon from the threat of Russian infantry rolling up their exposed flanks and encircling the Americans. Should the fight last any time at all, a serious possibility existed that they would all be surrounded and destroyed.

The Americans had to hit fast and hit hard or else find themselves on the losing end of the life-or-death struggle.

Whatever happened, Jensen was certain of one thing. This time, the Russian general would have to face him on his terms. For a fleeting moment, he wondered if that was going to be enough.

He'd soon have his answer.

The first enemy tank had entered the trail.

CHAPTER 5

When she arrived at the front of the line, Linda Jensen handed the three computer cards to a bored Air Force technical sergeant. Linda pushed open the weighty door. She headed out into the blowing snows of the tarmac. Her daughters, and the families of the men of her husband's platoon, followed close behind. The 767 was waiting.

As she walked across the open ground, even in the blizzard she couldn't help looking up at the plane. The aircraft was completely illuminated. The artificial glow of the tarmac's spotlights created a beautiful image. The bright lights striking the glistening fuselage were mixing with the falling snow and melding into one.

On her tail, the 767 had a giant eagle with wings stretching upward and talons reaching down as if to grasp an unseen prey. Under the eagle, the gold letters read EARLY EAGLE AIRLINES.

The plane had landed twenty minutes earlier. Air Force personnel were busily preparing it to depart within the next ten. A ground crew worked in a tremendous hurry to refuel the giant old lady.

Another crew was deicing the wings. Still more airmen scurried about in the storm, loading baggage and food onto the airplane.

Holding on to the handrail, Linda walked up the icy ramp. Upon reaching the top step, she entered the aging aircraft. Greeted by a pair of smiling flight attendants, she made her way down the narrow aisle and found seats 14A, B, and C. She and the girls stowed their carry-ons and sat down. For once, Amanda and Susan were too tired to fight over the window. When she settled in next to the aisle, Linda felt herself sink. Wave after wave of exhaustion washed over her.

Forty-four-year-old Linda Jensen had been an attractive young woman. Twenty years earlier, she'd met Robert at a dance at the Fort Bragg, North Carolina, recreation center. It hadn't been love at first sight. In fact, she really hadn't cared for him much. Still, he'd been a determined suitor. And his persistence had finally won her heart.

Her parents opposed her marrying a soldier. At twenty-four, however, she wasn't going to let that stand in her way. Now, after two decades of marriage, any real passion between the couple was a distant memory. Yet even without the passion, she loved her husband. And she was certain Robert loved her. The relationship was a comfortable one, which for Linda revolved around the raising of the girls.

As she sank farther into the uncomfortable airliner seat, Linda realized she hadn't slept in nearly two days.

The sudden evacuation had surprised them all. Given three hours' notice in the middle of a forbidding winter night, she'd thrown a few things together for herself and the girls. Along with hundreds of others, they'd left Regensburg at 6:00 a.m. in one of the many convoys that would depart throughout the day. Although she'd no responsibility for the families of the men of her husband's platoon, they'd naturally fallen in behind her for the two-hundred-mile trip to Rhein-Main. Many of the soldiers' wives were scarcely older than her daughters.

It was a journey that normally would have taken four hours.

In the midst of the blizzard, however, the autobahns were packed with deep snows. Beneath the fresh powder lay two inches of solid ice. As they normally did when the snows came, the Germans made no attempt to clear the roadways. Instead, they left the frozen asphalt to its fate and gathered around their hearths to wait out the storm.

With Military Police escorts, the convoy had driven north toward Nuremberg. What was normally a pleasant sixty-mile jaunt took the Americans well over three times what it should have to accomplish. Every hill on the autobahn, of which there were far too many, became a nightmare for them all. At first, the girls enjoyed piling out to free a wayward car from a snowbank. The game, however, had soon become tiresome, even for the energetic teenagers.

It didn't take long for the local populace to further complicate the Americans' fight for Rhein-Main and the flight that would take them home. Upon hearing rumors of the American evacuation, a few Germans had panicked. On this initial leg, the interference hadn't been too severe. Yet as the endless hours passed, the number of Germans joining in the movement west would steadily increase, causing further misery for them all.

In Nuremberg, the column waited for two hours while other Americans arrived from the north, south, and east. At midday, the expanded convoy headed west into the teeth of the blizzard.

On the road, the struggling Americans encountered the same problems as before. The severe weather and frightened Germans were taking their toll.

The column trekked on to Wurzburg, an hour's drive west of Nuremberg. And again, it was a journey that took much, much longer to complete. At 3:30, hungry and tired, they arrived. The onrushing darkness of a long winter's night was quickly approaching.

In Wurzburg, there was another extended stop while more dependents gathered. The convoy, now nearing seven miles in length, headed into the black night toward Frankfurt. On this stretch of autobahn alone, thirty-seven cars had to be abandoned. The overwhelmed MPs could no longer take the time to deal with those that became jammed in the unyielding snows or suffered mechanical problems.

Seventeen hours after leaving Regensburg, Linda Jensen drove through the front gate at Rhein-Main. She was exhausted, she was filthy, and she was ready for the nightmare to end.

With no relief driver, Linda had driven the long, dark hours through the blizzard. She had struggled with the weather, the MPs, agitated Germans, and her increasingly restless daughters. Waved through the air base's main gate by an air policeman's strong right arm, Linda entered Rhein-Main in utter relief. Another air policeman directed her to a sprawling parking lot, where hundreds of automobiles sat on the frigid pavement.

Linda located a distant spot and parked the family's modest car. She and the girls dragged their bags across the wide parking lot toward the beckoning warmth of the passenger terminal. They were soon within the small terminal with its broad expanses of plate-glass windows. There, a stunned Linda found thousands of earlier-arrived men, women, and children crammed into every inch of space within the two-story building.

It took ninety minutes in a line that refused to budge for Linda to check in. There was an hour wait for the restrooms. The Jensen women found themselves a tiny spot on the cold floor. There they sat throughout the endless night and all the next day amid screaming babies, tired children, and people who'd long ago run out of patience.

With over two hundred thousand American dependents to evacuate, the logistics of the monumental operation were already showing the first telltale signs of failure.

Linda watched one commercial airliner after another arrive and unload its cargo of soldiers. Eight hours earlier, the soldiers had kissed their loved ones good-bye and departed from their stateside bases. With every seat crammed with women and children, the planes would quickly turn around and head back across the Atlantic. During the painful twenty-four hours Linda huddled on the terminal floor, she watched as a continuous stream of dependents arrived to take the place of those who'd found their way onto one of the departing aircraft.

Finally, their turn had come. Their names had been called. The wives and children of the men of 2nd Platoon had gratefully stepped out into the blizzard and hobbled on board the old 767.

The nightmare was nearing its end. In another few minutes, they'd leap into the darkness and head for home.

Sitting in the captain's chair, Evan Cooper waited while the final passengers boarded. The past two days had been a nightmare for Cooper as well. A nightmare for which he'd been praying.

Cooper, a former Air Force fighter pilot and combat veteran, had followed his time in the military with ten years of flying for America West Airlines. Next had come a stint with United. Frustrated by all the hassles that went along with doing the only thing he truly loved, he rolled the dice.

Selling everything he owned, and a couple of things he didn't, he'd gone out a few years earlier and purchased the well-worn 767. He was mortgaged to the hilt, but he understood that every dream had its price. With this one plane, he started Early Eagle Airlines.

Cooper eked out a meager living and found ways to make the payments on the plane during the first couple of years by flying military and tourist charters. But as America continued to withdraw most of its forces from overseas and a lingering recession hit the tourist industry, his dream began to sour.

Thirteen months ago, he'd been forced to declare Chapter 11 bankruptcy to keep his creditors from shutting down his single-plane airline. He'd given up the luxury of his sparse one-bedroom apartment and moved into a tiny space above a noisy, foul-smelling hangar. He survived on the occasional bologna sandwich. Each month, Cooper somehow scraped together the money to continue making the payments on the plane. And so far he'd found just enough ready cash to keep his ex-wife from having him thrown into jail for failing to pay his child support. How much longer he could continue to do so was anybody's guess.

Two days ago, the phone had rung unexpectedly, with salvation on the other end of the line.

"Could you rearrange your commitments and take on ferrying troops to Europe?" the voice at Military Airlift Command said. "We'll give you as many flights as you can handle and guarantee you at least a week."

At the moment, Cooper's flights for the next seven days consisted of picking up a planeload of little old ladies in Pittsburgh on Thursday and flying them to Elko, Nevada, to play bingo.

"Yeah. I think I can handle that," Cooper said, suppressing the excitement he felt.

It would be stretching his plane to its limits, but a week of MAC flights would give him enough money to satisfy his creditors and his ex-wife for at least the next three months.

Cooper located a backup crew. He found some out-of-work flight attendants and notified his copilot there would be a paycheck after all. Forty-eight hours ago, he'd started flying troops to Germany. In two days, the 767 had completed three trips to Europe.

Their next stop would be Charleston to discharge their passengers. The backup crew would then make the short jaunt to Savannah. There, they'd collect a load of soldiers from the 24th Infantry Division and return to Rhein-Main. At Rhein-Main, another group of dependents would be eagerly awaiting their turn to board the plane.

Cooper was determined to continue the process for as long as MAC wanted.

As the tired plane taxied onto the runway, Linda Jensen looked at her watch in the dim light of the passenger compartment. It was nearly midnight. The girls were already asleep. Linda glanced around the cabin at the wives and children of the men of her husband's platoon. In eight hours, they would touch down in Charleston.

None of them had any way of knowing that at this very moment, their husbands were fighting for their lives in the blustery snows of the bloodstained border.

The plane with the Eagle on its tail roared down the runway. The 767 fought its way into the stormy January night and headed for home.

CHAPTER 6

January 28—11:49 p.m.
2nd Platoon, Delta Troop, 1st Squadron, 4th Cavalry
The German-Czech Border

Feeling its way as it went, the Russian armored column moved single file down the narrow, twisting trail. The division commander would have preferred to proceed cautiously. The proper procedure would have been to first send his foot soldiers to clear the woods of the elusive enemy before moving forward. His orders, however, were to seize the north–south highway without delay. By morning, he had to control the critical highway the entire fifteen kilometers north to where the British and American lines met. If he waited while his infantry secured the woods, most of his division would still be on the border when morning came. He was risking his armor by not supporting it with infantry, but orders were to be obeyed.

The leading components of the armored advance were nearly halfway to the north–south highway. In less than a kilometer, the forward elements would reach the roadway and turn north. So far, they'd encountered no further opposition after defeating the token American resistance at the border. Maybe Dmetri had been correct in his assessment of their opponent. Possibly after such a humiliating defeat, the enemy had abandoned its positions and was in full retreat.

At the front of the long column, the lead tank's massive hull scraped against the low-hanging branches. The tank warily eased around a sharp bend to the left. Two other T-80s and a BMP2 were close behind. All four disappeared from view around the curve.

Jensen waited until just the right moment. With his heart pounding in his ears and bile rising to his lips, he screamed into his headset, "Open fire!"

Renoir's and Richmond's gunners instantly launched TOWs. Using their periscopes' optical sights, they made minor adjustments during their missiles' brief flight. In the twinkling of an eye, the American missiles turned the first T-80 into a flaming mass of twisted metal. Ravenous fires reached back to eagerly lick at the steel treads of those behind it in the endless column. The lead elements frantically searched for the source of the attack. With a forty-seven-ton fireball preventing their movement forward and the massive column blocking their retreat, they were trapped. If they failed to locate the source of the ambush and quickly destroy it, they knew their lives would soon be over.

As the first TOWs tore from their launch tubes, Cruz ordered his Bradley onto the roadway. The fighting vehicle sprang from the cover of the deep forest and positioned itself in the middle of the trail. Renoir and Richmond opened fire with their Bushmasters on the BMP a few vehicles back of the burning tank. The Bushmasters' shells ripped gaping holes in the side armor of the Russian fighting vehicle. Thick smoke billowed from the wounded armored personnel carrier. The BMP's ten soldiers died in a matter of seconds beneath the deadly curtain of fire from the Bradleys.

Cruz's gunner located the second T-80. He hurled a stubby missile down the narrow path with devastating effect. The tank was quickly devoured. Another ear-shattering explosion rocked the night. A second pillar of fire stretched high into the sorrowful evergreens.

The third tank succeeded in its desperate attempt to find the source of the ambush. The T-80's machine gun opened fire on the American position. The turret of the monster swung to the left. The tank's gunner locked onto the Bradley sitting in the center of the trail. In a fraction of a second, he would unleash the awesome power of the T-80's main gun to annihilate the foolish Americans who dared to stand in the column's way. The Russian gunner prepared to fire his cannon. The time was nearly here. Without warning, three TOWs ripped into the tank's exposed belly. Its metal workings spilled forth onto the snows. A third blazing tank reached out to sear the majestic forest.

"Fall back! Fall back!" Jensen's voice screamed in their ears.

In fifteen seconds, the platoon had devastated the enemy. His ability to advance was gone. The remaining elements of the Russian column were hidden by the curve. Protected by the thick woods, they were unreachable by the platoon's guns. Jensen's men hadn't suffered a single loss.

Given a little time, however, the Russian commander was certain to dismount a powerful infantry force and crush the Americans. There was nothing more the platoon could accomplish. The time had come to run.

Jensen signaled the pair of soldiers guarding the platoon's right. The soldiers raced back through the fallen trees to the Humvee.

Sergeant Richmond raised his commander's hatch and motioned for the two soldiers protecting the left. They hurried through the heavy snows and disappeared up the ramp into the Bradley's rear compartment. The ramp closed behind them.

The platoon started its escape. With Cruz's Bradley providing protection for the fleeing soldiers, Renoir's team scurried onto the roadway and tore back down the winding trail. Richmond's fighting vehicle was soon clipping at his heels. With Jensen at the wheel, the Humvee soared from the woods a few seconds later.

While he drove, Jensen keyed his headset. He needed to ensure that Austin's group, waiting in ambush below, didn't fire upon their own platoon. In three previous wars, he'd seen far too many soldiers killed by friendly fire.

"Delta-Two-Four, this is Delta-Two-Five. Seth, are you there?"

"Yeah, Bob, we're ready and waiting."

"Seth, we're on our way. Don't fire. Say again, do not fire. It's us coming down the trail."

"Roger. We copy. Bring it on home."

In order to turn around, Cruz's Bradley backed into the spot Richmond's had just relinquished. The last of the Bradleys headed down the trail one hundred yards behind the speeding Humvee.

A few vehicles back of the raging fires of the lead tanks, two BMPs spotted a small opening in the trees. They carefully threaded their way through the obstacles on the forest floor. The BMPs warily eased onto the roadway in front of their burning comrades.

The T-80 directly behind the BMPs attempted to follow the personnel carriers through the narrow opening they'd forged in the woods. The tank, twice the BMPs size, faltered in its attempt to make it around its burning partners. It wedged itself in the heavy mantle of trees. The more the tank attempted to extricate itself, the more it succeeded in jamming its gargantuan frame ever deeper into the quagmire. The T-80 blocked any further use of the escape route the BMPs had found. The possibility of breaching the burning tanks was gone. And the impenetrable forest of ancient fir held no other means of escape.

Jensen's plan had succeeded. He'd trapped the Russian armored division at the border.

The BMPs were reentering the trail in front of the blazing tanks when they glimpsed the shadow of the final Bradley beginning its retreat. Throwing caution to the wind, the lead BMP commander gave chase. The second followed close behind as the lethal pair pursued the Americans down the unfamiliar path.

No one in the fleeing platoon was yet aware of the BMPs' success in breaching the barrier of burning metal. A lethal chase had begun.

The Bradleys rushed toward the safety of Austin's covering force. Renoir's and Richmond's vehicles sped past the deserted platoon building and through Austin's position without slowing down. The Humvee also hastened past the ghostly structure and was nearing Austin's force.

Cruz's team trailed.

At the last possible instant, Austin spotted the rapidly closing BMPs as they made the trail's final turn. He quickly aimed his Bushmaster at the onrushing threat. His gunner did his best to line up a clear shot at the leader. He was more than eager to release the first of his TOWs. But Cruz's Bradley was in their line of fire.

"Brownie, nail the bastards!" Austin screamed into his headset.

"Hector's in the way!"

"Foster, can you get the lead one?"

"Negative, Seth! The trail's too tight. There's no way to fire around Cruz."

"Hector, get out of the damn way! Hector, move your ass to the right!"

In the confined space, however, there was nowhere for Cruz and his men to go.

The final Bradley was nearing the platoon building when a Spandrel missile leaped from the lead BMP. The lethal missile ripped from its mooring and roared through the frozen night. With a mighty wail of protest, it struck the lightly armored rear of the Bradley. As it exploded beneath the impacting missile, the Bradley swerved sharply to the right. The crippled fighting vehicle slammed headlong into the staid building that minutes earlier had been the platoon's home. Inside the Bradley's burning wreckage, Cruz and his team were dead.

The BMPs continued their relentless pursuit of the American cavalry. The first, his lone missile fired, found a small opening and slid to the left to allow his partner to pass.

A second inviting target, the speeding Humvee, was one hundred yards beyond the demolished Bradley. In the new leader, the Spandrel gunner took aim. The smaller American combat vehicle was in his sights. In a few seconds, he'd be ready to fire.

But the Russian would never unleash his Spandrel. For he didn't have a few seconds left to live.

The Bradleys of Austin's force had beaten him to the draw. With Cruz out of the way, they locked onto the enemy armored vehicles. In quick succession, the American crews fired TOW missiles. Two struck the lead vehicle. The third hit the trailing one. Both BMPs erupted in hellfire and damnation, reaching high into the low-hanging heavens. For good measure, the Bradley commanders opened up with their Bushmasters to ensure no one survived.

And no one did.

A few hundred yards down the trail, Jensen keyed his headset once again. For the moment, he was uncertain of what had happened near the platoon building. While he dashed for safety, he was aware of the excited chatter on the radio. And he'd heard the explosions close behind. He didn't yet know, however, that Cruz and his men were dead.

"Form up just before the highway," Jensen said.

Renoir's Bradley skidded to a stop thirty yards from the trail's entrance onto the north–south roadway. The platoon began arriving at his position. The young sergeant dismounted. He ran to scout the blizzard-shrouded highway. Renoir threw himself into a snowdrift at the edge of the road. He brought his night-vision goggles up to his face.

He could see nearly a mile in both directions on the snowy asphalt. Behind him, there were tremendous explosions and constant distractions by the sudden flashes of light all along the border. But for as far as he could see, nothing was moving on the pavement.

While Renoir scanned their escape route, Austin's covering force arrived at the platoon's location. Jensen sent Marconi and a handful of soldiers scrambling to the rear to protect them. Once more, they needed to get organized. It was then that he realized they were short a Bradley.

"Who's missing, Seth?" Jensen asked, as Austin climbed down from his fighting vehicle.

"Cruz's team bought it, Bob. We saw the BMPs coming, but with his Bradley in the way, we couldn't get an angle on Comrade to get off a shot."

Midnight. In fifteen minutes of battle, the platoon's losses totaled seventeen. Even so, there was no time to mourn, for there were twenty-six lives Jensen could still attempt to save.

Kicking up the soft snows as he ran, Renoir hurried back to the platoon's position.

"Well?" Jensen said.

"I checked the road in both directions. There's nothing moving anywhere."

"Are you sure?"

"I'm positive, Sarge. The road's deserted."

"Well, it won't be for long," Jensen said.

"What're we going to do?"

"I wish I knew. One thing's for certain, we can't stay here."

So far, their leader's instincts had served them well. But now he faced a new dilemma. If they didn't get off the north–south highway and onto one heading west, his platoon would soon be trapped.

They had two alternatives. They could try to run north. In that direction, the highway headed northeast. Winding slowly away from the border for twelve miles, it would take the platoon nearly thirty minutes to reach the town of Selb. There they'd find a roadway leading to the west. Or the platoon could flee five miles south. There the highway connected with E48, the major east–west artery running through this section of Germany. That would place them three miles west of the border checkpoint manned by Echo Troop's 4th Platoon and a few miles east of the small German town of Schirnding.

Either way—north or south, it might already be too late. For all Jensen knew, the enemy could have breached the north–south highway in a number of locations. They could be trapped no matter which way he chose. And he knew that even if they were fortunate enough to reach one of the western-reaching highways, the Russians could be ten miles into Germany by the time the platoon arrived.

Jensen poked his head into the rear compartment of Austin's Bradley, where Jelewski and his radios had found a home.

"What's the word on the squadron net?"

"Real confusing," Jelewski said. "One thing's for sure, they've hit hard all up and down the border."

Information Jensen already knew from the sounds of the pitched battles raging both north and south of the platoon.

"Haven't been able to make much sense out of any of it," Jelewski added.

"Any word on whether they've breached our lines?"

"Can't really tell. Some units have failed to report in entirely. Others seem to be holding on okay. Russians are jamming our frequencies like crazy, so squadron's changing them constantly. I'm not getting much of it at all. But what I can tell you is that because of the weather, squadron says they can't get the Apaches into the air until morning. They're going to try to send one of the tank troops along with a couple of platoons of Bradleys our way, though."

"Get on the radio and tell them they'd better do a lot better than try." And Jensen made the decision that could end the lives of every member of the platoon in the next few minutes. "Tell them we've blocked an armored column's advance within a mile of the border but we can't hold any longer and we're retreating to take up a secondary position. Give them the map coordinates for E48 just east of Schirnding. If we can get there, that'll be the platoon's next position."

"Roger."

Jensen had chosen his next move. Now was not the time to try anything cute. They would head for the nearest east–west highway and pray they got there before the Russians did.

They needed to hurry. Their location was quite desperate. Jensen, however, had to make a second, equally important choice before they could hope to have any chance of escaping the hangman's noose.

Should they go fast or slow?

If they moved cautiously, the Russians were bound to arrive at the north–south highway's entrance to E48 before they did. If the platoon moved too quickly, however, what they'd done to the Russian column in the woods a few minutes earlier was probably going to happen to them. If enemy units had breached the north–south highway, this time 2nd Platoon would be on the wrong end of the ambush. Neither option was particularly attractive.

The platoon sergeant decided to do the only thing he could. The platoon would move fast. But he'd send out a sacrificial lamb to try to fool any wolves that might be waiting.

He would be the sacrificial lamb.

Bringing together as much of the battered platoon as he could, he hurriedly explained his plan. He would take two soldiers with him in the Humvee. One would drive, the other handle the machine gun.

They'd rush south as fast as they could. The five Bradleys would trail far enough behind to be out of sight. If the Humvee came upon an enemy trap, Jensen would try to spring it before the Russians realized he wasn't alone. It was the best chance he had of saving the platoon.

As Ramirez, head bandaged by the platoon medic, and Steele were without weapons, they were reluctantly elected to go with him. Steele climbed behind the machine gun. Ramirez got behind the wheel. Jensen sat in the passenger seat, ready to cry out over the radio at the first sign of trouble.

It was time to move. The Humvee cautiously poked its nose from the woods and headed onto the highway.

They were soon up to traveling speed on the deserted roadway. Going thirty miles per hour, they plunged through the deep snows. It was a speed the Bradleys could easily match.

It wasn't long before the Humvee completed the first terrifying mile. Jensen spoke into his headset, "Delta-Two, move out."

"Roger," Austin said.

One at a time, every few seconds, a Bradley hurtled from the woods and onto the open highway. In a little more than a minute, all five were on the narrow ribbon that would carry them south to prepare for the next battle. Again, hopefully on Jensen's terms and Jensen's terrain.

From a safe distance, the general surveyed the burning wreckage at the front of the stalled column. He turned toward the tall figure standing next to him in the snows.

"Well, Dmetri, what do you have to say about our foe now?"

"Comrade Commander, you were right in your estimate of the enemy. He turned out to be quite resourceful."

"How long did the lead battalion commander say it would take for his infantry to secure the woods?"

"At least three hours. Possibly more if we encounter serious resistance."

"What about this?" The general motioned to the burning wreckage. "How long before we can be under way again?"

"He didn't know, Comrade Commander. He can't begin clearing

the wreckage until he's certain all the ammunition inside the burning tanks has exploded. It might take many hours before we can extricate ourselves."

"Well, I'll tell you one thing, Dmetri. We'd better find a way out of here before morning. If the American air forces find us here at dawn's first light, none of us will survive."

The Bradley crews blindly followed the man who'd so far kept them alive. None of them needed their night-vision systems to find their way through the blizzard. To their left, scores of burning Russian and American vehicles created their own false sunrise in the east.

Jensen, his eyes fixed upon the fearful roadway, knew if all went well, the platoon would arrive at its next position in fifteen minutes. And if things didn't go well, they'd never arrive.

When the Humvee completed the second mile without incident, even the stoic platoon sergeant began believing his fateful decision had been correct. He glanced over at Ramirez. The private's hands were locked onto the steering wheel. The fear in Ramirez's eyes was undeniable.

"Keep alert . . . keep alert," he admonished his inexperienced companions. And himself.

The Humvee was three miles from E48. Their precarious luck needed to hold for a few minutes more. Much could still go wrong. The Humvee might not fool the enemy and spring a waiting ambush. The Russians could arrive at the roadway just after the Humvee passed, catching the trailing Bradleys. Or E48 could be crawling with Russian tanks when they got there.

"Come on 4th Platoon, Echo Troop, don't let us down," he muttered to himself.

Unlike Jensen's platoon, the doomed soldiers of Echo Troop's 4th Platoon didn't have a tactical edge over their opponent. Jensen had the twisting trail, which he used to its utmost advantage.

But 4th Platoon was responsible for a major four-lane highway into and out of Germany. They couldn't stop the enemy by destroying a few lead tanks. Hit three minutes after the attack on Jensen's men, they'd heard Jelewski's alert on the squadron net moments before the enemy slammed into them. It had helped.

Even so, it wasn't nearly enough. Now, twenty minutes into the war, all eight of the platoon's Bradleys lay burning at the border. All forty-three of the platoon's men were dead.

They'd held out for as long as they could, taking a dozen Russian tanks with them to their graves. But after a fierce struggle, an immense enemy armored column two thousand vehicles long was rolling west unopposed.

The Russians were three miles east of where Jensen's platoon would attempt to enter E48. And the Bradleys were four miles north.

While Jensen and the remnants of his platoon plowed through the night toward an inevitable meeting with the massive Russian column, he wondered out loud, "How the hell did this happen?"

CHAPTER 7

There'd always been that 20 percent in both the East and West who refused to accept the changes occurring at the end of the first Cold War. Instead of joining the new world, they continued on with a policy of fear and suspicion. In the East, they seized the opportunity a struggling Russia created. A new hatred was born, stronger and more resolute than ever.

This was a prideful people with a thousand years of history. And the degradations, real and imagined, felt by their ultimate defeat by the West in the last half of the twentieth century lay heavy upon far too many souls.

That was never more evident than by the aggressive, dictatorial actions in the second decade of the new millennium by the Russian President Vladimir Putin. While his nation's economy floundered and his people's suffering spread, he focused his single-minded attention on rebuilding a vast Russian military whose evolving power was capable of threatening even the strongest of his country's neighbors.

Russia steadily drifted away from the tantalizing promises of a democratic society and back toward those dark, terrifying days of repression and dread.

What Putin didn't understand, however, was that his actions would much too soon lead to his own ruin. As yet another crippling recession appeared to ravage the world, the unrest within his disjointed country soon grew well beyond his control. He'd been caught in a vise squeezing in from those on the left, who found themselves unable to feed their children, and those on the far right, who demanded he take even more extreme action to reclaim Russian's rightful place as the ruler of Eastern Europe.

That churning turmoil would quickly erupt into an all-consuming civil war.

Six years prior to Russia's surprise attack on that bitter German January night, the country had fallen. What they'd failed to win at the ballot box, the Communists and Nationalists rose up to claim in the streets. The coup was intense and bloody. The cruelty knew no bounds. Hundreds of thousands died. The lovers of democracy fought with the resisters of change to determine the destiny of the Eastern world. In the end, the West stood helplessly watching as the disheartened masses chose an ineffective, but familiar, Communist system over one that promised them a future filled with uncertainty.

It was over in a matter of weeks. When it was finished, the Communists had reclaimed their rightful place.

From the chaos of the new government emerged Cheninko.

He'd always been there—an unnoticed, second-tier leader of the Communist Party. In the confusion that followed the civil war, Cheninko saw his opportunity and struck. He seized power and held on to it with a viselike grip.

He'd been only seven when Stalin died. Yet in his mind's eye he remembered Stalin's years as the truly glorious ones for the Soviet Union. So he returned Russia to those dark and terrifying times. Purges, repression, and murder became Cheninko's path to attaining his vision of the new Russia. He knew, however, that his world would never be complete without the strength of a unified Soviet Union. And like his countrymen, he could never rest without the security of a communistic East to buffer his country from the frightening power of the West.

The brutal dictator's biggest obstacle in reaching such a goal was NATO's incursions into the East following the first Cold War. Many of those he needed to return to the Soviet sphere were firmly entrenched in the Western military alliance. He knew if the Russians invaded a NATO member, the Americans would have no choice but to fiercely respond to crush him. If he was going to succeed, his country would have to appear to have no direct role in the internal struggles and civil wars designed to topple the democratic leadership of the East one by one.

Aided by the same allies that had helped in the conquest of Russia, Cheninko's agents began harvesting the seeds of discontent in the countries of the East. Rivers of blood soon flowed. And again, the results were the same. Within two years, even the most progressive countries of Eastern Europe were back under the Communist thumb.

Within days of the Communists' return to power, each country withdrew from NATO and rejoined the Warsaw Pact.

A new Cold War, more gripping than ever, reached out a frozen fist to dominate the planet. The fences went back up. East and West were separated once more. A curtain of barbed wire and steel, mistrust and misunderstanding, seized the northern half of this tiny world.

Still, Cheninko wasn't satisfied. For he was convinced that Russia had yet to reclaim the preeminent world position that was rightfully hers. There was one thing standing in the way of obtaining that lofty goal.

Unified Germany.

The savagely horrific stories Cheninko had been told of the last world war were as vivid as if the battles had occurred yesterday. He knew Russian children could never sleep soundly in their beds as long as there was one Germany. In the previous world war, over twenty million Russians had lost their lives at the hands of a ruthless German invader bent on conquest. He wouldn't let that happen again.

The Russian nightmare could never be quelled without putting an end to the threat a unified Germany posed to Mother Russia.

Cheninko's single-minded purpose became separating the Germans, East and West, one last time.

His plan for conquest took form.

Cheninko had two powerful assets in East Germany. He would call upon both to return the East Germans to their proper place. First, just as there had been in Russia and Eastern Europe, in every major city there still existed a loyal cadre of East German Communists. Just as importantly, under the provisions of the Yalta and Potsdam Agreements, Cheninko had demanded and, after much saber rattling, received the right to return ten thousand Russian soldiers to East German soil.

The plan was simple. Cheninko would utilize these resources to realize the same result he'd effected throughout his Communist empire. He would disperse the gospel of dissatisfaction once more. He would use his eager band of German Communists to spread his brand of truth. And when the time came, ten thousand of his finest soldiers were waiting inside enemy lines to sway the battle. He was certain he wouldn't fail. With his sword of propaganda, he'd sever the German brothers.

Once again, blood would flow in the streets of Europe. This time, however, Cheninko would watch with great satisfaction, for the blood would be German.

What Cheninko couldn't comprehend, however, was the obsession the Germans held for the day their defeated country would be whole once more. The Russian nightmare presented by a unified Germany was matched by an equally vivid German nightmare that their country would again be torn apart. In the German mind, once the two Germanys had become one, nothing on earth was going to rip the East from the West's hands.

The time had come to finish the job—the time had come to return East Germany to the Soviet sphere. Cheninko's orders went out. First, his Communist cadre would take to the streets with banners, leaflets, and speeches. They would deride the policies of the West. They would point to their inability to care for their families without the jobs the latest recession had stolen from them. They would call for a general uprising to throw off their oppressors and return to the old ways. More than anything, they would search for an opening to create incidents of violence while looking the part of the innocent victim. It was a formula Cheninko had used on many occasions.

Cheninko knew it would be a few hours, a few days at most, before such an event would occur. The Communists would then put down their banners and pick up their stones and sickles.

Cheninko was right. In April, nine months prior to the beginning of the war, on the second day of their "peaceful" protest throughout all of East Germany, the justification the Communists needed appeared. It happened in Leipzig. A small group of men, women, and children "innocently" found themselves face-to-face with a roving band of neo-Nazis ten times their size. A push, a shove, a placard smashing a shaved skull, and the battle for East Germany had begun. The Leipzig police were slow to respond to the unanticipated crisis. Before it was over, three Communists, including a six-year-old child, lay dead.

Thousands took to the streets. In every city in the eastern half, with red banners held high, they staged "spontaneous" and "peaceful" protests intended to be neither spontaneous nor peaceful.

"The fascist murderers must be brought to justice!" they cried. There was blood in their voices and menace in their hearts.

"The fascists must be rooted out and destroyed!" they screamed.

"Long live the proletariat! Long live the Communist brotherhood!"

The battles were soon being fought. And blood did flow in the cobblestone streets of Germany. Each side justified the perversion through their own warped perceptions of the world.

The Germans of the West watched in horror as civil war struck like lightning in the East. When the German government's attempt to control the slaughter failed, Cheninko was certain his vision of the new world would soon be complete. In a short time, East Germany would be his.

Cheninko was convinced the bloated West would always be more concerned with holding on to its riches than in holding on to its East German brothers.

He was very wrong.

For two months, a civil war of unspeakable horror raged in the East. Sabotage, terror, and murder became the realities of East German life. The tide of battle swung decisively toward the Communists. Their victory was nearly complete.

It appeared to be over.

But much to the surprise of all involved, it wasn't nearly so.

CHAPTER 8

Enter the German savior—Fromisch.

From the depravity of the horrendous conflict, he arose. Manfred Fromisch, fifty-two-year-old leader of one of the strongest pre–civil war neo-Nazi sects. He was an evil man of no more than five feet. His deformed body was every bit as twisted as his ravaged mind. But his vision of the world was just as strong and compelling as Cheninko's. Fromisch brought order to the bitter struggle's chaos. He brought the Nazis back to prominence.

On the brink of losing the East, the new Führer was born. He marched out his brown-shirted thugs and defeated the Communists at every turn. His brilliance at orchestrating the horrific little battles of the narrow streets and dirty alleyways knew no equal.

Along with his skill at fighting, he brought an orator's tongue to the eager pulpit of the unhealed German psyche—the wounded national psyche that remained from the forced degradations of the last world war.

"Kill the Auslander!" Fromisch screamed.

"Kill the Slav!"

"Kill the Jew!"

"Kill! Kill! Kill!"

"Destroy the Communist menace!"

"Bring back our rightful place as the world's master race!"

"Germany for the Germans!"

"Deutschland uber Alles!"

At first, the Germans of the West refused to listen. They resisted the old siren songs.

In the end, however, when their government failed them, they reluctantly turned toward the savior's voice. They didn't want him, but they had little choice if they desired to hold on to a united Germany. Millions gritted their teeth and fell in behind Fromisch's banner. The dream of one Germany was just too strong.

The tide of battle turned. The East was pulled from the brink. With Fromisch at its head, the stream of blood became a flowing river. As summer dragged into fall, it was clear the struggle was over and the Communists would lose.

It was over for everyone except Cheninko. For he still had one card left to play.

For months, Cheninko's elite ten thousand had waited in their barracks for the order to come. On three occasions, when the Communist victory appeared imminent, Cheninko had considered issuing such a command. Each time he hesitated, however, for the timing had never been quite right.

Now, from deep within the Kremlin's walls, the secret orders went out to his commanders in East Germany. "Go out to protect the defenseless people from Fromisch's butchers," Cheninko said. "Pick your spots carefully. But entangle yourself in such a way that before the Germans realize what has happened, you're in the middle of the civil war. Destroy the serpent Fromisch and his venomous army of murderers. Relight the Communist flame in the hearts of the East German people. Return them to their rightful place within the Soviet world."

On an October day, when the leaves were dying and a pungent hint of the coming winter hung in the air, Communist men, women, and children were sent out. Acting upon Premier Cheninko's directions, they found themselves surrounded by a company of Fromisch's rogue army. The brave little band held their placards high. Just as they'd done many times before, Fromisch's grinning skinheads moved in for the kill. The results, as they'd been so often in the past months, would be incredibly swift and brutally certain. Not a single Communist would survive the unfortunate encounter.

But things don't always go as planned.

Instead, for the first time in months, the brown shirts found themselves on the wrong end of the slaughter. For from out of nowhere, a battalion of Russian soldiers emerged.

Fromisch's rabble excelled in a street fight. This, however, was no street fight.

It was over in twenty minutes. Outnumbering the skinheads seven to one, the Soviets left two hundred of Fromisch's maniacal henchmen lying dead on a blood-drenched street in East Berlin.

Three days later, the Soviets used the same tactic in Dresden. Another Russian battalion "stumbled" upon a slaughter in the making. Before it was over, scores of slain brown shirts sprawled in the gutters of a thousand-year-old alley.

Things were once again going Cheninko's way.

The time had come. The morning after the Dresden victory, using the death of a handful of Russian soldiers as their justification, the Soviet forces would take to the streets. They would ruthlessly hunt down Fromisch and his men. No mercy would be shown. No quarter would be given.

They wouldn't stop their onslaught until they'd wiped all traces of the brown shirts from the face of the earth.

The day broke on a clear autumn morning. The end was in sight. Within the week, East Germany would be firmly in Cheninko's hands.

When each Russian commander awoke, however, he found his barracks surrounded by a well-armed force of Germans twenty times his battalion's size. Faced with certain annihilation, all seven surrendered without a shot being fired.

Worldwide television captured the final humiliation. With the exuberant Fromisch at their head, the brown shirts marched the Russians to the Polish border and kicked them out of Germany.

Other than an occasional act of senseless sabotage, the battle for East Germany was over. East Germany belonged to Manfred Fromisch.

Germany's adoration for the man who'd saved their country was boundless. With national elections scheduled for early in the coming spring, the latest polls showed that Fromisch and his neo-Nazi party held nearly 80 percent of the vote in both the East and the West.

The next Chancellor of Germany would be Manfred Fromisch.

The next political party to lead the German nation was going to be the Nazis.

Defeat at the hands of Fromisch and his butchers was too much for Cheninko to bear. The horrors Nazi Germany presented haunted his every waking moment. It stole his fitful sleep. The anguish the Germans had wrought upon his country tore at the fabric of Cheninko's tortured soul.

On the day the first snow touched upon Moscow, Cheninko gathered his field marshals.

"You'll prepare a plan for the destruction of Germany."

"Yes, Comrade Premier."

"You'll be ready to attack within four months or face the consequences of your failure."

With thousands of their fellow officers dead at the hands of Cheninko's firing squads, or in the living hell of the gulags, there was no question of what the consequences would be.

There could be only one response. "Yes, Comrade Premier."

Unless the Germans turned away from the poison spewing from Fromisch's mouth, they would pay dearly for their decision. Cheninko would see to that.

The American President was backed into a corner. If he abandoned Germany, there would be no chance of using his great country's power to control Fromisch and swiftly push his vile Nazis aside. If he abandoned Germany, Fromisch would be free to do as he wished.

Yet if the President announced his acceptance of Fromisch, his country would appear to be giving legitimacy to those whose unspeakable acts had cost sixty million lives during World War II.

The President decided to do the only thing he could. He appeared on worldwide television in early December to announce his decision. Only a handful of his top advisors knew the true purpose behind his words. Not even America's closest allies were privy to the President's plans. He couldn't take the chance that Fromisch would uncover America's actual intentions.

"My friends. After much discussion, and with the backing of the House and the Senate, I have come to a decision on what America's policy will be toward the upcoming German elections. As we must do, we will respect the duly elected government of Germany, no matter what leader and form of government the free people of that nation choose to guide their future. America reiterates her position that the sovereignty of Germany, like that of all remaining NATO countries, will be protected against aggression from any source."

America had made the choice its interests dictated. America would do what it had to do.

America would pretend to back the Nazis until it could find a way to rid the world of Fromisch and his followers.

Unaware of the President's true purpose, Cheninko watched in utter disbelief.

In a rage, the Russian leader ordered the Soviet High Command to appear in his office within the hour to present its plan for the conquest of Germany.

CHAPTER 9

December 14—10:07 a.m.
Inside the Kremlin
Moscow

Comrade Cheninko sat behind his massive desk. He did nothing to hide the anger that showed in his eyes and blackened his soul. Five of the Soviet Union's highest-ranking military officers filed into the Premier's ornate office. The Admiral of the Soviet Navies was the first into the room. Next came the field marshals commanding Army Group North and Army Group Central. The Commander of the Soviet Air Forces followed them in. The last to enter was the junior officer in the group, Comrade General Valexi Yovanovich, the Director of Operations for the Soviet High Command. Unlike the fat old men who had come before him, the younger Yovanovich stood ramrod straight before Cheninko.

General Yovanovich prided himself on his powerful body, which was without a hint of excess. His dark, wavy hair, with the slightest touch of gray at the temples, accentuated his rugged good looks and square jaw. Yovanovich's booming voice and calm demeanor were every bit as powerful as his finely honed body. He was a man to be reckoned with, of which he was acutely aware.

They were here to present Yovanovich's plan for the conquest of Germany. Nervousness was etched upon the first four faces. Their discomfort showed in their stilted movements and furrowed brows. Only Yovanovich appeared to be at ease. Each knew it was the brilliant Yovanovich's performance that their lives depended upon.

Premier Cheninko wasted no time in getting to the point.

"Did you see what the American President said on television last night? How dare he back Fromisch and the Nazi pigs?"

"Yes, Comrade Premier, we saw," the leader of the Soviet Air Forces said.

"We have no choice now but to attack. Have you done what you were told? Have you devised a plan to destroy the Germans?" Cheninko said.

Each looked to Valexi Yovanovich.

"Yes, Comrade Premier," Yovanovich said. "With our plan, we'll conquer Germany in five days."

The others anxiously awaited Cheninko's reaction. They'd told Yovanovich not to make such bold statements. But as usual, he hadn't listened. Each knew that in the new Russia, bold statements were a one-way ticket to the gulags.

"What?" Cheninko said. "Five days?" There was disbelief on the Premier's face.

General Yovanovich had anticipated Cheninko's reaction. "Yes, Comrade Premier, with your help, we'll capture Germany in five days."

"My help?"

"Comrade Premier, I'm afraid we can't defeat the Nazis without your help. Your role in conquering Germany will be quite significant."

A smile came to Cheninko's face. The idea that he would play a major part in eliminating the Nazi threat to Mother Russia pleased him greatly.

"What help is it you'll need from me, Comrade General?"

"Comrade Cheninko, it would probably be best if I laid out our plan for you. Your role is quite important. It'll be more easily understood, however, if I explain the overall concept. Our plan covers every aspect of the conquest of our enemies. It involves four elements—deception, sabotage, power, and diplomacy. We've left nothing to chance. With this plan, we'll capture Germany in five days."

"Five days, Yovanovich. How can such be possible?"

"Because our enemies have been far too distracted in the past thirty-three years. The Americans' entire focus had been on destroying those who indiscriminately practice terror. While the Americans pursued their goal of destroying the fanatics, they had little choice but to let down their guard just a little nearly everywhere else in the world. In this relentless pursuit, they have exhausted their military both physically and psychologically. They spent years trying to eliminate an elusive foe they neither understood nor, until they became hopelessly bogged down in fighting, regarded as anything but a vastly inferior opponent."

"That may be true, Yovanovich, but I still don't see how any of that guarantees we can conquer Germany in so short a time."

"Comrade Premier, until you came to power, the Americans had felt far too secure in Europe. They had continued to reduce their forces in Germany from a Cold War high of three hundred thousand to barely twenty-five thousand. While they continued to maintain two divisions' worth of pre-positioned equipment in Germany, they left not a single combat soldier on German soil. And they kept just two functioning air bases. To tell you the truth, they may have had no other option but to divert their forces to the degree they did while they spent more than two decades hunting down the zealots. Once they ended most of their lengthy forays in the Middle East, they thought there would be time for their military to rest and heal. For that reason, when the new Cold War began, they were somewhat slow in responding to what was happening in Europe. They are clearly trying to rectify that mistake, but we are certain the force we presently face on the battlefield is one that we can conquer with relative ease."

"Do you believe we have an accurate estimate on the opposition that awaits us, Yovanovich?"

"Yes, Comrade Premier. Our intelligence is quite good. In the past couple of years, the Americans have returned two armored divisions and three cavalry regiments to Germany. We believe that while they are making plans to reopen a number of fighter air bases, for now we will battle only the two that remained after the American drawdown. At this moment, we estimate we face approximately one hundred thousand Americans along with the British, Canadian, and German forces.

We are confident that while the Americans have yet to fully decide to return to their earlier Cold War force levels, their recent reopening of their primary transport air base at Rhein-Main is a sure sign of their intent to greatly fortify Germany and Western Europe. I fully expect that if we give them a few more years, they will double their combat forces and increase their fighter air bases to at least four. But as they will see quite soon, the efforts they've made so far are going to be far too little and much too late."

"Comrade General, while they might only have two functioning fighter air bases within Germany," Cheninko said, "you cannot forget their air forces in England, Spain, Italy, Greece, and Turkey. And their significant seaborne forces."

"I'll get to that, Comrade Premier. But first I wish to address only the forces opposing us within Germany itself. As I just stated, the Americans are down to one-third the force we'd have faced during the first Cold War. A force we could've defeated then."

Another bold statement. Again, those present awaited Cheninko's reaction. Valexi Yovanovich was going to be either the next Premier of the Soviet Union or standing in front of a firing squad by the end of the week. And they knew they'd be standing with him.

Yovanovich never hesitated. He showed no outward concern for what the Premier's response might be.

"The British likewise had reduced their forces," Yovanovich said. "There are less than fifty thousand British and Canadian soldiers guarding the northern half of Germany. And as was demonstrated during the recent people's war to liberate East Germany, the German military force of three hundred thousand active duty and reserves wasn't even capable of dealing with a simple insurrection. The Germans demonstrated weakness in both leadership and organization."

"Yes, Yovanovich, you're correct. The German military did show such weaknesses. If it hadn't been for that vile dog, Fromisch, East Germany would be in our hands right now."

"Comrade Cheninko, do not concern yourself unnecessarily. Our plan will undoubtedly correct that problem in the very near future."

"It had better, Comrade General."

"Everyone in this room fully understands the consequences should we fail. But a close assessment of our opponent shows that victory is all but assured. When we totaled up the force we'll face within Germany itself, it came to 450,000. Their air forces consist of eight American fighter wings, three British, and fourteen German. They can muster eleven armored divisions—eight German, two American, and one British. In all, there are less than four thousand tanks waiting to oppose us. In a war as swift and decisive as this one, it is unlikely the Americans and British will be able to significantly reinforce the army we'll face in the field."

"But conquer Germany in five days, Yovanovich. Are you certain?"

"Comrade Premier, I'd stake my life on it. By the end of January, we'll have mustered 150 divisions. We'll be able to place a little over two million soldiers on the battlefield; 105 of these divisions are first-line. The remaining forty-five are reserve units with older T-62 tanks. In total manpower, we'll outnumber the enemy five to one. In air forces, our advantage will be three to one. In tanks, greater than twelve to one. And in artillery, twenty to one."

"But, Comrade General," Cheninko said, "certainly you know superior numbers aren't enough to ensure victory. What about the other factors . . . the sophisticated technology of the West, the fact that the Germans will be fighting on their own soil, and so on?"

There was firmness in Yovanovich's voice. "You're correct, Comrade Premier. Superior numbers won't be enough. That's why we've left nothing to chance."

Even the field marshals were beginning to be infected with Yovanovich's confidence. The Director of Operations was a shrewd man. And shrewd men didn't make statements that would lead to the living hell of the death camps unless they were certain of what they were saying.

"The fact that the Germans will be fighting on their own soil will actually be to our advantage, Comrade Premier," Yovanovich said. "We're certain the Americans and British will grudgingly trade ground for time in order to gain a tactical advantage. They'll be satisfied to dig in and force us to fight a costly war of attrition against strongly fortified defensive positions. But the Germans will feel the panic of the loss of their homeland. They'll feel the pressure to save their countrymen from our advancing armies. They'll be unable to show the patience a defensive army must demonstrate. Their panic will cause them to make mistakes."

"Such a point, Comrade Yovanovich, is well taken."

"My staff's convinced the Germans are going to blunder. And our plan's been designed to take advantage of every error."

A smile came to Cheninko's face. For the first time, he suspected that what Yovanovich was saying was actually true.

"We're going to take Germany in five days," Cheninko said.

It was time to throw caution to the wind and jump on Yovanovich's bandwagon. "Yes, Comrade Premier," the Commander of Army Group Central said. "As General Yovanovich said, we're going to take Germany in five days."

"All right, Yovanovich," Cheninko said. "So far, I'm convinced. Tell me about this plan of yours."

"Comrade Cheninko, let's start with the first of the four elements—deception. You're going to play a critical role in this part of our operation. As you are aware, sometime ago we told the world that the reunited Warsaw Pact would soon hold its first war games. This week, you'll announce that those war games will be the largest in history. The world will hear that fifty of our divisions will conduct this exercise right on the border with Germany."

"But, Comrade General, the West will scream to the high heavens if I make such an outrageous announcement," Cheninko said.

"Of course they will. But at the same time, you'll also announce a reopening of the SALT-VI nuclear disarmament talks. The Americans will be so relieved by your sudden willingness to resume the disarmament discussions that they'll ignore the threat posed by our war games. With honey in your voice, you'll tell the world a few days later that you wish a summit meeting with Fromisch as soon as the German elections are concluded. You'll stop making speeches the West would find even the least bit threatening. And through diplomatic channels, you'll begin making quiet overtures toward the Americans, British, and French. This, of course, will all be a ruse to hide our true intentions. In fact, even your announcement of fifty-division war games will be a lie. With your sweet words to protect us, we're not going to send fifty divisions to the German border. We're going to send the entire 150."

"Comrade General, that's fine. I'll deceive the diplomats. But how do you propose we deceive the American satellites that spy on our country every moment of the day? We'll need at least four full weeks of straining every last resource of the Soviet Union to bring 150 divisions to the jumping-off point for the attack. The Americans will recognize what we're up to on the very first day."

"Deception, Comrade Premier, deception. In the next two weeks, we'll secretly repaint the unit designators on every vehicle of our armies. The Americans are so proud of their satellites' ability to 'read the numbers on every truck in the Soviet Union' that they'll help with our deception. The equipment rolling forward will have the designations of exactly fifty divisions. No more, no less."

"But, Comrade General, the Americans can count, can't they?" the Premier said. "They know how many tanks make up fifty divisions."

A grin came to Yovanovich's handsome face. "The Americans know the only way we can get so much equipment to the war-games site is by rail. They'll anticipate massive use of our railway system. We'll use that to our advantage. We know what time their spy satellites typically photograph each area each day. So what we're going to do is make up many of our trains with identical cargoes. Say tanks being carried on the first three cars, followed by six BMPs on the next three, followed by a certain number of artillery pieces, and three more cars carrying tanks. It will take precise timing. But we're sending the trains west on an exact schedule. Every time a spy satellite takes a picture in a particular area, it'll see what appears to be the same train sitting at the same place in one of our rail yards. The Americans will see what they'll think is one train, when in fact it'll be a different train every day."

"Will such a ruse work?"

Valexi Yovanovich gave an honest answer. "That I cannot guarantee, Comrade Premier. I know it won't work forever. Nevertheless, I believe it's going to work long enough for us to surprise our enemies. Because in addition to the trains, we'll use the weather to our advantage. Our meteorologists tell us central Europe is blanketed by heavy clouds 80 to 90 percent of the time in the month of January. So many of the spies in space won't be able to see exactly what we're doing as long as the clouds are there to protect us."

"But, General Yovanovich," Cheninko said, "paint and clouds will help us confuse the satellites, but what about the spies the enemy has placed in our midst? By the second day of our efforts, the Americans will be receiving reports that something strange is going on. How do we stop that?"

"Comrade Premier, I don't propose we stop such reports at all. Instead of stopping them, which would only increase the Americans' suspicions, we're going to add to the reports. Using our double agents, we'll also report unusual activity in the Soviet Union. However, the reports from the double agents will do something the others won't. Their reports will explain the reason for such activity."

"And what will that be?"

"If you'll excuse my bluntness, Comrade Premier, the Americans would like nothing better than to see you overthrown. So we'll feed them reports that the actions within the Soviet Union involve an attempted coup. I mean no disrespect, but they'll be so overjoyed by the possibility of your overthrow, they'll eagerly ignore any other reports. The Americans will see only what they choose to see."

"My overthrow . . . very good, Yovanovich. That's just devious enough to be something I'd have come up with."

"Thank you, Comrade Premier. But there's still more to our deception. On the evening of the beginning of our battle to liberate the German people from the Nazis, we'll deceive the Americans once again. We've known for years that they believe they can defeat us because of our centralized leadership structure. Within a few hours of the beginning of the war, they'll send their aircraft to kill each of your field commanders and all the members of their staffs. As they did to the Iraqis in both their wars against them, they'll first attempt to destroy our air defenses, then wipe out our command and control. The Americans won't realize until it's too late, but our field headquarters won't be where they believe."

"Oh? And where will they be?"

"They'll be anywhere but where the Americans think. At the last possible moment, under the cover of darkness, we'll move all our command elements. We'll continue to move them to avoid their destruction. My staff has drawn up detailed plans for such movements and will furnish them to our field commanders at the appropriate time. To assist their survival, we've also developed a scheme to make the Americans believe our field headquarters have been eliminated. That'll buy your field marshals and generals further time to conduct the war rather than concerning themselves with Stealth fighters coming in the dead of night to end their lives."

"I'm sure the Army Group Central and Army Group North Commanders were relieved to hear that." With a widening grin, Cheninko looked at the two field marshals.

A smile came to both the field marshals' faces. "Yes, we were, Comrade Premier," the Army Group Central Commander said.

Cheninko turned back to Yovanovich. "Go on, General."

"Finally, to complete our deception, we'll let the Americans fool themselves once more. The Americans believe we'd never attack Germany during bad weather. They're convinced we could never sustain such a war if we attacked in anything but the best possible conditions. Their beliefs are correct. At least, they're correct if we were planning a drawn-out campaign. But we aren't. We're planning a five-day war. By attacking in the worst possible weather, we'll catch our opponent unprepared. We'll also have the added benefit of the weather hampering the American's fighter aircraft and attack helicopters. So our proposal to you, Comrade Premier, is that on the worst night during the last week of January or first week in February, we begin our quest to liberate Germany."

A huge smile came to Cheninko's face. It was obvious he was pleased with what he'd heard so far. "Deception, my dear Comrades, deception," the Premier said.

There was relief on the four senior officers' faces. Yovanovich's boasts were making sense. And their date with the firing squad just might be averted.

Yovanovich glanced at the others. He found an audience in full appreciation of what was being presented. Six sets of eyes shone with the same belief. *We will surprise our enemies. We will take Germany in five days.*

Yovanovich had Cheninko exactly where he wanted him, and he knew it.

"Comrade Premier, unless there's more you wish to hear about the first element of our plan, I'll move on to the second phase—sabotage."

"Please go on, General," Cheninko said. "I'm eager to hear what else you've got in store for our enemies."

"The West is particularly susceptible to sabotage. The Americans pride themselves upon their fancy computers and their sophisticated command and control. Yet in the past thirty-three years, they've done little to continue modernizing their infrastructure within Germany. They're very vulnerable. In the 1980s, they'd begun a complete redesign of their communications by installing a digital fiber-optic system. When the Cold War ended, and they withdrew the majority of their forces from Germany, the modernization project was slowly phased out. The existing fiber-optic system is much too small to handle the huge increase in forces over the past two years, so they've had to reopen their microwave communication sites to handle 80 percent of their command and control needs. There is little or no redundancy. By knocking out a handful of critical communication facilities, we can isolate Germany in the first few hours. To make our task even easier, these communication facilities are on isolated mountaintops miles from the nearest combat units. Unbelievably, these facilities have no security systems whatsoever. With their strategic communication system destroyed at the beginning of the war, the Americans' abilities to coordinate their efforts will be severely crippled. To aid in our efforts and cause further confusion, we also plan on destroying much of the German power grid, many of the primary German civilian communication systems, and as many cell towers as we can. We estimate that with over eighty million panicked Germans trying to use the cellular and landline systems, they will overwhelm the civilian communication network within hours of the start of the war."

Yovanovich paused to allow Cheninko to grasp the importance of what he'd just said.

"Comrade Premier, chop off the head, and the serpent dies. We'll isolate Germany in the first hours of battle. Without the ability to precisely coordinate their efforts, the inferior force we face on the ground will stand no chance. In the darkness of the first night, we're going to sever the American head and watch our enemy wither and die."

"Comrade General, is what you're telling me true? Is it going to be that easy?"

"Let me make myself clear, Comrade Premier. I never said it was going to be easy. Nevertheless, during the past decades, the Americans have made themselves quite susceptible to the destruction of their ability to control a war in Germany. And they haven't done nearly enough in the past few years to rectify that situation. We're going to take advantage of that susceptibility."

"Full advantage, Comrade Premier," the Army Group North Commander added.

"As soon as we disrupt their command and control," Yovanovich said, "we'll buy ourselves a number of hours in which to destroy those assets that stand in the way of our victory. We'll eliminate the Allied air bases and destroy the two pre-positioned armored divisions of weapons the Americans have waiting inside Germany for their reinforcements."

"How do you propose we do that?" Cheninko said.

"I'll get to that portion of the plan shortly, Comrade Cheninko. But first, let me address a significant point you need to be made aware of. With command and control in disarray and our attack taking place in the middle of the night, we'll have six to eight hours of free rein. It'll be at least that long before our enemy can mount any sort of coordinated counterattack."

"Of his air forces also?" Cheninko asked.

"If our plan works, we should have that critical night before we'll see significant air or ground forces. During those first confusing hours, we'll sabotage his efforts further. And once we've brushed aside the American and British border forces, we'll have those same hours for our armor to penetrate deep into the heart of Germany. Those first eight hours are critical. We'll put ourselves in a position to win, or lose our chance for victory, in the darkness of the first night."

Cheninko looked at his field marshals. "Then you'll place yourself in such a position no matter what the cost."

"Yes, Comrade Cheninko," the Army Group Central Commander said. "It will be done. We'll see to that."

"It's imperative that our divisions reach their objectives by sunrise of the first morning," Yovanovich said. "From east to west, we must have seventy kilometers of operating area throughout the length of Germany. If not, we'll be unable to disperse our massive army. And that would be fatal. By sunrise, no unit larger than company size can dare to remain together. We're certain the American weapons of mass destruction will be used on any target larger than that."

"Weapons of mass destruction, Comrade General?" Cheninko said. "Are you telling me the Americans will use nuclear weapons on our forces?"

"Comrade Premier, let me be perfectly clear. For nearly seventy years, the American strategy for defending Germany has included the liberal use of tactical nuclear weapons on the battlefield. We believe that given the opportunity, they'll use them against us. The Americans are convinced their only chance of winning will be by using their vast tactical nuclear arsenal. And, Comrade Premier, the interesting thing is the Americans may be correct. That's why our prime directive will be that there'll be no massing of forces after the first sunrise. We cannot tempt the enemy by presenting such an inviting target to him. Even if he chooses not to use his nuclear capabilities, his conventional weapons will be brought to bear on any massed units. By dispersing our force so widely, we'll greatly limit the Americans' ability to unleash the power of his B-2 and B-52 bombers. And we'll significantly reduce the effectiveness of his Tomahawk cruise missiles. Even so, our commanders won't want to see what his attack helicopters, ground-attack aircraft, drones, and Multiple Launch Rocket Systems can do to any armored units they find."

"Comrade General, you'll tell our commanders that I'll personally order their appearance before a firing squad if they violate that directive."

"I'll see to it, Comrade Premier. This brings us to the third phase of our plan—power. This phase will be completely coordinated with the sabotage phase. As our forces smash through the border, our sabotage teams will be disrupting the enemy's ability to control the war. By dawn of the first day, we'll have choked American command and control beyond its limits. With our air forces, we'll then clear an air corridor. Through this corridor, five airborne divisions will fly into the heart of Germany to destroy the NATO airfields, eliminate the American pre-positioned armored equipment, and capture every bridge over the Rhine River between France and Germany."

"Why not send our airborne soldiers in at the moment we attack?" Cheninko said. "Why wait until morning, giving the enemy a chance to get organized?"

"My staff looked at such a proposal, Comrade Premier. There were a number of problems involved in attacking with our airborne forces at the beginning of the battle. Remember, the attack will come in the middle of the worst night of winter weather we can find. The weather and darkness alone would cost us half our airborne force. And don't forget that the targets are deep within Germany. Even with surprise on our side, enemy aircraft would knock down many of our transports before they reached our airborne soldiers' jumping point. Those the enemy air forces didn't destroy, their Patriot missiles would feast upon. My staff estimates that less than 20 percent of our men would make it to their targets."

"But still, the element of surprise would be far greater with an airborne assault in darkness."

"Comrade Premier, such a plan won't succeed. The answer is an early-morning jump on the first day after we've secured the heavens. We'll still lose as much as 40 percent of our forces. But we anticipate success, even with such losses."

"Do the rest of you agree with General Yovanovich's analysis of the situation?"

"Yes, Comrade Premier," each said.

"All right, I'm not completely convinced. But I'll leave that decision in your capable hands, Yovanovich. Use our airborne forces as you see fit."

"Thank you, Comrade Premier. With the success of the airborne attacks, the sabotage phase is completed by noon of the first day. Well before that time, we'll have crushed the token enemy forces that control the border. And we'll be deeply into the power phase of the operation. Once our tanks break through the heavily forested border, we'll enter an area of Germany that is farmland and small villages. The enemy's ability to stop our advance will be greatly lessened in this open country. The moment the lead elements clear the border, two-thirds of our reserves will rush forward. If everything goes as planned, nearly one hundred of our divisions will be inside Germany by sunrise."

Cheninko's smile grew even wider. "One hundred armored divisions rolling into Germany. What a sweet sight that'll be."

"By dawn of the first morning, our tanks will be in Berlin and Nuremberg. We'll also have broken through and surrounded East Germany. We'll accomplish that task by sending a sizable force into the thirty-kilometer area north and south of the German town of Selb. It's at this point that the British and American forces meet. Once they penetrate the border, those divisions will turn straight north to isolate the East."

"East Germany will be in our hands on the first morning. Yovanovich, your plan is so much more than I could have hoped for."

"I'm flattered, Comrade Premier. My staff has worked day and night to ensure our victory. They'll be thrilled to hear of your compliments. As I stated before, sometime on the first morning, we'll finally encounter a strong armored defense. When that occurs, we'll maintain an unrelenting pressure on our opponent. For every tank we lose, another will come forward to take its place. And another will move forward to take that one's place, and another will move forward, and so on. Our enemy is well trained and powerful. But he has few reserves. For every tank we destroy, for every helicopter we shoot down, there'll be no replacement. We will never allow our opponent a single moment to breathe. Under our constant pressure, the enemy lines will crumble."

"And when they do, the Germans will learn what happens to those who chose to follow such an evil path."

"Yes, Comrade Premier. By noon of the first day, more than one million of our soldiers will be inside Germany. Thirty thousand tanks will be rolling west. We'll have solidified our hold on East Germany. And we'll be well inside the western half of the country. Because of the heroic efforts of our airborne soldiers, the enemy air bases within Germany will be no more."

"By noon of the first day. Remarkable, Comrade General."

"By the end of the first day, our tanks will surround Munich. At sunset on the third day, we'll enter Frankfurt. We won't be stopped."

"Wonderful, Comrade General. Your plans for our ground forces appear to be very well developed. But you've made no mention of our navies. What about their role?"

"Comrade Premier, as you directed, this war is for a single purpose. Our intent is to do nothing more than free the German people from the Nazis. For that reason, the navy's role is a limited one. Although no one could deny that it's certainly important. When the war begins, our navies will destroy any American ships they find in the Black Sea. They'll then block the Black Sea from any further entrance by our enemies. They'll also attempt to block the Baltic Sea and our Pacific coast from attacks upon the Motherland. Finally, a significant submarine force will rush into the Atlantic. Their orders will be to find and destroy any American aircraft carriers attempting to cross to support their countrymen."

"Very good, Yovanovich."

"Comrade Premier, there's a final phase to our plan—diplomacy. It's every bit as important as the combined power of our military. It cannot be overlooked. As I stated earlier, this part of our plan must begin immediately. You must tone down the tenor of your speeches. For the next seven weeks, you've got to treat the Americans as if they're our brothers, and the Germans like a long-lost cousin. Concessions will be hinted at. Talks will begin. We'll make it look like everything the West desperately wants is coming true."

"Yes, Yovanovich. If it'll destroy the Nazis, I'll do all those things and more. For the next seven weeks, I'll rock our enemies to sleep with a lullaby. Music that is soft and sweet to the Western ear."

"At the moment of our attack, our NATO country ambassadors will present an unmistakable demand—stay out of the dispute between the Soviet people and the despicable Nazis or suffer the consequences."

"Do you believe such an approach will succeed?" Cheninko asked. As he had already mentioned, he was well aware of the tremendous American airpower in England, Spain, Italy, Greece, and Turkey. No one needed to tell him that those forces were a definite threat to his country's ability to win the war.

"I've spoken at length with our diplomats, Comrade Cheninko. Faced with the prospect of a Nazi Germany and our threat to destroy them next, they assured me that at the very least Belgium, the Netherlands, Norway, Greece, and Turkey will agree. The Italians and Spanish will be more difficult. But in the end, we believe they'll also see the light. We don't know about the French. The Americans, British, and Canadians will, of course, refuse."

"After what the American President said on television last night, there can be no doubt of that," Cheninko said.

"No doubt at all, Comrade Cheninko. But nevertheless, no matter what the Americans do, you must remember one thing—we will take Germany in five days!" There was supreme confidence in Yovanovich's voice.

Cheninko's response was quieter but also unwavering. "Yes, Yovanovich, we'll take Germany in five days."

"So we've your permission, Comrade Premier, to put our plan into motion?"

"Yes, begin preparing for this operation immediately. Attack in late January or early February. Destroy the Germans once and for all."

That night, for the first time in many months, Cheninko's nightmares of the horrors a Nazi Germany presented to his country didn't appear to disturb his tortured sleep. The Russian Premier slept like a baby.

At 11:45 on the evening of January 28, in every NATO country except Germany, the Soviet Ambassador presented himself to the head of state. The announcement was made that the Russians were only interested in protecting themselves against any further threat from the Nazis. All were assured there was no intent to do anything but stop the Germans. The Soviet grievance was with Germany and Germany alone.

Each leader was told if they helped the Americans fly a single aircraft against the Warsaw Pact, they would be next after the Russians finished with the Germans. As had been predicted, Turkey, Greece, the Netherlands, Norway, and Belgium complied with the ultimatum. They had little choice. Italy and Spain wavered. Neither officially agreed to the Soviet terms. But in the end, neither would allow American aircraft into or out of its airspace. France refused the Russian demands and prepared to go to war. The United States, Great Britain, and Canada made clear threats of their own in response to the Soviet demands. The Soviet Ambassadors were left with no doubt of the three countries' resolve. Even with all that had happened in the past few months, they would never abandon Germany.

The gauntlet had been thrown down. And the challenge had been accepted.

The third great European war in just over one hundred years had begun.

CHAPTER 10

Two weeks prior to the Russian attack, the President sat in the Oval Office, listening to a debate on whether to declare a military state of alert. Present at the meeting were the Director of the CIA, the Secretary of Defense, the Chairman of the Joint Chiefs, the Secretary of State, and the Ambassador to the Soviet Union.

The President leaned back in his chair and placed his hands behind his head. "So what you're saying, General Larsen, is there's no doubt in your mind that the Russians are preparing to attack."

"That's correct, Mr. President," the Chairman of the Joint Chiefs said. "Both the CIA and military intelligence are telling us the Communists plan to invade Germany in the next few weeks. There have been unmistakable signs that the entire Warsaw Pact has mobilized."

"Great. First Fromisch, now this. What else can go wrong?" The President looked at the Director of the CIA. "Chet, before we discuss the Russian situation any further, what's the latest word on the German elections?"

"Pretty much the same as before, Mr. President. With three months to go before the Germans go to the polls, Fromisch's lead is slipping a little. But it was so large to start with that there's little doubt he's going to win."

"Even so, keep after it, Chet. If we can find a way to discredit him and keep him from being elected without anyone finding out what we did, I'd be a happy man. With a guy with Fromisch's past, there must be tons of things we could dig up on him."

"I've got some of my best people working on it, sir. But after how poorly the German government did during the civil war in East Germany, there doesn't seem to be much hope of turning them away from Fromisch no matter what nasty little things we come up with between now and April. And with the Russians mobilizing at this very moment, we've got a lot more pressing problems than Fromisch. Within a month, we could find ourselves in the middle of a full-fledged war if we don't act and act fast."

"Mr. President, let me reiterate again that State Department sources tell us the Russian mobilizations have occurred because of serious threats to the Cheninko regime. Not because of some so-called plan to invade Germany," the Secretary of State said. "I can understand the CIA and military's concern. But there's no threat to us whatsoever. Premier Cheninko has privately assured me that the rumors of an attempted coup are, in fact, true. He's asked that we not overreact to what are nothing more than the internal struggles of the Soviet people."

The President turned back to the Director of the CIA. "What do you think, Chet?"

"I believe, Mr. President, that there's more to this than a few hotheads trying to overthrow Cheninko."

"Do you know that for sure?" the President asked.

"No, sir, I don't. The reports from our operatives in Eastern Europe are not at all consistent. Some of our most reliable sources are telling us there was, and still is, a real threat to the Cheninko regime. But . . ."

"Boy, wouldn't it be nice to see that bastard overthrown," the President said.

"Yes, sir, it would," the Secretary of State said. "And even if he's not overthrown, this is bound to play right into our hands. My people are convinced that this attempted coup is the reason why Cheninko's made so many gestures of peace in the past few weeks."

"So, Mike, you're fairly certain Cheninko's trying to protect his rear with this alleged mobilization?" the President said to the Secretary of State.

"Yes, Mr. President. This is nothing more than a power struggle within the Soviet Communist Party. For the past one hundred years, they've had them every so often, just like clockwork. This one's no different."

"Mr. President," the Secretary of Defense, his voice hoarse from his recent throat-cancer surgery, said, "if Cheninko was afraid of losing his grip on the Communist Party, why did he send fifty of his best armored divisions to the German border?"

The President turned back to the Secretary of State. "Well, Mike, have you got an answer to that one?"

"Sure. He announced there'd be war games weeks ago. If he calls them off, he looks vulnerable to those wishing to succeed him. And he also looks weak to his allies in the Warsaw Pact. He's got plenty of divisions available to protect his interests in Moscow. Why call off the war games and admit there's a problem within his regime? If he did so, he'd be encouraging those who oppose him."

"Mr. President, let me reiterate again, the intelligence community's convinced the Russians are up to no good. This overthrow thing's a red herring to throw us off the track," the Director of the CIA said.

"But can you prove that, Chet?"

"No, Mr. President, we can't. The satellites tell us something's going on that isn't quite right. And many of our operatives are saying the same thing. But there's nothing you'd call proof."

"Mr. President, if I could interject here," General Larsen said. "As we speak, there are fifty Russian divisions waiting to begin three weeks of so-called war games on the border with Germany. If we don't move this minute to reinforce our forces and evacuate our civilians, we're going to be too late."

"Mr. President, my people," the Secretary of State said, "have been working day and night for the past three years to come to terms with the Cheninko government. With the gestures Cheninko's made in the past month, we've finally got an opportunity to normalize relations. If you do what General Larsen's advocating, you'll be sabotaging the State Department's efforts. The SALT-VI negotiations are scheduled to begin next week. If we do what our military's proposing, the Russians are bound to back out of those talks."

"Mr. Ambassador, you've been sitting here taking this all in. What do you think we should do?"

"Well, Mr. President," the ancient politician, darling of the party, said. "I've been meeting with the Russians face-to-face for over a year. And while I don't trust the Communist sons of bitches, I believe the Secretary of State's correct in his assessment of the situation. We've never had a better opportunity to deal with Cheninko than we do now. I've sat staring out my window in the embassy in Moscow watching the strange events, and I've reached the same conclusion as the Secretary of State. The rumors on the streets in Moscow say that the mobilization is in response to an internal struggle for power."

"And you believe those rumors are true?"

"Yes, Mr. President, I do."

It was becoming painfully obvious to the three who favored an immediate response to the Russian threat that they were losing the argument.

"Mr. President," the Secretary of Defense said, "if you don't order a full mobilization of our armed forces, I want you to understand the consequences. We can't win a ground war in Europe if the Russians attack."

"And we'll lose any opportunity to win the Second Cold War if we choose to do anything as provocative as mobilizing our military every time the Communists sneeze," the Secretary of State said.

"Very well. I've heard both sides. Does anyone have anything further to add?"

When no one responded, the President announced his decision. Like all decisions in Washington, he knew the losers had to be allowed to save face.

"Mike, I want you to prepare a communiqué to Premier Cheninko. I want it sent under my signature. Express, once again, our displeasure with his decision to conduct his war games so close to the German border. Tell him in the strongest possible terms that I'll hold him personally responsible for any incidents between his forces and ours. Make it clear the United States will not tolerate any further acts of aggression against members of NATO."

"Yes, Mr. President," the Secretary of State said, doing his best to hide the glee he felt from his triumph.

"I also want everyone to understand," the President said, while looking at the losers, "that this decision's not irreversible. Bring me proof the Russians are preparing to attack, and I'll change it immediately. Is that clear?"

All present nodded, stood, and filed from the room. As protocol demanded, the winners didn't start slapping themselves on the back until the losers were out of sight.

The Americans had taken the bait.

America's best chance for victory had been thwarted. There would be no mobilization of the country's military forces in time to meet the grievous threat.

"Mr. President, we've got the proof," the Director of the CIA said into the secure phone line. "We're convinced the Russians are planning an attack in central Europe. I need an audience with you immediately."

"That's fine, Chet. Inform the Secretary of Defense and Chairman of the Joint Chiefs. How much time are you going to need?"

"At least an hour."

"All right, I'll clear my schedule from three this afternoon on. How's that?"

"Just fine, sir. I'll notify the Secretary and Chairman and bring my best analyst to show you what we've found."

"Okay, Chet. You're on for three."

On January 25, three days prior to the Russian attack, the CIA had gathered enough information to have a legitimate chance of overturning the President's earlier decision.

CHAPTER 11

When the Director of the CIA arrived at the White House with his photo analyst, his nemesis, the Secretary of State, was waiting.

"Chet, the President told me you've uncovered some information about a big Soviet plot to attack Germany," the Secretary of State said.

"That's right, Mike. My boys have come up with some pretty convincing evidence."

"Before we go in to see the President, mind sharing what you've found?"

"As a matter of fact, Mike, I do." And with that, the Director of the CIA turned and walked into the waiting area outside the Oval Office.

General Larsen and the Secretary of Defense arrived. The group was ushered into the President's office. After the usual pleasantries, the President got right to the point.

"What have you got, Chet?"

"Mr. President, the first thing I want to do is show you some photographs and have Benson here go over them."

The Director spread six enlarged photographs across the President's desk. The assembled group pressed in close.

"Yeah, Chet, six photos of a train sitting on a railroad siding. So what?"

"Mr. President," Benson, a thin man in his late thirties, said, "these aren't pictures of one train sitting on a siding. These are pictures of six different trains identically made up, sitting in the same position on the same siding on six different days."

"What?"

"That's right, Mr. President," the Director of the CIA said. "The Russians have prepared these trains to look as identical as possible. But they're definitely not pictures of the same train. They're pictures of six different trains, taken on six different days."

"I don't understand. Why would the Russians make up six identical trains and park them in the same place on the same siding on different days?"

"It's simple, Mr. President," Benson said. "They wanted us to believe it's the same train. We've gone back over hundreds of pictures taken in Eastern Europe this month. And they're all showing the same kind of ruse."

Even the Secretary of State had to admit interest in what was being brought to light. "Why in the world would they do that?" he asked.

"Only one reason," Benson said. "They're moving more than fifty divisions to the border, and they didn't want us to figure out what they're up to."

"And until today, it had worked," the Director of the CIA said.

"Well, I'm still confused," the President said. "Tell me how you know it's six different trains."

They were now in Benson's element, and for the first time the CIA's top analyst relaxed. "Mr. President, look at this first picture. It was taken on January 3. The others were taken on January 6, 14, 15, 21, and the last one was taken this morning. The reason there are just six pictures is the weather over this portion of Poland has been clear enough for the imagery satellites to photograph only six times this month. We're in the process of looking at the radar satellites' images for the cloudy days to see if we can piece a pattern together. The siding you see is in the railway station in the small Polish town of Konin, 150 miles from the German border. As you can make out," Benson said while handing the President a magnifying glass, "the train consists of an engine pulling fourteen cars, with a tank on each of the first nine cars and artillery pieces on the last five."

The President took a close look at the first picture. "Okay, I see that."

"Look at the other pictures, Mr. President. An engine, nine cars carrying tanks, followed by five cars carrying artillery pieces."

The President slowly examined each photo. "All right."

"Let's look again at the first train. You can clearly read the unit designation on the tanks. Do you see those, Mr. President?"

"Yeah, I can make them out okay."

"Now check the numbers on the tanks in the other pictures."

The President took a minute to go back and forth between the original picture and the other five. "They're the same."

"That's correct, Mr. President. But they're six different trains."

"Are you sure?" the Secretary of State asked.

"We're absolutely certain," Benson said.

"How?" the President said.

"Because in the last two pictures, the tanks are old T-62s, now primarily used by Warsaw Pact reserve forces. In the first three pictures, the tanks are T-72s. But in each picture there are the slightest of discrepancies. In the fourth picture, the tanks are T-80s. They're definitely six different trains, carrying six different cargoes made up to look identical."

"Have you examined pictures of the border areas?" the President asked.

"Yes, sir, we have," the Director of the CIA said.

"And how many Warsaw Pact Divisions were you able to identify?"

"Exactly fifty, Mr. President. When we did the examination, however, it wasn't the pictures of the border that bothered us as much as something else. That something was the area from ten to fifty miles behind the border. What we found there is that the Russians have laid out tremendous amounts of camouflage netting. We really don't know what's being hidden beneath the netting. But we do know there's so much of it in place, they could be hiding as many as one hundred armored divisions."

"And it could be nothing more than dirty laundry and mess tents, couldn't it," the Secretary of State said.

"Mr. President," the Director of the CIA said, "we believe this is the smoking gun you wanted to see. These pictures, and the reports of our operatives in the field, leave no doubt that the Russians are up to no good."

"But what exactly are they up to?"

"We don't know for sure, Mr. President. We can only speculate. But the logical answer is that they want us to believe there are fifty divisions at the German border, when, in fact, there are many more."

"And why would they bring more than fifty divisions to the border and go to such pains to disguise what they're doing?" the Secretary of Defense said. "Quite simply, the only answer is that they're preparing to attack."

"Now, hold on there," the Secretary of State said. "You're telling the President that based upon a few strange events in a handful of pictures, we should assume the Russians are planning to start a war with us?"

"What other explanation could there be?" the Secretary of Defense said.

"Lots of them. Two come to mind immediately. First, bringing all these divisions west could be nothing more than an obvious reminder to the people of Poland and the Czech Republic of who the boss really is. Second, Cheninko might be testing our intelligence capabilities. He might be doing this to see how strong our ability to detect such an action is."

"Come on, Mike," the Secretary of Defense said. "You want the President to believe that the Russians would spend the kind of money it took for this elaborate ruse just to see how quickly we'd spot it?"

"That's exactly what someone like Cheninko might do."

"General Larsen," the President said, "didn't your people once tell me that the Communists would never attack in the dead of winter?"

"Ah . . . yes, sir, we did," the General said. "We've always believed that when the winter weather's combined with our capabilities to disrupt their supply lines, they couldn't sustain a war in central Europe in anything but the best conditions. And for that reason, they'd never attempt it."

"Are you now changing that estimate?"

"No, Mr. President, I'm not. I still believe the Russians can't sustain a ground war in the middle of winter. What I do believe, however, is that based upon the intelligence information we're looking at, they're going to try. Sir, I'm convinced the Russians are going to attack. And they're going to attack soon."

"Mr. President," the Secretary of State said, "the General's admitted the Russians would never attack in the middle of winter, yet he insists they're going to. General, do you want the President to declare war on the Russians based upon a handful of pictures of trains?"

"No, sir, I do not. What I hope from the President is for him to allow this country's military to do its job."

"General Larsen, what do you want me to do?" the President said.

"Mr. President, if we're going to have any chance at all, we need an immediate mobilization of our forces, both active and reserve. What I'm asking you to do is to raise our alert status to Defcon Two and declare a full military mobilization."

"And there goes the SALT-VI talks right out the window! The press will have a field day with that one," the Secretary of State said. The Secretary of State had decided the time had come to play his trump card. He knew the mention of the President's worst fears—that the press would be all over him again—would work. With the presidential election ten months away, and the President in trouble in the polls, he was terrified of the slightest hint of bad publicity. "Mr. President, if you declare a mobilization, the Russians could possibly take it as a sign that we're about to declare war on them. With all those Russian divisions on the German border, who knows where that could lead? We might cause the Russians to attack, not because they want to but because they'll view our actions as forcing them into it."

"Mike, you've got a valid point there," the President said.

"Mr. President, everyone's aware of the importance of the SALT-VI talks. We all want to see a continuation of the nonproliferation of nuclear weapons," the Director of the CIA said. "But we're talking about a bigger issue. We're talking about a Russian attack in central Europe in the next few days. At this point, that's got to be more important than any other consideration."

"Does it, Chet? I'm not so sure."

"Mr. President, you must order a military mobilization immediately," the Secretary of Defense urged.

"No, I think Mike's made some sense here. We can't take such drastic action based upon a few photographs. I believe we should do something, though. General, what is the minimum response we could undertake without tipping off the Russians about what we're up to?"

"Mr. President, the response we should undertake is a complete mobilization of America's armed forces, active and reserve. If we can't do that, then we should first evacuate all American dependents within one hundred miles of the border. Next, we need to strengthen our ground forces and ready our fighter aircraft on the East Coast to move to Europe. Then, we must reinforce our highest-priority needs. I'd begin with at least one battalion of Patriot missiles and as many field hospitals as we can muster. We're critically short of medical personnel in Germany. And our present air defenses aren't strong enough to stop a determined enemy. Finally, we need to place our forces in Europe on alert against a Russian attack."

"General Larsen, I agree with you on everything except the part about placing our troops in Europe on alert," the President said. "That would just be too provocative. Can we do the rest of what you suggest without creating too much suspicion?"

"Mr. President, we can begin moving the 82nd Airborne and at least part of one of our armored divisions to Europe, one battalion of Patriot missiles, and a few field hospitals without raising much suspicion at all. We can also send a few wings of fighters over at the same time, without anyone's noticing. If challenged, we'll claim we needed to call an unscheduled test to see where the weaknesses are in our ability to reinforce our units in Europe under winter conditions. As far as moving the dependents nearest the border, we can probably get away with that for a little while before things get out of hand."

"Good, let's take that approach, then. Get on it right away."

"But, Mr. President, we really do need to put our units in Europe on alert."

"No, General, that would definitely tip everyone off." Especially the press, the President thought. "If you can bring me some information about what's under those camouflage nets . . . you know, get some pictures of that . . ." The President stood and started escorting them to the door.

"Mr. President, there's an intense storm scheduled to hit Europe in the next few hours," Benson said. "We'll probably not be able to get any definitive photos for another four days. Not before January 29 at the earliest."

"Well, bring them to me then, and we'll revisit this entire issue," the President said.

He closed the door behind them and returned to his desk. There was still much more to do today. The Iowa caucuses and the New Hampshire presidential primary were only a few weeks away, and he didn't like what the polls were saying.

CHAPTER 12

January 29—12:05 a.m.
2nd Platoon, Delta Troop, 1st Squadron, 4th Cavalry
On the Way to E48

The lead elements of an immense Russian armored column were inside Germany. One thousand tanks, one thousand BMPs, and hundreds of support vehicles rumbled down E48.

A single Humvee was headed for the same highway. Five Bradleys trailed a mile behind.

Now two miles from where the north–south highway and E48 met, the Humvee ran through the blizzard unopposed. The firing along the border had nearly stopped. Jensen knew it wasn't a good sign. So far, they'd completed three miles of the fateful journey without seeing a soul. Neither friend nor foe had been encountered. Jensen understood, however, that the real test lay in front of them.

"Seth, everything okay back there?" he whispered into his headset.

"Yeah, Bob. We're all fine. How 'bout you?"

"Quiet as can be. Haven't seen a thing. But that could change at any moment. So keep your guard up."

"Roger."

Jensen scanned the road ahead. Every one of his senses was keenly alert. At thirty miles per hour, the Humvee plunged through the fearful night. The platoon sergeant knew they could die in an instant without ever realizing what had occurred. In the next mile, or around the next curve, an enemy rocket could be waiting.

Deep within the forest, the Humvee's tires churned through two feet of virgin snow. Time stopped. Every moment was a tortured eternity.

He glanced at Ramirez. The young private stared straight ahead. The cavalry soldier continued to grip the steering wheel with all his might. Fear was etched onto every feature of his gaunt face. Despite the freezing temperatures, beads of sweat trickled down Ramirez's forehead and appeared on his upper lip.

Jensen returned to watching the ominous path. A few more eternities passed.

Just over a mile to E48.

The lives of the cavalry squadron's fifteen hundred men rested squarely upon Lieutenant Colonel David Townes's sturdy shoulders.

For squadron commander Townes, the time spent on the border was always exceptionally difficult. With weapon in hand, nearly half the squadron's soldiers stared across a few hundred yards of open ground at a person they'd been indoctrinated to hate. An enemy who stared back at them, also with weapon in hand.

During his unit's month at the border, he'd seldom slept. For the past two weeks, however, he'd not slept at all. With the Russians conducting their massive war games, sleep had become a luxury the squadron commander could no longer afford. He worked twenty-hour days, struggling to hold together a squadron responsible for defending fifty miles of the border of a free country and its eighty million citizens. With his meager force, he was charged with protecting two major highways—E48, which ran within a mile of squadron headquarters at Camp Kinney, and E50, forty miles south.

Townes had spent the evening going over the disturbing intelligence reports that had wound through a half dozen levels of command before finally finding their way into his hands. The reports left little doubt. The squadron was face-to-face with at least ten Russian divisions.

Fifteen hundred Americans were up against 110,000 Russians. For every member of 1st Squadron, there were more than seventy of the enemy. Neither the squadron commander nor any soldier under his command had the faintest illusion about stopping the Russians should they decide to advance into Germany. That had never been their mission. Their job was to be the trip wire. They were here to delay and harass their opponent for as long as they could. And Townes, like Jensen, understood there was only one way to accomplish such a task—by bleeding and dying in the snows of Germany.

The men of 1st Squadron were here to give up their lives.

The squadron commander's assets were quite limited. Six hundred of his soldiers were on the border at any moment. Fifteen miles behind them, at Camp Kinney, he had in reserve an equal number of cavalry soldiers who'd come off twenty-four hours at the border at eight this morning. David Townes also had at his disposal two hundred support soldiers—cooks, clerks, and mechanics. His most valuable assets were two troops, each with twelve top-of-the-line M-1 Abrams tanks, and a squadron of twenty-one tank-killing Apache helicopters.

Townes's last meeting with his staff had been three hours prior to the Russian attack. With the threat the enemy posed clear for all to see, the meeting had been quite animated.

"Sir," the squadron aviation officer said, "I have to recommend that if something should happen tonight, you don't commit the Apaches to battle in the middle of a blizzard. We can't afford the losses such an order might create."

"Captain Marks, I thought your Apaches were capable of fighting in all weather conditions." There was disgust in the quick-tempered Townes's voice.

"They are, sir. But with the tactics we employ, our losses could be tremendous. I only have twenty-one Apaches. And three of those are deadlined for parts. The weather's supposed to break by morning. If the Apaches have to be ordered into combat, I recommend that you wait until then."

Townes knew that his subordinate was correct. The Apaches' strongest ally was surprise. Their approach was to fly into battle at full speed with their skids skimming the treetops. They would catch the enemy unaware, killing him before he could counterattack with his air-defense weapons. This tactic, however, had its costs. Despite their sophisticated guidance systems, the squadron commander had lost Apaches on night-training missions in perfect weather. Even the most careful pilot could inadvertently fly into telephone wires.

"All right, Marks. If anything happens, we'll hold the Apaches back until morning."

The meeting concluded a few minutes later, with Townes directing the duty officer to not commit the Apaches. It was this information about the disposition of the Apaches that Jelewski received on the radio moments before the platoon began its desperate run toward E48.

Townes had left the drab squadron headquarters at a little before eleven for some much-needed food, and possibly a drink or two, at the tiny officers' club on the far side of the compound. While he trudged through the falling snow, he realized there were three long days before the squadron's month on the border would be completed. In seventy-two hours, he would finally be able to let down his guard a little and settle in for a well-earned rest.

At 11:45, Townes was sitting alone at a table next to a frost-covered window in the nearly deserted officers' club. The squadron commander had just devoured a last satisfying mouthful of schnitzel. He was about to order a bourbon and water when Brown's TOW ripped into the first T-80. A ball of fire filled the eastern heavens. In rapid succession, additional fireworks rushed skyward. Townes, a veteran of Iraq and Afghanistan, knew it could mean only one thing. He scrambled to his feet and raced from the club at full speed. Running as fast as he could through the deep snows, it took him five full minutes to retrace his steps to squadron headquarters.

At midnight, as Jensen's platoon screamed onto the north–south highway, the squadron commander realized the full implications of the attack. All along the border, 1st Squadron was falling back or being wiped out.

As 2nd Platoon neared the beckoning crossroads, twelve tanks, with sixteen Bradleys in support, were heading out of Camp Kinney to find a blocking position on E48. An equal force was preparing to race south to support the squadron's platoons protecting E50 and the enemy's access to the historic city of Nuremberg.

Help was on the way for the squadron's border forces. There was, however, no chance of the first column of tanks and Bradleys covering the twelve miles to the intersection where Jensen's platoon would enter E48 before the Russian column reached the same point. The deadly M-1s were going to be too late to aid Jensen's retreating platoon.

If David Townes hadn't been a man willing to change his mind, Jensen and his men would've been racing toward their certain deaths. A death waiting to greet them in the form of one thousand Russian tanks.

The last report from the platoon blocking E48 hadn't been encouraging. Twelve tanks and two platoons of Bradleys weren't going to be enough to stop the growing Russian juggernaut. Blizzard or not, Townes had to play his trump card.

The Apaches had to attack. If they didn't, by the time the weather cleared, Camp Kinney would be thirty miles behind enemy lines. He could chance losing the Apaches in the vicious storm, or he could wait and lose them on the ground.

Townes scooped up the telephone and dialed a three-digit number. It rang twice before the squadron aviation officer answered.

"This is Colonel Townes. Get the Apaches into the air."

"But, sir, I thought we agreed to keep the Apaches on the ground until morning. The weather's no better than it was, and . . ."

"Dammit, Marks, you heard me! My whole command's getting slaughtered out there. If we don't do something immediately, by morning this camp's going to be well behind enemy lines. And the pilots flying your Apaches will be speaking Russian. Get nine of them into the air and on their way up E48. Do it now! I want the other nine ready to leave for E50 in the next half hour."

In the time it took Jensen's platoon to travel the first three miles south, nine grotesque killers were climbing into the blizzard and roaring toward the border.

E48 was near. The Humvee started up a long incline. It was the final hill the Americans would climb before descending into the majestic valley where the highways intersected.

"Halt just before you get to the top of the hill," Jensen said.

When they neared the crest, Ramirez brought the vehicle to a stop. Motioning for them to stay put, Jensen grabbed his night-vision goggles and leaped from the Humvee. In a crouch, he ran through the blizzard to the apex of the hill. Jensen threw himself down in the deep snows. From the hilltop, he had an unrestricted view of E48 as it ran through the winding valley below. He lay perfectly still, trying to get a feel for his surroundings. It didn't take long for him to realize the awful truth about the platoon's situation.

He heard them before he saw them. Like the tremors that followed an earthquake, the rumble of a thousand tanks shook the earth beneath his motionless form.

There was much movement to the east. Jensen pulled the night-vision goggles up to his face. When the goggles covered his morose eyes, the strange green world returned.

There they were, an endless column of Russian armored vehicles stretching for untold miles to the east. Jensen quickly scanned the area in front of him for any signs of activity. The intersection of the two highways was deathly silent. He slowly panned to his right, searching the forested valley to the west for any signs of the enemy. There was nothing anywhere. The Russians hadn't yet made it to where the highways met. He turned back to calculate the distance from the enemy column to where the roads converged. It didn't take long for him to have his answer.

His battered heart sank. The lead tank wasn't more than a mile from the crossroads.

The platoon was trapped. Their luck had run out. Jensen's mind soared through his options, desperately searching for an answer.

If they made a run for the crossroads, they'd be wiped out before any of the platoon's vehicles reached E48. Even if they somehow made it to E48, they'd have to race west through the valley floor. The Russians would have them in their sights for at least five minutes. There'd be no chance of escape for the fleeing Americans.

They could turn around and head seventeen miles north to Selb. Maybe they'd have better luck upon arriving there. Unfortunately, he sensed it was far too late to attempt such a desperate maneuver. The Russians would soon penetrate the north–south highway in a number of locations. Even with the sacrificial lamb out front, the platoon would undoubtedly be ambushed and killed before they made it halfway.

Maybe they could wait for the squadron's twelve Abrams tanks to arrive. Possibly they could escape then. But Jensen knew that by the time the tanks made their way from Camp Kinney, the Russians would be five miles farther into Germany. And the platoon would be trapped forever behind enemy lines.

They could abandon their vehicles, fade into the woods, and fight a guerrilla action on foot. But 2nd Platoon's strength lay in the power of its Bradleys. Deep within the protective forest, they might hold out for a few days, possibly longer, before their position was uncovered.

That, however, had never been their mission. The platoon was here for one reason. They were here to slow the Russians for as long as they could.

They could attack . . .

E48 was much too broad for the five Bradleys to do to this column what they'd done to the earlier one. E48 was four lanes wide. And on both sides of the highway, there were large open areas before reaching the impenetrable woods. They would have to destroy at least thirty enemy vehicles to have any hope of blocking the powerful column's advance.

With so small a force at his disposal, there was no chance of that occurring. Jensen knew they wouldn't succeed. They couldn't stop the Russians. Nevertheless, from their hilltop vantage point, they might be able to create a bit of havoc for at least a little while. With the two-

and-a-half-mile range of their TOWs, they could possibly destroy as many as ten or twelve tanks before the Russians figured out what had hit them.

Jensen understood what would happen next. The enemy would locate the origin of the strike. Once they did, the Russians would pull back out of range of the Bradleys. They'd then open fire with their massive cannons. The first salvo, likely to be from a hundred tanks, would end the brief skirmish. There'd be no chance of surviving. With one swish of the Russian elephant's tail, the mosquitoes' lives would be over.

With any luck, however, they could slow the elephant down for as much as fifteen minutes. The exchange of twenty-six lives for fifteen minutes of precious time was the best Jensen could do.

It was settled. With five Bradleys, the men of 2nd Platoon, Delta Troop, would attack two thousand Russian armored vehicles.

While he lay in the snows planning the battle, the Bradleys arrived behind him. Jensen returned to meet the dismounting vehicle commanders.

"Seth, send scouts out one hundred yards in each direction."

The last thing they needed was an enemy unit stumbling upon the unprotected platoon.

Two soldiers scrambled in each direction to find defensive positions.

Jensen drew the vehicle commanders together. The Russian column continued its steadfast movement into Germany. He had little time to organize the attack.

The fire had gone out in the platoon sergeant's expressive eyes. "We're too late," he said. "A Russian armored column's a mile from the intersection. We'll never make it if we try to escape on E48. And it's too late to turn around."

While they huddled together in the storm, taking in their leader's pronouncement, each sneaked glances at the others in the group. Disappointment was everywhere. They were all experienced enough to know the significance of Jensen's words.

"Our only option is to attack. Maybe we can slow them a little." While they listened, Jensen explained his hasty battle plan. "This road's only wide enough for three Bradleys to fire at one time. Here's what we'll do. Brownie, you set up on the left. Seth, you're in the middle. Foster, you've got the right. Renoir, you and Richmond line up single file far enough behind Seth that you can pull right around him. I want every shot to count. You vehicle commanders are to fire the TOWs. Brownie and Foster, take your time and pick out a couple of good targets. Fire off both your TOWs. Then have your driver back far enough off the line for Renoir or Richmond to move into your firing position. Do that before you begin reloading your missile tubes. Seth, wait until Brownie and Foster finish firing before you open up with your TOWs. Then back up to reload, making room for Brownie or Foster to fill your spot. You guys keep firing, trade positions, reloading, and firing again for as long as you can. Whatever you do, don't fire your Bushmaster or machine gun. The muzzle flash will give our position away immediately. Has everyone got it?"

Five soldiers nodded their understanding.

"Let's go get them, then," Jensen said. Deep within his parka, an uncontrollable grin crept onto the platoon sergeant's weathered face at the realization that this just might be his life's end.

The quick meeting broke up. Jensen guided Brown into position on the far left, with just enough of the Bradley's turret peaking over the crest of the hill for Brown to select his targets and fire his TOWs. Austin's team slid into the middle. Foster was soon in place on the right. Richmond and Renoir lined their Bradleys up twenty yards behind Austin's. Both anxiously waited to pull forward and enter the fray.

The Bradleys in place, Jensen crawled forward through the snows to the crest of the hill. He brought his night-vision goggles up to his face once more. The platoon sergeant located the steadily rolling lead tank. Traveling at twenty miles per hour, the lumbering ogre was a quarter mile from where the roads met. On the gentle slope, a mile above the crossroads, Jensen's force watched the tanks crossing the final distance to the intersection. Brown and Foster selected their victims and waited for the command to fire. There was no need to hurry. With so many inviting targets from which to choose, Jensen wanted to ensure the first few shots were easy ones.

In a handful of minutes, the small group of Americans would be wiped out. But in doing so, they would buy their countrymen a little extra time.

Second Platoon was going to go down fighting.

In thirty seconds, the lead tank would reach the intersection. The monstrous image was in the crosshairs on Brown's periscope.

While the snows fell upon them, the bloodied platoon waited. The soldiers held their breath as the eternities continued to torturously tick past.

CHAPTER 13

January 29—12:11 a.m.
2nd Platoon, Delta Troop, 1st Squadron, 4th Cavalry
On the North–South Highway a Mile from E48

From out of nowhere, the leading tank and the two behind it suddenly exploded.

The stark violence startled both the Russians and the American platoon. Unaware of the Apache's change of orders, Jensen was just as confused as the enemy. The burning tanks lit up the midnight battlefield once more. A new false daylight devoured the night. Jensen threw off his night-vision goggles.

For an instant, he believed one of his crews had panicked and fired. But that couldn't be the answer. One TOW couldn't destroy three tanks. And three tanks had been destroyed. Mines? It couldn't be that either. There hadn't been time for anyone to lay them.

Just then, a T-80 opened up with its antiaircraft machine gun. Instantly, Jensen's quick mind solved the puzzle. It could only be one thing—helicopters!

Searching the low skies, Jensen caught a shadow roaring through the valley. A glimpse really. But enough to tell him that the cause of the sudden infernos had been Apaches. Jensen had seen the unmistakable silhouette of a sleek Apache Attack Helicopter.

At night, the helicopters' olive drab image appeared to be jet-black. After watching the Apaches on numerous night-training missions, the cavalry soldiers had anointed the squadron's lethal avengers with an appropriate name.

"Black death" had arrived on the battlefield.

The nine two-man tank-killer teams had thundered out of Camp Kinney within minutes of the squadron commander giving the order. It was a scene right out of *Star Wars*. Each crew was sealed in its futuristic cockpit. In the helicopters, the target-acquisition officer sat in front of and below the pilot. Their sophisticated night-vision equipment was positioned over their passionless faces. Their instrument panels were aglow from a multitude of dials and gauges. At treetop level, in the middle of the night, in the middle of a blizzard, at 180 miles per hour, they rushed toward the border.

When they neared the target area, the attackers split into three groups. At full speed, the first group roared straight down the valley a few feet above the ground. They found the Russians exactly where they'd anticipated. While they continued to hurtle toward the huge formation, each locked onto one of the leading tanks. Nearly as one, they unleashed a Hellfire missile from beneath their obscene helicopter. The missile rocketed out. With the target-acquisition officers' guidance, the Hellfires smashed into their targets. A trio of tanks was instantly destroyed.

The victorious helicopters veered sharply to the right. A single T-80 commander figured out what had happened. He fired a handful of belated rounds from his antiaircraft machine gun in their general direction. The Apaches disappeared over the tree line.

With the Russians' attention turned southward toward the fleeing helicopters, a second group of tank killers roared in from the north. This group fired long bursts from their 30mm chain guns at a jumbled mass of BMPs a quarter mile back in the column. The thinly armored upper skins of six BMPs were ripped to shreds. The BMPs started to smolder, then to burn brightly. But the second group of Apaches wasn't done yet. Each fired a Hellfire missile. A T-72, then another, followed by a third, were soon blazing.

A few more feeble antiaircraft shots were fired at the attackers. The helicopters passed over the trees untouched. In the wake of this attack, the final group of Apaches zoomed directly down the valley floor. Taking the same path for their second run, the original trio was ten seconds behind them.

Hellfire missiles rained down upon the column once again. This time the six Apaches ran straight down the roadway, staying over the target significantly longer than during the first two runs. As the leading group veered left into the forest, and the second disappeared to the right, a dozen armored vehicles exploded. Heaven-searing flames erupted everywhere.

The Russians were stopped dead in their tracks.

It was like watching a highly skilled cat play with a terrified mouse.

This mouse, however, wasn't defenseless. For this was a mouse with very sharp teeth. In this game, a careless cat could soon find himself the mouse's meal.

The cat formed up for another run.

From the snowy hilltop, Jensen and his Bradley crews watched as the Apaches tore into the column. When the Russians faltered and began to retreat, the platoon sergeant saw his opening. He leaped up and ran to Jelewski's position in the rear of Austin's Bradley.

"Jewels, get me on the Apaches' net as fast as you can!"

Jelewski reached over and adjusted the radio dials. He handed the handset to Jensen.

"What's today's call sign for the Apaches?"

"Vulture," Jelewski said.

Jensen put the handset to his parched mouth. "Vulture-One, Vulture-One, this is Delta-Two-Five. Say again, this is Delta-Two-Five."

From the cockpit of the lead helicopter came the response in the officious voice all pilots seem to use. "Roger, Delta-Two-Five. This is Vulture-One. Go ahead."

"Vulture, have five Bradleys on north–south highway, one mile north of your position. During your next run, we're going to join in on the attack. After we fire, we'll try to escape west in the confusion. Don't fire on us. Repeat, we are friendlies, don't fire on us."

"Roger, Delta-Two-Five. We copy. Welcome to the party."

"Roger, Vulture, good luck."

Jensen hurried back to the crest of the hill to verify the tank column was still withdrawing.

"Ramirez! Steele! Get all the scouts in as fast as you can. We're getting the hell out of here."

The pair ran off in different directions.

Jensen spoke into his headset. "Change of plans guys. Here's what we're going to do. The Russians are falling back, but they're still within range. Next time the Apaches attack, we're going to open fire. With any luck, the bastards will never figure out that there's firing coming from a second position. Take your time selecting your targets. Let's make every TOW count. Once your missile tubes are empty, rather than backing up to reload, head straight down the hill as fast as you can toward E48. We'll try to get away before the Russians spot us. Whatever you do, don't look back. Just keep going. Form up in that big apple orchard just this side of Schirnding. Any questions?"

There were none.

While three Apaches commenced another run, this time from the south, the first pair of scouts returned.

"Into Brown's Bradley," Jensen said.

The scouts hurried into the Bradley's rear compartment.

The Apaches pounded the disorganized column with Hellfires and chain guns. Hades' fires grew in the valley below. Thunder roared and lightning flashed with each new explosion.

Brown locked onto a fleeing tank near what had been the front of the column. He released his first TOW. While it flew toward its target, its fins popped out and a light appeared on the missile's rear. Using his periscope to guide it, Brown adjusted its flight toward the struggling Russian tank. In seconds, the missile covered the mile and a half. The TOW slammed into the armored vehicle with tremendous force. Half-ton pieces of flaming metal spewed into the snowy air.

Three T-72 commanders had guessed right. Each had been waiting for the next helicopter attack to come from the south. They opened up with their tanks' antiaircraft guns and main cannons. A cannon shell ripped through the center of a soaring black helicopter. Spinning wildly out of control, the shattered remains of the Apache smashed into the woods north of the roadway.

The firing of the T-72s attracted the attention of Foster and Brown. A pair of TOWs swept from their tubes. Each began the process of homing in on its target. While the TOWs were in flight, another group of Apaches raced over the treetops. As the TOWs destroyed two more tanks, the Apaches opened up with Hellfire missiles once more.

"I'm out of here," Brown, his missile tubes empty, yelled into the radio. And down the final mile of the north–south roadway, the first Bradley raced.

While Richmond moved forward to take Brown's position, a second set of scouts ran up and entered the rear of Foster's Bradley.

Austin had been tracking what he believed to be a command tank a mile back in the column. The moment Brown cleared the hilltop, Austin fired. It was a long shot. More than two miles. But it was still within the TOW's range. The missile's flight seemed to take forever. Austin, however, never faltered. The TOW ran true. In a blinding explosion, the lead battalion's commanding officer died. The confusion at the head of the accursed column was now complete.

Foster launched against the final of the three T-72s involved in downing the Apache. Just as his missile neared the stationary tank, its commander decided to start his retreat. At the last possible instant, unaware that certain death was bearing down upon it, the T-72 moved. The TOW missed by inches. It passed in front of the tank and smashed into a snowbank near the tree line.

"Shit! I missed the son of a bitch. I'm out of here, too." And with that, Foster's Bradley charged over the hill. Following Brown's lead, it disappeared down the snow-clogged path leading to E48. Austin fired his second TOW toward a scurrying BMP. Within its walls, ten Russians died the instant the missile's powerful nose struck. One more funeral pyre was added to the multitudes in the flaming valley below.

As Austin's second missile rammed home, Brown's team turned

west onto E48. At thirty-five miles per hour, the Bradley hastened to escape.

Two more scouts arrived and scurried up the open ramp at the rear of Richmond's Bradley. The hatch closed behind them. Renoir moved the final Bradley into position.

It was Austin's turn to try his luck on the highway. "We're gone!" he yelled. The third Bradley crested the hill and raced to slip the hangman's noose.

The disorganized Russian column, filled with fire and death, continued to withdraw. With Austin out of the way, Richmond hurled a TOW at a T-80. The sergeant led the speeding armored vehicle by too much and missed the inviting target. As the last sprinting scouts appeared through the storm with Ramirez and Steele, Renoir fired the first of his missiles. Another BMP's crew didn't have long to live.

"Load up! Load up!" Jensen screamed at the top of his lungs. He could barely be heard over the tumultuous sounds in the valley below.

The final scouts raced to the rear of Renoir's Bradley. Out of breath, Ramirez and Steele ran to the Humvee.

The third group of Apaches, again running right down the flaming valley floor, attacked the retreating column. Death poured from the heavens in the form of Hellfire missiles and 30mm chain-gun fire. This time, however, the cat was far too greedy and spent too much time feasting on the mouse. While the Apaches roared down the length of the endless column, fifteen tanks opened fire. A curtain of deadly fire closed in on the Americans.

The trailing Apache's rotor was crushed by a pair of direct hits. The low-flying helicopter smashed into the flaming wreckage of one of its earlier victims. One hundred yards farther into the valley, the lead Apache was struck by no fewer than ten antiaircraft shells. Its pilot attempted a steep turn to the right, away from the line of fire. The Apache exploded in midair. The middle Apache banked sharply to the left to avoid the sudden explosion of its brother. It somehow survived its scrape with death, disappearing over the treetops.

Foster's Bradley turned onto E48 and plowed west through the storm.

Jensen was on his headset once again. "Forget about firing your TOWs. Let's get out of here while we still can!"

The words still ringing in his ears, Richmond's Bradley tore from the platoon's hiding place. It leaped over the hill and was gone. Renoir followed a few seconds behind. The Humvee trailed what remained of the platoon.

The Americans would still need some luck. After the mauling they'd taken, the Russians were furiously pulling back from the battle site. Should they spot the fleeing mosquitoes, however, they were still easily within range to quickly end all of the cavalrymen's lives. Fortunately, the panicked enemy was much too busy searching for death from above to concern themselves with anything else.

With the Russians watching the dagger-filled skies for the next attack, Jensen's men slipped away, one vehicle at a time. Each raced west to escape the valley floor. When they slid around the corner onto E48, the three soldiers in the Humvee could feel the intense heat from the tangle of burning giants a quarter mile away. Every few seconds, more rounds would cook off, exploding in the raging fires. With each new burst, the Humvee's crew would involuntarily duck. They understood the next explosion they heard could be from the 125mm cannon of an alert enemy tank that had spotted the fleeing Humvee. Although Jensen knew if that happened, they would never hear the sound of the detonating shell before it killed them all.

Both sides had had enough.

Licking their wounds, the six surviving Apaches turned and headed for home. Behind them, scores of ravaged armored vehicles lay burning in the snows. An impassable wall of death and destruction reached from tree line to tree line.

The Apaches, with a helping hand from Jensen's platoon, had blocked E48.

The Humvee rounded a final forest curve and disappeared.

CHAPTER 14

January 29—12:25 a.m.
2nd Platoon, Delta Troop, 1st Squadron, 4th Cavalry
Outside the Town of Schirnding

At the end of the burning valley, the forest gave way to an area of small farms and modest villages. Two miles ahead lay the town of Schirnding. On its eastern edge, an ancient apple orchard dominated both sides of the highway.

The magnificent orchard was a beautiful sight during the platoon's drives to the border in April, when the trees were beginning to bloom, and again in July, when the apples were ripening. The orchard was pretty in a different sort of way in October, when autumn's vivid hues tumbled down in torrents upon the passing soldiers.

During the platoon's drives to the border in January, however, there was nothing attractive about the ghostly trees that hung still and lifeless in a cold gray world.

The platoon began assembling along the roadway in the bleak orchard. First, Brown and his men arrived, driving through the trees and stopping near the edge of the quaint town. Foster and his crew were a mile behind.

With the continual explosions, it was impossible to know what had happened to those they'd left behind. Each new arrival quickly got out of his Bradley to peer back down the snowbound roadway to see if anyone else had survived. One by one, the lumbering fighting vehicles arrived safe and sound. And when the Humvee was spotted in the distance, there was actually a feeble cheer from the spent platoon.

The Humvee eased to a stop beneath a gnarled apple tree. When its occupants exited, the excited soldiers crowded around to celebrate in earnest their continuing good luck.

"Sarge, did you see how many of those bastards we killed!" Marconi said.

"Yeah, Comrade's finding out he's going to be one dead mother if he messes with 2nd Platoon," Richmond added.

With a wave of a gloved hand, the platoon sergeant put an end to such talk. The last thing they needed at this moment was to let down their guard. "Knock it off, you guys. This war ain't over. Not by a long shot. We've still got a lot of work to do." Jensen turned to Austin. "Seth, have you put out scouts?"

"Well, no, not yet, Bob."

"Then, dammit, get to it. We're out in the open here. If the Russians catch us like this, we're all dead."

Again, scouts were dispatched in every direction to protect the platoon.

Jensen examined their new defensive position. He'd driven through here hundreds of times. But unlike the border trail, the platoon sergeant had never given much thought to how to defend it.

While he looked around, it occurred to him that this wasn't the ideal spot for the platoon to make its stand. Nevertheless, this time he had little choice.

Once E48 passed through the small town, the roadway entered open country. It would stay that way to the town of Marktredwitz and Camp Kinney. If the Russians broke through at Schirnding, they'd have considerably more freedom with which to operate. If the enemy got past Jensen's platoon, it was going to be nearly impossible for the outmanned cavalry squadron to stop them. Jensen had no alternative than to make his stand here.

He went over to where Jelewski was standing. "Jewels, tell squadron we're setting up to defend this position."

"Can't," Jelewski said. "In the past few minutes, the Russians have begun jamming the entire frequency spectrum. They're apparently putting everything they've got into making sure this squadron can't further coordinate its efforts. There's nothing but static and noise everywhere I turn."

With communications cut off, Colonel Townes would no longer be able to control the desperate battle. From this moment on, it would be up to isolated groups of men, like the ones standing in the lifeless orchard, to fight on alone.

There weren't many options on the open ground. Jensen would try to hide the Bradleys at the front of the wide orchard and hope for the best.

Under normal conditions, the cavalry soldiers would dig a sloped hole deep enough to cover each of the Bradleys up to its turret and gun systems. The Bradley would then be driven into its fighting hole. This would accomplish two things. First, it would make the Bradleys more difficult to discover. And second, the ground in front of each position would protect the Bradleys, creating challenging targets for their opponent to attack and kill.

They probably had the time to prepare such positions. Jensen suspected that the battered Russian column was going to take many hours to re-form, breach the burning barrier, and move forward once more. But even so, there would be no Bradley fighting holes dug on this night.

The problem wasn't the Russians. The problem was the miserable weather. The ground beneath the deep snows was frozen solid. With their small entrenching tools, it would be impossible for the cavalry soldiers to break through the rock-hard surface.

It was the Wisconsin-born Austin who came up with the idea. "Bob, let's build snow forts between two trees and use them to conceal the Bradleys. It won't provide the protection being dug in would, but at least it'll make us difficult to detect."

Austin had built hundreds of such fortresses of snow in his days as a young snowball warrior. The East Texan Jensen had never seen a single one. Still, the idea didn't sound half-bad.

"Well, it's better than nothing, Seth. Pick out firing positions for the Bradleys and begin concealing them. I'll work on setting up the supporting fields of fire."

Before preparing for the forthcoming battle, Jensen decided to do one more thing—get any remaining civilians out of the village. Once the attack commenced, there probably wasn't going to be much of a village left. He assumed most of the townspeople had awakened and fled the moment they heard the first exchange of gunfire. Nevertheless, he needed to make sure. He found Steele and Ramirez leaning against the Humvee.

"Go knock on every door in this stupid little town. If you find anyone, tell 'em to get the hell out of here as fast as they can. Check all the cellars, too. That's where they'll be hiding if anyone's still around. Ramirez, you take the north side of the road. Steele, you've got the south."

"But, Sarge," Ramirez said, "this place must have at least two hundred houses in it."

"Then I guess you'd better get your asses in gear. I want you to finish up and be back here by three at the latest. I've got plenty more planned for you two to do. Now beat it."

The reluctant pair started shuffling up the highway.

"You'd better move faster than that if you don't want the Russians using you for target practice," Jensen said.

Ramirez scooped up a big glob of snow. He made himself a hurried snowball. The private hurled it at his platoon sergeant. It missed by a mile. Ramirez and Steele took off running, each headed for the first farmhouse on his side of the highway.

Jensen trudged back to see where Austin had placed the Bradleys. The five fighting vehicles were all in a straight line at the front of the orchard. Each was about one hundred yards from the next. Each was between a pair of apple trees. Three were on the left side of the road. Renoir's was on the far left, three hundred yards from the highway. Foster's was in the middle. Austin's was nearest to E48. The remaining Bradleys were on the right. Richmond's was one hundred yards away. Brown's was in the extreme right-hand position.

With the Bradleys emplaced, the crews began dismounting. In the flickering half-light emanating from the fires in the east, each team started building a snow wall in front of their armored vehicle. If time permitted, they'd build the barrier far enough across to connect with the broad trees on both sides of them.

Fifteen years ago, playing in the snows used to be fun, Austin thought. He scooped up another armload of snow and placed it on the wall rising in front of his Bradley. Fifteen years ago, the wars he saw in the movies looked like fun, too. An ironic little chuckle escaped his lips. Oh well, at least building the fort was taking his mind off the numbing cold.

Once or twice each minute, from five miles away in the tree-lined valley, another secondary explosion would reverberate throughout the crisp night.

While the Bradley crews worked to hide their positions, Jensen broke off three dozen small branches from a nearby apple tree. If the Russians gave him the time, he'd get all the firing stakes in place. Still, he knew that even with adequate time, he didn't have enough men to set up a decent defensive position.

In the coming battle, he'd leave two soldiers to fight from each Bradley. One would handle the TOWs, the other the Bushmaster and machine gun. There was no reason to have a driver; the platoon had nowhere to go.

Including Jensen, that would leave sixteen infantrymen on the ground to support the Bradleys. Two troopers would assist each fighting vehicle, consuming ten of his men. Two more would be set out on the northern edge of the orchard to protect the left flank. Another soldier would be placed on the southern edge to protect the right. The final pair would take the Humvee and find a position inside the village to protect the platoon's rear. For all Jensen knew, Russian units could be west of his location and the platoon's position already surrounded. The last thing he wanted was to prepare for an attack from the east and find himself fighting an enemy coming from the west.

No matter which way he arrayed his modest force, its position was going to be vulnerable. No matter what he tried, there were going to be holes in his lines in every direction. What he would do, in whatever time the enemy allowed, was get the most from what was left of the platoon.

Taking two soldiers, he initiated the tedious process of working out the best positions for the men on the ground. He'd start with the infantry support for the Bradleys nearest the highway. Austin's would be first.

He placed a soldier thirty yards to the right of the fire team. Jensen worked with the young trooper to plot out his position. Once determined, two branches were shoved into the snow a few feet in front of the location. The branch placed on the left marked the left boundary of the defender's firing area. The second branch, placed on an angle to the right, marked the right firing boundary. This was the soldier's field of fire. The soldier would be responsible for engaging everything coming within the boundaries of his sticks. Normally, the firing positions would overlap so more than one cavalryman would be available to engage any battlefield target. With so few men, however, overlapping fire was a luxury the platoon wouldn't have.

With the first supporting position laid out, Jensen told the anxious private to "dig in." To conceal his position, the soldier started creating his own miniature version of the Bradleys' snow forts.

Jensen moved to the other side of Austin's Bradley to place the second of his men. Jelewski would go into the position thirty yards to Austin's left. With Jensen, the specialist laid out his field of fire. When the branches were in place, he turned to Jelewski.

"Get your position set. Once it's ready, head over to the nearest farmhouse, find a phone, and make an attempt to contact the squadron."

"But, Sarge, there are only two civilian landlines going into Camp Kinney, and there are likely to be thousands of Germans calling the camp hoping to find out what's going on. So it's going to be impossible."

"I know, but we've got to try. Give it no more than an hour, then come back."

The conversation completed, Jensen headed back to the highway to collect two soldiers to support Richmond's position.

After everyone was settled in, the platoon sergeant would place himself in the center of the coming battle. He'd build his own snow fort on the right-hand side of the highway, just a few feet from the wide road. When the Russians broke through at Schirnding, they'd have to do it by going through him.

When he reached the highway to collect the next pair of soldiers, a final driver turned off his Bradley's rebellious engine. The orchard should've been silent. Yet much to their chagrin, the windswept world around them was filled with fearful sounds.

The cavalrymen heard the unmistakable squeal of a tank column. The entire platoon froze. The enemy had taken them by surprise. The Americans were going to be caught in the open without proper defensive positions. Jensen pulled his night-vision goggles to his face. He frantically searched the entire length of the snow-covered ribbon of asphalt for signs of the impending attack.

There was nothing there. Other than the swirling snows, he could find no movement whatsoever on the two miles of E48 visible from the orchard. While he stood looking to the east, he slowly realized the awful truth. The sound wasn't in front of him. The noise of the lethal tanks was coming from the rear. And it was growing louder.

Austin stood holding an armload of snow one hundred yards away.

"Seth, get word to the Bradleys that the enemy's behind us!" Jensen yelled. "Tell them to crank their turrets around and get ready to repulse an attack from the west."

When Austin acknowledged the command, Jensen turned to the soldiers nearest the roadway.

"Let's go!"

Six soldiers, rifles in hand, raced with their sergeant toward the town. What the pitiful group was going to do to stop an armored column not a single one of them had a clue.

The instant the lead tank's immense hull eased around the narrow corner, its commander spotted Ramirez and Steele. The African-American private was pounding on a door. His partner was standing on the corner across the street from him, casually drinking a beer. Neither had a weapon.

The menacing tank closed to within a few feet of the defenseless soldiers.

The commander's hatch opened and a head popped out.

"Who the hell are you two?" the tank troop commander asked over the noise of the M-1s' engines.

Ramirez placed his right arm behind his back in a feeble attempt to hide the beer. "Well, sir, our sergeant told us to get everybody out of this town."

"That's great, but who the hell's your sergeant, and where the hell is he?"

"Sergeant First Class Jensen, sir. We're what's left of 2nd Platoon, Delta Troop. Our sergeant's up there." Ramirez pointed down the roadway. "He's getting our Bradleys ready for the Russians."

"How many Bradleys, and where are they?"

"They're in the orchard on the other end of town, Captain," Steele said. "We've only got five left. The Russians got the other ones when we fought them up at the border."

"So you men have seen some action?"

"Shit yes, sir. You think I got this bandage on my head for nothing?" Ramirez said. He neglected to mention it was cement, not bullets, that had caused his injuries. "We've been in two battles already. Musta killed a thousand of those sons a bitches."

Next came the question Ramirez had hoped to avoid.

"Where'd you get the beer, son?"

"Well . . . ah . . . you see, Captain, there's this *Gasthaus* right up the street and . . ."

"You mean you found a *Gasthaus* open in the middle of the night, in the middle of a war?"

"Well . . . it . . . it wasn't exactly open, sir."

Jensen and his men scrambled from doorway to doorway, edging up the ageless street. The squeaking of the tank treads had stopped. The soldiers knew the tanks were no longer on the move. Unfortunately, the rumble of tank engines was extremely close. So they also knew the tanks were right around the next bend. When he reached the corner, Jensen signaled to Marconi to cover him. Ever so carefully, Jensen peeked around the bend.

There stood Ramirez and Steele in the middle of the street passing out bottles of beer to an entire troop of 1st Squadron tank crews.

"Ramirez!"

Hearing the thunder in his sergeant's voice, Ramirez let go of the two beers he was carrying. They dropped harmlessly into the snows.

"Marconi, go back to the orchard and tell Austin it's a false alarm. Tell him to continue preparing for an attack from the east."

"Will do, Sarge." In a slow trot, Marconi took off for the orchard. He was sure glad he wasn't in Ramirez's or Steele's shoes right now.

Jensen stomped over to where his wayward privates stood staring at the ground. As he opened his mouth to begin a richly deserved tirade, Jensen spotted the captain standing in the open hatch of the tank above the pair.

"Oh, sorry, sir. Didn't see you there." Jensen didn't salute. He and the captain knew that when the shooting started, the saluting stopped. "Sergeant Jensen, 2nd Platoon, Delta Troop."

"That's all right, Sergeant. Captain Murphy, Commanding Officer of Bravo Troop. I know you didn't send your men out to serve as bartenders for a bunch of tank jockeys. But after your privates told me about all the Russian tanks waiting up ahead, I thought we might have one final beer for the road. I mean, at this point, what's it going to hurt?"

Jensen thought about it, reached down, and picked up one of the bottles Ramirez had dropped. "You know something, Captain, I believe you might be right."

The captain and his vehicle commanders dismounted. While they enjoyed what was likely to be the last beer of their lives, Jensen reported on what had happened to his platoon. His audience froze in midswallow when he told them he suspected the Russian force the Apaches had chewed up consisted of at least three armored divisions.

Even if the attack helicopters had destroyed the one hundred armored vehicles Jensen believed they had, there were still over nine hundred Russian tanks and an equal number of BMPs with which to contend. Captain Murphy considered the possibility of a second beer. They knew their vastly superior tanks could run circles around the Russians. Even the T-90 had little chance against the M-1. A well-trained American tank unit could easily destroy three or four times its number in enemy armor. This, however, was eighty tanks to one.

Jensen glanced at his battered watch. It was 12:58. The war was one hour and thirteen minutes old. He wondered how many eternities that had been.

The final drops of strong beer savored, Captain Murphy walked toward the front of the orchard with Sergeant Jensen.

While they walked, they came up with a plan.

CHAPTER 15

Army Sergeant Larry Fowler drove the two-and-a-half-ton truck out the gaping nose of the C-5 cargo plane. On the back of the truck sat a modest-sized metal compartment with a small rear door. Clear of the plane, Fowler's ground guide, Private First Class Jeffrey Paul, scrambled into the truck's passenger seat. All around them, C-5s were in the final stages of disgorging their cargo—a Patriot missile battalion.

The first thing Fowler noticed was that the Germany he'd left over a year earlier was the same. Although, Fowler had to admit, the snow was deeper than he'd ever remembered seeing in any of his previous German winters. The damp cold of Europe was quite a change from the high desert air of El Paso. Fowler's truck inched across the tarmac. It took its place at the rear of the Charlie Battery line.

"Sure is cold out there," Jeffrey Paul said, trying to make conversation.

"This is your first time in Germany, isn't it?" the thirty-year-old Fowler said.

"Yeah," Paul answered. He wrapped his arms around himself in a symbolic attempt to stay warm.

The final battery vehicles exited the C-5s. Two ten-ton tractors pulling Patriot missile launchers eased in behind Fowler's truck. A huge wrecker joined the end of the line. Identical convoys belonging to the other three batteries of the Texas battalion finished forming around them on the well-lit tarmac.

All sat waiting. Ninety-six noisy engines idled in the bitter cold. While they waited, Fowler continually pumped the gas pedal, revving his faltering truck.

A quarter mile away, a trio of commercial airliners were loading passengers. Twenty yards to Fowler's left, the battalion commander and the battery commanders stood talking near the Bravo Battery column. The quick meeting broke up. Captain Allen, Charlie Battery commanding officer, walked to his Humvee. He said a few words to the first sergeant. The first sergeant got out of the Humvee. He marched down the line of vehicles tapping on the hoods and motioning for the drivers to get out of their trucks.

"Fowler, shut it down and head up to the command vehicle," the first sergeant said as he passed by. "The battery commander wants to talk to all the drivers and officers."

Fowler turned off the engine, shoved open the door, and climbed down. Head bent, he walked through the falling snows past the twenty battery vehicles in front of his own. Cold or not, it was exhilarating to get out and stretch his legs after twelve hours crammed in the noisy passenger compartment of a C-5. Two dozen drivers and a handful of officers crowded around the grim-looking captain. The fierce winds kicked up. The snows grew heavier. To see, the late-arriving Fowler was forced to peek over the top of a camouflaged shoulder.

"Ladies and gentlemen," Captain Allen said, "we hadn't told you earlier, but just over an hour ago, the Russians attacked Germany. From what we've been able to find out, this is an all-out assault." In the bitter cold, the battery commander's breath was visible with every fateful word. "We're involved in a war here. So far, the Russians have confined themselves to sabotage and a massive ground thrust into Germany. The battalion commander just received word that at this moment, the Russians are pushing through the border in a number of places. They're beginning to drive west."

Captain Allen paused. He needed to ensure his people grasped the seriousness of the situation. As he looked at their stunned faces, there was no doubt everyone understood. Each face stared into his in disbelief.

"The Warsaw Pact air forces haven't been heard from yet. That, of course, is subject to change at any moment. A massive air attack is expected sometime in the next few hours and could occur at any time. For that reason, we'll be moving out without delay."

Thirty sets of eyes nervously scanned the low-hanging heavens.

"Here are the assignments the battalion commander handed out. Alpha Battery will go north to reinforce the 5th German Patriot Battalion at Munster. Bravo Battery stays in the middle of Germany to support the American 3rd Patriot Battalion at Giessen. Delta Battery is to remain here at Rhein-Main in reserve. Charlie Battery . . ." Everyone strained to hear their unit's assignment.

". . . everything south of Heidelberg. Our job's to reinforce the American 6th Patriot Battalion. Alpha Battery, 6th Battalion's Engagement Control Station is deadlined awaiting parts and is out of action for at least five days. We'll be traveling to Stuttgart to take their place. Ladies and gentlemen, we're going south."

"Sir, how far south is Stuttgart?" someone asked.

"About one hundred miles straight down the autobahn," Captain Allen said. "Here are the engagement-team assignments." He glanced at the list he'd hastily prepared. "Lieutenant Miller and Staff Sergeant Magruder. Lieutenant Morgan, you and Sergeant Fowler will pair up. Lieutenant Little and Sergeant Owens. Should we need a fourth engagement-control team, Lieutenant Smithson and Staff Sergeant Cherno. Does everyone have that?" Captain Allen searched their faces. When there was no reply, he said, "Good. Get ready to pull out. We leave for Stuttgart immediately."

The quick meeting broke up. The soldiers hurried back toward their vehicles. Lieutenant Barbara Morgan reached out and grabbed Fowler by the sleeve when they neared the rear of the convoy. Beneath her cap, her bobbed red hair was visible as it cradled her attractive neck. The ruddy-faced Fowler could see the freckles running unimpeded across the bridge of the pretty lieutenant's nose.

At five feet seven, Fowler stood eye to eye with her. Although he'd never admit it, he had a tendency to overcompensate for his lack of height, especially when dealing with women.

"Sergeant Fowler."

"Yes, ma'am."

"Have you ever been to Germany?"

"Yes, ma'am. Before I went to Fort Bliss for Patriot training, I spent a couple of years in Ansbach."

"Good. Then at least one of us will know what they're doing." She gave him a captivating smile. The sweet smile hid her growing apprehension.

Fowler scrambled back into his truck. The lieutenant climbed into the passenger seat of the Humvee in front of him. He felt good about drawing her as his partner. Working with her had always been easy. And they'd made quite an effective team at killing the enemy during the mock battles the battery had fought against the computers. He hoped their successes wouldn't change now that the enemy could shoot back.

Besides, she was extremely easy on the eyes—an important thing for a newly divorced man to consider, even in the middle of a war.

There had already been some indications that Lieutenant Barbara Morgan held similar thoughts about the sergeant with whom she would share duty in the Engagement Control Station. After one too many drinks at last month's battery Christmas party, they'd found themselves parked on a lonely desert road in the backseat of her car. An hour of alcohol-induced embraces had ended with fifteen minutes of heavy groping but no more.

Since then, she hadn't been cool toward him. But neither had she given any sign that the relationship would go any further. For the past five weeks, she'd acted as if the Christmas party had never happened. She hadn't been hostile, but she hadn't been particularly friendly, either. For whatever reason, since Christmas she'd treated him in the professional manner officers had of dealing with NCOs.

Fraternization between officer and enlisted soldier was certainly more common than it had been. Nevertheless, it remained officially unacceptable behavior. As far as either knew, no one suspected there was anything between them. For that matter, at this moment neither of them knew themselves if there actually was.

All around them, the vehicles came to life. "All right, let's roll," Fowler said. He restarted his truck's engine.

The three convoys crept toward Rhein-Main's front gate. Fowler followed Lieutenant Morgan's Humvee. Her Humvee followed a ten-ton tractor pulling a Patriot launcher and its four deadly missiles.

When they neared the gate, the bright lights on Rhein-Main's tarmac suddenly went out. The lights inside the passenger terminal also were extinguished. Thousands of cramped men, women, and children were plunged into darkness.

A mile east of the air base, the north–south autobahn waited. Ahead of them, Alpha and Bravo Batteries turned left and headed north. Charlie Battery swung south onto the snow-covered autobahn. The six-lane roadway was deserted. For Fowler, not having to deal with the insanity of German drivers while trying to guide his truck in this horrendous weather was a relief in itself.

In Charlie Battery's twenty-four-vehicle convoy, a dozen huge tractors pulled the launchers and replacement missiles. Using only the sliver of illumination provided by their blackout lights, they felt their way south at twenty-five miles per hour. The vehicles spaced themselves two hundred yards apart. The convoy's drivers soon discovered that even at this snail's pace, there was no sure way of stopping in the snow and ice.

If a Russian air attack was imminent, they needed to get to Stuttgart as quickly as they could. They were sitting ducks as they chugged down the eerie autobahn. They understood that if the Russians caught them on the empty roadway, their lives would soon end. Spread out or not, a handful of determined MiGs could destroy the entire battery with relative ease. Nevertheless, with their massive loads, they couldn't go any faster than they were.

It was better to make twenty-five miles an hour than to helplessly stand by the roadway while the wrecker fought to pull a ten-ton tractor out of a snowbank. Worse yet was the possibility of sliding a tractor into a ditch and watching as four missiles, each with two hundred pounds of high explosives in its nose, slid off your trailer and bounced along the ground.

Even a gentle touch of the brakes became an adventure. While they fought to cover the treacherous miles, more than one of the convoy's drivers watched in terror as the trailer he was pulling passed in front of the tractor he was driving.

Ten minutes into their dangerous run, Fowler spoke his first words since beginning the journey. "Put a clip in my M-4."

"What?"

"I said, put a clip in my M-4. And while you're at it, put one in yours, too."

"Why?"

"Because, my friend, you and I are at war. The Russians attacked over an hour ago."

Without another word, Paul reached over and loaded thirty-round ammunition clips into the pair of M-4s sitting between them.

The relentless storm pelted the windshield. It overwhelmed the wipers, making it impossible for Fowler to see. He could neither locate Lieutenant Morgan's Humvee in front of him nor the launcher that trailed two hundred yards behind. In the middle of the convoy, he drove on alone.

Fowler fought every inch of bleak roadway, doing all he could to keep his precious cargo safe. Without the Engagement Control Station nestled on the back of his truck, the trailerloads of deadly missiles would be worthless. He strained with the last of his fading strength, fighting the merciless elements with nothing but his blackout lights to guide him. Every few minutes, he would signal his companion to take a rag and swipe at the windows.

Jet lag sank deep into the canyons of Fowler's weary mind. Exhaustion washed over him. He'd never been more miserable in his life. He tried with all his might to ignore the undeniable fact that in the past day and a half, he'd hardly slept. A couple of catnaps were all he found time for while his unit furiously prepared to rush to Germany. Now, at least, he understood the urgency.

Ever so slowly, the horrid miles slid past for Fowler and the convoy while they drove through the night toward an unknown destiny.

Inside the truck, Fowler's thoughts were racing.

Outside, the world was strangely quiet.

CHAPTER 16

With his parka pulled tightly around him, Airman First Class Arturo Rios drove a small tractor across the snow-covered tarmac. It was one of those little yellow tractors used around airports to take luggage out to the planes. But Rios wasn't carrying luggage. Behind his tractor trailed a long line of two-thousand-pound bombs.

Twenty-year-old Arturo Rios worked as an armaments loader for a wing of F-16 Falcons. Mainly, he drove the yellow tractor back and forth to the ammunition-storage area in an isolated corner of the base. There, while the young airman sat daydreaming, a crew of loaders would prepare his lethal convoy. Rios would then carry death across the base to the flight line. At the flight line, others waited to take the bombs and attach them to the belly of an F-16.

It wasn't a glamorous job. And if Rios ever made a mistake, it wasn't going to be a job with any longevity.

Tired of his mundane life in Miami's Little Cuba, Rios had joined the Air Force to see the world. In eight months in Germany, he hadn't seen much of the world yet. But he'd seen the two miles between the ammunition dump and the flight line often.

For the young airman from balmy Miami, this first, frigid German winter was pure misery.

In the past few days, he'd noticed a marked increase in the activity on the base. There was a definite sense of urgency in the work on the flight line. But so far, no one had bothered to explain why. His hours in the blizzard's bone-crippling cold had grown longer. And his trips to and fro with his lethal cargo had become nonstop.

Three squadrons of F-16s from South Carolina had arrived at Ramstein earlier in the day. Rios had spent the last five hours taking munitions to the South Carolina fighters.

Rios pulled up in front of a reinforced bunker where a South Carolina F-16 waited to receive the last two bombs from this tractorload. Master Sergeant Arnold, chief of the flight-line crew, spotted him. Arnold walked through the falling snow to where Rios sat in the open tractor.

"Rios, I've been looking for you. As soon as you drop off these bombs, you need to report to the base armory."

"Why? What's up?"

"I don't know, but we got word a few minutes ago that all augmentation air police need to report to the armory. Your name was on the list. You did two months of augmentation training, right?"

"Yeah, back in September and October."

"Well, then get over there as soon as you finish here."

"Okay, Sarge."

Fifteen minutes later, with his head down to shield his face as he trudged through the blowing gale, he started the lonely walk to the base armory. When Rios arrived, a madhouse greeted him. In rapid succession, people hurried in and out the doorway to the modest room that served as the base's weapons-distribution center. Inside the dingy room, Rios passed a dozen airmen sitting cross-legged on the floor, furiously disassembling, cleaning, and reassembling boxloads of never-before-used M-4s. An air policeman in a wire-mesh cage motioned the bewildered airman over.

"Name?" the air policeman said.

"Arturo Rios."

"Rios . . . Rios," the air policeman said, while scanning a lengthy list on his clipboard. "Ah, here we are . . . Rios, Arturo J. Let me see your I.D. card."

Rios dug into his pocket, withdrew his identification, and handed it through a small opening in the screen. After a cursory glance, the air policeman returned it.

"Okay, Rios, wait here while I get your equipment."

The air policeman disappeared through a doorway into a weapons-storage area. In less than a minute, he returned with a large, heavy machine gun cradled in his arms. In each hand, the air policeman carried a metal ammunition container. He clumsily opened the door through the screen and brought out the machine gun and ammunition. He placed them in Rios's arms. At over 125 pounds, the gun and its tripod weighed nearly as much as the slight airman.

"You're checked out on .50 calibers, aren't you?" the air policeman asked.

"Yeah, I spent two weeks on them during augmentation training."

"Good. There's a Humvee waiting outside. Go out there and tell the driver to take you to defensive position fourteen on the eastern perimeter of the base."

"Why? What's going on?" Rios asked.

"Man, didn't you get the word? The Russians attacked the border over an hour ago. We're expecting some kind of attack on Ramstein anytime now."

Unlike the Army, which took the position that every soldier was an infantryman first and whatever else he was second, the Air Force's approach was to concentrate on making their airmen proficient at the primary job they performed. Without the distractions his Army counterpart faced, an Air Force technician was hands down more proficient at performing the same tasks. The downside to such an approach was that should it ever come to ground combat, the airman, while not completely helpless, was nevertheless at a severe disadvantage.

The Air Force's solution was to leave the primary combat role to the air police. The air police would be supplemented by the air base's augmentation force, individuals who'd been released from their primary duties and given a period of combat training. Only in a dire emergency would the average Air Force technician be compelled to fight.

Army and Marine Corps Vietnam veterans were ripe with stories about Communist attacks on air bases. Inevitably, two little guys in black pajamas would sneak through the wire of an American air base and attempt to destroy an airplane or two. As soon as the fighting started, airmen from all over the base would race to the scene of the battle—with their cameras.

There was even a recorded case where a pair of malnourished figures attacked the world's largest B-52 base. At the moment of the attack, there were five thousand airmen on the base. The base's commanding general called a small Army camp five miles away for reinforcements.

As was typical of most air bases, on the evening of January 28, the M-4s of the thousands of Ramstein airmen were still sitting in their original grease and wrappings in unopened containers.

The Humvee stopped in front of a heavily sandbagged, horseshoe-shaped position on the isolated eastern end of the sprawling base. The bunker was directly in front of the air base's primary runway. It was less than fifty feet from the chain-link and barbed-wire security fence. Thirty yards beyond the fence lay a dense woods. The air policeman helped lift the machine gun from the vehicle and assisted Rios in setting it up. The task completed, he shoved the metal ammunition containers into the airman's hands. Without another word, the driver got back into his Humvee and disappeared into the blizzard.

Rios adjusted the machine gun's positioning. Satisfied, he opened one of the containers. He removed an ammunition belt and placed it in the machine gun. The confused airman did a little housekeeping, brushing away the snow from the top of the sandbags. Then, all prepared for an attack, he sat wondering what else to do.

Rios began doing the only thing he could—staring into the foreboding woods and waiting for the Russians. Outside the wire, the branches of the muddled evergreens drooped beneath the weight of the heavy snowfall. The wind eerily whistled through the trees. Biting snow fell upon the anxious airman's world of sand. The night was pitch-black.

Time stopped.

After what Rios believed to be two hours and was in fact twenty minutes, a flight of three F-22 Raptors raced down the runway toward him and took to the night. The stealth fighters passed directly over Rios's head. Each screamed into the eastern sky.

A few minutes later, a second group of Raptors thundered down the runway, roared ever so closely over Rios's position, and disappeared into the blizzard. They were followed by a flight of F-35s.

Throughout the night, the pattern would be repeated, with flights of F-22s, F-35s, or F-16s heading down the runway right at him. At the last second, each would leap from the ground and vanish into the eastern darkness. The fighters would later return to be refueled and re-armed. They would then race back down the runway toward the forlorn airman once more.

The thunder of the jet engines would temporarily deafen Rios. Even so, he really didn't mind. For the activity broke the monotony. It provided a distraction from his mounting fears on a surreal night that had no end. Alone with his lethal weapon and his frightening thoughts, Rios waited in his isolated bunker of sand and snow.

Above the fierce storm's immense layer of clouds, the stealth aircraft roared through the twinkling winter's night sky toward the Czech border at nearly fifteen hundred miles per hour. In each, a single pilot sat. The trio of fighters carried identical pairs of thousand-pound bombs. Air-defense missiles hung from their wings and were positioned in the bays below the F-22s' bellies, ready to destroy any MiGs that were unfortunate enough to cross their path. Vulcan 20mm cannons waited for close-in air-to-air battles or ground-support attacks.

Each of the American pilots was exceptionally skilled. All three were supremely confident. And there was absolutely no reason for them not to be. Their fighters were arguably superior to any in the world. They could handle both air and ground targets with relative ease. Because of their stealth capabilities, any MiGs that wandered too close would be nearly helpless against them. No enemy radar, whether in an approaching aircraft or on the ground, was capable of accurately identifying and combatting the F-22s.

It wasn't because the Stealths were invisible to the radars. That would've been impossible. Instead, their unique design caused the aircraft's image to be deflected in various directions rather than reflected directly back. The radar would receive a confusing, disorganized image that it was unable to recognize and interpret.

The formation's primary target, the first of the new war, was an air-defense battery near the Czech city of Pelzen. After vanquishing the air-defense system, their secondary objective was to destroy the Central Army Group Command and Control Center the missile battery protected. The targeting information upon which the mission was based was the last imagery satellite pictures of the western Czech Republic, taken four days earlier.

With the blizzard masking the targets, the stealth pilots would be forced to use their infrared systems to deliver their payloads with pinpoint accuracy. This wasn't going to be easy. Or at least that's what they thought. Nearing Pelzen, the three couldn't believe their good fortune. Like the foolish Iraqis had done on the first night of Desert Storm, the Russians had turned on their air-defense radar. The signal from the radar served as a homing beacon for the planes. The Russian target had put out a "come and get me" sign.

The lead aircraft made a silent run at the radar. The pilot released a bomb at precisely the right moment. Using the radar's own signal, he guided his deadly cargo toward the objective. The radar exploded in a fiery flash of light.

With the air-defense system immobilized by the first F-22, the other two fighters were free to concentrate on taking out the command and control center. The target was more difficult to acquire than the radar had been. But the pilots found it exactly where the intelligence reports told them it would be. A rambling house sitting alone in the middle of a farmer's field, the command center was easily identifiable by the bristle of radio antennas on its roof. Even with the late hour, there were half a dozen well-lit rooms within the building. Outside, a number of combat vehicles sat in the falling snows. It was far too easy for the skilled Americans.

The F-22s locked onto the target. Each released a single bomb. With absolute precision, the pilots guided the munitions toward the large house. The target was instantly vaporized by the force of two thousand pounds of high explosives.

None of the pilots had needed his second bomb to complete the mission. With smiles upon their faces, they turned and headed home to Ramstein. When they landed, each passed a few arm lengths above a frightened Cuban-American airman's bunker just off the eastern end of the runway.

The wing commander met the triumphant pilots as they rolled to a stop. "How'd it go?" he asked when the flight leader climbed down from his aircraft.

"Piece of cake," the major said. "The assholes had their radar on. We followed it in and destroyed both the primary and secondary targets. These guys are as dumb as the Iraqis. Even the Taliban knew better than to do something this stupid."

The four walked into the operations center feeling quite good about their country's chances of vanquishing another aggressor. Ground crews raced to refuel and rearm the aircraft for their next mission.

Prior to the attack on the radar installation, the Russian lieutenant had been quite concerned. The headquarters staff had departed long ago, moving their command center thirty miles south. There had been ample time to get the entire command element moved after nightfall, even if they'd struggled with the fearsome elements in doing so.

They left the communication antennas on the roof of the old farmhouse. The moment the staff set out, the lieutenant and his men drove the old, worthless vehicles up and parked them in the same positions the staff's vehicles had been in earlier. The lieutenant turned on some lights within the building. Not so many as to be obvious. But enough to make the enemy believe their opponent was either foolish or careless.

Now, however, the essential element in the deception was giving him trouble. The ancient radar, worth only what a Moscow junk dealer would give for it, was acting up. He'd started it at exactly midnight. Nevertheless, the lieutenant could only get it to remain on for a few minutes at a time. Without a working radar, it would be nearly impossible to fool the Americans into believing their raid upon Central Army Headquarters had been successful. He had no options. Rather than leaving for the new headquarters' location, he and his privates would have to stay and baby the old grandfather of a radar until the Americans attacked. They found themselves some protection in a gully a few hundred yards west and waited.

By 3:00 a.m., the lieutenant had made a dozen trips to the radar. In each instance, he'd coaxed it into working once more. He'd gotten the radar running a final time and had walked a short distance away when the first thousand-pound bomb dropped from the sky.

Death came to claim him in a whisper from above. He never heard it. He never saw it.

Had he lived, he would've been proud to know his mission was a complete success. He'd fooled the Americans and saved Central Army Headquarters from any further attack. At least for the time being.

In the darkness of the first night, all over Poland and the Czech Republic, American, British, and German aircraft went after the Warsaw Pact's command and control with a vengeance. The Warsaw Pact air forces sat on the ground, aware of what was happening but content to wait for their moment to come. Only in the wee hours of the morning, when the British attacked two air bases in central Poland, did the MiGs rise up to meet the challenge.

In nearly every case, the NATO pilots reported that their missions had been a complete success. Enemy command and control had been decimated. The ability of the Russians to coordinate their war efforts had been severely damaged. Their leadership had been eliminated.

But the Americans were mistaken. General Yovanovich's ploy had worked. All the Russians had lost was of value to the scrap heap. By sunrise of the first day, less than 8 percent of the Warsaw Pact's command and control had been destroyed.

And American command and control was in serious trouble.

CHAPTER 17

The communication center sat on a hilltop in a thick forest of green and white. It was fifteen miles from the nearest German village. Bristling with microwave dishes, its tower rose a hundred feet above the tallest of the ancient evergreens. Nestled next to the prefabricated metal communication control building were a large satellite ground-station dish and its associated equipment.

Nine minutes after the Russian tanks burst through the border, the five-man Spetsnaz commando team struck. Each commando's dress was as black as the darkest night. Each had painted his face in a thick layer of camouflage chalk. Each carried an automatic machine pistol and a satchel charge. Each was a proficient killer, the match of any in the world.

On their bellies, three of the commandos crawled the final quarter mile through the forest's floor. The chain-link fence that surrounded the facility was their destination. With their wire cutters muffled by a thick cloth, they cut a hole in the fence at the rear of the compound. They were soon inside. While a ghostly figure kept watch, his partners began attaching explosive charges to the legs of the communication tower and the satellite dish.

Just inside the compound sat the guard shack. The remaining pair of saboteurs crept through the shadowless forest to within a few feet of the tiny structure. The security for the Langerkopf communication site, the third largest American facility in Germany, consisted of a single airman with a Beretta pistol strapped to his hip.

A night-shift crew of eleven was working inside the communication building. They had no weapons. The M-4s of the fifty-person Air Force detachment were stored at their headquarters a mile down the mountainside.

The Spetsnaz team leader silently covered the final few feet to the guard shack. In a single motion, he cut the airman's throat. Without ever realizing what had happened, the American dropped into the snow. The commando dragged the lifeless body across the roadway. A glistening trail of red marked the path he'd taken. He hid the dead airman behind one of the American cars parked across from the communication building. The leader quickly returned to protect his partner. His accomplice started connecting the plastic explosives to the windowless metal building. The expert job was soon completed. The leader signaled the members of the team at the tower and satellite dish. The timers were set.

The saboteurs melted back into the woods. Five minutes later, two simultaneous blasts leveled the mountaintop. The tower toppled sideways, tumbling into the pristine forest. The satellite dish was vaporized. The communication control center burst into a thousand fragmenting pieces.

There wouldn't be enough left of any of the airmen to bury.

At the same moment, identical teams of deadly assassins were attempting to infiltrate the mountaintops where the two largest American communication centers were located. At the world's biggest military communication facility, the Army site at Donnersberg, luck was with the Americans.

A soldier had been sent down to the barracks area to pick up a box loaded with sandwiches and snacks for a hungry night shift. The saboteurs were just beginning to set their explosive charges when the soldier's car crested the snow-swept hill. The first thing the American saw was the body of the site's sole guard lying by the gate. The next thing that came into the headlights of his rusting Fiat was five black-clad figures. The soldier knew that at any cost he had to warn those inside the building. He slammed his hand down on his car's horn and held it there. The horn's wail crushed the night's silence, alerting those inside.

The pair of commandos nearest the gate raced toward the old car. While they ran, the Russians drew long knives from the sheaths on their hips. The American locked his doors and continued sounding the horn. A forearm smashed the driver's side window, shattering the glass. A silver blade flashed in the darkness. In the assassin's expert hands, the grisly task was effortlessly completed. Another American had succumbed. But before the Russians ended his life, the soldier had sounded his horn for nearly twenty seconds.

From inside the facility, a head poked out the main door to see what the commotion was all about. Two quick bursts from a machine pistol cut him down. He fell back into the building and lay bleeding on the polished tile floor. The Spetsnaz team rushed to set their charges.

Unlike the defenseless airmen at Langerkopf, twenty M-4s sat in weapons racks inside Donnersberg's main entrance. The Americans tore open the racks and pulled out the M-4s. The storage locker next to the racks yielded ammunition clips and a wooden crate filled with bullets. While the technicians readied their ammunition clips, a warning went out to every communication facility in Germany.

As he watched helplessly as one of his men died on the cold white floor, the staff sergeant in charge of the night shift picked up a microphone and pushed the speaker button.

"This is Donnersberg. We're under attack from an undetermined enemy force. Say again. To all sites. Donnersberg is under attack. Take whatever action is necessary to protect yourselves."

At the sixty American strategic communication sites throughout Germany, the soldiers and airmen scrambled to secure their facilities. Their survival, and the ability of the generals to control the coming war, depended upon it.

At Langerkopf, the warning arrived a split second too late. The airmen heard it. But before they could react, the tumultuous blasts ended their lives.

After issuing his warning, the Donnersberg supervisor picked up the phone and quickly dialed the barracks area. At the unit headquarters a half mile down the mountain, seventy soldiers were awakened. They rushed to dress and join the eighteen attempting to protect the hilltop. Nearly all American military communication within Germany went through Donnersberg. Each knew that without Donnersberg, command and control would be forever lost.

But fate, and hunger, had given them a chance. Individually, the communication specialists were no match for their highly skilled opponents. Still, the soldiers were reasonably well trained in the use of these basic weapons.

Inside the communication center, seventeen soldiers waited for their shift leader to give the word. The staff sergeant looked at his men as they held their rifles at the ready.

Outside, the commandos rushed to finish the job. Their presence had been discovered, but they were far too practiced to panic. Their task was nearly complete. Without interference, in a minute, no more, the timers would be set.

"Half out one door, and half out the other," the staff sergeant said. "Whoever's out there must be stopped. We've got to hold on until the rest of the unit gets here."

The Americans burst through the facility's two doors. The commandos were waiting. Before they could reach the snows, six soldiers were felled in a curtain of automatic gunfire. The staff sergeant was the first to die as he led his technicians in their counterattack. The eleven survivors knew it would be five long minutes before any of the reinforcements would arrive. Until then, it was up to them. They dove for cover and frantically searched for the enemy. A black figure was spotted. The Americans opened fire. The Russians responded with their automatic weapons. In a blinding flash, the hilltop erupted in an intense firefight. The muzzle flash of a rifle gave a second intruder away. The Americans returned his fire. One by one, the five commandos were identified and battled.

The first of the assassins fell dead from a soldier's chattering M-4.

Two more Americans went down. One of the soldiers lying in the falling snows screamed in agony from a bullet-shattered kneecap. Next to him, his friend was silent and still. Muzzle flashes from both sides lit up the night.

The clock was moving. The sands of time were beginning to run out for the killing team. A second of the saboteurs was struck in the chest by American fire. He dropped into the snows. The odds were now nine against three. Still, even though outnumbered, the advantage remained with the deft assassins. The American survivors knew, however, that if they could hold on just a little longer, they were going to have a chance of saving the critical mountaintop. The struggle continued. More precious seconds ticked by. Torturous minutes slowly passed as bullets flew in both directions.

Over the sounds of battle, the surviving commandos heard a long line of cars beginning to churn up the mountainside. They knew they'd failed. They disengaged. Firing as they went, all three fell back. The first of the reinforcements—eleven soldiers crammed into a late-model Dodge and an old Volkswagen—reached the top of the hill. Others were close behind. At the edge of the compound, they piled out of their cars and raced through the gate. The mountain was alive with gunfire. And the reinforcements were growing by the minute.

The Russians were overwhelmed. A third and shortly thereafter a fourth of the enemy was caught in the relentless crossfire of the reinforcements and the original defenders. The final commando, the leader of the deadly group, ran toward the rear of the compound. With incredible ease he scaled the ten-foot perimeter fence in a hail of gunfire.

While he straddled the wire, the soldiers heard him scream. He dropped to the ground on the other side and staggered into the darkness. In seconds he was gone. The soldiers let him go. None of the Americans was eager to follow the deadly assassin into the black, chaotic forest.

He would never be found. The only trace of him would be a thick trail of blood leading down the mountain that would disappear in a few days, along with the melting snows.

In the morning, the explosive ordnance team would shake their heads in disbelief. If the sandwiches had arrived thirty seconds later, the commandos' mission would have been a complete success and America's chances of strategically controlling the war nearly gone.

Half the American microwave communications between Germany and England, and from there on to the States, had disappeared with the loss of Langerkopf. The other 120 channels went through a single facility—Feldberg. The only other modern American satellite relay in Germany sat next to the Feldberg communication control station.

As at Langerkopf, the security at Feldberg consisted of a single airman with a 9mm Beretta. The airmen's M-4s were two miles down a snowy hill at the detachment's headquarters. Hearing Donnersberg's warning, the Feldberg night-shift supervisor issued an order for the fifty airmen below to gather their weapons and rush to the top of the mountain. Once more, sleeping Americans were roused.

The Feldberg supervisor placed half his crew, six unarmed men, near the fence line to watch for any sign of the enemy. They had no weapons, so they wouldn't be able to defend themselves. Nevertheless, they could provide a warning. The six airmen stood in the shadows inside the fence. After a quarter hour in the freezing cold, the airmen were growing far more concerned about the pain in their extremities than the possibility of an enemy attack.

The five-man killing team sent to eliminate Feldberg was late. Fifteen minutes late. They'd left their safe house on the outskirts of Frankfurt right on schedule. But they'd taken a wrong turn within minutes of starting their journey. Driving a sputtering Opel down unfamiliar streets in the middle of a blizzard, the team leader had missed the turn-off. In the darkness, he'd driven three miles in the wrong direction before realizing his mistake.

The twenty-mile trip to Feldberg was to take no more than fifty minutes, even in this weather. Instead, the commandos had taken ninety to arrive at the end of a deserted farm road near the base of the high mountain. They'd tossed caution to the wind and scrambled up the mountainside at breakneck speed.

At any cost, their target had to be destroyed.

Five black-clad figures, protected by the forest's oppressive darkness, reached the hilltop. The commandos split up. Three crawled through the snow to the rear of the compound. The communication tower and satellite ground equipment was their objective. The second team moved toward the front gate. The American guard shack was right in front of them.

The first team muffled their wire cutters and snipped a hole in the chain link near the tower.

From the shadows, an airman screamed, "Someone's at the fence! Intruders near the tower! Intruders! Intruders!"

A commando crawled inside the wire, drew his knife, and hurled it toward the sound. The knife's blade found its target. The voice in the darkness shrieked. The wounded airman dropped to his knees, clutching at the knife deep within his chest. The remaining killers rushed through the hole. The trio was upon the airman in a flash. The American let out a final scream.

"Dammit! Where the hell are you guys?" the shift supervisor screamed into the telephone. "We're under attack up here!"

"Hang tight. They left five minutes ago. Should be there anytime."

Ten cars were churning up the steep, snow-covered roadway. They were nearing the top. The guard leaped from the shack and drew his Beretta. He fired two rounds toward the tower. The sound of his firing crackled through the windswept night. The hurried shots missed everything.

The second set of assassins was hidden in the trees fifteen feet from the guard shack. They opened up with their machine pistols. The guard went down.

The commandos' mission had been foiled. The pair stepped from the forest and ran inside the gate. Each blindly fired automatic rifle bursts into the walls of the prefabricated aluminum communication control building. The rounds ripped through the thin metal walls and tore into the communication equipment. Half the critical equipment on the Feldberg to Martlesham Heath, England, link was torn to shreds. Sixty of Feldberg's 120 channels to England disappeared as the gunfire tore the sophisticated electronics equipment apart.

The commandos stopped to reload. They could hear the automobiles coming up the hill. The cars were growing louder by the second. Both turned toward the ominous sound.

One of the Americans was standing undetected in the area behind the night shift's row of parked cars. He crept over to his own. He opened the driver's door and crawled inside. Lying flat on the floorboard, he dug his keys from his pocket. The airman shoved the key into the ignition.

In one motion, he bolted upright and started the engine. The airman threw the car into gear and floored it. Tires spinning wildly, the car fishtailed. It smashed into the car next to it and spun back to the left. With snow flying from every crevice, it roared straight for the menacing black figures near the gate. The assassins turned toward the onrushing car. At the last possible instant, the commando leader dove out of the way. The other saboteur froze. The car smashed into the stationary figure, scooped him up, and, in a mighty crash, impaled him on the fence.

The leader leaped to his feet. He ran to the car. With blood streaming down his face, the driver looked up. The airman's eyes held an instant of recognition. The leader stuck the nose of his machine pistol close to the windshield and squeezed the trigger.

The rescue convoy was quite near.

The sappers at the rear of the compound spotted another of the airmen hiding in the darkness near the building. They opened fire. Half a dozen bullets slammed the American against the wall. His lifeless body crumpled to the ground. Trails of blood oozed down the side of the building.

One of the assassins ripped the satchel from his back. He set the timer for ten seconds and tossed it toward the satellite terminal. The satchel landed within a few feet of the satellite dish. The charge exploded, leaving behind nothing but an unrecognizable mass of twisted, smoldering metal.

The line of cars crested the hill. They roared toward the compound. The commando leader was right in front of them. As they sped toward the gate, the three passengers in the first car stuck their M-4s out the windows. They started firing. Caught in the open, the saboteur ran toward the rear of the facility. His companions waited near the communication tower to cover his escape. They returned the Americans' fire.

It was an eighty-yard run through deep snows with the soaring cars clipping at his heels. The ruthless killer was in incredible physical condition. But the distance was much too great. Like a pack of hungry wolves, the line of cars raced after the fleeing figure. The commando leader blindly fired as he ran.

The first car closed in for the kill. From twenty yards away, the airmen unleashed a long burst from their M-4s. Lines of bullets danced across the leader's back. The saboteur somersaulted in the snow. He sprawled forward, face buried deep within the drifts. He was already quite dead.

Nevertheless, the Americans were in no mood to take any chances. For good measure, the speeding car ran over his bloody corpse.

With their leader out of the way, the remaining commandos fired everything they had. A hail of bullets smashed the first automobile's windshield. The driver took a round to the face. The car spun out of control. The airman sitting next to him grabbed for the steering wheel. It was, however, too late. The speeding car veered to the left and smashed into the base of the burning satellite equipment. The automobile burst into flames. All four airmen were trapped by the raging fires.

The airmen in the next pair of cars raced side by side through the compound. Six M-4s returned the three commandos' automatic-pistol fire. Two of the invaders fell. The wounded saboteurs dragged themselves toward the hole in the fence. The opening was just a few feet away. Another burst of gunfire from the swarming Americans, and the pair moved no more. In a desperate attempt to save his own life, the final saboteur ran for the fence. He squeezed through the hole and disappeared into the darkness. Twenty airmen leaped from their cars and raced to the wire. They started firing in the direction the black figure had taken.

The commando wouldn't get far. The next day they would find his bullet-riddled body in a thorny thicket one hundred yards down the hillside.

The sabotage of the American strategic communication system was over for the moment. But the Russians weren't finished yet.

General Yovanovich's plan called for four initial targets—the three largest military communication facilities in Germany and one of the smallest. Langerkopf, where the site had been destroyed. Donnersberg, where a shift of hungry soldiers had survived. Feldberg, second only in size to Donnersberg. And on the top of the Zugspitz, the highest mountain in the German Alps, a tiny relay that served as the only American communication link with Italy. If all of the sappers had succeeded, communication between America and her field commanders would've nearly disappeared. In Germany, communication between the air bases and the ground forces the fighter aircraft were intended to protect would be severely handicapped. America would fight this war almost blind.

As it was, the loss of Langerkopf and the two satellite ground stations destroyed significant portions of the communication system, crippling the Americans. Langerkopf served as one of only two facilities connecting Germany and England. And it also tied together the majority of communications west of the Rhine River. The American fighter bases at Ramstein and Spangdahlem received most of their communication services through the destroyed site.

Even with their losses, the sabotage hadn't caused the crushing defeat of American command and control General Yovanovich had envisioned. The Americans had been staggered by the swiftness and intensity of the Russian attacks. They had to do something to restore their ability to strategically control the war or face certain defeat against the superior armored forces pouring through the border.

Precious time was passing. There was no more of it to waste if the Americans were going to have any chance of winning the war. They had to overcome the saboteurs' destruction.

And they had to do it now.

CHAPTER 18

In his warm two-bedroom apartment, Army Staff Sergeant George O'Neill fell asleep next to his wife, Kathy. The twenty-eight-year-old O'Neill had decided to stop studying at about 11:30, when the couple's nineteen-month-old son, Christopher, awoke and started his nightly screaming. It had taken George forty-five minutes to calm the child and return him to his dreams. Christopher quieted, O'Neill slid into bed next to his wife. Snuggling next to her on the brutally cold night, George decided that a prolonged bout of lovemaking just might be in order. But when his amorous advances didn't awaken Kathy, he gave up and rolled over. In a short while, he fell asleep.

As he drifted off, O'Neill should have been more concerned than he was. He was aware that an evacuation of dependents had begun. Even so, he believed it would be another two weeks before the Stuttgart area, well to the west of the border, would be affected by the order.

With the Warsaw Pact's war games scheduled to end in a few days, O'Neill was confident the evacuation order would be rescinded long before it would threaten to separate him from Kathy and Christopher.

The gangly George O'Neill wasn't a handsome man. And he wasn't very comfortable around people. Unlike her husband, the irresistible Kathy O'Neill was quite attractive. Petite, with shoulder-length blond hair and a pixie smile, she was a real charmer. Everyone who met smiling Kathy took to her immediately. Her zest for life was obvious to those with whom she came into contact. Many times, as she stood in the bathroom watching George shave, a silly grin would come over her sweet face. For as she stared at him, she would realize there was no doubt she'd married Ichabod Crane. Nevertheless, she loved her Ichabod. And she knew her Ichabod loved her. To Kathy's credit, when she'd met George, she'd taken the time to look beyond his features. What she found hidden there was a man of substance. Now, four years into a wonderful marriage, she knew her instincts had been correct. For her, he was the perfect husband. And for George, there couldn't have been a better wife.

They were truly soul mates. Fortunately for both, the bond between them was immutable. For like many marriages, theirs had suffered tragedy. Within days of arriving in Germany, the couple's firstborn child, Emily—a four-month-old, bright-eyed baby girl—had died of sudden infant death syndrome.

It was Kathy who'd found her. And it was Kathy who'd borne the brunt of the grief and guilt that followed. Alone all day and most evenings while George went to work or attended college classes, she'd suffered in silence. Luckily, within three months of Emily's death, Kathy had become pregnant with Christopher. And while she'd never fully recover from the taking of her first child, Christopher's arrival had eased the pain. With Christopher in her arms, her boundless love for life had returned.

A classic underachiever, O'Neill had enlisted in the Army eight years earlier because he couldn't figure out anything better to do with his life. It was Kathy who'd given him the direction he needed. Despite an extremely challenging job, since his arrival in Germany O'Neill had attended the University of Maryland's on-base college program. For thirty months he'd carried more than a full load of classes. He'd given up his lunch hours, his evenings, and his Saturday mornings to sit at uncomfortable wooden desks in the base education center.

As the couple's last six months in Germany neared, O'Neill was three months away from completing his bachelor's degree in business

administration. Four courses to finish, and he would be a college graduate. He took great pride in the fact that if he received an A in these
final classes, he would graduate summa cum laude. Or as he'd told
Kathy after a particularly demanding week, "thank the laude."

After a full day's work, he would devour a hasty meal. A quick kiss
for mother and child, and he would hustle off to class until nine. Af-
terward, he'd study until late into the night. He slept little. On the
weekends, he'd have a firm grip on a textbook from the moment he
awoke until well after dark. Without someone as supportive as Kathy,
O'Neill would never have been able to maintain the torrid pace he set
for himself. Even the patient Kathy had expressed how nice it would be
when she finally got her husband back. Yet each believed the sacrifices
they were making would be worth it.

During the past year, he had received well-paying management
offers from a handful of America's leading telecommunication companies. And while the couple's decision wasn't yet firm, it appeared that
when they left Germany, they'd also leave the Army behind.

He'd been asleep for scarcely fifteen minutes when the phone in the
living room began to ring, shattering his brief peace. He glanced over
at Kathy. His soundly sleeping wife was just beginning to stir. In a fog,
he stumbled out of bed and headed for the living room. Christopher's
renewed screams were added to the unexpected clamor. O'Neill grabbed
the phone and was surprised to find Navy Petty Officer First Class Mike
Gallagher on the other end of the line. George did his best to clear away
the cobwebs and overcome his confusion at the unexpected call. In
thirty months, no one from his unit had ever disturbed him at home.

"What's up, Mike?" O'Neill asked.

"Sorry to bother you, George, but Defcon One was called an hour
ago. They've got me calling all the guys who live on the base. Report to
the office as soon as you can. I've still got to notify Benning and White-
hall. See you when you get here."

Without waiting for a response, Gallagher hung up. O'Neill stood
in the middle of the living room, telephone still in his hand, while his
addled brain tried to accept what he'd just heard. He couldn't shake his

disbelief. This had to be a dream. Defcon One could only mean one thing—his country was at war.

Christopher continued to wail. Kathy hurried into the child's room. O'Neill returned to the bedroom and started putting on his uniform. While he finished lacing his boots, Kathy wandered in holding the now-contented toddler to her breast.

"What's going on, George?" she said.

O'Neill figured that until he found out what was happening, the less he said the better.

"Don't know, Kath. That was Mike Gallagher on the phone. He said they need me to come back to the office for something."

"How long are you going to be gone?"

"He didn't say, but it might be all night."

O'Neill threw on his field jacket, wrapped an olive-green scarf around his neck, shoved his hands into his gloves, and put on his cap. With a kiss for mama and baby, he hurried from the second-floor apartment. He raced down the cold steps and out the front door. The moment he stepped through the doorway, the fearsome blizzard smacked him across the face. Any cobwebs lingering in his brain instantly disappeared.

The couple's car was buried beneath two feet of snow and ice. Rather than fighting to free it, O'Neill decided to walk the half mile to his office. He pulled the scarf up around his ears and started down the cobblestone street. With every step he took, the snow and ice crunched beneath his feet. The iridescent glow of the base's ancient streetlamps surrounded him. There were other shadowy figures in the narrow streets purposely heading in different directions. But he never noticed. His mind was far too preoccupied with the implications of what Gallagher had told him.

Near the small base's western fence, O'Neill bounced up the steps of a single-story office building. He swung open the glass door. He stopped to pull out the identification badge hanging from a chain around his neck. A quick flash of the badge for the MP sitting at the desk just inside the doorway, and he continued on his way.

O'Neill went by his office and threw off his jacket, scarf, hat, and gloves. He returned to the hallway and headed toward the operations center. Other than a few lights being on that normally wouldn't have been at this time of night, things appeared quite normal. Maybe this really was nothing more than a dream.

At the end of the hallway, he entered the code into the cipher lock and threw open the door to the Defense Information Systems Agency's European Division Operations Center. In the middle of the white windowless room, four metal desks were pushed together. Next to each was an assortment of communication equipment—printers, computers, telephones, microphones, and speakers. From this room, all American strategic communication from Iceland to Turkey was managed.

Around the clock every day of the year, the operations center was manned by a shift of four. The four—an officer and three NCOs—controlled three hundred communication facilities, three satellite systems, and a trio of huge, computerized message centers. As the agency's members knew, you couldn't get a pencil to Europe without the communication system they controlled.

Rather than finding four people when he entered the operations center, O'Neill found fifteen. All but two were members of the agency. The strangers—a three-star general and a captain who was most likely the general's aide—stood at the far end of the modest room beneath a large map of the European communication system. The general was talking with the agency's director, Air Force Colonel John Cossette. Standing at the edge of the group was the agency's deputy, Marine Colonel Charles Hoerner. O'Neill was too far away from their conversation to hear what was being discussed.

George O'Neill was one of the specialists assigned to the Defense Information Systems Agency's European Division. The organization was manned by seventy handpicked soldiers, airmen, sailors, Marines, and Department of Defense civilian employees. In theory, the assignment of each service's top communication specialists to the agency sounded good. In practice, however, the agency was bound to struggle in the coming days while trying to find a way to let the generals control the conduct of this war. For political reasons, it was staffed by people from each service. Yet the vast majority of the worldwide military communication network was operated by the Air Force and Army.

The sailors assigned to the agency were excellent electronic technicians. They were far superior to their Army counterparts, but they were trained for shipboard and ship-to-shore communication, a vastly different system than was used on the ground in Europe. The agency's twenty-eight sailors and Marines would be of little help in the days to come. Much of the remainder of the staff were officers or civilian electronics engineers whose sole purpose was to design orders in response to new circuit requests. In neither the Air Force nor the Army did the officers play any active role in running the communication facilities. Since the development of the worldwide communication net in the 1950s, the system had been under the total control of the NCOs of both services.

As O'Neill stood in the operations center, he counted the number of people within the agency with enough on-site experience to keep the system going in a crisis. There were six. Six NCOs to direct all strategic communication within Europe and from Europe to America. Besides O'Neill, there were two Army Sergeants First Class, Rojas and Mitchell. There were three Air Force NCOs—his coworker in the quality-control section Senior Master Sergeant Denny Doyle, and Technical Sergeants Goldsmith and Becker, both of whom worked on operations-center shifts not presently on duty. While he looked around the room, he realized of the six people who would lead the fight against the chaos that was bound to follow, he was the only one present.

The other five NCOs lived in the military housing complex at Ludwigsburg, twenty-five miles north. With the autobahn essentially shut down by the blizzard, it would be some time before any of them would arrive.

Next to the four controllers' desks, the communication equipment was chattering wildly. The shift, consisting of an inexperienced Navy lieutenant, a petty officer first class, and two Air Force NCOs, looked overwhelmed. Other than the general's animated conversation with Colonel Cossette, everyone in the room was just standing around.

Marine Major Michael Siebman, O'Neill's lunchtime jogging partner on those rare occasions when college classes weren't in session, spotted him standing by the door. Siebman wandered over.

"When'd you get here?" Siebman asked.

"Just a minute ago, Major. How long have you been here?"

"About twenty minutes, I guess."

"What in the world's going on?"

"Word is the Russians attacked a little over an hour ago. Full-scale assault, from what I've overheard."

"I . . . I . . . Major, I don't understand."

"Neither do I. But there's no doubt about it, Russian tanks have crossed the border. From the looks of things, their war games were apparently just a ruse to hide their true intentions."

"Who's the general talking with Colonel Cossette?" O'Neill asked.

"General Oliver, Chief of Operations for European Command Headquarters."

"What's he doing over here?"

"EUCOM's mad as hell. Their circuits to the Pentagon and many of the major European commands were knocked out when we lost Langerkopf. The entire system's in disarray."

"Lost Langerkopf?"

"Yeah, we lost Langerkopf a few minutes after the Russians attacked. No one seems to know for sure what happened, but we do know that sappers hit Donnersberg and Feldberg at about the same time that Langerkopf went off the air. Donnersberg's fine. Feldberg survived, but they lost one of their two supergroups to Martlesham Heath and their satellite ground station. Almost everything between Germany and England's been knocked out. And apparently there's little communication going into and out of the air bases at Ramstein and Spangdahlem."

O'Neill didn't have to look at the map behind the general's head to know what it all meant. No one in Europe knew the American communication system better than he did.

"What have they done about it so far?" O'Neill asked.

"I don't know. I guess that's why the general's over here. From what little I've overheard, no one seems to know what to do."

"Aw shit!"

O'Neill brushed past the major and headed for the Navy lieutenant sitting in the lead controller's chair.

CHAPTER 19

"Lieutenant Templeton, have you ordered the sites to start rerouting the highest-priority circuits?" O'Neill asked.

"What?"

"What have you guys done to reroute the highest-priority users we lost when Langerkopf went down and we lost a supergroup between Feldberg and Martlesham Heath, and the Feldberg and Langerkopf satellites, sir?"

"I'm sorry, Sergeant. I don't understand."

"What I mean, sir, is that we should've started determining an hour ago who the highest-priority users are and rerouting them onto the remaining sixty channels to England. We then need to see which of the most critical circuits going to our air bases at Ramstein and Spangdahlem went through Langerkopf so we can reroute the really important ones through Donnersberg."

The general and the colonels stopped their conversation in midsentence. General Oliver rushed across the room to where O'Neill was standing. The others followed in his wake.

"Sergeant," the general said, "are you saying we can do something to restore our communications with England and the States?"

It certainly wasn't every day that a staff sergeant had a conversation with a general. But O'Neill understood, despite his uneasiness, that the situation called for him to ignore the stars on the general's uniform and do what needed to be done.

"Yes, sir. The 20 percent of our communications on the fiber-optics system is still safe and will likely remain that way. Of the rest, we're not going to be able to restore everything. But we can give you some of it. We've still got sixty channels on the microwave system into Martlesham Heath. We've lost our two major satellite terminals, but we've still got twelve channels on the old satellite from Landstuhl to Arlington, Virginia. We can also give you forty-eight more channels to the States through Coltano, Italy, and onto an undersea cable there. After that, or whenever you want if you need them sooner, we can give you a few circuits into the air bases at Ramstein and Spangdahlem."

"Why wasn't this done before now?"

"It should've been, sir. Forty years ago, the entire process was supposed to be computerized so that it would automatically happen in this kind of situation. Unfortunately, Congress cut the project from the budget when the phasedown in Europe began, so it never got started. I've been told back then our communications was almost as good as anything AT&T could've provided. But without the funds, there has not been any real change to the system in all that time. So we'll have to do the rerouting and restoration manually."

"How long will that take, Sergeant?"

"Sir, you tell us what you want, and we'll get you a circuit back online about every five minutes. All that's necessary is for you and your staff to let us know what you need and when you need it, within the limits I just gave you, and we'll take care of the rest from here."

The general scooped up the nearest phone and dialed the European Command Operations Center in the middle of the base.

"This is General Oliver. Give me Colonel Morrison immediately."

"Yes, sir," Colonel Morrison said a few moments later.

"Charlie, look I'm still over here at DISA. They tell me that if we let them know what our priorities for circuits are, they can handle it for us. Get the staff on it right away. I'll be over in a few minutes to give you the details."

"Will do, sir."

The general hung up the phone. He turned back to O'Neill. "They're already on it. We'll start letting you know what we've absolutely got to have just as soon as I get back to my office."

"That'll be fine, sir."

"Anything else, Sergeant?"

"No, sir. Just tell your staff not to wait. As soon as they know the first few circuits, get back to us. We'll start working on getting them in immediately."

"Very good."

Without another word, the general turned and headed for the door. His aide was right behind him. When the door closed behind them, the two agency colonels turned back to O'Neill with relieved looks on their faces.

"Thanks, Sergeant O'Neill," Colonel Cossette said. "Are you certain you can do what you just promised the general?"

"Absolutely, sir."

"What are you going to need from us?"

"Sir, the first thing I'm going to need is access to the routing databases for every circuit in Europe. There are over four thousand of them, and we lost about a thousand when Langerkopf went down. So it's going to take some effort to get the most important ones working again. All I really need at the moment is to get into Lieutenant Templeton's computer so I can bring up the database files."

The colonel motioned for Templeton to make room. O'Neill grabbed a nearby chair and slid in next to him.

"What else?"

"As soon as EUCOM calls back, we'll need someone to work the phones. Lieutenant Templeton will do just fine. Finally, we need anyone not involved in the restoration of communications to go somewhere else. We're going to need all the room we can get."

"All right. Is there anything I can do?"

"Lots of things, sir. Mainly we'll need you to run interference with the brass. We can handle the technical end of it from here, but only if we don't have every general in Europe trying to give us orders. So I'd like you or Colonel Hoerner to be in here at all times."

"Don't worry about that, Sergeant. You concentrate on doing what you promised General Oliver, and we'll take care of the rest."

"Sir, it's really not a problem. It'll just take a little time."

It was only a matter of minutes before the phone on Templeton's desk rang.

"Sergeant O'Neill," Lieutenant Templeton said, "General Oliver's on the phone for you."

O'Neill took the phone from the lieutenant. "Staff Sergeant O'Neill speaking, sir."

"Sergeant, we're ready on this end. There are twelve circuits we've got to get in as soon as we can. I'm going to turn the phone over to my chief of staff, Colonel Morrison, to work with you guys."

"That's fine, sir. We're all set here. General, this will work better if we keep someone on both ends of the line at all times until we get everything up and running. These first few are going to take awhile until we get the bugs out of the process and everybody's working together."

"I understand, Sergeant. We'll keep someone on this end of the phone until we get the job completed. Here's Colonel Morrison." Oliver handed the phone to his deputy.

"Sergeant O'Neill, is it?" the colonel said.

"Yes, sir."

"General Oliver tells me you're going to be able to handle this for us."

"Yes, sir. Just give me the four-digit designator for the first twelve circuits, and we'll take it from there."

"Well, let's see. We must have Kilo-Quebec-Seven-Victor, our primary presidential strike command circuit, back in just as soon as we can. Make that your top priority. I'm sure the President's nowhere near ready to order any kind of nuclear strike or anything like that against the Russians, but should he at some point decide it's come to that, without that circuit, he won't be able to do so."

O'Neill wrote the circuit designator on the notepad on the senior controller's desk.

Colonel Morrison continued to talk. "Then we've got to have Echo-Charlie-Twenty-Seven from here to Air Force Headquarters at Ramstein and also Alpha-Six-Thirty-One, as soon as we can get it, for the National Security Agency folks in Augsburg to be able to talk to their headquarters in Virginia. The next . . ."

"All right, sir, I've got it," O'Neill said. "It'll probably take an hour, possibly a little more, to get these first twelve up. In the meantime, I'm going to turn you over to Lieutenant Templeton. Each time we get a circuit back, we'll notify you so someone can verify the circuit's working. Just keep on giving the lieutenant a list of the circuits you want, and we'll work it throughout the night."

"Okay, Sergeant, we'll do that."

O'Neill handed the phone to the lieutenant. He took his notes and started working through the database. The typically shy O'Neill certainly had no desire to be in the spotlight. But shy or not, he understood the significance of the job he was doing. Without an ability to communicate, the war effort would be fragmented and disjointed. In all likelihood, that would prove fatal. All the fancy American technology would be of little value if they couldn't fully coordinate its use. And no matter how uneasy he felt when dealing with higher-ups, O'Neill wasn't going to let the fact that he'd been shoved into the limelight stand in his way.

He found the correct database and located the appropriate pages to begin working on returning the presidential strike command circuit to service. He ran his finger down the screen, checking the crucial communication channel's routing—the White House to the Pentagon, up through Nova Scotia and across Greenland, from there to Scotland, to Martlesham Heath on the English coastline, through a relay in Holland, to Feldberg on the supergroup the saboteurs had destroyed, then to Donnersberg, and finally arriving in Stuttgart.

O'Neill visibly relaxed, his confidence growing. He knew they all wouldn't be this easy. But this one was a piece of cake. Just one leg of the four-thousand-mile journey to worry about, and communications with the White House would be restored. All he had to do to allow the President to talk to his European Headquarters was to move the circuit at Feldberg onto the working supergroup to Martlesham Heath. From there they'd be home free.

He located a lower-priority circuit to preempt and wrote down its position on the Feldberg–Martlesham Heath link. O'Neill picked up the microphone in front of him. By pushing the microphone button, he would be in instant contact with every communication facility in Europe.

"Feldberg, this is DISA."

"DISA, Feldberg," came a voice from the battered mountaintop.

"Martlesham, this is DISA."

"Go ahead, DISA," said an airman at the Air Force site on the English coast.

"Okay, guys, we're starting with Kilo-Quebec-Seven-Victor. Feldberg take it from Supergroup One, Group Three, Channel Eight, to Martlesham and move it to . . ."

Five minutes later, a first critical communication circuit was up and working. With the highly skilled George O'Neill taking the lead, more would soon follow.

The Russian plan to eliminate American command and control had so far failed. The Americans had been staggered by the sabotage. But General Yovanovich's promise to Premier Cheninko to sever the American head hadn't yet occurred. The Americans had been crippled by the commandos, but they were far from dead.

What the Americans didn't know, however, was that Valexi Yovanovich still had a few tricks up his sleeve.

The monumental chess match between the gangly American sergeant and the implacable Russian general had many more moves yet to play before the war would reach its end.

At stake were the outnumbered Americans' chances of controlling the burgeoning conflict.

CHAPTER 20

The expensively clad figure dangled in the darkness one thousand feet above the precipice. Seventy-mile-per-hour winds buffeted him. The blowing snows tore at his anguished face. The blizzard slammed him relentlessly against the side of the icy overhang.

He had no choice. To save his life, he slid the one-hundred-pound pack from his back. He let it drop into the abyss. His life now depended upon a thin nylon line, the sole artery connecting him to his fellow climbers. With their powerful arms, the other two commandos lifted him out of the void and onto the side of the mountain.

He staggered to his feet.

The fall really hadn't been his fault. They were five hundred feet above the area they'd surveyed earlier in the week. In the darkness, the leader had fallen into the undetected crevice.

The mighty storm ripped at the trio. Their heavy ski outfits were little defense from the blizzard's fearsome sting. Icy particles tore pieces of flesh from their exposed cheeks. They had no protection from the fierce elements. At nearly ten thousand feet, they were well above the tree line.

They turned to continue their torturous climb toward the mountain's peak. The crest of the Zugspitz, the highest mountain in Germany, was still a few hundred feet above them. Even with their superb conditioning, every step was agony as they struggled toward the top.

The commandos had arrived in Garmisch a week earlier. Their cover as ordinary tourists here for a ski vacation had been a convincing one. Each day, with their backpacks full, they would take the ski lift up the Zugspitz. The lift would deposit them two thousand feet beneath the mountain's summit. From there they'd hike ever higher up the mountain, often coming within a thousand feet of the peak.

They'd scaled the heights to deep-powder ski, to ski the snows no one else had skied. At least that was their story.

In reality, they were mapping the trail as far up the mountain as they possibly could. A trail they would follow a final time when the command came. On their first day on the slopes, they dug a cave in the snow. There, they made a daily deposit of weapons, explosives, and climbing gear. Each day they would stay on the mountain working out the climb for as long as they could without arousing suspicion. They would then break powder and ski down the steep mountainside. The three were magnificent skiers. Each was much admired by the mountain's enthusiasts as they made their way down from the fearful heights.

Not a single person noticed that while their backpacks were full on the way up the mountain, they were empty when they returned to the lodge.

They were the darlings of the ski season on the Zugspitz. All three were blond, powerfully built, and captivatingly handsome. All three were vicious, brutal killers.

Rich Swedish students, they told the beautiful women who lounged by the chalet's gigantic fireplace. Their English and German were impeccable. Between them, they'd conquered many of the pampered kittens who curled by the fire lapping up every word of the assassins' contrived tales. Nearly all of their conquests had been wealthy American girls. Girls eager to try anything to relieve the boredom of their meaningless existence, if only for a fleeting moment.

Not a bad assignment, each commando told himself, while heading back to his room late in the evening with another empty-headed admirer on his perfectly tanned arm. The saboteurs had even become friends with a group of American soldiers on holiday in the Alps. They liked the amiable soldiers much more than they cared for the shallow girls who were so eager to be a night's entertainment.

Not a bad assignment at all. At least until tonight.

Their contact in the chalet's dining room had given them the signal at breakfast. The mission was on. In the afternoon, the team loaded their backpacks a final time. The trio told the indulgent ones by the fire that after they made one last ski run, they had to drive to Munich on business. But not to worry, they'd be back by morning.

The killers had suffered a shock when they arrived at the ski lift at a little before three. The lift had been shut down. The chairs that reached well up the mountain sat still and silent. Without the lift to carry them the majority of the way, they'd never make it to the top of the Zugspitz in time.

They rushed into the lift building. The pimply-faced teenager who ran the lift sat staring out an icy window.

"What's going on here, Franz?" the leader asked. "Why isn't the lift running?"

"They closed it down, Mr. Ardesen. There are high winds on the mountain, and it's too dangerous to ski. So they told me to shut it down."

"Franz, we've got to go into Munich on business tonight. We want to make one more run down the mountain before we do."

"Sorry, Mr. Ardesen. They told me to shut it down."

"I understand, Franz, but all our lives we've wanted to ski a mountain in these kinds of conditions. We've been waiting for a challenge like this forever. Now you're telling us we're going to miss that chance."

"I really am sorry, Mr. Ardesen, but that's what they told me."

"Look, you like us, don't you, Franz? And you know what great skiers we are. So why don't you open the lift long enough to let us go up, then shut it back down again."

"I can't, Mr. Ardesen. If I did, and somebody saw me, it could mean my job."

"Well, maybe if we made it worth your while . . ." The leader reached into his pocket and withdrew a huge wad of euros.

The boy's eyes grew wide. He'd never seen so much money in his entire life. And the ski lift ran just long enough to deposit the darlings of the Zugspitz at a place far up the jagged mountain.

Shortly after dark, dressed in outfits belonging to the commandos, the waiter and two of his accomplices drove the saboteurs' Mercedes out of the chalet. They headed down the road that led to Munich. They made sure to wave from a distance at the pampered ones who watched the car drive away.

The trio fought their way to the very crest of the mountain. One hundred yards away were the twinkling lights of their objective. The killers moved toward the small compound. Every few feet, they stopped and watched. There was no guard. Taking out a pair of wire cutters, they ran in a low crouch the final yards. A few quick snips, and they were inside.

The pair of airmen on duty at the relay on top of the Zugspitz had heard Donnersberg's warning two hours earlier. They'd gone to the building next door and awakened the six companions who shared with them the most isolated assignment in Europe. After an uneventful hour, the master sergeant in charge of the facility told the others to go back to bed. Shortly thereafter, he retired himself. They felt safe and secure on their mountain perch. After all, for seven months of the year the only way to gain access to the communication site was by helicopter. Even in the middle of summer, in the best of weather, it took a snowcat to get to where the eight lived.

There was a blizzard blowing on the mountain. And it was the middle of the night. Nothing could be better protection from the enemies of the outside world. The airmen felt so protected in their home of ice and snow that they'd never uncrated their M-4s. The weapons sat in a metal storage container on the far side of the compound.

Their coworkers snug in their beds once more, the two airmen returned to their game of gin rummy. While they played, they listened to the activity between the communication sites and the voice at DISA who continued to restore the critical circuitry. As a radio relay, they had no direct role in the activity. Their sole function was to keep two microwave radio systems—one from Donnersberg to the top of the Zugspitz and the other from the Zugspitz to Coltano, Italy, on the air. None of the circuits broke out at the relay. Their involvement in George O'Neill's efforts was little more than that of interested spectators. Donnersberg and Coltano would take care of the rest.

The door burst open. The blowing snows poured into the room. The airmen's cards flew in every direction. The startled pair looked up to find themselves face-to-face with a figure dressed in an expensive ski outfit. The intruder was holding a machine pistol. He motioned for the airmen to raise their hands.

Next door, the barracks entrance also flew open. Snow rushed in upon the sleeping airmen. An arm reached inside and tossed a grenade onto the floor. The arm disappeared. The perpetrator dove for cover in the snow. Five seconds later, the exploding grenade killed all six airmen. To make sure the job was completed, a second commando appeared in the doorway. He fired a long burst from his black machine pistol into the room.

The moment the explosion sounded next door, the saboteur in the communication building gunned down his captives with two quick pulls of his automatic pistol's trigger. The airmen fell dead on the floor.

With the enemy eliminated, there was no need to hurry. The commandos removed the plastic explosives from the two remaining satchels. Even without the leader's backpack, they had more than enough to finish the job. The leader attached explosives to the legs of the communication tower. A second killer prepared the communication building for destruction. The third placed charges throughout the small barracks, moving an occasional body part aside to complete the job. In twenty minutes, they were ready. They set the timers for half an hour and hurried down the dark mountain as fast as they dared.

Five hundred feet below the peak they stopped beneath a large rock formation and waited. Six minutes later a trio of explosions rocked the Alps. American strategic communications between Germany and Italy were no more.

They cautiously made their way back down from the heights. The descent wasn't as physically challenging as the climb had been. Even so, it took every skill the commandos had to safely reach the chalet. At a little before seven they crept through the lobby and up to their rooms. Not a soul was around. It was hours before the guests sleeping in the warm chalet would awaken for brunch.

Early in the afternoon, the Swedish gods would be seen skiing the mountain a final time. As they hurriedly packed their Gucci bags, their panicked admirers paid scant attention to them. In a few hours, the rich young women would cross the border into Austria to continue their holiday safe from the war.

For the first time ever, the boy failed to show up for work at the ski lift. Just before dark, they found his body in a snowbank near the building where the chalet's workers lived. His throat had been cut. His pockets were empty.

Unaware that the Zugspitz relay had been destroyed by the commando team moments earlier, George O'Neill continued to work at keeping the Americans in the war.

"All right, Coltano, are your patches all set?" O'Neill said into the microphone.

No response.

"Coltano, are you ready?"

Still no response.

"DISA, this is Donnersberg. We've lost Coltano."

"God dammit!"

"What's wrong?" Colonel Cossette asked.

"We've lost everything going south to Italy, sir." He held the microphone to his lips. "Zugspitz, what's the story with Coltano?"

Silence.

"Zugspitz, what the hell happened to Coltano?"

More silence.

"Zugspitz?"

O'Neill took a moment to gather his thoughts.

"Lieutenant Templeton, tell Colonel Morrison we've lost the forty-eight channels to the States through Italy. Tell them I'm going to redirect the eight circuits I already ran through Coltano onto the Landstuhl satellite."

He'd been holding the old, second-generation satellite's twelve channels as his final reserve. But now he had little choice. All he had left were those twelve and the sixty channels through Feldberg to Martlesham Heath to satisfy the needs of every command in Germany.

General Yovanovich's noose was tightening.

"Donnersberg," he said into the microphone, "Landstuhl, we're going to take the following circuits and move them onto the satellite . . ."

Twenty minutes later, the bus from Ludwigsburg pulled up in front of the building. Fourteen of the agency's personnel flashed their badges and entered. O'Neill looked up from the computer to see the faces of the five other people in the organization capable of doing what he was doing standing in the operations-center doorway.

It was 3:35 a.m. As Air Force Senior Master Sergeant Denny Doyle entered the operations center, O'Neill noticed that his coworker was carrying a suitcase.

"Looks like you've got your hands full," Doyle said.

"You can say that again. Where the hell have you guys been?"

"Oh, you know, mostly playing tag with our bus and every parked car in Stuttgart. There's not an undamaged fender between here and Ludwigsburg. What's the situation here?"

O'Neill began briefing the five on what had happened and the actions he'd so far taken. In midsentence, O'Neill stopped. "Denny, what's with the suitcase?"

"Man, you must've been busy. You and I are on our way out of here, remember?"

"Jesus, I forgot about that in all the excitement."

Should war be declared, the plan called for European Command Headquarters to immediately dispatch a staff to England to set up a backup command location.

From everything O'Neill had been told in the past thirty months, Patch Barracks wouldn't be around much longer. It was common knowledge they were sitting at one of the Russians' first-strike targets. The belief was by this time tomorrow, few buildings at the American headquarters would be standing. Six members of the organization would accompany the EUCOM backup staff to England. They'd prepare to run all communication activities from the Hillingdon communication facility on the outskirts of London. Colonel Hoerner, Major Siebman, Senior Master Sergeant Doyle, Petty Officer First Class Gallagher, Technical Sergeant Becker, and Staff Sergeant O'Neill were to head to England at the first sign of trouble.

"You'd better turn things over to us, so you can get home and grab a suitcase," Doyle said. "We're leaving on the next plane to England, old buddy."

"Oh my God! Kathy! Christopher! What about them?"

"They'll get evacuated with all the other dependents, I guess," Doyle said.

"But they're not supposed to be here. They promised us we'd have at least two weeks' notice of any Russian attack. They said there'd be plenty of time to get all the dependents out of harm's way."

"They also said the Russians would never be crazy enough to actually attack us. Looks like they were wrong on both counts."

"Denny, I'm not going. I won't leave my wife and baby here by themselves."

"You really don't have a choice, George. You know we're going to need you in England. Now, if you want to spend a little time with that beautiful wife of yours before we leave, you'd better get your butt in gear."

George O'Neill raced out of the operations center. His mind was spinning. He absentmindedly put on his gear and left the building. As he headed for his apartment, he wondered how he was going to break the news to Kathy.

Locked deep in thought, he didn't notice that the snows had stopped. The storm was gone. The sky above held a beautiful moon and hundreds of shimmering stars. It was 4:00 a.m. In four hours there was going to be an incredible winter sunrise over Germany. But George O'Neill wouldn't be there to see it.

In an hour, he'd have to somehow find the courage to leave his wife and child sitting in the middle of a war while he escaped to the safety of England.

CHAPTER 21

1st Platoon, Alpha Company, 2nd Battalion, 69th Armor,
   3rd Heavy Brigade Combat Team, 3rd Infantry Division
Wurzburg

The first sergeant rushed down the ancient barracks' second-floor hallway, throwing open doors and rousing his men. The final door on the left side of the cavernous structure Hitler had ordered built flew open. An arm reached in and flicked on the lights. The booming voice of the tank-company first sergeant filled the room, shattering the slumber of the soldiers inside.

"Warrick, Richardson, up and at 'em. Division's called an alert. Form up in the company area in ten minutes."

Seeing the soldiers stir, the first sergeant hurried to the other side of the hall to continue his distasteful task.

"God dammit," Specialist Four Anthony Warrick said, "another stupid alert."

He sat up and rubbed the crusty sleep from the corners of his eyes.

"What time is it?" Tim Richardson asked.

"Man, I don't know . . ." Warrick looked across the room at the clock radio on his bureau. "Shit . . . it's only one o'clock."

The specialist and sergeant reluctantly left the warmth of their beds. Richardson used his forearm to rub away the moisture from the window next to his bunk. He peered through the glass.

"Christ. It's still snowing like crazy out there."

"Wonderful," Warrick said. "Just what we needed. Standing outside in the freezing cold until some idiot up at division decides he's had enough fun for one night."

"What the hell's going on?" Richardson said. "We just had a practice alert last week."

Warrick shrugged his shoulders in response to his tank commander's question. Each threw on his camouflage uniform. With minutes to spare, Richardson hurried down the hall. He pushed open the door to the foul-smelling latrine with its rusting pipes and dripping faucets. He stuck his head beneath the nearest one. The young sergeant ran cold water over his face until he could stand it no longer.

Richardson stared into the mirror while dragging a comb through his auburn hair. The twenty-three-year-old face looking back at him was boyish and pleasant. The eyes in the mirror were bright and blue. Although tonight they stared back at him with a bloodshot tinge at their edges, the result of too many liters of German beer consumed a few hours earlier.

The gregarious M-1 commander was well liked by everyone within the tank company. Nevertheless, only the eleven other members of his platoon felt they knew him well. And even they had to admit that when it came right down to it, none of them really ever knew what Tim Richardson was thinking. There was a distrust Richardson held for people, which caused him to keep even his closest friends at arm's length. Those sentiments could be traced directly to an exceptionally harsh and abusive childhood.

Richardson ran back to his room. He grabbed his parka, hat, and gloves. He threw these final articles of clothing on while flying down the second-floor hallway toward the middle of the building. Once there, he hurled himself down the wide stairs.

He pushed open the barracks door. A blast of arctic cold rocked him to his very soul as he stepped from the building. So much for finding a way to rid himself of the alcohol still running through his veins.

"Son of a bitch!" he screamed.

The snows pelted him as he hurried to his place on the far left of the company formation. All three of his M-1 tank's crew members were waiting in the darkness when he arrived. Tony Warrick and his tank's driver, PFC Jamie Pierson, looked as miserable as Richardson felt. At the end of the short line, the face of the tank crew's newest member, Private Clark Vincent, was as emotionless as ever. All three had their backs turned to the driving winds. But their feeble efforts were of little use against the biting snows that pummeled them.

"Jesus," Richardson said. "Do you believe this shit?"

"Who's the clown that came up with this brilliant idea?" Warrick said.

"Probably some second lieutenant up at division who got bored on staff duty and decided to have a little fun."

"Whoever he is, he's got to be crazy," Warrick said. "I vote we find out who he is, go up to division, and kill him."

"Nah, Tony, we can't do that," Jamie Pierson said. "Someone told me that if you kill a second lieutenant, they get real mad and punish you by not letting you go into Wurzburg for two whole weeks."

"And I heard," Vincent added, "that they also kick you off the company bowling team for six months."

The three of them stared at Vincent in complete disbelief. This was the most any of them had ever heard the young private utter in his brief time with the M-1 crew. In his six weeks serving on Richardson's team, Vincent, the tank's new loader, hadn't said more than one word at a time, and then only on rare occasions. And most of those words had consisted of a single syllable.

Richardson was the first to recover from Vincent's actions. "There you have it, Tony. No second lieutenant's worth that."

"Then it's settled," Warrick said. "We won't kill him. We'll just go up to division and hurt him real bad."

Although the longer they stood, and the more miserable they became, the better the murder idea sounded.

The first sergeant walked to the front of the formation in the purposeful strut all first sergeants seem to instinctually develop. He looked at the men huddled in the company area. If the elements were bothering the first sergeant, he would never show it.

"Company, fal-l-l in!"

The soldiers snapped to attention. Each held his head high while looking straight ahead. The windblown snows tore at their faces. Not a soldier flinched. Not a soul blinked. No matter how uncomfortable they were, once called to attention, they would never move until allowed to do so.

"Re-e-e-port!"

The four platoon sergeants did an about-face in the snow to look at their platoons. Staff Sergeant Greene, 1st Platoon Sergeant, repeated the command, "Report."

After 1st Squad reported, Richardson said, "Second squad, all present." He saluted Greene. Greene returned his salute.

When the platoons had reported to their sergeants, each sergeant did an about-face once again. Greene waited until the first sergeant looked his way.

"First Platoon, one man unaccounted for," Greene said. He saluted the first sergeant. The first sergeant returned the salute and moved on to 2nd Platoon.

Six of the tank company's men were absent. Four were married soldiers who hadn't yet arrived. The other two were tankers who'd found a willing *Fraulein's* company. Both were presently snuggled under thick German comforters on opposite ends of the gray streets of Wurzburg.

The report taken, the lieutenants moved forward from their positions at the rear of the platoons. The platoon sergeants exchanged salutes with the platoon leaders. Each sergeant moved to the rear of the platoon to stand where his lieutenant had previously stood. Lieutenant Mallory now stood in front of 1st Platoon.

The company commander came forward. He faced the first sergeant. The first sergeant reported to the captain. They also exchanged salutes. The first sergeant turned and strutted around to the back of the formation.

"At ease," the company commander said. He paused for a moment and stared into the faces of the soldiers under his command. It was obvious that he was searching for just the right words. "Men, I don't know any other way to tell you this. So I'm just going to say it. Russian armor attacked in force about an hour ago. The German border's been overrun. As of this moment, we're at war."

Even in the midst of a blizzard, the body language of the soldiers evidenced the surprise each felt. Like so many others on this night, Richardson wondered what it all meant to him. He didn't ponder anything as esoteric as how many more sunrises he would see or what his own end would be like. At twenty-three, he still felt the complete invincibility of youth. The possibility of his death wasn't remotely comprehensible. Instead, he focused on something far more concrete and tangible. The first thing to enter his mind was how cold his feet always got and how many extra pairs of socks he should take along in his tank.

"The battalion commander's gone up to brigade to receive our battle plan and marching orders. While we're waiting for the orders to come through, each of you is to go into the barracks and get your field gear ready to go. We'll fall you out again when we're set to move. Until then, I recommend you stay in the barracks and keep as warm as possible. I'll send someone to the mess hall for coffee and donuts."

Protocol called for the company commander to turn the company over to the platoon leaders, who would turn the platoons over to the platoon sergeants, who would dismiss their men. But enough was enough. The captain wanted his soldiers inside as quickly as possible. So he dispensed with the formalities and dismissed the company himself.

The tankers wandered back into the ancient barracks. In silence, each soldier went to his room and took down his previously prepared field bags from the top of his locker. Richardson grabbed a handful of extra socks. He stuffed them into one of the bags and placed the bags in his doorway.

The soldiers began mentally preparing for the task that lay ahead. A half hour went by. The coffee and donuts arrived. There was muted talk, whispering really, but nothing more.

The tankers waited on the company commander, who waited on the battalion commander, who waited on the brigade commander, who waited on the division commander. The division commander waited on Army headquarters in Heidelberg. Heidelberg waited on European Command Headquarters in Stuttgart, who, thanks to George O'Neill's efforts, was talking with the Pentagon. The Pentagon spoke with the President.

Another half hour went by. Richardson went back into his room and flopped down on his bed. He looked up at the peeling ceiling and waited some more.

The President released the Pentagon to do their job. The Pentagon talked to Stuttgart. After a dozen tries, Stuttgart finally got through to Heidelberg. An hour passed. It was 3:00 a.m. Russian tanks were pouring into Germany. Richardson wandered down to the first floor for another donut and a second cup of coffee.

Heidelberg spoke to the division commander. The division commander called the three brigade commanders together and told them which battle plan to implement. The brigade commanders returned to their brigades. They called the battalion commanders together. The battalion commanders were briefed on the battle plan. Richardson sat in the second-floor hallway with his back against the wall and his legs sticking straight out. He stared at the lifeless, cream-colored wall on the other side of the hall. The battalion commanders returned to their battalions.

The battalion commanders called the company commanders together. The company commanders returned to their companies and informed the platoon leaders of the plan.

The first sergeant ran across the company area. He shot up the icy steps and burst through the heavy wooden doors.

"Everybody form up outside!" he yelled.

His voice reverberated throughout the three-story barracks.

The tankers scrambled in every direction. They grabbed their gear and ran down the same steps the Nazi tankers of World War II had used nearly ninety years earlier. The ghosts of those long-dead warriors watched from the twilight shadows as the Americans of Alpha Company raced out the door for the final time. The Americans disappeared into the darkness in their rush to meet the enemy.

When he stepped outside, the first thing Richardson noticed was that it was even colder than before. The fierce winds ripped at his face while he ran through the deepening drifts. The second thing he noticed was that the blizzard had stopped. He dropped his heavy field bags into the snows and took his place in line.

They dispensed with the formalities. Formalities were for peacetime armies. The company commander headed to the front of the formation.

"Men, we've gotten the word to move out. Your platoon leaders have been briefed on the battle plan. The 3rd Brigade will be heading south on Autobahn A7 to take up defensive positions. I've sent to the motor pool for trucks to take you to your tanks. If I don't see you again before we leave, I want to tell you all good luck and good hunting. Remember, you're American soldiers, the finest trained and best equipped in the world. Every one of you knows the capabilities of your M-1s. There's not a tank in the world that can stand up to the Abrams. And there's not a division in the world better than the 3rd Infantry. Platoon leaders, take charge of your platoons and prepare your men for battle."

The company commander and the lieutenants saluted. The captain returned to the orderly room to see if there were further instructions from battalion. While they waited for the trucks, Lieutenant Mallory briefed the eleven men of his tank platoon on their objective and their mission once they arrived. The division's organization chart called for each tank platoon to have four tanks. Like a number of platoons within the 3rd Infantry, however, Mallory's platoon was short a tank crew.

They would limp into battle with only three M-1s.

Hitler's fears of his military had been so great that throughout Germany he'd built numerous small kasernes and barracks so there'd never be too great a concentration of soldiers at a single location. At the end of the Second World War, the Americans simply moved into those scattered locations. The fifteen thousand men of the 3rd Infantry Division were housed on eight kasernes in and around Wurzburg.

From each of the eight bases, every few minutes a platoon of three or four tanks or a similar number of Bradleys departed.

At 4:00 a.m. on that terrifying morning, Richardson's seventy-two-ton M-1A2 rolled forward. The three tanks edged out of the motor pool and turned south onto Autobahn A7. For hours, the rumble of armored vehicles could be heard all over the city.

The Americans' organized response had begun.

CHAPTER 22

Carl Stern, veteran anchor for the evening news segment, stared down at the piece of paper he'd been handed during the commercial break. He pondered the significance of the words he would read. From behind the camera he heard, "Fifteen seconds, Carl." Stern adjusted his silk tie and straightened his immaculate suit jacket.

"In five . . . four . . . three . . . two . . . one."

"This just in to the WNN news desk," Stern said. "An unconfirmed White House source has intimated that clashes have occurred on the German border between American military units and elements of the Warsaw Pact earlier this evening. These clashes have apparently resulted in at least a handful of casualties on both sides. For more on this story, we take you to WNN's Pentagon reporter, Patricia Moore."

The picture switched to an attractive woman in her early thirties wearing a charcoal blazer and matching skirt. She was standing inside the main entrance to the Pentagon.

"Thank you, Carl. So far, the Pentagon has refused to confirm or deny a report, which leaked from the White House, of possible skirmishes between American forward units and forces of the Soviet Union. I can tell you, however, that activity here is unusually heavy for this time of the night. All of the joint chiefs are still in the building. Rumor among the Pentagon press corps is that many high-ranking officers who'd left for the evening have been recalled. Other than that, there's little information coming out of official sources here. Minutes ago, it was announced that the Pentagon has no plans to hold any unscheduled press conferences this evening. Back to you, Carl."

"Thanks, Patricia. We take you now to Steven Dillard at the White House." The picture changed to a man in a tan trench coat, his dark hair blowing in a cold Washington wind. A well-lit image of the White House was in the background. Stern continued to talk, "Steven, what can you tell us from the White House?"

"Carl, twenty minutes ago, a high administration source told me that clashes have occurred between Russian and American soldiers along the border of Germany. The source, who wasn't willing to be quoted on camera, said details at this point are quite sketchy. As our viewers probably know, Warsaw Pact war games, involving as many as fifty Russian combat divisions, have been going on at the German border for the past two weeks. White House Press Secretary Randolph Wilkerson told me that the President has been aware of the possibility of something like this occurring because of the close proximity of the Warsaw Pact and Allied units. Our source, and Press Secretary Wilkerson, confirmed that there have been some casualties on both sides from the skirmishes. Neither, however, is able to provide us with any further details at this time."

Dillard paused. The picture on the screen returned to Carl Stern in the Boston studios. "Thanks for your timely report, Steven. We'll get back to Steven and Patricia as further information on this late-breaking story becomes available."

The picture changed to an unhappy man with an upset stomach holding the latest pink cure.

From now until the end of the war, WNN would be America's most popular television station.

CHAPTER 23

January 29—4:00 a.m.
2nd Platoon, Delta Troop, 1st Squadron, 4th Cavalry
Outside the Town of Schirnding

With gloved hands wrapped around his canteen cup, Robert Jensen took another sip of strong coffee. After Ramirez and Steele arrived with the steamy liquid a few minutes earlier, both had been removed from the shit list—at least until their next stupid stunt. Against an ageless apple tree, the platoon sergeant knelt in the modest snow fortification he'd hastily constructed. He was fifteen feet to the right of the critical four-lane highway. The platoon's firing positions were all laid out. The apple branches had been in place for quite some time. The cavalry soldiers were as ready as they could be for the Russian attack.

Within the last hour, the weather had changed for the better. After three wretched days, the snowfall had ended. The skies above were clearing. A full moon and a handful of shimmering stars, their glow distorted by the bitter cold, peeked through the early-morning darkness. Around the lifeless orchard, the world was eerily still. For the past thirty minutes, there hadn't been a single secondary explosion in the death-filled valley below. The fiery destruction the Americans had inflicted four hours earlier was no longer impeding the Russian column's ability to advance.

Jensen lifted the metal cup for another taste of bitter coffee. As he did, the terrifying sounds of two thousand armored vehicles resonated from the valley floor. With the cup poised at his lips and the ebony liquid's pungent aroma filling his nostrils, the platoon sergeant froze. It took just seconds for his senses to confirm what he already knew. The thunderous noises were definitely there.

It could only mean one thing—the enemy was on the move. The Russian armored divisions were headed west once more. Their thrust deep into the heart of Germany was back under way. This time there was no possibility that the Americans could prevent the powerful column from escaping the bloody valley.

The platoon sergeant had tried to find a way to keep the Russians from breaching the woods. He'd sent Austin and a handful of scouts scurrying back into the valley on foot. They'd made a desperate attempt to find an ambush spot for Captain Murphy's tanks. If the M-1s could surprise the enemy prior to his escaping the restrictive mass of evergreens, the cavalry soldiers would still have a chance. Murphy's tanks would be greatly outnumbered, but in the narrow valley's confines, the overpowering Abrams tanks would've had an excellent opportunity of blocking the immense column's actions once again.

Jensen's hopes, however, had been dashed. His desperate plea for one final miracle had gone unanswered. When Austin and his men arrived in the valley, the woods were swarming with Russian infantry. The Americans had barely escaped with their lives.

Austin, unharmed but dejected, had returned with nothing but bad news. The staff sergeant's discouraging report forever sealed the cavalry soldiers' fates. Deep within the forest, hundreds of white-clad figures were moving forward. Scores were carrying armor-piercing weapons— weapons capable of destroying any tanks, even the nearly indomitable M-1. Faced with such a threat to his meager force, Murphy's Abrams tanks dare not enter the burning valley.

There would be no opportunity for another ambush before the Russians freed themselves from the woods. The platoon sergeant and tank troop commander would have to return to their original plan. It was a good plan, capable of inflicting the utmost casualties upon the invaders. Nevertheless, both understood there was little chance for victory. Still, it was the best they could do against such overwhelming odds.

With the Russians on the move once more, Jensen would've given anything for a way to contact squadron headquarters. How nice it would be to call the Apaches forward a final time. But it was no use. Jewels said the enemy still had the squadron's frequencies jammed, and his lengthy attempt to contact the squadron by landline had failed miserably. With so little time remaining before the Russian attack, there was no way for 2nd Platoon to alert the Apaches.

To a man, the waiting Americans knew they were alone.

The minutes slowly passed. Jensen took a final, slow drink of hot coffee. Out of the corner of his eye he caught the movement—movement from the east at the point where the highway left the forest and entered into open farmland. He pulled his night-vision goggles up to his face. There they were, an unending line of Russian armored vehicles. The lead tanks were clear of the woods. The point elements of the advancing enemy were two miles from the apple orchard.

Jensen's heart sank once more. His spirits were as spent as his weary body. He knew the truth. No missile-laden savior was going to swoop down from the heavens to save his depleted platoon. There were going to be no miraculous escapes this time.

He prayed his instincts were wrong. Deep inside, however, he realized there would be no help.

Isolated by the lack of communications, Lieutenant Colonel David Townes had spent the last four hours guessing what his next move should be. The six returning Apaches' victory on E48 had been welcome news. Nevertheless, the cavalry commander's joy was short-lived. By 2:00 a.m., messengers had arrived from the squadron's southernmost areas. The units protecting highway E50 had been smashed. The Russians were pouring into Germany. Rather than releasing the last of his reserves, Townes decided to wait to see what the squadron of tanks and supporting Bradleys he'd sent south two hours earlier could do to slow the enemy.

At 2:30 a.m., on a desolate stretch of roadway halfway between the border and Nuremberg, the American cavalry attacked a five-division armored force. Twelve M-1s and sixteen Bradleys met three thousand Russian armored vehicles.

By 2:40 a.m., every American was dead.

The cavalry soldiers did everything they could. Using their superior skills, they destroyed three of the enemy for every loss of their own. Even so, their efforts barely slowed the Russians down. Minus one hundred vehicles lost to the Americans, the herculean force continued its relentless push toward Nuremberg.

At 4:00 a.m., another scout arrived with word from the south. The Russians had advanced fifty miles inside Germany. The enemy was two-thirds of the way to Nuremberg. Unless stopped, in two hours they would capture the infamous city.

All fifteen Apaches took to the skies. Forty-eight of the sixty-four Bradleys Townes had in reserve roared south at breakneck speed to intercept the massive column.

The squadron commander had heard nothing further about the Russian tanks the Apaches had stopped four hours earlier on E48. He sent his final sixteen Bradleys up the highway. They would wait for the enemy three miles east of Camp Kinney.

Four hours into the war, he'd nothing left in reserve but two hundred cooks, clerks, and mechanics.

As the column's T-72s emerged from the woods, they fanned out across the countryside. They rumbled forward across the heavy snows. The earth trembled beneath their massive weight. The tanks rolled irrepressibly on.

Jensen's men were waiting. In six minutes, the Russians would reach the barren apple trees. Shielded by fortresses of snow, five Bradleys lay hidden in the orchard. The Americans watched the overpowering enemy's steady progress. The platoon's soldiers could hear their hearts pounding in their chests. They could feel the blood rushing through their veins. Fear was etched on every face. The Russians would soon be upon them.

Four hundred yards behind the point elements, the lead division's commander breathed a sigh of relief as he left the nightmarish valley filled with so much suffering. Two battalions of his T-72s and BMPs were in the clear. Others would soon follow. Within the next couple of hours, every vehicle in the endless column would finally free itself from the confining woods.

The advancing tanks and armored personnel carriers were entering an area of open farmland. The general smiled a brief smile. Nothing on earth had the power to stop the three divisions now. There was little chance they'd be embarrassed by their opponent again. The tank-killing American helicopters would be forced to come out and fight in the open. The Apaches would be easy prey for the column's two hundred air-defense weapons. The enemy's fighter aircraft would also be vulnerable. They'd have to think twice before braving an attack on the westward-rolling armada. Death awaited those who dared to challenge the power the division commander controlled.

The fleeting smile disappeared. An hour earlier, he'd been certain his life was over. There was no doubt the Army Group Central Commander had been serious when he threatened to put him in front of a firing squad of men from his own division. After their thrashing by the American helicopters, all three divisions had been trapped behind an impenetrable wall of hellish flames. Too late to turn the huge column around in the narrow space. And impossible to go forward.

For four hours, thirty thousand men had been unable to extricate themselves from the barrier of exploding shells and red-hot metal.

It was his fault. That he knew. The blunder was his and his alone. He'd kept his air-defense missiles and guns in the rear. He'd hoped to protect them until they were really needed. He was certain the enemy wouldn't dare risking his attack helicopters in such horrible weather. No Russian commander would've taken such a gamble. But he'd guessed wrong. And the American cavalry commander's bold move had inflicted a terrible toll. His division had been caught by the enemy's swift strike. If the Americans had struck again, the entire column could've been destroyed. Fortunately, however, the enemy hadn't been heard from since the Apaches' surprising attack. He couldn't understand why. The only answer the division commander could find was that the token enemy forces they faced at the border were even weaker than they'd been led to believe.

Even so, they were forty kilometers behind schedule. They had to hurry if they were going to free the seven-mile-long column from the woods well before sunrise. If they failed to do so, their enemy, weak or not, would send his fighter aircraft to find and destroy any units still trapped in the narrow valley passageway.

He'd been careless. One more careless act, and the Army Group Central Commander promised to come forward once again and personally pull the trigger that would end his life.

There would be no more carelessness. Of that he was certain. He was out of the woods. And nothing was going to stand in his way.

The plodding tanks and BMPs were three hundred yards from the lifeless orchard. Twenty abreast, they churned through the deep drifts toward the deserted village. The tiny force awaiting them remained undetected. In the Bradleys, the TOW operators and Bushmaster gunners took aim. Unaware of the American presence, the enemy continued on. The moment of truth had arrived. The time for a final desperate battle had come.

Jensen keyed his headset. He took a last look at the overwhelming force coming toward them.

"Open fire!" he screamed.

From one hundred yards apart, five TOW missiles leaped from their firing tubes. Little more than a blur, each roared a few feet above the blowing snows. They raced across the open ground. Their victims would never know what hit them. The missiles reached their targets at nearly the same instant. On the tip of each TOW seven pounds of high explosives detonated upon contact. Five simultaneous explosions rocked the winter night. For thirty miles around, a soul-searing sound crushed the early-morning stillness. In the village four hundred yards away, every window shattered.

Just inside the timeworn town, a razor-sharp cascade of glass poured down upon Ramirez and Steele as they waited in the Humvee to protect the platoon's rear.

In unison, five forty-seven-ton roman candles lit up the skies like the light of a thousand moons. An irresistible wave of flesh-consuming heat emanated in every direction. Fifteen Russian soldiers died in less than a heartbeat. The stark violence of the battlefield was unmistakably clear.

The Bushmaster cannons opened up on the approaching armor while the TOW operators quickly selected a second target. The surviving T-72s staggered but came on. The supporting armored personnel carriers ground to a stop. From the rear of fifty BMPs, figures dressed in white ran in every direction. More than three hundred Russian foot soldiers spread across the open ground. They rushed forward with their rifles spewing death. The American infantrymen answered with their chattering M-4s. The night was suddenly filled with gunfire.

The division commander took stock of the enemy. It only took a moment to determine that the pitiful force challenging the might of his rolling armada was insignificant. A handful of armored vehicles supported by a small group of infantry. Nothing more than a minor irritant. Right now, however, he was in no mood for irritations, minor or otherwise. The column was well behind schedule. If they fell any further behind, a bullet to the head would be his reward.

Four of the five Bradleys fired a second volley of screaming TOWs. Three tanks and a BMP met the same calamitous fate as had befallen their countrymen a few seconds earlier. Four brightly burning pillars joined in lighting up the dreadful night.

In the fifth Bradley, Austin also fired. Unfortunately, rather than racing across the battlefield to destroy its victim, the TOW dropped harmlessly from its tube. The missile skidded along the ground for a few feet and stopped.

"Shit! A damn misfire!"

It only happened about 5 percent of the time with the highly reliable TOWs. Still, it wasn't a good omen for the embattled defenders.

In near unison, the Bradley crews retracted their firing tubes. Each began reloading. For the next two minutes, the Bushmasters would have to go it alone.

The division commander saw his opening.

"All units pinch in toward the orchard and finish them off. Do it now and move on."

Five rows of Russian armor headed straight toward the apple orchard.

The moment the first explosion occurred, four Bradleys from Captain Murphy's force sprang from their hiding place at the edge of the village. They roared up the highway two by two. It would only take a half minute for them to arrive at the front of the orchard. That, however, was going to be too much time for them to be of any help to 2nd Platoon. In thirty gruesome seconds, Jensen's men were decimated.

One hundred yards to the platoon sergeant's right, Sergeant Richmond reached back for a replacement missile. A T-72's 125mm cannon shell ripped through the snow wall in front of his position. The shell drove headlong into the stationary Bradley. It bored through the fighting vehicle's seven inches of frontal armor and detonated inside the command compartment. Richmond's Bradley exploded. Another fireball crushed the fleeting darkness.

On the far left, a foot soldier supporting Renoir's position took a bullet in the face from an AK-47.

Renoir was positioning a TOW in its firing tube when half a dozen rounds from a BMP's 30mm cannon ripped through the thinner armor on his Bradley's turret. Both Americans were killed instantly. For good measure, a nearby T-72 finished off the crippled Bradley with a single shell from its main gun. The horrific fires were growing with every passing heartbeat.

Austin's Bushmaster gunner returned the favor, repeatedly striking the commander's compartment of a charging BMP. Hatches on the top of the BMP sprung open. Two frantic figures clambered from the smoking vehicle. A lethal burst from Jelewski's M-4 struck both. The Russians crumpled half-in, half-out the open hatches. Neither moved again.

Beneath Jensen's deadly fire, four white-clothed Russians went down in quick succession. Somewhere on the right, a cavalry soldier screamed.

The turret of a T-72 turned. Its main gun lowered. Austin had a TOW in its firing hole. From point-blank range, the T-72 fired. Austin's shattered Bradley leaped into the air. Flaming chunks of jagged metal and minute fragments of fragile flesh flew in every direction.

A white-hot piece of aluminum the size of a giant fist landed upon the prone Jelewski. The searing metal burned through the soldier's clothing. His parka burst into flames. The soft flesh between his shoulder blades started to sizzle. The platoon radio operator shrieked in agony. He dropped his rifle and rolled onto his back. Jelewski frantically clawed at the burning aluminum. The metal fell into the snows.

One by one, the ground soldiers of 2nd Platoon were isolated, engaged, and eliminated. By the time Murphy's four Bradleys completed their suicidal rush through the orchard, only six of the fourteen American infantrymen were still firing.

The quartet of Bradleys raced past the barren trees. They roared into the center of the fray. On the right, the lead Bradley never got off a single round. A BMP beat him to the draw. A Spandrel missile smashed into the fighting vehicle, setting it ablaze. Its crushed steel treads moved no more. The remaining Americans fired TOWs into the oncoming tanks. As the TOWs struck, three more huge flaming candles melted the night's new drifts.

Sergeant Foster fought to keep his head. His second TOW was entering its firing tube. Next to him in the compartment, Marconi continued to fire the Bushmaster. The last thing Foster would ever hear was Marconi's dejected, "Aw, shit."

The young soldier had recognized that a Russian tank's long barrel was pointed straight at them from two hundred yards away. A huge explosive round escaped from the tank's main gun. Foster and Marconi never heard the night-shattering "whoosh" the round made. The shell hurtled across the flaming field in less than an instant. It smashed full force into the fighting vehicle. Four of 2nd Platoon's Bradleys were enveloped in roaring flames. A single one remained.

Brown fired a TOW from his reloaded tubes. The missile slammed into a T-72.

One of the Bradleys on the highway fell prey to a charging BMP. The American vehicle's fiery wreckage slammed into an apple tree twenty yards to Jensen's left. The ancient tree was soon ablaze.

The other two fired a second missile with devastating effect. Beneath the striking TOWs, more earthshaking explosions rocked the bitter night. The Russians pounced on the surviving pair of Bradleys. Two T-72s fired, and the third of Murphy's fighting vehicles was gone. The last, its missile tubes empty, turned to make a desperate run for the safety of the village. The Bradley hadn't gone far before the power of the enemy fell upon it. Another scorched and twisted mass of unrecognizable metal was created by the impact of striking shells.

On the far right, Brown fired his second replacement TOW. Like a comet searching the heavens, burning pieces of a defeated BMP soared into the bright night. It was Brown's sixth kill of the war. It would be his last.

All attention turned to the sole surviving American vehicle. A T-72 quickly isolated and, in a vivid display of its immense power, destroyed the final Bradley of 2nd Platoon.

Jensen and Jelewski continued to return the Russian fire.

From the safety of his command tank, the Russian general surveyed the killing ground. A smile came over him once again. The brief skirmish had gone exactly as he'd hoped. Despite being surprised by the enemy, his men had responded quickly. Just what he'd needed to save himself from the firing squad. He'd suffered some losses. Yet his losses were trivial in the grand scheme. The encounter had been little more than a minor bump in the road for his rolling armada. In scarcely three minutes' time, his lead units had finished off the small force of enemy armor. The threat from the foolish Americans was over. The fierce little battle was at its end. There were only two inconsequential infantrymen with whom to deal, and the column would be advancing again. At least that's what the division commander believed.

The Russians had taken the bait. As Jensen and Captain Murphy had anticipated, the firing from the orchard and the rush of the four

Bradleys into the middle of the nasty conflict had focused the enemy on the area surrounding the highway. With their tanks concentrated in the center of the battlefield, the Russians' flanks were extremely vulnerable.

He'd sacrificed his platoon, but the plan had worked exactly as Jensen had hoped.

The time had come to spring the Americans' trap. At just the right moment, identical groups of six M-1s and six Bradleys appeared north and south of the orchard. Thirty-two foot soldiers struggled through the waist-deep snows to support the armored vehicles.

Firing as they went, the Americans smashed into the enemy's soft flanks. They ripped into the exposed sides of their gigantic foe. Fireworks blazed in all directions. Four . . . five . . . six Russian tanks fell in the first seconds. The Americans surged forward, determined to take the fight to their opponent. Confusion gripped the field. M-1s and Bradleys waded deep into the T-72s and BMPs. Cannon shells and TOW missiles roared through the grievous morning. Explosion after explosion rocked the fallow fields.

The M-1s were over twenty tons heavier and technologically superior. Their frontal armor was nearly impenetrable. The American crews were the best in the world. They struck a severe blow on the lead division's armor. The slaughter went on without letup. If they had had twice their number, the Americans could have stopped the enemy in his tracks. But without pause, Russian tanks and BMPs kept appearing from the woods and moving toward the orchard.

In the end, the odds were just too great for the Americans to overcome. As each Russian armored vehicle fell, ten more rushed to take its place. As each American was destroyed, the rest were that much more susceptible to being overwhelmed.

All around the apple orchard, the fierce struggle continued for a full fifteen minutes. By the time the last M-1 was surrounded and dispatched, the Americans had eliminated 141 enemy vehicles. The cavalry soldiers had destroyed their opponent at a four-to-one ratio.

Yet when it was over, the inevitable had occurred. The American armor had been overwhelmed.

With Murphy's sudden appearance on the battlefield, the majority of the fighting swiftly shifted from the center of the staid orchard to its flanks. Hidden behind a wall of snow, Robert Jensen hammered away at a squad of infantry attempting to advance up the highway. He stopped firing for a moment to retrieve a replacement ammunition clip. Over the sounds of the ongoing armor struggle, an enemy soldier took careful aim and squeezed the trigger of his AK-47. The bullet tore through Jensen's modest snow fortress, catching him squarely in the upper thigh. It missed the bone but ripped an exit hole the size of a silver dollar in the back of the platoon sergeant's leg. A crippling pain surged up his spine, settling deep within his brain. Despite his valiant efforts, he dropped into the snows and struggled to regain his footing.

Seeing their antagonist fall, a Russian soldier ran forward. He tore the pin from a hand grenade. The white-clad figure hurled it from forty yards away. The throw came up short, a full ten yards short. Lethal pieces of the exploding grenade rushed out in every direction in their determined quest to maim and destroy. Propelled at incredible speed, death ripped through the winter air. A thumbnail-sized chunk of steel found its mark. A glancing blow of daunting metal struck Jensen on the left side of his face. It lodged in his skull just above the temple. The fragment missed his eye by less than an inch. The platoon sergeant fell to the ground and moved no more.

A pair of Russian soldiers rushed up the roadway to within a few feet of their wounded foe. The time had come to finish off the tenacious American. The infantrymen raised their rifles. Each took aim and slowly began to squeeze the trigger.

The sound of firing echoed across the center of the battlefield.

CHAPTER 24

January 29—4:15 a.m.
2nd Platoon, Delta Troop, 1st Squadron, 4th Cavalry
Outside the Town of Schirnding

Both Russians tumbled into the deep drifts in front of the wounded platoon sergeant's position. Ever-expanding pools of red formed beneath their lifeless bodies. Their squad reacted slowly, confused by what had just happened to their comrades. Another brief burst of gunfire, and two more perplexed figures fell. The bewildered Russians retreated, looking first for cover and only then for the source of the unexpected attack.

A second infantry squad rushed forward to support the first.

Up the highway the Humvee roared, with Ramirez at the wheel. Standing behind the machine gun, Steele fired round after round to protect the fallen leader of 2nd Platoon.

The moment the Humvee reached the front of the orchard, Ramirez leaped from the vehicle. He ran the fifteen feet to his sergeant. Steele continued to fire, holding off the Russian infantry. Ramirez looked at Jensen's motionless form. The young soldier bent down to pick up his wounded leader. As he did, a bullet slammed into Ramirez's right shoulder. Blood spurted from the new wound. The stunned Ramirez took one look at his latest injury and slumped facedown in the snow.

Steele glanced at the fallen figures. Neither Jensen nor Ramirez was moving.

"God dammit! Ramirez, get your ass up!"

He squeezed the trigger on the machine gun, pinning the Russians down once more.

"Get up, God dammit! Don't leave me out here alone!"

He knew they'd all be dead in seconds if he left the machine gun and tried to help his wounded countrymen.

Ramirez slowly raised himself on his left arm. He shook his throbbing head, fighting against the unbelievable pain. Waves of nausea washed over him. The right shoulder of his parka was turning a deep shade of red. He staggered to his feet. The Russian squad's fire was homing in. Still more enemy infantry were closing with their position. Ramirez could hear the whistling bullets striking all about them. Round after round ricocheted off the Humvee's metal frame or stung the snows near the Americans.

He grabbed Jensen's arm. The private torturously dragged him across the snow toward the Humvee. As he did, a bullet ripped through Jensen's left boot. Blood rushed from the platoon sergeant's foot.

Pulling Jensen behind him, Ramirez crossed the open ground to the idling Humvee. A crimson trail marked his way. With a superhuman effort born of necessity, he lifted the much larger sergeant and dumped him into the passenger seat. Ramirez raced around the vehicle and crawled behind the steering wheel. With his left hand, the private reached across and threw the Humvee into gear. He shoved the gas pedal to the floor and jerked the steering wheel to the left. The hard tires spun in the snow, digging for the frozen ground below. The Humvee fishtailed as it whirled about. It rushed away from the orchard at full speed. Standing behind the machine gun, Steele lost his balance and tumbled to the floor.

They never looked back.

The Humvee raced through the village. It headed down E48 toward Camp Kinney. Ten icy miles to cover with a badly bleeding, one-armed driver and a passenger near death from three severe wounds.

While the Humvee sped down E48, the last American tank succumbed. With the exception of the constant secondary explosions, few sounds of battle invaded the ancient orchard. Of the blocking force, a single soldier was still firing. In his position thirty yards to the left of the burning wreckage that housed the charred remnants of Austin and his gunner, Aaron Jelewski continued to fire after the destruction of the last Abrams. A squad of Russian infantry moved in. They encircled his fortress of snow. Hundreds more were running toward his position.

It was hopeless. Jelewski threw down his weapon and raised his arms over his head. A lieutenant and three private soldiers rousted the badly burned American from his hole. They walked him back toward the maze of flaming tanks. The blazing remains of nearly two hundred armored vehicles were strewn about the snowy field as if haphazardly tossed there by some vengeful god.

The command tank rushed forward. It stopped a few feet from the prisoner. The division commander climbed down from his tank. He walked over to the captive. Jelewski stood with head high. The defiance in his eyes was unmistakable. The general took one look at the proud American, drew the pistol from his hip, and shot Jelewski dead with a single round to the head.

"We have no time for prisoners, Lieutenant," the general said over the sounds of the continual secondary explosions.

Without giving it a second thought, the division commander climbed back onto his tank. The armored vehicle drove away.

The horrific battle at the orchard had been the division commander's second blunder of the war. As had been promised by the Army Group Central Commander, his bullet to the head would also soon come. At sunrise, for his miscalculations, both in the valley and outside Schirnding, he'd receive the same summary fate that had befallen Aaron Jelewski.

"Is he alive?" Steele said. The concern was evident in his skittish voice.

"Man, I'm not sure if I'm alive." Ramirez glanced at the twisted form in the seat next to him. "I can't tell if he's breathing or not."

"We'd better get there soon."

"I'm doing the best I can. Now that the snows have stopped, this road's starting to ice over. And I can't lift my right arm at all."

"You want me to drive?"

"Hell, no. I want you to get ready to kill any Russian bastard you see."

"Shit, I've been doing that. You see how many of those sons a bitches I got back there?"

"Yeah. You did great, man."

"So did you," Steele said.

"You know what, after what we just did, we're a couple of damn heroes."

But neither felt like a hero. Other than the intense pain in Ramirez's shoulder and the numbness that gripped them both, they felt nothing at all.

They drove on in stunned silence. The Humvee plunged through the frightful darkness toward Camp Kinney. Each distressing mile was without end. Ramirez blocked out everything but the here and now. He battled with every ounce of dogged determination to keep moving west. Focus on the road. Focus on the ice and snow. Forget about your friends lying dead a few miles back. Forget about how much your mangled shoulder hurts. Forget about all the blood oozing down your back beneath your parka. Try to forget. Try to forget everything.

And, eventually, the torturous miles did pass.

Three miles from Camp Kinney, the Humvee was forced to stop at a roadblock. Two platoons, the squadron's final sixteen Bradleys, waited to defend the highway. Anxious soldiers crowded around the Humvee.

"Who're you guys?" a lieutenant asked.

"We're 2nd Platoon, Delta Troop," Ramirez said.

"Where's the rest of your outfit?"

"They're dead. Everybody back there's dead, Lieutenant. And if you don't get out of my way, my sergeant's also going to be dead pretty soon. This guy saved our ass so many times tonight that I'd really like to return the favor."

"Sure, okay. Just one more thing before you go. How many Russians are there, and where are they?"

"There's about a thousand Russian tanks a few miles behind us," Steele said. "Don't worry, Lieutenant. You'll see them for yourself soon enough."

Steele's response had the desired effect. The soldiers instinctively stepped back. The Humvee raced off once more, this time with the fifteenth-century spires of Marktredwitz visible in the darkness ahead.

When the Humvee neared Camp Kinney's front gate, Ramirez didn't slow down. Two MPs stepped into the roadway. They signaled for the speeding vehicle to stop. The next thing the MPs knew, they were diving into the dirty snows on the sides of the narrow entrance.

The maniacs in the Humvee roared into camp. The MPs leaped to their feet. Each drew his Beretta and lifted his arm to fire at the intruders. They found themselves staring into the barrel of the Humvee's machine gun. One look into the stone-cold, African-American face behind the gun, and they knew the soldier meant business. Their arms went down as quickly as they'd gone up.

Absolutely nothing, neither heaven, nor earth, nor MP, was going to slow Ramirez and Steele.

Ramirez raced toward the rear of the drab compound. At the last possible moment, he mashed the Humvee's brakes. The vehicle skidded to a stop in front of the dismal gray building that served as the squadron dispensary. At the command center next door, Colonel Townes saw the Humvee arrive.

Desperate for news, he hurried to meet the vehicle. Townes hoped it was a messenger with word of the battle on E50 to protect Nuremberg. Or someone who could explain the endless fires in the eastern sky above E48. What he found was the hapless trio.

Townes looked at the distorted figure in the passenger seat. He knew the face. For the moment, however, the name escaped him. He glanced at the baby-faced privates. My God, they're so young, the squadron commander thought. At this moment, hundreds of soldiers, exactly like these, are dying lonely deaths out there in the German snows.

At least he believed they were young until he stared at their faces a moment longer. A terrifying look pulled him deep within their haunting eyes. Inside, he found two very old men, who in the past five hours had seen far too much of life.

"Let's get some help over here right now!" Townes said. "Get a stretcher out here! Hurry it up!"

Two medics appeared from the dispensary with a stiff stretcher of green canvas. They laid the stretcher on the cold ground. Robert Jensen was gently lifted from the seat and placed upon it.

The senior medic took his stethoscope, held up Jensen's parka, and started moving the cold instrument around on his chest. He next checked the wounded cavalry soldier's wrist, searching for signs of a pulse.

"Is he alive?" the squadron commander asked.

"Just barely. I'm picking up a faint heartbeat."

"Good. Get him inside. I don't want to lose even one more man if we can help it."

The medics lifted the stretcher and carried it into the dispensary. The exhausted Steele climbed down from the rear of the Humvee. He struggled to help Ramirez out of the driver's seat. Behind Ramirez, the seat was thick with blood. While they fought to maintain their balance in the snows, Colonel Townes spotted the heavy red stain.

He turned to Ramirez. There was true sadness in the squadron commander's voice. "I'm sorry, Private. I saw the bandages on your head, but in the confusion didn't notice your other wound. Can you make it into the dispensary?"

Ramirez's false bravado spewed forth a final time. "Hell, sir, I've been hurt worse than this just walking down the street in East L.A."

But the truth was that without Steele's support, Ramirez would've collapsed on the spot. Townes gingerly cradled Ramirez's injured shoulder and walked with the pair toward the dispensary. When they neared the building, Ramirez and Steele spotted the long rows of bodies lying in the snows. Each was covered with a thin plastic sheet that blew in the biting winds, revealing the grisly secret hidden within.

Inside the cramped dispensary, they found a madhouse. The squadron doctor, his physician's assistant, and six medics were attempting to save the lives of two dozen badly wounded soldiers. The conversation was stilted and terse. Harried people ran in every direction. The stain of fresh blood was everywhere. The three stood frozen in the doorway, watching the macabre scene unfold.

The physician's assistant and a combat-experienced medic were frantically working on their newest patient.

"What's his blood type?" the PA asked.

The medic grabbed Jensen's dog tags. He held them between two fingers long enough to make sure he didn't make a mistake.

"A positive, sir."

"Any A positive left?"

"Nope, got a couple of bottles of A negative."

"Well, use them, then. Give him at least two pints."

The medic fought his way to the refrigerator. While he waited for the blood, the PA recorded Jensen's vital signs and began checking his injuries. The festering head wound brought immediate concern.

"Doctor, when you get a chance, you'd better take a look at this one."

Ramirez collapsed. He dropped to his knees on the bloodstained floor. Colonel Townes helped Steele drag him to the only open examining table.

A medic hurried over to take a look at the latest in a lengthy line of problems.

"Get some blood into him, too," the PA said.

"Blood type's O negative," the squadron commander said while looking at Ramirez's dog tags.

"Oh shit," the medic said. "Only one O negative left."

"Use it anyway. Then follow it up with some plasma," the PA said.

Cradling two pints of blood, the other medic rushed back to Jensen. He shoved a long needle into an exposed vein and taped it in place. Moments later, he did the same with the platoon sergeant's other arm. A quick check of his efforts, and he was on his way to help with Ramirez.

"We can handle it from here, sir," the medic said as he gently moved the squadron commander away from the table. He hoped Colonel Townes would take the hint and leave the hectic room.

Townes didn't miss his meaning. He turned to Steele. "Let's go outside, Private. I need to ask you some questions about what's going on up there."

"All right, sir," Steele said.

They headed for the door. For Steele, it was a welcome relief to leave the gruesome dispensary without its appearing that he was abandoning his buddies. They walked outside into the darkness and the unrelenting wind.

"What unit you with, Private?"

"Second Platoon, Delta Troop, sir."

"Were you the ones making all that noise up on E48 a while ago?"

"Yes, sir. Us and Captain Murphy and his tanks."

"What happened to everyone else?"

Steele's answer was little more than a whisper. "I think they're all dead, sir."

"You say you think. Do you know for sure?"

"No, sir. I mean we didn't see everyone die. But I'm pretty sure the Russians got them all."

"Where are the Russians now?"

"Right behind us, sir."

"No one to stop them before they get here?"

"Only one between them and us are those Bradley crews we talked to outside town."

"No one else?"

"No. No one else, sir."

Not the answers Townes had hoped to hear. But at least he now knew where the squadron stood.

"Thank you, Private. Stick around, I might need to ask you some more questions later on."

Steele nodded in understanding. The squadron commander turned and walked toward the command center. It was time to plan one final, hopeless battle.

It was little more than a slaughter. The sixteen Bradleys never had a chance on the open ground. As soon as they were spotted, the Russians unleashed an immense barrage that nothing could survive. Remaining outside the TOWs' range, the tanks destroyed their opponent without facing a single effective shot from the squadron's Bradleys. At most, the eighty-six American lives slowed the Russians enough to add ten precious minutes to the West's time.

The sounds of the battle so near Camp Kinney created an even greater sense of urgency in the dispensary's activities.

"We've got to get the wounded out of here," the doctor said.

"We've still got one medevac chopper and four ambulances," the senior medic said.

"Then let's get moving right now. If we wait any longer, it's going to be too late."

The PA continued to work on Jensen.

"What about this one?" he said. "You think he'll survive the helicopter ride to Wurzburg?"

"What's his status?" the doctor asked.

"I've got the bleeding stopped. And I've bandaged his foot and leg. But his head wound's very serious."

"If we don't have room on the medevac for everyone who needs to be on it, leave him here."

In three wars, the senior medic had never left a wounded countryman behind. And he wasn't about to start now.

"We'll have room for him," the medic said.

You're damn right you will, Ramirez told himself. Even if I've got to crawl outside to get the machine gun off the Humvee and kill me a doctor, Sergeant Jensen's going on that helicopter.

The medics carried the most serious cases out to the waiting medevac. Robert Jensen, still unconscious, with IVs attached to both arms, was loaded onto the twenty-year-old Black Hawk.

The wounded in less need of immediate attention were placed in the ambulances. The instant the last patients were loaded, the ambulance drivers tore out the front gate.

With Steele's help, Ramirez slowly walked to the helicopter. The two stood looking at each other for what seemed a long time. Neither knew what to say. Finally, the medic signaled that Ramirez needed to board. With his good arm, he patted Steele on the shoulder. Ramirez reached out, and the medic pulled him onto the helicopter. He gave Steele a thumbs-up. The medevac lifted off the ground. It spun around and headed west toward the Army hospital at Wurzburg. Steele gave a half-hearted wave as it soared overhead in the darkness.

The squadron commander watched the medevac take to the skies. The time had come to organize the last of his forces. The two hundred men were given everything left in the squadron's arsenal—M-4s, grenades, machine guns, and twenty-four shoulder-mounted light antitank weapons. Nothing that would stop so powerful an enemy. But that had never been their job. They'd always been here to trade their lives for precious minutes of time.

While this final element prepared to leave camp, a messenger arrived. The Apaches and Bradleys sent south had failed to stem the tide. All had been destroyed. Nuremberg, and its five hundred thousand citizens, had fallen to the Russians. In all, over five million Germans were already behind enemy lines.

The last two hundred men rolled out of Camp Kinney. They headed east, hoping to slow the enemy just a little more. The squadron commander rode in a Humvee that had served its country well. Next to him, his driver sat in a seat with a large bloodstain on its upper right corner. Standing behind the squadron commander, Steele waited with his machine gun at the ready. In a few minutes, the two—the African-American private with the haunting baby face and the ancient look in his eyes, and the disheartened squadron commander—would die together on a blustery winter night.

The soldiers of the border would never see the light of the glorious morning that dawned two hours later. By 6:00 a.m., of the fifteen hundred men of 1st Squadron, fifty-nine were still living. Only two dozen of those weren't wounded.

The proud cavalry squadron was no more.

With their lives, they'd bought the West six hours to prepare to meet the challenge.

In the spring, the apples would bloom again on the scarred trees of the ancient orchard. But the soldiers of 2nd Platoon wouldn't be there to see them.

The Black Hawk would cover the 120 miles in under an hour. At a little before eight, with his life hanging by a thread, Sergeant First Class Robert Jensen was rushed into surgery. At that exact moment, 4,500 miles away, the 767 with the frightening eagle on its tail landed in Charleston, South Carolina. Half-asleep, the exhausted Jensen women walked down the ramp and into the Charleston Air Base Military Airlift Command Terminal.

When she entered the warm terminal, Linda handed a third set of computer cards to an Air Force sergeant. Not a single passenger was yet aware that eight hours earlier, their husbands and fathers had begun fighting and dying in the bloody snows of Germany.

CHAPTER 25

January 29—6:00 a.m.
United States Army Air Field
Stuttgart

A green bus with U.S. ARMY on its sides stopped near the C-17 transport. The large aircraft's four engines were already running. The passengers began exiting the bus and walking up the C-17's rear ramp. George O'Neill was the last to leave the tired bus. He reluctantly trailed the other five members of his agency as they trudged toward the waiting plane.

O'Neill tossed his suitcase into the jumbled pile in the back of the aircraft. He dropped into the seat between Denny Doyle and Major Siebman. The forty members of the European Command backup team quickly settled in. The cargo aircraft was soon roaring down the runway. It disappeared into the darkness.

O'Neill slumped farther into his seat. The flying time to England would be under two hours. In 120 minutes, he would be five hundred miles from Kathy and Christopher.

Circling high over the Rhine, the Airborne Warning and Control System's AirLand Battle controllers noted the takeoff of the plane from Stuttgart. Inside America's prize command and control system, the AWACS computers instantly processed the data on the departing aircraft.

The AWACS was carrying its maximum crew of twenty-nine, both officers and enlisted. Twenty-three of them, including the aircraft's tactical director, were women. For the past six hours, the AWACS controllers had been waiting for the MiGs to appear in the east.

Yet for six tedious hours, the skies had remained quiet. They knew a Russian air attack was inevitable. At this point, the battle controllers didn't understand why it hadn't occurred hours earlier. Why the Russians were waiting made no sense at all. The longer they waited, the more time the Americans had to prepare for the coming battle. Inside the AWACS, the controllers were edgy and tense. They sensed that even though there had been no sign of the enemy, the attack would undoubtedly be launched before the sun rose.

The Boeing E-3 Sentry sat well back of the battlefield. Its radar searched the eastern sky. It would report the moment the first enemy aircraft was spotted. Using its pinpoint guidance, the Allied fighters and air-defense systems would then attack and destroy. Because of the AWACS, the Americans firmly believed they could overcome the Warsaw Pact air forces' numerical superiority.

Despite the three-to-one odds against them, with the AWACS, the West could dominate the skies. Without it, America's plan for a precisely integrated AirLand Battle would be unworkable.

Seventy miles north of London, three airmen departed an aging English taxi at the front gate to Mildenhall Air Base. The airmen briefly held up their identification cards for an air policeman to see. They were just three of many entering the American base in the darkness and fog of an English winter.

The main gate's air policemen had watched a steady stream of airmen arrive at the base in the hours since midnight, as units located their members and ordered their recall.

By 6:00 a.m., the air policeman who passed the trio through had grown tired and a little lazy. If it had been daylight, or he'd been at all suspicious, he would've noticed that the pictures on the identification cards and the faces into which he made a cursory shine of his flashlight weren't the same. The air policeman would've also noticed that the three were wearing fatigue uniforms whose necks were splattered with fresh blood.

A mile back down the narrow country lane leading to the air base, the bodies of the airmen whose faces matched the identification cards lay in a rock-strewn field a few hundred yards from the asphalt. They were clad in only their underwear. Their throats had been slit from ear to ear.

It had been an expert job.

Once inside the base, the "airmen" walked down the main road for a quarter mile. They turned right onto a quiet side street and headed toward the communication tower. The high tower was easy to find, even in the misty darkness.

One hundred yards from the base communication facility, the commandos melted into the shadows of an abandoned wooden barracks. They scouted the area to make sure no one was about. Satisfied that their presence had gone unnoticed, two of the saboteurs crawled beneath the rotting building. Three machine pistols, an equal number of satchel charges, and a radio were waiting. They gathered the weapons and charges, and when the third signaled that the coast was clear, the pair reemerged. Hidden by the fog and predawn drizzle, the Spetsnaz team started the final preparations for their task.

The killers attached silencers to the ends of their weapons. Another quick glance around, and they headed toward the base's central communication building.

They'd trained hundreds of hours for this assignment. At last, their time had come.

Another isolated German mountaintop, hidden in a thick evergreen forest, was the sole remaining target on General Yovanovich's list.

The sapper team that crept through the darkness was greatly reinforced. Twenty-four skilled assassins were headed for the Air Force communication facility at Schoenfeld. They understood that unlike the earlier attacks at Langerkopf, Donnersberg, and Feldberg, this time the Americans would be alert and ready. And like their comrades preparing to attack at Mildenhall, they also understood they could not fail.

Whatever it took, the objective had to be eliminated. At all costs, Schoenfeld had to be destroyed.

When they neared the top, the leader silently signaled. The commandos split into equal groups of six. The plan called for them to assault the facility from all four sides at once.

Russia's chance for victory was hanging in the balance.

While they soared through the star-cluttered heavens, O'Neill spoke not at all. The shock of leaving behind the two people he loved more than life itself was overwhelming. Kathy and Christopher were sitting at what would be one of the enemy's first targets. And he could do nothing to save them. He'd placed his family's lives into the hands of others. He'd boarded that bus. George O'Neill had done what he had to do.

An hour after leaving her, the last lingering kiss from the only woman he'd ever loved hung on his lips like a heavy mist. He could still see the kiss, but he just couldn't touch it anymore.

He'd arrived at their apartment at a little after four. The instant George opened the door and saw her standing there cradling Christopher, he knew Kathy was aware of what was occurring.

"Is it true what Mrs. Williams told me?" she said. "Have the Russians really attacked?"

The look on his haggard face gave her all the answers she needed. The rumors racing through the housing area at the speed of light were, in fact, true. Kathy held her sleeping child ever tighter.

"I've got to be back at the office in an hour, Kath. They're sending me to England to set up a backup operations center."

In the painful silence of the next moments, she began to fathom, as her husband already did, that she and Christopher were soon going to find themselves alone in the middle of a war without George to protect them.

They moved to the bedroom. George started packing. Kathy took Christopher to his room and laid him in his crib next to a frost-covered window. While George continued preparing to leave, Kathy started silently caressing his dark hair. He wrapped his arms around her. Tears rolled down both their faces. Kathy took him by the hand and led him over to the bed.

He would make love to his wife tonight after all.

They stood on the second-floor landing. His suitcase was at his side. Their parting had been bearable for George only because of the urgency of ensuring that Kathy understood what she needed to do.

"They're going to evacuate you as soon as they can. With any luck, Kath, by this time tomorrow you'll be sitting in your mother's kitchen while she spoils rotten the grandchild she's never seen. Get a bag packed right away. Don't bother with anything but the essentials. While you're waiting, stick close to the other women in the building. If the Russians attack, don't hesitate. Grab Christopher and get down to the basement as fast as you can. Do you understand? Don't wait for anything; get downstairs."

Huge tears streamed down her cheeks. "I understand."

George looked into her beautiful eyes a final time. He hoped she truly understood. Her life, and the life of their child, depended upon it.

He took the sleepy toddler and gave him a final hug. He turned to Kathy. Their final kiss went on for a very long time. Without further words, he grabbed his bag and disappeared down the steps. She stood staring at the door long after he was gone.

High in the Eiffel Mountains, fifty miles northwest of Frankfurt, the forty airmen of Schoenfeld waited. The sabotage at Langerkopf, Donnersberg, and Feldberg had occurred six hours earlier. The assault on the Zugspitz was three hours old. Not a single attack on American communications had been reported since. Still, the airmen protecting Schoenfeld felt no sense of security. The airmen of Langerkopf and the Zugspitz had felt safe. And they were all dead.

Ten of the detachment's airmen, M-4s at the ready, prowled the perimeter fence. Five were inside the chain link. Five others were hidden in the frozen tree line beyond the wire. Every airman knew the value of the prize they guarded.

It was two hours before the German sunrise.

Crawling on their bellies, the assassins inched through the snows to the edge of the compound. Each of the four teams included a commando with a sniper's rifle. The snipers attached silencers to the ends of their single-shot weapons. From the protection of the woods, the killers lay watching the communication site. In no time, they identified the Americans lurking in the shadows inside the fence.

One of the airmen in the trees outside the compound foolishly lit a cigarette. A second coughed. His location was pinpointed. A third stamped his feet in the bitter cold.

But two of the Americans hidden in the woods went undetected.

Six commandos crept forward to eliminate the three airmen they'd spotted outside the fence. Each commando's right hand grasped a razor-sharp knife. They were on the airmen before the Americans realized what had happened. It was over in seconds. With blood dripping from their throats, the airmen fell dead. The Spetsnaz leader signaled. The snipers silently fired. Four airmen inside the compound went down. Two of the Americans cried out as they dropped to the frozen ground. The fifth guard, the one nearest the gate, turned toward the final sounds of his fallen friends. Two black figures raced from a nearby thicket. Each plunged his knife deep into the airman's back. He died before he could sound the alert.

Twenty-four lethal black forms moved forward as one. The six on the west side rushed through the gate. The other teams quickly cut holes in the chain link.

The pair of Americans in the woods waited until the moment was just right. As the commandos breached the fence, the airmen opened fire. Caught in the open, a pair of wounded Russians fell. A third soon joined them.

The firing alerted the thirty airmen inside the communication building. Even so, the commando leader saw no reason to panic. There were only two doors out of the facility. And five automatic pistols were trained on each. To bring the situation under control, all he needed to do was eliminate the unseen enemy in the woods.

The doors of the windowless building burst open. Four Americans rushed headlong from each. They were cut down before their feet hit the ground.

Another commando was felled by the firing from outside the wire. His comrades blindly fired into the trees, trying to pin the Americans down. The leader identified the muzzle flashes in the woods. He signaled one of his teams. They retraced their steps through the gate. The leader knew it wouldn't take long to encircle and kill the two airmen. Another commando collapsed, little left of his face from the blast of an airman's M-4.

Inside the communication building, the Americans were trapped. A desperate call went out.

"This is Schoenfeld. We're under enemy attack. Repeat, we're under enemy attack. Ramstein, you've got to get us some help up here quick."

Sixty miles away, the Ramstein communication facility responded. "Hang tight, Schoenfeld, we're on it."

Six commandos circled the fence line. The two Americans outside the wire were surrounded and trapped. Even so, before they died the determined airmen eliminated three more saboteurs.

To save Schoenfeld would require the close support of helicopters. Four Army Black Hawks lifted off from Kaiserslautern, ten miles closer than Ramstein to the battle scene. Each helicopter carried multiple machine guns, rocket pods, and six infantry soldiers. The Black Hawks had more than enough firepower to deal with the force attacking Schoenfeld. If they could just get there in time.

The Black Hawks raced through the black void with their throttles full out. At this distance, it would take nearly twenty minutes for the helicopters to reach the mountaintop. Until then, the airmen trapped inside the building could do nothing but pray.

The commando leader was aware of the possibility of an American counterattack. Once his sapper team was discovered, he knew exactly how much time he would have. And that time was beginning to run out. The commandos rushed about, preparing their explosives to destroy the hilltop. The team leader personally attached the charges to the one thing that absolutely had to be eliminated—the AWACS ground station.

The Americans' greatest fear had been of an all-out Russian air assault to break through and shoot down the unarmed AWACS. But with seventeen AWACS aircraft waiting in England to take the defeated one's place, General Yovanovich had spotted a far simpler solution. All the Russians had to do was demolish the two locations on the ground where the plane's data entered the American strategic communication system. With the ground stations destroyed, a fully coordinated AirLand Battle plan couldn't be implemented.

Schoenfeld and Mildenhall had to be eliminated.

Without the ground stations, the AWACS team would still see the MiGs the moment they left their runways. But the AWACS computers would be greatly hampered in providing the detailed data and maps of the battlefield to anyone on the ground.

Without a completely operational AWACS, a tremendous blow to American command and control would be struck.

At Mildenhall, it was almost too easy. Well inside the protective fences of the air base, the communication facility had no fences of its own. It sat on a peaceful side street near the center of the base. There was no guard.

With satchel charges and machine pistols in hand, the killing team ran through the gray morning toward their target. Two stood guard while the third placed the plastic explosives onto the AWACS ground-station equipment. When that task was completed, they moved on to the base's communication tower and building.

With the explosives in place, the team leader checked his watch. Their mission was on a precise schedule. They couldn't destroy their target too soon and alert the ground station in Germany that the AWACS was the next sabotage target. He set the timers. The commandos ran back across the road. They crawled under the abandoned building to wait. Their machine pistols were at the ready.

The trio lay hidden, watching from beneath the old building's decomposing floor. In three minutes, the electronic timers would set off the powerful detonations. At that moment, the airmen at Schoenfeld cried out about the commando attack. The Mildenhall shift supervisor decided that prudence called for a quick check of the area around his site. Through the fog, the Spetsnaz team saw the facility's door open. The shift leader took two steps down the rain slick steps and tumbled to the ground. Thinking their supervisor had fallen, the pair of airmen following him out the door burst into laughter. In an instant, they lay dead next to him. A single bullet to the head had taken each life.

A short time later, a tremendous explosion demolished Mildenhall's AWACS ground-station equipment. A second blast soon followed. The tower toppled sideways. Its twisted wreckage crashed into the exploding communication control building. With the loss of the communication center, the ability to coordinate their air base's efforts with the outside world disappeared.

Beneath the abandoned barracks, at shortly before seven on a dismal English morning, the leader tapped out the message in Morse code . . . "m-i-s-s-i-o-n-a-c-c-o-m-p-l-i-s-h-e-d."

The commandos crawled from beneath the rotting building and joined the growing group of curious airmen who'd gathered at the site of the explosions. As the air police dispersed the crowd, the saboteurs disappeared into the mist.

It hadn't been as simple at Schoenfeld. Yet the task was nearly completed. The explosives were all in place. The commandos disappeared into the woods. Their leader remained behind. He set the timers to go off in thirty seconds. If the fuses were any longer, he ran the risk, however slight, of the Americans inside figuring out what was happening and rushing out to disconnect the charges. No matter how remote the possibility, he couldn't afford to take such a chance.

The final timer set, the leader ran for the gate as fast as his strong legs would carry him. In the difficult conditions, however, the distance was far too great to cover in such a brief time. He never had a chance.

The force of the blasts caught him just as he reached the gate. His crushed body was tossed thirty feet into the air. The mountaintop was leveled. While he lay dying, a wide smile spread across his broken face. The mission had been a complete success. Schoenfeld was no more.

A second victory signal was sent to General Yovanovich.

Five minutes away from reaching the hilltop, the Black Hawks saw the massive explosions in the darkness ahead. They knew they were too late to save the communication facility.

But the Americans would soon exact their revenge for the slaughter at Schoenfeld. During the next three hours, the helicopters would mercilessly hunt down every member of the deadly commando team. By ten o'clock on a beautiful winter morning, the last black figure had been identified and killed.

Within minutes of receipt of the second message, the MiGs rose from their bases. From all over Eastern Europe, they took to the skies and roared west. In the first quarter hour, over one thousand Warsaw Pact fighters soared into the heavens. Thirty minutes later, from deep within the Ukraine, seventeen hundred transports and three hundred fighter escorts left the ground. Inside the transports were five divisions of Russian airborne soldiers.

The AWACS battle team saw every plane as it left the runway, but was nearly helpless to do anything about it. They could still guide the Allied pilots once they were airborne. There was little way, however, for the AWACS computers to precisely communicate with the widespread ground forces and air defenses to provide the detailed coordination so necessary to an integrated, highly complex AirLand Battle plan.

Forty-five minutes later, the C-17 carrying George O'Neill touched down at Upper Heyford, England. As O'Neill plodded down the ramp, his outlook was as dreary as the cold, damp, English morning that greeted him.

The outmanned Americans, their command and control crippled, were in deep trouble.

CHAPTER 26

January 29—7:15 a.m.
Charlie Battery, 1st "Cobra Strike" Battalion, 43rd Air
   Defense Artillery Regiment
A Deserted Parking Lot on the Eastern Edge of Stuttgart

The majority of the Patriot convoy had arrived at a few minutes after six. It had taken five interminable hours for the battery to complete the treacherous journey south. Fowler's arms ached from the strain of their icy autobahn adventure.

Eventually, they were all present. And they were more or less in one piece as the soldiers worked in the darkness to prepare the deadly Patriot battery for combat. The mangled fenders on a number of the huge tractors showed the results of their constant battle with the storm. The battery's drivers had experienced far too many frightening entanglements with unforgiving guardrails. The wrecker had been so busy pulling vehicles out of snowbanks that the convoy had stopped waiting for those who needed such help. As it was, the last of the eight launchers, being pulled by the wrecker, hadn't arrived until fifteen minutes before seven.

"All set back there?" Fowler asked.

He turned in his chair to look down the narrow aisle. A few feet behind him, between the rows of electronic equipment on both his left and right, Jeffery Paul stood with his head pressed against the low ceiling in the Engagement Control Station.

Paul spoke into his headset. He looked up at Fowler a few seconds later.

"The communication van says everything's ready. The final launcher's been hooked up and is set to go. All thirty-two missiles are online. The last regiment report said no enemy aircraft have been sighted, but we need to stay alert because there's some kind of trouble with the AWACS."

"What kind of trouble?"

"They didn't know for sure. All they said was that for some reason they'd stopped receiving data from it a few minutes ago."

Fowler turned to look at the pretty lieutenant sitting next to him in the front of the cramped compartment. In the confined space, the pair was so close that he could feel the warmth of her body next to his.

"Okay, Lieutenant Morgan, we're ready to engage the enemy anytime you are."

Even though his hands were quivering at the thought of the challenges that might lie ahead, Fowler smiled a reassuring smile. She smiled a nervous smile in return.

"Let's do it, then," Morgan said.

Nineteen months ago she'd walked across the stage at Ohio State University to receive her bachelor's degree. The last thing that would have entered Barbara Morgan's mind on her graduation day was the possibility she'd be involved in a fight to the death in Germany less than two years later.

But life isn't always kind.

Shortly after the commencement ceremony, on what was to be her wedding day, her husband-to-be had failed to appear. Twenty-one days later, her offer of a well-paying Wall Street entry-level position had been unexpectedly withdrawn. In three weeks' time, she'd suffered two crushing blows. Staggered by her misfortunes, she'd desperately needed to get away. She went out to find herself. Within a month, the Army found her.

The lieutenant and sergeant reached out and started flipping switches and pushing buttons from the countless selections on the electronic panels positioned above and around their side-by-side radar screens. The Engagement Control Station sprang to life. In front of Fowler and Morgan, the identical screens started feeding them information.

Unlike older radars, where the target would only appear on the screen when the radar swept by it, the advanced Patriot radar didn't sweep at all. Anything in the sky would remain constant on the screens at all times.

Thirty small triangles, each representing an aircraft, appeared at various locations on their screens. Most of the triangles were well to the east, near the German-Czech border. The movement of the triangles indicated that the aircraft were circling in no discernible pattern. Fowler and Morgan watched the activity in the predawn sky. Six of the thirty triangles were racing east.

The six appeared to have just taken off from one of the American air bases in central Germany. Another six, having left their positions at the border, were headed west.

"They aren't in our sector, and I'm certain they're friendlies," Morgan said. "Even so, just to make sure everything's working okay, I'm going to interrogate the flight headed west."

"Sounds like a good idea to me, Lieutenant."

Barbara Morgan activated the IFF—the interrogator, friend or foe. She directed it to interrogate the formation's lead aircraft. The Patriot's computer transmitted a coded signal to the unidentified fighter. The signal asked the plane to identify itself by sending back the proper response. In the nose of the leading F-16, the signal was received. The correct answer to the interrogation was transmitted back to the Engagement Control Station by the fighter's computer.

Upon receiving the appropriate reply, the Patriot's computer placed a friendly symbol next to the aircraft's triangle on both screens. The system was working fine. For no other reason than to calm her nerves, the lieutenant continued to interrogate the fighters in the formation. In seconds, friendly symbols appeared next to all six triangles.

Sitting in the right-hand chair, Morgan's job for the next four hours consisted of identifying any approaching aircraft. There were only three possible identification symbols. An aircraft was friendly, hostile, or unknown. Dealing with the friendlies and hostiles was easy. The friendlies would be passed through the protective air-defense net. The hostiles would be turned over to Fowler to be shot down by a screaming Patriot missile.

The unknowns would be Morgan's most critical task. Deep within their windowless world many miles from the soaring aircraft, it would be difficult for the Patriot crew to determine whether or not to fire on an unknown. There was always the possibility that a friendly aircraft's transponder had malfunctioned, or combat had damaged the fighter and it could no longer answer. The air-defense system couldn't allow enemy MiGs to get through. Yet it was considered bad form to shoot down one of your own planes.

With no way for the aircraft to identify itself as a friendly, the onus was on the pilot to show that he belonged to the good guys. On the radar screens, the Patriot identified a prearranged corridor. If the pilot entered the narrow corridor and made the proper turns within its boundaries, Morgan would allow it to pass unharmed. All the pilot had to do was remain inside this invisible, crooked crosswalk in the sky, and he or she would be home free.

Hopefully, the sleepy pilot had been paying close attention during the early-morning mission briefing. If not, they would pay for their carelessness with the loss of their life.

They watched the friendly triangles disappear from their screens as the F-16s landed at Spangdahlem Air Base, 160 miles northwest of the battery's position.

"Looks like we're in business, ma'am," Fowler said.

Morgan opened her mouth to respond. As she did, the eastern edges of the radar screens started to fill with wave after wave of never-ending triangles. By the untold hundreds, the triangles suddenly appeared. All were headed west at a high rate of speed.

The long-anticipated Russian air attack had begun.

With the AWACS' guidance, huge numbers of Allied fighters should have risen up to meet the enemy near the Czech border. That was what the American battle plan said would occur. But with the AWACS crippled by a lack of communications, the air bases were slow to respond.

Instead of meeting the Russians with an equal number of fighters, the Americans met them with two dozen F-16s out of Spangdahlem. The F-16s had been circling the border waiting for a Warsaw Pact attack. Twenty-four found themselves pitted against one thousand.

The idea was simple: have the twenty-four delay the enemy to buy enough time for the American, British, and German fighters to scramble into the sky. Using the AWACS, the NATO air forces would be coordinated with pinpoint accuracy to stop the enemy in its tracks. The AWACS would then further coordinate the American and German air defenses to strike down any intruder lucky enough to get through the deadly curtain of fighters.

With the AWACS ground stations destroyed, however, such a response didn't occur. The AWACS was designed to instantly feed the Russian attack data through Schoenfeld or Mildenhall to every wing at the nine Allied fighter bases in Germany and six in England. At the fifteen bases, the defenders would rush to their planes. Within minutes, the skies would fill with lethal Allied defenders. Without the attack data, however, it never happened. Instead, all the AWACS commander could do was speak into her headset to the operations center at Ramstein.

"Ramstein, this is Colonel Howard, technical director of Sentry One. For some reason that both of my communication specialists are at a loss to explain, all of our ground communication links have gone dead. The Soviets have launched a massive air strike. Enemy strike force of approximately one thousand aircraft launched at zero-seven-twenty. All headed west. Every available fighter from all bases must take to the air to meet the enemy threat. AWACS will control the fighters once they're airborne. Say again. Launch all Allied fighters at once. Did you get that, Ramstein?"

"Roger, Sentry One," the major in charge of base operations said. "We copy. Will have my team notify Ramstein's wings and the remainder of the Allied bases immediately."

The AWACS commander had done what she could to alert the defenders. While waiting for the American, British, and German fighter aircraft, she returned to coordinating the force she had available at the moment—twenty-four F-16s.

At Ramstein, the major turned to the three sergeants who comprised his staff.

"You heard Sentry One, we've got to get every possible plane into the air. I'll begin notifying Ramstein's fighter wings. Sergeant Brennan, contact Spangdahlem base operations and relay the information. Once you've finished that task, get in touch with the American air bases at Mildenhall and Lakenheath and order their fighters to cross the English Channel to engage the enemy as soon as they can. Let me know when you've completed that assignment. There will no doubt be a great deal more to do."

"I'm on it, Major Coleman." The sergeant picked up the phone to call Spangdahlem and initiate the first of his actions.

"Sergeant Rodgers, you've got the German air bases. Contact each one immediately," Coleman said.

"Will do, sir," she said. Like her predecessor, she was quickly on the telephone.

"Sergeant Mitchell, you take the English air base in Germany first, then begin contacting the ones in England."

"Got it, sir."

Satisfied by his team's efforts, one by one the major called each of Ramstein's wings and relayed Sentry One's order. It would take him nearly seven minutes to alert and scramble all of Ramstein's fighter aircraft.

Score after score of pilots and their support crews began racing to the aircraft waiting in the darkness of the hangers or on the icy tarmac.

Sergeant Brennan needed four tries to get through to Spangdahlem. But in scarcely more than a minute, a second base operations center was beginning to pass on the call to arms to its pilots.

The MiGs roared through the heavens at over one thousand miles per hour.

Brennan attempted to contact the two American fighter bases in England. He first tried Mildenhall. Unaware of the Spetsnaz team's destruction of Mildenhall's communications, he made eight fruitless attempts before finally giving up. Lakenheath was next. But he had no better luck getting through to the other American base. With the shortage of available circuits between Germany and England, no matter what he tried, all the frustrated airman heard was a busy signal.

The Russian fighters were almost twenty miles closer than they'd been sixty seconds earlier.

Even before the commandos' successes, American attempts to communicate with their NATO allies had been a joke. There were far too few interconnect points between the separate American and NATO systems. The most important of those interconnections had occurred through a microwave link between the NATO facility at Bad Kreuznach and the American facility at Schoenfeld.

Schoenfeld was a smoking ruin.

The other pair of sergeants tried notifying the German and English air bases in the northern half of the country. Without Schoenfeld, it was a call that would be impossible to complete.

The MiGs came on.

"Major, this isn't working. Spangdahlem's operations center's been notified," Brennan said, "but no matter what I try, I can't seem to get through to either Mildenhall or Lakenheath."

"I've gotten ahold of no one, sir," Rodgers added. "Not a single German fighter base has been alerted."

Major Colemen looked at the final member of his team. Mitchell shook his head, indicating he'd also met with complete failure.

"What're we going to do, sir?" Rodgers asked. "Obviously, we need to try something else if we're going to have any chance at all of completing our mission."

Coleman stared at Rodgers and Mitchell, his mind racing. "Get onto German civilian landlines and keep trying. I'm not sure if that will work any better than what we've already attempted, but don't give up no matter how long it takes. We've got to get in touch with the Germans and British."

Without further word, both began furiously dialing, attempting to get an outside line. They would quickly discover, however, just how overwhelmed the civilian communication system was. Millions upon millions of harried souls had overpowered its capabilities many times over. And an annoying busy signal was all that greeted the frantic airmen's every effort.

Outside, they could hear thunderous scores of American F-16s, F-22s, and F-35s coming to life and heading for the runways. The response, while incomplete, was getting under way.

In the middle of the absolute chaos within Germany, Coleman knew reaching England by landline was beyond impossible. But there was one thing his team could still try.

"Sergeant Brennan," he said, "do you have any friends at Lakenheath or Mildenhall?"

"Lots of them, sir."

"Any chance you've got their cell-phone numbers?"

"Got a handful of close friends at Mildenhall and a few at Lakenheath programmed into my phone."

"I've got the same. You take Mildenhall. I'll go after Lakenheath. If you get through to anyone, explain the situation and have them contact their base operation's center immediately."

"Will do, sir."

Both the sergeant and the major were soon on their cell phones, desperately attempting to break through the snarl of maddening busy signals that also greeted them.

It would take a frantic hour's effort for Major Coleman to contact an old friend at Lakenheath. By then, Lakenheath's fighters would be too late to influence the outcome of the air battle that raged throughout the skies over Germany.

They would never reach Mildenhall.

Twenty-four F-16s met the Russians at the German border. Like Jensen and his platoon's hopeless stand on the snowy ground below, the pilots knew they were here for one purpose—to buy precious minutes of time. In the sparkling darkness preceding the dawn, twenty-four attacked one thousand. The battle was joined.

The Americans were clearly better. Better aircraft. Better pilots. Although not so much better that they could withstand the ridiculous odds they faced.

The F-16 pilots expected the skies behind them to hurriedly fill with American, British, and German fighters. It didn't happen. The Americans began responding out of Ramstein, and minutes later out of Spangdahlem. But without effective command and control, the British and Germans didn't arrive in time to be a significant factor in the initial air battle of the new war. At Mildenhall, the Americans never left the ground. With the sluggish Allied reaction, the Russians were in a position to gain temporary control of the skies over Germany. For the moment, that was the only thing they wanted. One hour's control of certain parts of the skies over their ancient enemy was all General Yovanovich had asked of them.

The majority of the Russians blew through the screening force of F-16s like they weren't even there. One thousand MiGs were inside Germany. In bits and pieces, two hundred scattered American fighters would eventually race east to challenge them. In what would be recorded as the classic duel in the short history of man's flight, the world's greatest aircraft met in the enveloping darkness that masked the coming morning. High over central Europe, the talented American pilots battled the MiG-29s and Su-35s to the death.

It was a far different form of air combat than any of the pilot's grandfathers had experienced in these same skies during the Second World War. Eighty-three years earlier, a pilot's anguished defeat had been up close and filled with gut-wrenching emotion. But as the years passed and technology leaped forward, death in air combat had become almost sterile and impersonal. Rather than pitched battles with machine guns blazing and the pilots so near they could see the terrified look on their vanquished opponent's bloody face, the Americans and Russians dueled from vast distances.

The American Sidewinder and Sparrow missiles and the Russian Archer and Aphid missiles ripped through the remorseless skies from up to forty miles apart. And when armed with AIM-120 AMRAAMs, the American planes' range grew by nearly three times that.

Sitting in front of their screens, Fowler and Morgan watched the burgeoning air battle. With each passing minute, the clashes multiplied. The Patriot team's reaction to what they were witnessing was part fascination and part horror as the triangles from the west and the triangles from the east tore into each other. Death was coming to scour the heavens and weed out the unworthy.

A hundred miles from the closest clash of pilots and planes, they could see the tiny images of the air-to-air missiles streaking through the sky. Upon impact, the losing triangle would distort and break up. Any trace of the defeated aircraft would then disappear from the screen. The battle raged for half an hour, with neither side gaining a clear advantage. More of the triangles from the east than triangles from the west were falling. Still, the American victories weren't so overwhelming as to overcome the enemy's five-to-one edge. The mesmerized pair sat staring at their screens as the Russian steamroller slowly pushed their opponent back. The American pilots faltered.

The Russians came on. Holes appeared in a number of places in the American fighter defenses. By their sheer numbers, the MiGs broke through. Russian aircraft poured into the heart of Germany.

Behind the American air forces, the air-defense units braced for the attack. Close to the front, the Stinger shoulder-mounted missile and other shorter-range systems were assigned the task of supporting the ground units. Those weapons didn't have the capabilities to stop the high-flying Russian fighters headed for the rear of the American defenses.

Patriot and Hawk waited. The role of these long-distance killers was to protect the air bases, command and control centers, and support systems. Shoulder- and Humvee-mounted Stingers were also assigned to work in unison with their more powerful brothers. With their five-mile limit, the Stinger would try to protect the vulnerable close-in area created by a diving aircraft that the Hawk and Patriot couldn't activate in time to defeat.

Only Patriot and Hawk stood between the onrushing enemy and the total destruction of America's strategic assets. As the Americans had done to the Iraqis during Desert Storm, and later in the second Iraq war, the first objective of the Russian air armada was to destroy the thing that could destroy it.

Patriot and Hawk had to die.

In the early 1990s, a joint American and German proposal called for the permanent assignment of seven American and four German Patriot battalions within the Republic of Germany. If the original plan had been carried out, the Russian attack on that January morning would have been met by forty-four Patriot batteries. Each battery would have been capable of firing thirty-two missiles without reloading. The seven hundred surviving MiGs would've been greeted by twice their number in Patriot missiles.

At one billion dollars per battalion, however, such peacetime expenditures for Patriot hadn't been politically supportable. Instead, there were two German and two American Patriot battalions assigned the task of protecting the critical assets of the West from the threat approaching in the dawning skies. One of the plan's original Patriot battalions had been diverted from Germany for duty in Saudi Arabia. Another had been given to the Israelis as part of the Desert Storm agreement. The final three battalions had arrived in Germany only to be deactivated and sold to the Japanese.

With the arrival last night of Fowler's battalion, the West presently had twenty firing batteries with a little more than six hundred missiles inside Germany. Unfortunately, four of those batteries containing over one hundred missiles would be of no use in the coming battle.

Delta Battery of the Texas battalion was trapped on Rhein-Main Air Base by the ever-growing flood of panicked German refugees. They'd just received word to set up on Rhein-Main itself. It would be another hour before they'd be ready to fire their first missile. And three of the sophisticated Patriot batteries—two American and one German—were presently down with maintenance problems and would never join in the fray.

Without the four batteries, the remaining sixteen stood poised with slightly under five hundred missiles to engage seven hundred MiGs. The Patriot batteries knew they'd be the enemy's first objective.

Nevertheless, the Patriot was going to be a difficult target for any attacker, no matter how determined, to kill. It couldn't be said they were impossible to destroy, for the Patriot could be conquered. What they were was hard to discover from the air. With their passive radar systems, they didn't put out any easy-to-track radar emissions. Yet given enough time, the Russians would detect the Patriot's signal. And once that signal had been discovered, the MiGs would move in for the kill.

The Patriot needed nine seconds after launching for its huge missile to activate and kill. It was far too large to handle close-in targets. If a fighter could get inside the system's defenses, the Patriot would be unable to defend itself. From that point on, the MiG would stand an excellent chance of fooling the little Stinger missiles and destroying the Patriot. All it would take was a single air-to-ground missile into the Engagement Control Station, and the Patriot, no matter how many missiles still waited on its launchers, would be out of the war forever. For that reason, in wartime a Patriot battery never stayed anywhere for more than eight hours. Four hours was even better.

From this moment on, nearly one-quarter of the Patriots that survived the initial attack would be unavailable as they shut down, moved, and reinitialized.

Early in the century, the American military had phased out the Hawk Missile System. But when the threat reappeared in the East, with a Hawk battery costing one-tenth the price of a Patriot, the decision was made primarily for budgetary purposes to reactivate them for use in Europe by both the Germans and the Americans.

The seven older Hawk systems, each with eighteen missiles, made for an even easier target. With its three radars emitting strong signals, the Hawk provided a clear beacon for the Russians to follow straight to their objective. The Hawk batteries were twenty to fifty miles in front of the Patriots. It was Hawk that would engage the first wave of Russian fighters.

The MiGs came on.

The Americans waited. Their missiles were at the ready. While they steeled themselves for the attack, they were unaware the Russians had mapped each Hawk and Patriot battery.

The moment the war began, just as the Russians had anticipated, the air-defense units moved from their permanent locations to new firing positions. Russian operatives watched every battery move to its new location.

Sitting in an ancient car on a distant hilltop overlooking Rhein-Main, three men in worn overcoats had used night-vision equipment to detect the new Patriot battalion's arrival at a little after midnight. From the moment the three batteries drove out of the air base's main gate until they arrived at their destinations, they were never out of sight of a vast web of Russian spies.

Thirty minutes prior to the launch of the Russian armada, the last message on the American and German air defenses had been transmitted. As the MiGs broke through, they knew exactly where every Hawk and Patriot battery was emplaced.

The three American and four German Hawk units prepared to fire. Normally, they'd have sat with their radars off until the last possible moment, depending on the AWACS to tell them the precise instance to turn on their systems. But with the AWACS' ground communication capabilities destroyed, the Hawk batteries were on their own. Without the AWACS, the only way they could see the enemy was through their own radars.

As the Russian fighters burst deep into Germany, the Hawk batteries turned on their equipment. Their radars started putting out loud, clear signals. Each unit knew they'd signed their own death warrants. The air-defense crews were well aware that their radars' strong emissions would lead the enemy right to them. Still, they had no choice.

The outer net of Hawks began to die. The American battery at Wurzburg was the first to fall. Its crew fired two missiles—two successful kills—before a MiG-29 broke through and rammed a rocket into the Hawk Engagement Center. The rocket had followed the homing beacon the Hawk radars had provided straight to the target.

One hundred miles north, a dozen MiG-29s demolished the German battery at Cuxhaven. Not a single Hawk missile had been fired. The MiGs then turned their attention to the German battery fifty miles south at Friesing. One, and then another, and finally a third of the MiGs tumbled from the sky from the determined German battery's missiles. The fighters fought their way through the beleaguered Hawk's defenses. The battery succumbed in a hail of air-to-ground missiles.

The remaining four Hawk firing batteries remained in the fight. At least for the moment.

The Russians roared deeper into Germany. The time had come to challenge the immense power of the Patriot.

Scores of westward-moving triangles headed toward their targets.

CHAPTER 27

January 29—8:11 a.m.
Charlie Battery, 1st "Cobra Strike" Battalion, 43rd Air
    Defense Artillery Regiment
A Deserted Parking Lot on the Eastern Edge of Stuttgart

Six triangles leaped from the melee. They raced toward the southwest. Unless stopped, they'd reach their objective in the next five minutes.

"Here they come!" Morgan said. "I'm starting the interrogation."

"Ready to target as soon as they're identified," Fowler said. "Paul, it's too early to tell if the MiGs are heading for us. But just in case, notify the three Stinger teams to get ready to repulse a fighter attack. Then tell the communication van to direct everyone to get away from the launchers and take cover."

"Roger."

"First two aircraft have been identified as hostile," Morgan said. "Authorized to engage when they are within fifty miles." She could feel the first sticky beads of sweat rolling down her spine.

"Roger, Lieutenant. Verify on my screen, first two aircraft are hostile. Beginning targeting information. Hostiles are approximately eighty miles out and closing. Am locking into the computer." Fowler started typing on the keyboard in front of him. "Will intercept the moment they're in range."

Less than thirty miles, and the enemy fighters would be within the giant missile's reach. With their present speed and course, that would occur in precisely ninety seconds.

"Roger," the lieutenant said. "Verify engagement procedures have begun on first two targets. Last four aircraft have also been identified as hostile. Final four are cleared for engagement."

"Locking in coordinates on the final four targets. Computer has been directed to engage the moment they're within range." Fowler's mouth was so dry that his lips clung to his teeth and fought against his anxious words.

"Verify four additional targets are locked in and engagement sequence has been initiated," Morgan said while staring at the symbols on her screen.

"Paul, notify regiment that we're in the process of engaging six hostile aircraft," Fowler said.

"Roger. Notifying of ongoing engagement."

There was nothing more to do. The computer would take it from here, automatically selecting the missiles and firing once the targets came within fifty miles of the Patriot.

The Patriot's nearly flawless kill rate might be slightly lower at so great a distance. But at this moment, the air-defense team didn't care. They were far more concerned with another problem. Nearly all of the American Patriot air-defense systems had received a software upgrade more than a decade earlier. Each Engagement Control Station could now engage up to nine aircraft simultaneously. Unfortunately, the missile system that Fowler and Morgan were controlling had been repurchased from the Japanese a few months earlier. The system had never received the updated software. All four of the battalion's Engagement Control Stations were scheduled for the upgrade within the next three months. At the moment, however, that was of little comfort to the air defenders. During the coming war, the Patriot computer they were controlling could only fire at and engage five targets at any one time. And six were on the way. Any way they looked at it, one of the rapidly closing aircraft wasn't going to be attacked until a first had been destroyed.

If they waited too long to engage the MiGs, there was a real possibility of the final aircraft breaking through. It was a chance they dare not take.

Fowler and Morgan stared at the screens. One by one, the seconds ticked by. The triangles continued their unyielding march across the ever-brightening heavens. With each passing instant, they grew closer to the battery. The determined MiGs inched ever nearer to the Patriot's firing point. The Americans could do nothing but watch as death crossed the skies intent on claiming them.

At least there was nothing for the Patriot soldiers to do for the first minute. Sixty seconds behind the initial group, a second set of six triangles suddenly appeared. They were followed moments later by another pair, and behind them a final aircraft. All were on the same flight path as the first group. There was little doubt they were coming for the Patriot.

Morgan instantly recognized the immense danger. She started interrogating the first of the nine new triangles bearing down upon them.

"Got them yet, Lieutenant?"

"Identification coming in," she said. "Lead aircraft in second flight is hostile. Cleared for engagement."

"Lead aircraft identified as hostile," Fowler said, so the lieutenant could verify he understood her command. "Beginning engagement procedure."

"Second and third aircraft also identified as hostile," Morgan said. "Cleared for engagement on second and third aircraft."

"Roger. Beginning engagement of . . ." He stopped in midsentence as the screens flashed new information.

Even as the data for the later flights was being fed into the system, the computer and radar were locked onto the original targets. While Fowler typed in the command to track and target the newer aircraft, the computer recognized that the first MiG had reached the firing point.

The computer selected a missile from the number six launcher and gave the command to fire. Belching hellfire and brimstone, a two-thousand-pound missile rocketed out of the launcher's top left canister. A sleek nineteen-foot killer raced skyward at incredible speed. The instant the missile was launched, there existed a 98 percent chance of a successful kill. In all likelihood, the pilot in the intruder was already dead. The Russian just didn't yet know that his fleeting life had come to an end.

"Confirm launch of first missile at . . ." Fowler glanced at his watch. "Zero-eight-fourteen. Paul, notify regiment of first launch."

"Roger. Notifying regiment of initial launch at zero-eight-fourteen local time."

They would have preferred to stop and follow the flight of the missile as it rushed into the heavens at nearly four times the speed of sound. At two thousand miles per hour, the Patriot would reach the oncoming enemy fighter in just over forty-five seconds. But if they wanted to live to see another day, the crew in the Engagement Control Station didn't have forty-five seconds to spare. There were still fourteen aircraft roaring at them through the first frigid rays of the early-morning sunrise. All had a single goal in mind—end the Patriot soldiers' existence.

Fowler and Morgan returned to the fight.

"Targeting second and third fighters in second flight," Fowler said.

The computer grabbed a missile from the number two launcher and hurled it into the sky. Two seconds later, it fired a third missile, this time from launcher number eight. Three missiles appeared on their screens. Each was rushing into the heavens to seek and destroy. Two more pilots, as yet unaware, had less than a minute remaining.

There were twenty-nine missiles still waiting on the launchers to bring havoc to the German skies.

"Confirm second and third firings also at zero-eight-fourteen," Fowler said. "Notify regiment of further launches."

"Notification under way," Paul said.

"Confirm hostile on second flight aircraft four, five, and six," Morgan said.

"Roger," Fowler answered. "Targeting second flight of aircraft four, five, and six."

Thirty-five miles away, the onboard radar of the first fighter recognized the threat streaking toward it across the heavens. The aircraft screamed for its pilot to take evasive action. The lead triangle broke from the pack and attempted to dive thirty thousand feet to the ground below. The Russian hoped he could conceal himself in the ground clutter and lose the incoming missile. But the pilot's desperate maneuver was bound to fail. The Patriot's highly sophisticated computer immediately readjusted the missile's flight. The missile matched the fighter's every move. Even if by some miracle the pilot reached the sheltering ground, the Patriot system was far too advanced to be fooled. The missile, twice as fast and far more agile than the fighter, wouldn't relent as it locked the MiG in its death throes and narrowed the distance between them with each passing moment.

The Patriot computer fired a fourth missile, again selecting one from the number six launcher. Right behind it, a fifth missile, from launcher number one, roared off its platform. The computer had reached the maximum number of aircraft that could be simultaneously engaged. Until one of the missiles destroyed its target, or failed in the attempt, no further firings would occur.

In the first flight, all but the trailing aircraft were being hunted down by the great birds of prey. With their radars warning them that certain death was on the wing, the pigeons scattered to the four winds. Only the final fighter in the group continued its persistent quest to eliminate the world's premier destroyer of airplanes.

Fifteen miles behind the first flight, the second group of six came on. Given enough time, the Patriot would deal with each and every one of them.

The only question remaining was whether there would be enough time.

"Confirm two more firings at zero-eight-fifteen," Fowler said.

"Paul, tell the Stinger teams to prepare for target acquisition," Morgan said. "I think we might need them."

"Notifying Stinger teams and confirming firings with regiment."

Morgan began interrogating the final three aircraft.

"The two fighters in the third flight confirmed as hostile," she said. "Begin targeting."

"Roger. Confirm hostiles in third flight of two aircraft," Fowler said, his eyes never leaving his screen.

The first missile reached out a sharpened talon to seize its helpless victim. The MiG-29 exploded, disappearing like a vapor from the slowly brightening sky. The Patriot confirmed the kill. A small tic-tac-toe symbol appeared over the aircraft's triangle. The tic-tac-toe started to flash. In a few seconds, the scattered pieces of the destroyed fighter fell from the heavens. And the tic-tac-toe disappeared from the screens.

Fowler glanced at his watch once again. "Confirm initial kill at zero-eight-fifteen," he said.

"Roger," Morgan said. "Kill confirmed at zero-eight-fifteen."

A sixth missile leaped from its launcher. It raced to meet the final fighter in the initial flight. There were five missiles in the air, eight more fighters targeted, one enemy plane destroyed, and a final unidentified aircraft with which to deal.

The clock was ticking for the Patriot crew. Any mistake at this point, no matter how small, would likely be fatal.

Another blinking tic-tac-toe flashed over one of the fleeing triangles. A second Russian aircraft was no more.

"Second kill at zero-eight-sixteen," Fowler said. His voice was businesslike, masking the feelings of panic within him that were increasing by the second.

"Confirm second kill at zero-eight-sixteen," the lieutenant said. She half turned in her chair. "Paul, pass on to regiment, second confirmed kill at zero-eight-sixteen."

"Roger. Second confirmed kill at zero-eight-sixteen."

The four triangles being hunted were heading away from the battery's location. But the other nine were coming on fast. None of the six aircraft in the targeted second flight had yet been fired upon. They were thirty miles away and growing nearer. At a thousand miles per hour, they roared toward the Patriot team.

If the enemy wasn't stopped, Fowler and Morgan had just over a minute to live.

With a second fighter destroyed, the Patriot launched once more. Fire roared from beneath the number two launcher. Another long missile, silhouetted in the lingering shadows of the growing sunrise, leaped from its launch tube. The pilot in the lead aircraft in the second flight would never see the coming day.

"Confirm firing of a seventh missile at zero-eight-sixteen," Fowler said. As he watched the images on the screen, his concern continued to grow. There were still far too many of the enemy needing to be engaged and little time remaining to do so.

"Roger. Firing confirmed."

A third flashing tic-tac-toe appeared on the screens. Somewhere in the dawning skies over southern Germany, another pilot's life had ended.

"Third kill recorded," Fowler said.

"Third kill confirmed."

Paul didn't wait for them to tell him to notify regiment. He started relaying the latest firing and kill information on his own.

Ten miles behind the second flight, the pair of hostiles also raced toward the Patriot battery. A few miles behind them, a lone aircraft trailed.

Morgan began interrogating the last fighter. The Patriot computer ordered the radar to send out the identification code. In the nose of the American F-16, the message was received and the proper response transmitted. A friendly symbol appeared next to the trailing triangle.

"Final aircraft is friendly. Do not target," Morgan said. "Say again. Do not target final aircraft. Aircraft has been identified as friendly."

"Understood," Fowler said. "Confirm on my screen that final aircraft is friendly."

The second flight continued to close with the Patriot battery. If they didn't stop the MiGs, Fowler and Morgan had forty-five seconds before a fiery death in the form of air-to-ground missiles would reach down to claim them.

The computer hurled another Patriot into the skies. The second fighter in the second flight would be its next victim. It would be a few more seconds, however, before the high-flying Russian would realize that he'd been abruptly transformed from hunter to hunted.

The straining jet engines of fighters four and five in the first flight gave their pilots all they had. Still, it wasn't nearly enough. The Russians were vastly overmatched. The steadfast missiles closed with their targets. Two more flashing tic-tac-toes found their way onto Fowler's and Morgan's screens. Another pair of MiGs had vanished from the early-morning sky.

The Patriot was free to fire once again. Launchers five and seven roared to life. A pair of missiles carried death into the heavens at Mach 3.9. Only fifteen miles separated the Patriots from their targets. In less than thirty seconds, the killers would span the distance between themselves and the planes.

Once again, all the Patriot engagement team could do was stare at their screens while the computer and the radar coordinated their maximum load of five missiles.

The first four fighters in the second flight ran in different directions. Each pilot clung to the desperate hope that he could somehow find a way to save his frail life. The final two fighters in the flight continued their determined quest to reach the air-defense battery. Fifteen seconds passed. The pair of MiGs closed to within ten miles of their target. Beneath their sleek wings and bloated bellies, their missiles glistened in a blinding morning sun's first rays.

Fowler and Morgan watched the two triangles nearing the battery. Another pair of hostiles was ten miles behind. The air defenders understood they had little time left.

"Paul, tell the Stingers to prepare for an attack!" Morgan said. "Targets are north-by-northeast."

Paul spoke into his headset once more.

"This is going to be close," Fowler said.

As the first pair entered a steep dive, the MiG pilots armed their air-to-ground missiles. The Stinger gunners pointed their shoulder-mounted air-defense weapons toward the heavens. With the five-mile limit of their small missiles, all the Americans could do was stand their ground and wait. They could see the black dots in the sky growing quite large, but were helpless to do anything about it. Behind the diving fighters, three more dots in the rising sun were coming quite near.

The MiGs would release their missiles just as they reached the three-mile point. They'd be close enough to have a decent chance of hitting the target, yet far enough away to keep the Stingers from locking on and firing in time to stop the attack. At that distance, they'd also be near enough that a Patriot missile wouldn't have the time to activate and find the plunging fighters before the MiGs found them.

In fifteen seconds, Fowler, Morgan, and Paul would reach their end.

A Patriot smashed into the last fighter in the first flight. Tic-tac-toe. The computer instantly fired upon the first of the diving aircraft. The MiG was eight miles away. Five miles from its firing point, it came on. The pilot saw the Patriot launch. But he knew that at so short a distance his only chance of escaping was by destroying the Patriot computer before its missile destroyed him. He had to make it to the three-mile point before the Patriot did.

He'd never release his missiles. Twice as fast as the MiG, the Patriot reached up to pluck it from the skies with three miles to spare. The MiG exploded six miles above the Engagement Control Station. A ball of fire tumbled to the ground a few hundred yards east of the American battery.

Undeterred by what had happened to its brother, the final aircraft in the second flight continued its teeth-rattling dive. The Stingers waited. They strained to obtain a lock onto the plunging fighter. Each gunner begged to hear the firing tone ringing in his ears. The MiG was nearly ready to unleash its ordnance. There was a single mile to cover before he would launch a handful of lethal missiles. It was too late for either the Patriot or Stingers to intercept the fighter in time.

Fowler, Morgan, and Paul had eight seconds to live.

They stared at their screens. Disbelief spread across their faces. Fowler gripped the computer keyboard with all his might. He could sense the hair on his arms standing straight up.

From out of nowhere, the plummeting fighter's radar suddenly warned the Russian that he was under attack. The confused pilot hesitated, uncertain of what his aircraft was trying to tell him. He'd seen the Patriot destroy his partner, but he was convinced the Patriot hadn't fired again. Much too late, the resolute Russian realized the missile that would decimate his aircraft wasn't reaching up from the ground to find him. The missile that was coming to end his life was approaching from the rear.

The F-16 Falcon was twelve miles behind the diving MiG. The two fighters just ahead of the American pilot had led her directly to the attack on the Patriot battery. She watched her display as her Sparrow missile raced across the sky toward the diving enemy. The Russian reacted to this new threat to his survival. He broke off his dive and soared upward at incredible speed. Nevertheless, the American kept her Sparrow right on target. The chase was short and sweet. A fireball erupted in front of the Falcon as the MiG died beneath the speeding Sparrow's attack.

As the MiGs began disengaging from the earlier air battle, it hadn't taken the AWACS commander long to determine what the enemy was up to. Unable to directly warn the air-defense units, the AWACS did the best it could. The Sentry One commander issued an urgent order for any available aircraft to intercept the Russian fighters. The lone F-16, her wingman killed moments earlier, had chased fourteen MiGs across the German skies in their one-hundred-mile journey to destroy Charlie Battery. The American pilot knew she couldn't stop all fourteen, so she bided her time. Running with her radar off to hide her presence, she waited for the Patriots to do most of the dirty work for her. With the seconds in Fowler's, Morgan's, and Paul's lives down to single digits, the F-16 struck.

The final pair of fighters was just beginning their own dives when the Sparrow raced right between them and smashed into the MiG a few miles ahead. For the first time, the Russians realized they weren't alone. Both took severe evasive action.

One right after the other, four Patriots destroyed the fleeing fighters of the second flight. The Patriot computer fired on the final pair of MiGs. The F-16 saw the dual launch. She pulled well away and waited for the Patriots to finish the job.

The MiGs also saw the Patriot fire. With barely ten miles between prey and killer, they knew there'd be no chance for escape. Their own tic-tac-toes were scant moments way.

Within seconds of each other, the pair exploded.

With the destruction of the last of the MiGs, the F-16 turned and headed north to Ramstein.

Inside the small van, the blood returned to the Americans' faces as the final of the hostile triangles was covered by the flashing symbols. A warming wave of relief washed over them.

None was able to muster the strength to utter a single sound after so narrow an escape. They sat in self-imposed silence for nearly a minute.

"Confirm thirteen missiles launched and thirteen kills recorded," Morgan finally said.

"Roger," Fowler said. "I confirm thirteen missiles fired and thirteen kills. Paul, notify regiment."

"Notifying regiment of thirteen launches and thirteen kills."

They were elated to be alive. But there was no time for celebration. Letting their minds wander too far from the images on their screens could still be fatal. They returned to the task at hand. As the air battle continued, the hundreds of triangles were far more scattered than they'd been earlier.

There was nothing within seventy-five miles of the Patriot battery. And to their relief, no indications that another attack on their position was imminent. For the moment, there was little to do but observe the surviving triangles as they battled and died in the blood-tinged skies over Germany.

The report came in thirty minutes later.

"Oh, man, you're kidding!" Paul said into his headset. "Are you sure about that?"

He looked into the curious faces staring up at him from the front of the compartment. "Regiment says that seven of the sixteen Patriot batteries and all of the Hawk firing units were destroyed by enemy fighters. Alpha and Bravo Batteries both bought it."

The Patriot community was a small one. While they looked into each other's startled eyes, Fowler and Morgan understood they'd lost many friends on this bright winter morning. They also knew if it hadn't been for a smart American pilot, their names would have been added to that list.

It was Fowler who would break the second bout of prolonged silence that enveloped the crowded space.

"Jesus Christ!" he said. "Take a look at this!"

The screens started filling with triangles once more. In an endless stream, they poured across the Czech border.

Before it was over, two thousand hostiles would cover nearly every square inch of both screens.

Seventeen hundred transports carrying five divisions of Russian paratroopers, and three hundred escorting fighters, were headed deep into Germany.

The next phase of General Yovanovich's plan was about to commence.

CHAPTER 28

January 29—12:31 a.m. (Eastern Standard Time)
World News Network Studios
Boston

The anchorperson sat behind the desk during the commercial break. A makeup artist stood over her.

"Ten seconds, Bonnie," the director said.

In millions of homes around the world, the television screen changed from one of a happy man driving a shiny new car to a picture of the American and Soviet flags clashing with the words THE BATTLE FOR GERMANY running across its bottom. The theme music for the war, primarily trumpets and percussion instruments, blared. When the music ended, the picture changed to the smiling anchorperson.

"Welcome back. This is Bonnie Lloyd at the WNN news desk in Boston. We've just received word from our Berlin correspondent, Stewart Turner, that Berlin has fallen to the Russians. For more on this story, we take you to Berlin and WNN's correspondent, Stewart Turner."

The picture changed to a handsome man in his late twenties standing on a snowy rooftop in the middle of the German capital. Turner held a microphone with a gloved hand. He was wearing a heavy overcoat and thick scarf to protect himself from the stark cold. His breath was visible with every word he spoke.

"Thank you, Bonnie. I'm reporting to you from the roof of the Sheraton Hotel in the center of downtown Berlin. It's eight thirty in the morning here. And as you can see behind me, the sun has fully risen.

The winter storm that held Europe in its powerful grip for the past few days dissipated late last night. The dawn has broken clear, but cold.

"The Soviet forces are visibly in control of this ancient city, so symbolic of the reunification of Germany. Russian tanks are absolutely everywhere. They've taken up positions at all the main intersections inside the city. So far, there's been little resistance from within Berlin itself. From time to time, gunfire and shelling can be heard in the distance."

The camera swung away from Turner and toward the edge of the rooftop. The cameraman slowly panned up and down a wide boulevard.

"The streets are empty except for the movement of the Russian tanks. In the distance, you should be able to make out the Brandenburg Gate."

The cameraman focused on the massive monument so filled with German history. A dozen tanks could be seen sitting beneath its wide arches.

The camera returned to Stewart Turner. "Other than that, this city, taken by complete surprise by the swift nighttime attack, is quiet and still on this shocking winter morning."

"Stewart," Bonnie Lloyd said, "we've heard rumors from some pretty reliable sources that most of what used to be East Germany is now under Soviet control. Can you confirm or deny those rumors?"

"No, I can't, Bonnie. Similar rumors have circulated through the press corps here in Berlin. But so far they're just rumors . . . What?" With a puzzled expression on his face, Turner looked at his cameraman. "Hold on for a second, Bonnie. My cameraman is indicating that there's some kind of activity in the street below us. We're going to attempt to give WNN's viewers a look at what's going on."

The camera swung over the side of the hotel rooftop. The picture showed five Russian soldiers dragging a pair of men in civilian clothing out of a building on the other side of the street. The men were shoved against a wall. In front of millions of television viewers, the Russians opened fire with their automatic weapons. Both men were killed instantly. They slumped to the ground. The soldiers turned and walked away. The crumpled bodies lay where they'd fallen.

There were five seconds of stunned silence in both Berlin and Boston. The producer cut away from Berlin and cued Bonnie Lloyd.

"I'm told that we've temporarily lost our picture from Berlin," she said. "After this commercial break, we'll be back to speak with our White House correspondent Steven Dillard and, following that, with WNN's military analyst, retired Colonel Philip McPherson."

The screen changed to the already familiar picture of the American and Soviet flags clashing with the bold words THE BATTLE FOR GERMANY beneath them. The war's theme music sounded for a few seconds.

The picture switched to a happy group of attractive men and women romping on the beach while enjoying their favorite beer.

CHAPTER 29

Arturo Rios sat in the sandbagged bunker. His hands were frozen on the .50-caliber machine gun's grips. He stared into the snow-laden evergreens on the other side of the chain-link fence. The sun's slow rise had caused his spirits to rise also. As its first rays peeked through the shimmering trees, its false promise of winter warmth reached out for him. There'd only been twenty minutes of daylight, but Rios was beginning to accept that the interminable night was finally over. For the past seven hours, he'd believed it would never end.

Seven hours. A lifetime while he crouched alone in the darkness and peered into the sinister trees on the far side of the icy wire.

The day had broken cold, but clear. The snows had stopped hours earlier. And as was common after a winter storm, not a cloud could be seen in a bright blue sky. He'd left Miami to see the world. One of the things he'd always wanted to see was snow. Yet as the blizzard pelted his exposed position, he'd concluded that he'd seen enough of it to last him for the rest of his days.

He shivered in his world of sand. The airman had long ago lost all feeling in his hands and feet. An hour earlier, a truck had arrived with a huge breakfast. So he was no longer hungry. He was, however, feeling one emotion quite strongly.

He was feeling utterly ashamed.

Much to his embarrassment, his active imagination had gotten the better of him during the night. Certain he'd seen movement on the other side of the fence, Rios had twice fired at shadowy enemy soldiers who existed only in his inventive mind. On both occasions, his firing brought reinforcements running from every direction. There was nothing out there, of course. Just the wind and snow, and a mind that insisted on making its own reality. Rios took no comfort in the fact that nearly every .50-caliber position on the lonely eastern perimeter had fallen prey to these same frailties at some time during the torturous darkness. The firing had become so commonplace that by night's end, the reinforcements barely responded at all.

Flying at an altitude of twelve hundred feet, scores of Antonov An-12 cargo planes neared their destination. Inside the belly of each "Cub," sixty of Russia's finest soldiers rose to their feet and turned toward the open door. A frigid wind rushed in to greet them. Each removed the powder-blue beret from his head, shoved it into his pocket, and replaced it with a helmet. Weighed down by their equipment, they waited for the light to turn green, signaling for them to jump.

They were the elite parachutists of the 3rd Regiment, 105th Parachute Division. Each of the division's soldiers was bursting with boundless pride. The 105th had received the most honored role. Its three regiments had been assigned the task of destroying the most important targets. The American air bases at Ramstein, Spangdahlem, and Rhein-Main were their goals. And to the men of the division's 3rd Regiment had gone the greatest prize of all—Ramstein, headquarters of the United States' air forces in Europe.

Two other airborne divisions had been chosen to attack the six German fighter bases—a pair in the southeast near Munich and four in the northwest. Another division would seize the bridges over the southern portion of the Rhine River. If the bridges couldn't be held, they would be demolished.

The final division, the 103rd, was the second most honored. It would send one regiment against the British air base in the northern part of the country. A second regiment would attack and lay waste to the Americans' two divisions of pre-positioned armored equipment near Kaiserslautern. The 103rd's final regiment sat on the ground in the western Ukraine. They anxiously waited to join the battle. The moment word was received that any of their countrymen had failed to eliminate their objective, the reserve regiment would take to the air to annihilate and destroy.

The Russians were taking a huge gamble—a risk justified by the potential reward. They were using nearly all the cargo aircraft in the Military Transport Aviation fleet to carry their airborne soldiers deep into Germany. Thirty-six thousand of the Soviet Union's best and brightest, and the tons of equipment that supported them, were on a flight path fraught with danger. For thirty minutes, each Cub had been carrying its sixty soldiers deep inside the borders of the enemy country.

The Warsaw Pact's air attack had opened a number of corridors into the heart of Germany. In addition, three hundred MiGs were escorting the transports. Even so, the slow-flying cargo planes were vulnerable. They were easy targets should they inadvertently stray into the path of the surviving Allied air defenses. And with the vast range of their missiles, the American F-35s, F-22s, and F-16s were quite capable of circumventing the protective cover provided by the MiGs to reach out and kill.

General Yovanovich had estimated that even with the earlier efforts of the Russian fighter aircraft to clear the way, there would be significant losses. His evaluation had been correct. One by one, the persistent Americans picked off over three hundred of the plodding planes. By the time the Russian transports reached their drop zones, 20 percent of the parachutists lay dead in fallow farmers' fields throughout Germany. Twenty percent of their combat vehicles had also been destroyed. Shot down by NATO fighters or air-defense missiles, one out of five of the lumbering planes had plunged to the earth or exploded in the brilliant blue sky.

Unlike the Americans, whose last division-level combat jump had occurred during the Korean War, the Russians believed in a strong airborne presence. The parachute divisions were the pride of the Soviet military and the Soviet people. America had reduced her airborne units to one airborne division and one air-assault division used primarily as light, mobile fighting forces. But the Russians retained eight divisions of airborne soldiers. The Russian airborne divisions were self-contained. Their combat vehicles, and everything they needed for battle, parachuted in with the divisions' soldiers.

Between the combatants, there were marked philosophical differences in the use of airborne forces. These were based primarily upon the attitudes the competing countries had toward the acceptable levels of losses of its military. The Americans couldn't withstand the close scrutiny the exceptionally high casualties of an airborne campaign brought. They'd long ago given up such tactics. For the Russians, however, there was no press or active voice in the citizenry to question their military decisions. Eighty percent losses were regrettable. Nevertheless, if it took such casualties to accomplish the mission, so be it. The common good would always outshine the individual life.

Despite the stark contrast in the competing countries' approaches to the use of their airborne forces, there was a single characteristic that tied the American and Soviet airborne soldiers together. Like the soldiers of the American 82nd Airborne Division, their Russian counterparts had a proud history of battle to uphold. The American airborne soldiers in their burgundy berets, and the Russian airborne soldiers in their berets of powder blue, correctly considered themselves to be some of the truly elite combat soldiers in the world.

Inside the lead Cub, the light turned from red to green. In a steady stream, sixty paratroopers plunged out the door and into a winter sky's icy nothingness. Each hurtled toward the frozen ground below.

All around them, the lethal regiment's soldiers did the same.

While Arturo Rios sat rejoicing at the coming of the sun, ten miles away, close to two thousand of Russia's best soldiers rained down from the sky like a frightful summer storm.

All over western Germany, a rain of billowing white parachutes began to fall—a torrential rain of terror for those who dared to stand against it.

Even with the 3rd Regiment's losses in the German skies, three hundred combat vehicles cascaded from the passing aircraft. The armored equipment dangled on the ends of huge triple parachutes. Along with the parachutists, the vehicles fell into the farm country northeast of Ramstein.

As with any combat jump, there are mistakes. The strong winds shift at a critical moment. A pilot miscalculates the jump point. Equipment and soldiers descend into wooded areas. Parachutes fail to open. While they drop into the mantle of solid white, many soldiers miscalculate their impact point with the frozen ground. An ankle is twisted, a leg is broken, a knee is smashed. A neck is snapped by a misdirected parachutist's encounter with the highest reaches of a mighty evergreen. Two chutes become hopelessly entangled in the close quarters, and a hapless pair of soldiers plummet together to their death.

General Yovanovich understood that another 10 percent of the men and equipment would never rise from the drop zone to join in the battle.

As the 3rd Regiment's parachutists rose from the snows, the unit was down to 70 percent of its original strength. Seventeen hundred highly skilled men and two hundred and fifty combat vehicles would soon be on their way to Ramstein. Their prize was the total destruction of the great American air base.

Waiting to contest them were four thousand lightly armed airmen. At stake were the Americans' last hopes of ruling the skies.

Arturo Rios sat at the end of the runway with an amused grin on his face as his wandering daydreams took him to the warm winds of home. His reverie was shattered as two Humvees screeched to a stop behind him. The Humvees were filled with anxious airmen cradling M-4s.

"All right, everybody out," the first Humvee's air-police driver said. The airmen climbed out of the vehicles.

"Wright, Goodman, Michaels, Wheatley, Wilson, and Velasquez.

You're to support this defensive position and everything for one hundred yards each way. Rios here . . . You are Rios, right?"

"Yes, Sergeant."

"Rios is the only one of you with combat training. So even though he's the lowest-ranking airman out here, you'll take your orders from him when it comes to defending this section of the fence. Does anyone have a problem with that?"

The fidgeting airmen knew they were out of their element. No one said a word.

"Good. Let's hurry up and get the sandbags out of the Humvees," the air policeman said. "We need to get some more bunkers set up right away. The Russians could be here any minute."

With the air policeman's fateful words, Rios's daydreams became nothing more than distant memories. Unsure of what was happening, he gripped the machine gun even tighter. Along the lengthy fence line, other Humvees were disgorging men and sandbags to support the .50-caliber positions.

The Cuban-American airman watched the ominous woods for any sign of the enemy while his countrymen rushed to prepare the new positions. A small bunker was hastily thrown together fifty yards to the left. An identical one was quickly erected on the right. When they were finished, the air policemen returned to their Humvees to grab some final items. They headed back to the main bunker.

"Here, you're probably going to need these." The air policeman put two additional ammunition containers on the ground next to the machine gun. His partner laid a dozen hand grenades on top of the sand.

Before Rios could respond, the duo rushed to their Humvees and sped away. The new arrivals crowded around the bunker, waiting for him to take charge.

Rios only knew one of the six airmen. He turned toward him. "Goodman, what the hell's going on?"

"Man, haven't you heard? The Russians just parachuted thousands of men in a few miles from here. The air police told us they're certain they're on their way to wipe out Ramstein."

"Hey, does anyone remember which end of this thing I point at the Russians?" Wheatley said while fumbling with his M-4.

"Don't you think we ought to get organized?" Goodman said.

"What do you want us to do?" another asked.

For Rios, his brief stint in the Air Force had involved only taking orders. He'd never before had to give one.

"Well, I guess the first thing we need to do is not all be standing in one place. Let's put two of you guys in each of the new bunkers. And two of you stay with me." Rios pointed at Wheatley and Velasquez. "You and you, take that bunker."

Clutching their rifles, the airmen picked up a couple of hand grenades and ran over to the bunker on the left.

Rios pointed to Michaels and Wright. "You and you, take the other one."

The pair also grabbed their rifles and some of the grenades. They ran off to the right.

"Goodman, that leaves you and . . ."

"Wilson," the chubby-faced airman with the broad grin said.

"You and Wilson with me."

CHAPTER 30

As they'd practiced untold times, the moment the men of the 3rd Regiment picked themselves up off the ground, they raced to their vehicles. In two minutes, the drop zone was secured. In ten minutes, seventeen hundred parachutists were rolling onto an icy roadway. The air base's main gates, on the northern and western fences, would be their primary objective. When they left the broad field, a company of parachutists, 140 of the regiment's best men, split from the column. The smaller force raced away at top speed. They headed straight for their goal—the woods outside the sprawling base's eastern fence.

Ten miles to the southwest, the air base waited. The giant base looked upon open country on its northern and western fences. The southern and eastern perimeters were on the edge of a heavily forested area. The attack plan was simple. The regiment would send a parachute company into the eastern woods. Their purpose would be to provide a powerful diversion. On foot, the 140 would strike the eastern fence, hoping to fool the Americans into believing that the primary assault was coming from the east. As soon as the Americans reacted to the ploy, the main force would use their armored vehicles to smash through the northern and western sides of the base.

The bulk of the initial offensive, the feint at the eastern fence, would be directed at Arturo Rios and his small band.

So far, everything was working precisely as planned. Thirty minutes after first touching German soil, 140 of the world's finest soldiers slipped into the heavy woods on the eastern edge of the air base. They started threading their way through the thick blanket of evergreens. It wouldn't take long to reach their objective.

From the moment the regiment touched down, American scouts had observed their every action. They'd seen the smaller force entering the eastern woods. They'd watched the larger column heading straight for the open sides of the air base. American intelligence had been solid. The Ramstein base commander wasn't fooled by the Russians' plan. The force preparing to attack the eastern fence concerned him. He knew, however, that it was the main column he had to stop.

For the moment, the base commander's assets were quite limited. Almost all of his fighters were still involved in the air battle, had been shot down by MiGs, or had just returned to be rearmed and refueled. The timing of General Yovanovich's plan had counted on the Americans finding themselves in just such a predicament.

As the Russians neared, all the Ramstein commanding general had at his disposal were five A-10 Warthog ground-attack fighters and six rescue helicopters. He ordered the A-10s and the helicopters to take to the sky and attack the invader's main column.

There was no time to lose. The determined parachute regiment was five miles from the air base and closing fast. If not stopped, they'd hit both gates in ten minutes. The A-10s roared down the runway toward Rios's bunker. They leaped from the ground and headed north to intercept the enemy regiment.

The stubby Warthogs churned through the low skies in search of the lengthy column. With the parachutists so close, it took no time at all for the American pilots to locate the target. In the snowy meadows northeast of the base, there were Russian vehicles everywhere they looked. The open ground of the killing field was in front of them. The Americans dove headlong toward the surging regiment. Their aircrafts' seven-barrel cannons blazed. The first of the Russian armored vehicles burst into flames. A second quickly followed. Fire and smoke billowed forth, choking the pristine skies.

The battle for Ramstein had begun.

At the precise moment the A-10s slammed into the leading edge of the main column, the parachutist company in the woods initiated an all-out assault on the eastern fence. A desperate struggle erupted on all sides. Hand grenades, mortars, and automatic gunfire ripped into the Americans. Fierce soldiers with powder-blue berets in their pockets rushed toward the fence.

"Here they come!" Rios screamed. He squeezed the trigger on his machine gun, firing round after round into the snow-covered trees on the far side of the wire.

His countrymen's M-4s soon joined in.

A second of the elite division's parachute regiments moved through the open country toward the smaller American fighter base. Fifty miles northwest of Ramstein, Spangdahlem and its three thousand airmen braced for the Russian attack.

A half dozen Warthogs, each armed and ready for battle, tore out of the air base to slow the hundreds of vehicles of the widespread Russian column. The A-10s, one of the greatest killers of armor in the world, ripped into the determined regiment. With the mighty cannons in their noses spewing certain death, and four five-hundred-pound bombs at their disposal, the A-10s charged straight for the oncoming parachutists. By the end of the tough little Warthogs' first pass, trails of thick smoke filled the skies over a broad area. The sounds of battle spread far and wide. The Russian light armor wilted beneath the intense air attack.

The Warthogs had been built specifically for a war in central Europe. Like the Apache helicopter, they'd been designed to hit and run. The slow fighter's greatest ally was the deep woods of the vast German forests. But the area around Spangdahlem was somewhat open country. There would be few places for the A-10s to hide. And the Russian parachute regiment was teeming with air-defense weapons.

The American attack had scarcely begun when the first of the Warthogs exploded, the victim of a shoulder-mounted air-defense missile. Its fiery remains fell to earth.

Still, the A-10 pilots were undeterred. The stodgy Warthogs struck again and again. Each time they dove straight for the Russian column. They dropped bomb after bomb. The grotesque aircrafts' lethal noses blazed with lightning bursts. Their magazines spewed forth death and destruction from the ugly planes at a rate of two thousand armor-piercing 30mm shells per minute. They ripped through the tops and sides of the thinly armored airborne vehicles. The American pilots clawed at the enemy with everything they had. Each knew that his wife and children were in the base's housing area.

This was no battle for God and country. It was going to be much more personal for the pilots and airmen of Spangdahlem. Their families' lives were on the line.

With each brief squeeze of their cannon's trigger, two, sometimes three or more, Russian armored vehicles died at the hands of the Americans. With each passing A-10, ten . . . fifteen . . . twenty Russian soldiers were killed. With each determined run, carnage ripped at the enemy column.

And with nearly every pass, another of the slow-moving A-10s pitifully tumbled from the skies beneath the Russians' fusillade of air-defense missiles and guns. Even so, the surviving A-10s fought on.

Neither side would give an inch. Ignoring the horror all around them, the tenacious parachutists kept coming. Relentlessly, the determined enemy column pressed on through the raging fires. Every second, they were growing nearer to their objective.

At Spangdahlem, the airmen watched the clouds of smoke filling the morning sky. The black plumes were getting closer. The sounds of battle were drawing near. With each new explosion, it was becoming more and more evident that the Russians would soon be at their doorstep.

Another pair of A-10s leaped into the sky. That was the last of them. The remainder of Spangdahlem's Warthogs were on missions at the front lines or not yet ready to return to combat. And as at Ramstein, the base's fighters were, for the moment, out of the war. Behind the A-10s, four Air Force helicopters with machine guns mounted in their doors rose into the blue. They were rescue helicopters, not intended to perform any combat mission beyond protecting themselves. But they were all the base commander had left.

The A-10s made pass after pass, wreaking havoc on the enemy column. The Russians responded with a lethal curtain of antiaircraft fire. By the score, the parachutists died. And one by one, the Warthogs dropped from the smoldering skies until there were no more. It was suicidal, but as the final A-10 fell, the helicopters bolted forward and attacked. With their machine guns blazing, they dove at the Russians.

The rescue helicopters were easy prey for the regiment's bristling air defenses. By the end of their first pass, the few identifiable pieces remaining from each of the defeated helicopters were smoldering in the snows. Every crew member was dead.

The Russians had suffered severe losses. That, however, wouldn't stop the parachute regiment.

There would be no feint at Spangdahlem.

The airborne soldiers' primary armored vehicles were their BMD-4s. The twelve-ton, extremely fierce BMDs were a cross between a small tank and an armored personnel carrier. Each carried a crew of three and five infantry soldiers. Each had an exceptionally impressive array of weapons, capable of inflicting severe harm on even main battle tanks. These nasty little scorpions carried an immense, highly deadly sting. Fifty of the regiment's BMDs had survived the A-10s' onslaught. With the BMDs in the lead, over 150 combat vehicles carrying twelve hundred men roared toward Spangdahlem's main gate.

The Russians rammed headlong into the air base. The Americans responded with everything they could lay their hands on. The air police had three dozen LAWs—light antitank weapons—and six armored cars armed with .50-caliber machine guns. The BMDs' armor, while stout in the front, was less than an inch thick on its rear and sides to allow for their transport and drop with the airborne forces. An airman with an M-4 rifle posed no threat to them, but the LAWs were more than a match for their opponent. And the heavy machine guns could easily rip right through a BMD's thin side armor.

As the first BMD raced through the air base's main gate, an air policeman raised a LAW to his shoulder and fired. The BMD erupted in flames. For a moment, the blazing armored vehicle blocked the attackers' entrance onto Spangdahlem. At full speed, another BMD raced up behind its burning brother. The second BMD slammed into the destroyed vehicle. It slowly shoved it through the front gate. Others dashed into the opening the BMD had created. The Americans fired their armor-killing weapons and fell back. Using their 100mm main gun, Bastion missiles, 30mm autocannon, and machine guns, the BMDs burst through the overmatched defenders. They attacked in every direction. The slaughter had commenced. Twelve hundred expert killers were far too many for the base's inexperienced defenders to handle. The LAWs and armored cars had slowed the initial advance. Yet within minutes, Russian vehicles were roaming the flight line. They raced onto the runways and headed for their objectives.

For each Russian soldier lost, five airmen went down. The Americans fell back once more. With satchel charges in hand, the airborne soldiers raced into the hangars and fortified bunkers. The A-10s, F-22s, F-35s, and F-16s burst into flames. Tremendous explosions filled the morning as countless numbers of America's fighter aircraft died on the snowy ground at Spangdahlem. The vicious fight for control of the air base went on unabated. Hand-to-hand combat raged from building to building and from room to room.

In the middle of the desperate battle, a 100mm shell soared into the base's massive ammunition dump. The explosion of thousands of missiles, rockets, and bombs was as powerful as that of a small nuclear device. It leveled everything in its path for two miles in all directions. A surging fireball rose thirty thousand feet into the air. Two-thirds of the base collapsed beneath its crushing shock wave. On both sides, hundreds died from the detonating armament's all-consuming blow. The explosion could be heard seventy-five miles away.

An hour into the battle, it was clear to the American base commander that all was lost. He issued the only order he could. Everyone was to retreat to protect the six thousand women and children trapped in the housing area. Two gates to the south remained in American hands. They had to get the dependents out while there was still time.

The airmen fought with everything they had to defend their families. Car after car filled with terrified dependents rushed out of Spangdahlem. They raced down an icy, winding road toward the safety of the Army installation at Kaiserslautern, forty miles to the southeast. Children watched in horror as their fathers died trying to protect them. Thirty-one women and nineteen children were killed during the attack. More than two hundred were wounded. Four thousand fleeing women and children would evade capture. Two thousand more were trapped when the final routes to freedom were overrun by the parachutists.

Fifteen hundred American corpses lay in the stained snows at Spangdahlem. A handful of airmen had escaped. The rest of the base defenders found themselves prisoners of war, two hundred miles inside their own lines.

One-fourth of Spangdahlem's fighters had been downed during the Russian air attack. Half had been destroyed by the paratroopers. The final one-quarter were presently involved in the air battle or were away supporting the intensifying combat at the front lines. Those still in the air would never return to Spangdahlem. Instead, they would fly across the Channel to land at Lakenheath.

With vengeance in their hearts and revenge in their souls, they'd carry on the struggle for Germany from England.

Spangdahlem was no more.

In their Humvees and trucks, a battalion from the recently arriving 82nd Airborne Division was rushing toward the air base. But with frantic Germans clogging every roadway, they'd be too late to save Spangdahlem. By the time they arrived, not a building would stand or an aircraft survive.

The shooting of the defeated base defenders would soon begin.

Forty yards away, a parachutist stepped from behind a broad tree. He hurled a hand grenade over the high fence. The grenade fell nine feet short of the large bunker. Rios fired upon the figure that had thrown the grenade. The machine gun's .50-caliber shells waltzed across the Russian's chest. They tore huge holes in his upper body. The mortally wounded Russian tumbled into the tangled branches.

"Get down!" Rios screamed.

The seven Americans clawed at the frozen ground. The hand grenade exploded. Sharp-edged metal flew in all directions. Inside their sandbagged worlds, the airmen could hear death whizzing by. Lethal pieces of the grenade smashed into the sandbags and burrowed for the cowering airmen. The layers of sand overwhelmed the deadly metal. Safe in their brown world, not a scratch found its way onto any of the airmen.

Four additional A-10s were ready to enter the battle. They screamed down the runway. The Warthogs rushed to meet the enemy in the open country three miles north of Ramstein.

The Russians on the eastern fence threw everything they had at the small group of defenders. They pressed their advantage. The widespread line of Americans struggled to hold on. There would be no further help for the airmen fighting at the distant fence. The base commander had no choice.

The general could do nothing further to protect the eastern edge of the base. He would hold his reserves and wait for the major assault soon to commence at the base's main gates. And he'd pray that, somehow, the desperate defenders on the eastern perimeter wouldn't fail.

"Let 'em have it!" Rios screamed.

He struggled to his knees and flailed away at the tree line once more. His machine gun's deep tones were joined by the staccato sounds of the M-4s. They fought to hold on against the superior Russians. All up and down the sprawling eastern fence, the parachutists fired their automatic weapons. Their primary goal was the elimination of the main bunkers along the lengthy defensive line armed with the powerful machine guns. The Americans futilely attempted to match the enemy's firepower.

Sixty Americans on the open ground, with a few sandbags to protect them, fought 140 proficient killers protected by the sheltering woods. Over the raucous songs of the guns, anguished screams could be heard all along the expanse as defenders and attackers alike succumbed to the withering fire.

Fifty yards to Rios's right, Michaels took a bullet to the face. The bullet's entry hole was no bigger than a dime. The exit hole in the back of his head was the size of the airman's fist.

On Rios's team there were now only six.

CHAPTER 31

R hein-Main had been one of the last major assets returned to the Germans during the American phasedown. And it had been one of the first given back to the Americans as they slowly initiated the process of rebuilding their forces in Europe. The air base had been back in American hands for a little over eighteen months and was finally reaching full operational status.

At the immense transport air base, the Americans were struggling to hold on against the fiercely determined Russian onslaught. The Rhein-Main base commander had no attack aircraft he could call upon to protect his installation. But because his base was enclosed in a thick forest, he did have a tactical advantage. The forest forced the Russians to focus the bulk of their attack at a few central locations. The main thrust had come at a small rear gate hidden in a thick mantle of snow-covered green. Deep within the woods, the Americans clung to the rusting gate with every ounce of courage they could muster. For fifteen minutes, a handful of air police armed with LAWs and three heavy machine guns held the narrow gate against an attacking force of two hundred armored vehicles.

At the main gate, the Americans had succeeded for the moment in beating back a smaller attack.

With the trees to conceal them, the regimental commander sent the rest of his parachutists out on foot to probe at the fences for weak spots.

There were many.

On the southern and western fences, the Russians crushed token resistance. After blasting gaping holes in both, they exploited them to the fullest. Three hundred parachutists scurried through the southern fence and pressed on toward the flight line. One hundred broke through the western wire.

At the back gate, the air police crumpled. One hundred and eighty soldiers of the 82nd Airborne Division had arrived on a commercial airliner fifteen minutes prior to the attack. Armed with only the M-4s they'd carried with them on the plane, they rushed to the rear gate.

Sixty-five of the seventy-three men and women of Delta Battery, 1st "Cobra Strike" Air Defense Artillery Battalion, hurried to back up the 82nd Airborne.

Having finished taking on a load of women and children, two commercial airliners taxied onto the runway. Without waiting for clearance, they roared down the asphalt and soared into the skies. Both pilots reported there were enemy soldiers everywhere they looked on the ground below. On the tarmac, a third airliner was being refueled. Its passenger manifest of over two hundred were running from the overflowing terminal. They rushed to board the waiting plane.

In the terminal building, thousands more were in near panic as the sounds of battle raged around them. Six air policemen burst through the doorway. They tossed M-4s to the four airmen working inside the terminal.

"Down! Everybody down!" an air policeman yelled. The air police raced back outside to take up defensive positions.

On the wide tarmac, a parachutist brought his missile up to his shoulder. He fired at a refueling C-17 cargo plane. The C-17 burst into flames. The fuel truck sitting next to the plane was soon consumed by the growing inferno. The thunder of the exploding truck could be heard for miles around. Flames spread across the far end of the tarmac. Black, noxious smoke covered a broad area. A second Russian took aim and fired at the huge C-5 next in line. The giant plane erupted. The roaring tarmac fires were soon out of control.

In the base housing area, a vile street fight sprang up. With women and children cowering in their homes, parachutists and airmen battled from house to house. But the Americans were no match for the enemy's superior numbers and fighting ability. They fell back, taking as many of the dependents with them as they could.

Things had grown critical on the flight line. Now in command of the entire area, the Russians methodically destroyed the eight airplanes they found sitting on the ground. The last to fall was the commercial airliner. With a shoulder-mounted missile, a parachutist blew the refueling aircraft apart. On board, every one of the women and children were killed.

Near the rear gate, the lightly armed soldiers of the 82nd Airborne Division fought with incredible bravery. They clawed at the Russians with everything they had, clinging to their defensive positions under ever-increasing pressure from their merciless opponent. They knew they had no chance against the power of the overwhelming enemy.

The BMDs broke through the beaten burgundy berets. They rushed down the tree-shrouded road. The three Stinger teams of the Patriot battery stood in the middle of the roadway. As one, the Stinger gunners fired at the oncoming BMDs. The air-defense missiles were as devastating against the armored vehicles as they would have been against a MiG. A wall of flames rose at the front of the Russian column.

The blow from the Stingers didn't even slow the parachutists down. They slammed their combat vehicles into the burning barrier and shoved their dying comrades into the woods. The Stinger teams hurriedly prepared to fire a second missile.

Three miles north of Rhein-Main, the commander of the German provisional guard battalion protecting Frankfurt International Airport watched the thickening clouds of smoke rising in the morning sky. He heard one tumultuous explosion after another from the American air base. The German leader listened to the sounds of the nearby battle. He braced his National Guard unit for an assault against Frankfurt Airport. After forty-five minutes, with no attack on his position and no enemy in sight, the German commander gambled. He ordered half his force, two companies of his armored unit, to move south to reinforce the Americans at Rhein-Main.

It was a decision that could potentially change the course of the battle. The Americans were falling back in every corner of the base. They faced certain defeat. But sixteen immensely powerful Leopard 2 tanks, supported by a company of mechanized infantry, were on their way. In fifteen minutes, they'd arrive at Rhein-Main's main gate.

Thirty parachutists moved toward the passenger terminal. The six air policemen defending the terminal building opened fire. The first volley from the airmen dropped a third of the enemy. Even so, the Russians came on.

The parachutists fired their automatic weapons at the air police guarding the terminal. Struck repeatedly by rifle fire, every plate-glass window on the south side of the building erupted at nearly the same instant. Shards of jagged glass leaped from the exploding windows. They tore into the frightened masses huddled together on the terminal floor. The screams of a thousand terrified voices filled the crowded building.

Eight adults and four children lay dying from the razor-sharp storm that poured down upon their heads. The blood of fifty others fell upon the cold tile.

One by one, the Russians eliminated the air policemen protecting the building. As the last American outside fell, two parachutists raced toward the terminal. Each carried a fragmentation grenade in a sweating palm. They burst through the terminal door.

It happened in slow motion. Yet it happened in the blink of an eye. The first pulled the pin on his grenade. He lobbed it into the middle of the room. The second hesitated. He realized in an instant what the pair had stumbled upon. He refused to follow his countryman's lead and attack the defenseless throng. The grenade remained in his hand. The parachutists turned and ran back toward the door. Shooting over the heads of the women and children, the airmen inside the terminal opened fire on the fleeing figures. Bullets ripped into the pair. The Russians slammed into the shattering glass door and were impaled upon its broken pieces.

The live grenade lay on the floor a dozen feet from where, ten hours earlier, Linda Jensen and her daughters had sat waiting for their names to reach the top of the manifest.

The closest airman was thirty feet from the grenade. He threw his rifle down. The airman hurdled the frightened masses blocking his path. He lunged toward the grenade. He had to get to it before it was too late.

He nearly made it.

As he reached out his hand to grasp the waiting time bomb, its five-second fuse expired. The resulting explosion sliced the airman into a thousand pieces. Deadly steel fragments ripped through the building. For thirty yards in every direction, the angel of death came to call.

Near the back gate, the final surviving Stinger team fired a third missile. Another BMD erupted beneath a missile's lethal nose. And for the third time, the Russians came on. The soldiers of the Patriot battery tried to rally once more. It was, however, no use. There was nothing they could do to stop the irrepressible Russian tidal wave that washed over them. When it was over, only fourteen of the American air defenders would still be alive.

The breakthrough at the rear gate was complete. The parachutists' vehicles roared through the trees toward their objectives. The time had come to finish the destruction of Rhein-Main and put an end to the uneven struggle. With their victory at the rear gate, the Russian commander was convinced nothing could stop his regiment from the successful completion of its mission. The total destruction of the American air base was minutes away.

The German tanks sped through the main gate. The armored personnel carriers of the German infantry were close behind. The Leopards burst onto the runway.

The Russian column broke free from the woods. Sixteen German main battle tanks were waiting. Undaunted, the parachutists charged straight for their ancient enemy.

Shell after shell ripped into the Russian vehicles. Still, the parachutists continued their maniacal rush from the forest. A meager response with a few Bastion missiles and their 100mm main guns was all they could muster against the German tanks' overwhelming power. With glee, the Leopards slaughtered hundreds of the cocksure invaders of their homeland.

In their armored personnel carriers, the German infantry started hunting down the remaining parachutists. The surviving Americans soon joined in. A rout was under way. But this time it was the parachutists who'd come up short. The Russians fell back. Finally willing to accept defeat, two hundred parachutists melted into the deep woods on the southern and western ends of the base. Fifteen hundred of their comrades hadn't been so lucky.

The cost in American lives had been tremendous. But bloodied and battered, Rhein-Main still stood.

Thirty yards to Rios's left, four parachutists rushed the chain link. They knelt at the base of the fence and furiously cut at the wire.

"Get them!" Rios screamed.

Wheatley and Velasquez signaled their understanding. Velasquez provided covering fire. Wheatley rolled onto his side, pulled the pin on a grenade, and leaped to his feet. He hurled the deadly grenade. It sailed over the fence and rolled to a stop a few feet from the Russians. In a blinding flash, the parachutists were torn apart.

Wheatley lay on his back in a pool of scarlet snow. He'd never know of the success of his efforts. The firing of a dozen rifles had cut the exposed airman down moments after he threw the grenade.

Then there were five.

North of Ramstein, the A-10s ripped into the Russian light armor with all the fury of the deepest pits of hell. With their cannons blazing, they made pass after pass. The Americans cut the attackers down to size. Death-filled plumes reached into the endless heavens.

And one after another, Russian air-defense weapons knocked the determined Warthogs from the sky. Neither side would concede an inch in the life-and-death struggle unfolding a few miles from the critical American air base. Second by second, the unspeakable angst grew.

Eleven minutes after the A-10s pounced, one hundred Russian vehicles lay burning outside Ramstein. Four hundred paratroopers were dead. And the twisted wreckage of every A-10 was smoldering in the snows. Six rescue helicopters attempted to follow up on the Warthogs' successes. Yet just as at Spangdahlem, they were brushed from the sky without a second thought.

One hundred and fifty combat vehicles moved toward their objective.

To Rios's right, two primary bunkers were wiped out at nearly the same instant. A pair of .50-caliber machine guns were gone. Two hundred yards of chain link was wide open. The Russians rushed forward. They broke through the wire in front of the defeated positions. Thirty parachutists were quickly inside. They fanned out, determined to crush the final pockets of resistance on the eastern fence.

Mortar shells rained down upon the remaining Americans. Wide craters pockmarked the eastern end of the runway. Velasquez never heard the round that landed inside his bunker.

Now there were just four.

CHAPTER 32

January 29—9:05 a.m.
102nd Parachute Regiment
The Rhine River Valley

The Rhine River valley is some of the most beautiful country on the planet. Covered in a black forest of evergreens thicker than found anywhere in America, deep mountain gorges cut by the proud river run for hundreds of miles as the lazy waters meander from Switzerland to the Atlantic Ocean. In the south, the river separates France and Germany. In the north, it runs through Germany's largest cities on its scenic journey to the sea.

The six thousand four hundred men of the 102nd Parachute Division weren't nearly enough to take and hold the bridges in the heavily populated areas to the north. They weren't even going to try. They had a single task: cut the broad bridges in the south, separating France and Germany. In all, there were twenty bridges between the two countries. Six major expanses were absolutely critical to the parachutists' plan.

They would do whatever was necessary to seize the six bridges. Once they were within their grasp, at the first sign of trouble, all six would be destroyed. The division would also take and hold as many of the smaller bridges as they could. Those they couldn't ensnare would be damaged to the point where they'd be of no further use to the enemy.

The Russians anticipated stiff resistance from the Germans on the eastern side of the spans and from the French on the western ends. But in the first confusing hours of the war, even the most valuable of the bridges was being guarded by a handful of lightly armed German provisional guards.

The parachutists swooped down into the Rhine valley like the Mongol hordes. Six hundred attacked each of the major bridges, overwhelming the outmanned guards. In minutes, the Russians eliminated the German defenders. They controlled the eastern approaches to each of the major spans. The parachutists started working their way across the wide bridges. They had no idea what they'd find waiting for them on the French side. Cautiously, the Russians moved forward.

Leapfrogging from position to position, the blue berets neared the far ends.

The western sides had been abandoned. The three customs agents at each border checkpoint had fled at the first sound of gunfire. The Russians started preparing fortified positions on both ends. Demolition teams rushed to ready each for destruction at the first sign of trouble.

Groups of two hundred attacked the fourteen smaller spans. Within a half hour, twelve were in Russian hands. The final two had been destroyed.

Ninety minutes after their arrival on German soil, the parachutists held the southern half of the Rhine River. The fortification of their positions was rapidly undertaken. One way or another, the French would never be allowed to set foot on any of the bridges. And the Germans would never be allowed to take any of them back.

After little more than ten hours of war, a direct attack east by the French army was an impossibility.

Five powerful French armored divisions would arrive at the great river as the sun soared high on the war's first full day. Rather than attacking the Russians holding the spans or heading north to cross into Germany in areas still in Allied hands, the French also began digging in, creating immense defensive positions on the western side of the Rhine. It was quite apparent that the French had little taste for the monumental fight unfolding to the east. Defending Germany, especially a Nazi Germany, wasn't something over which they truly cared to spend even a single drop of their young men's blood.

Despite the fervent pleas and unrelenting political pressure applied by the British and Americans, they would never join in the fight.

A parachutist grimaced in anguish as a trio of machine-gun bullets ripped into his upper body. Rios's eighth kill of the morning fell into the snows.

The number of invaders inside the fence was continuing to swell. Half of the sixty airmen assigned to protect the eastern perimeter were dead. In the center of the fence line, a single American machine gun remained. A score of parachutists concentrated their fire on Rios's position, pinning the Americans down. The blue berets worked their way across the runways, intent on surrounding the last real opposition.

"Rios, they're getting around behind us!" Goodman yelled.

"Keep firing into the woods. I'll do what I can to stop the ones inside the fence."

Rios grabbed the heavy machine gun. Cradling the weapon's smoking barrel in his arms, he picked it up and swung it around so he could fire upon the enemy advancing on the right. The red-hot barrel burned through Rios's clothing. The nerves on his forearms screamed as his skin began to fry. He slammed the gun down in its new position.

BMDs rammed through Ramstein's northern and western gates at the same instant. The air police focused everything they had on stopping the enemy before they could gain access to the base.

LAW missiles ripped through the air. Machine-gun fire tore into the parachutists. A chorus of explosions filled the morning. And as at Spangdahlem, the American defenses weren't nearly enough. The Russians never hesitated. They continued to apply wave after wave of intense pressure on the air police.

Within eight horrific minutes, the resistance at both gates had crumpled. The parachutists poured onto Ramstein.

A grenade landed at Wright's feet as he fought on alone in the sandbags to Rios's right.

Then there were only three.

At the same moment that their countrymen moved to destroy the NATO air bases, a few miles outside Kaiserslautern another parachute regiment advanced on the last of America's critical assets.

Two divisions of armored equipment sat in endless rows inside a giant supply depot. More than five hundred M-1 tanks and an equal number of Bradley Fighting Vehicles waited to be claimed by American units arriving from the States. There were a thousand Humvees armed with machine guns or TOW missiles and endless formations of trucks. One hundred and forty-four Apache helicopters sat in the snows, along with twice as many Black Hawks and Kiowas. Artillery pieces and air-defense weapons also were positioned in lengthy lines, poised for the Americans to come and take them. Each piece of equipment had been superbly maintained. Each was armed and battle-ready.

A company of military police, a little less than two hundred men, guarded the depot. As the confident parachute regiment poured down from the early-morning sky, that was all they expected to encounter. Intelligence had confirmed those facts five hours earlier. What the regiment had no way of knowing was that minutes after their departure from the Ukraine, a battalion of soldiers from the 82nd Airborne Division, accompanied by two companies from the 24th Infantry Division, had arrived at the depot to outfit themselves for battle. The Americans, having endured an eight-hour flight across the Atlantic and an additional three to make their way the sixty miles from Rhein-Main to Kaiserslautern, were in an extremely foul state of mind and more than ready to take it out on anything that crossed their path.

Seventeen hundred marauders were advancing on the pre-positioned supplies. They believed they'd find a small, determined force of MPs fighting with nothing larger than Humvees. What they were going to encounter, however, were two hundred MPs, eleven hundred American airborne soldiers armed with TOW missiles and machine guns, along with nearly four hundred soldiers from the 24th Infantry in the Bradley Fighting Vehicles they'd drawn from the depot.

Seventeen hundred were going to meet seventeen hundred in a battle that was absolutely critical to America's fading hopes.

Just outside the depot, the 24th Infantry hid forty Bradleys in the thick trees. They waited for the Russian regiment. Three times that number of 82nd Airborne Humvees were in support.

The parachutists roared toward their objective. Unaware of the overpowering force hidden at the supply depot, the regimental commander implemented his battle plan. He sent six hundred of his parachutists into the deep woods surrounding the target. On foot, the Russians stealthily moved through the heavy mantle of trees, intent on encircling the depot.

Given thirty minutes' warning of the parachutists' attack, the American battalion commander had anticipated such a move. The Russian action had already been countered. When the parachutists entered the forest, hundreds of American airborne soldiers lay in the shadows waiting for them.

The Russian regimental commander was a fearless man of legendary exploits in Cheninko's recent wars for Eastern European liberation. Once his soldiers in the woods engaged the thin defensive force of MPs, he'd make a frontal charge down the main road entering the depot. He was convinced his regiment would annihilate the MP company in a matter of minutes. He'd then set about the task of destroying the American equipment. Two hours from now, there wouldn't be a single combat vehicle standing in the depot.

Inside the woods, the parachutists edged forward. From all four sides at once, they'd hit the MPs. They'd tighten the noose around the Americans' necks and wait for the main column to smash through the defenders. It wouldn't be much longer until the besieged MPs would all be dead.

Deep within the forest, the Russians crept silently through the misty shadows. Their attack would commence as soon as they made contact with the MP company's scattered sentries.

The 82nd Airborne Division's soldiers were waiting.

The element of surprise was with the Americans. The burgundy berets hid in the twilight. They watched their opponent moving cautiously through the trees. Step by step, second by second, the Russians drew closer to the trap.

A burst of gunfire chattered in the forest. It was followed by another, and shortly thereafter by a third. With incredible intensity, the battle exploded in every corner of the snowy woods. The Americans caught their counterparts unprepared for the fierce attack that enveloped them. With rifles, grenades, knives, and fists, the two sides fought to the death in the forest's darkness.

In the woods, it was going to be no contest. The Russians had been taken by surprise, and they'd pay dearly for their mistake.

The regimental commander thought the gunfire in the trees signaled the beginning of his men's attack on the MPs. He ordered the long column forward. They charged down the winding road toward the depot. The decoys, four MP Humvees, sat on the roadway just ahead of the final curve. Each Humvee carried a single TOW missile. The Russians spotted the MP vehicles. In his command BMD, the regimental commander smiled a broad smile. The force waiting to challenge his regiment was exactly what he'd anticipated. At breakneck speed, they roared toward the MPs. Each American fired his TOW, destroying the leading edge of the onrushing column.

The parachutists barely slowed down. As they'd practiced over and again, the Russian vehicles shoved their burning comrades out of the way and continued on.

The Humvees disappeared into the woods on both sides of the road. The regimental commander smiled a second time. This was going to be even easier than he'd believed. The parachutists raced toward the depot.

It would soon be over. The American armored equipment would be destroyed and Russia's victory in the war assured. Around the next curve lay their prize. The column rounded the final turn.

Twenty Bradleys were waiting to greet them. Another twenty rushed in behind the parachutists. The 82nd Airborne's Humvees edged forward on both sides to complete the encirclement.

Ambush.

The trap had been sprung.

Untold numbers of TOW missiles ripped through the air from the Bradleys and Humvees. Bushmaster cannons laid down a deadly curtain of fire so thick that nothing on earth could withstand it. It was a supremely powerful blow. Half the Russian column disappeared in the first thirty seconds. The regimental commander lived just long enough to realize that his miscalculations were going to cost the lives of the brave men under his command.

The Bradleys moved in for the kill. The staggered Russians regrouped and fought back. Given the overwhelming force they faced and their ever-mounting losses, they knew they had little chance, but that was of no importance.

The BMDs were one-half the Bradleys' size. On their sides and tops they had one-seventh the Bradleys' armor. Even so, the BMDs were certainly not defenseless. Those that survived the initial onslaught quickly responded with Bastion antiarmor missiles and 100mm shells. The Bastions, one of the most powerful tank-killing weapons in the world, took a toll on the Americans, destroying a number of Bradleys and their crews. Their 100mm main cannon shells, however, were less effective in addressing the dire threat that imperiled the entire column. Most of the powerful Russian shells damaged the Bradleys' heavy frontal armor but failed to penetrate it, allowing the Bradleys to fight on.

Time after time, a BMD would get a clear shot with its cannon only to have the shell explode against the Bradley's hull without piercing the protection of its laminated, reactive armor plating. The Bradley crew would then quickly dispense with the BMD.

At Spangdahlem, the slaughter was under way. But at Kaiserslautern, it was the Americans who mercilessly butchered their opponent.

It was over in ten minutes.

With untold scores of vehicles burning on the roadway, the deputy regimental commander called for a full retreat. There was nothing else he could do.

The Americans pursued the remnants of the retreating parachute regiment across the German countryside. The burgundy berets would chase them all the way back to Russia, or follow them into hell, if that was what it would take to finish the job. Leaving the MPs behind, the Americans hunted down the scattered survivors.

When it was over, and the losses on each side had been totaled, the American victory was overwhelming. Fifty-three Americans were dead. Another eighty-seven were wounded. Seven Bradleys had been destroyed. Twenty-three Humvees had succumbed. Over sixteen hundred of Russia's finest soldiers had perished. The final few dozen were deep within enemy territory as they fought to save their lives. In the coming days, nearly all would be tracked down and killed by German territorial units or captured by angry mobs of German civilians.

The parachutists didn't fare well at the hands of the mob. A few were literally torn apart. Others were shot or hanged in ancient town squares. Their bodies were left to rot or thrown to the vermin. Only a handful lived to tell the tale of what had happened on a sunny morning outside of Kaiserslautern.

Of the hundreds of combat vehicles the Russians had come to destroy, one tank and a self-propelled howitzer were lost. A second M-1, and an Avenger air-defense missile system, had been damaged.

For now, the further arriving American reinforcements of the 82nd Airborne and the 24th Infantry Divisions would find the equipment they needed waiting outside of Kaiserslautern.

Despite their setbacks, even on the first morning of the war, one thing was clear to the American leadership. If they could hold on for fourteen days, enough reinforcements would arrive to turn the tide of battle. In all likelihood, if they were still bleeding and dying in the fields of Germany two weeks from now, America would win this war.

But the generals knew that would only be true if the Americans controlled the skies. And they couldn't do so unless Ramstein still stood.

CHAPTER 33

A pair of missiles ripped into the main aircraft maintenance hangar. The six fighter aircraft inside the huge building were engulfed in a roaring inferno. Thirty airmen were trapped by the fierce explosions. The all-encompassing fires soon consumed them. Two more death-tinged clouds reached into the restless skies over Ramstein. Thick trails of virulent smoke masked the battle, frustrating attacker and defender alike.

On the eastern fence, Rios's machine gun sang out against the advancing Russians. Forty parachutists were inside the wire. They were desperately trying to cover the ground necessary to wipe out the Americans' last heavy gun. Rios caught them in the open.

Five invaders fell in rapid succession from the mayhem spewing forth from the machine gun's barrel. In an hour of battle, twenty Russians had died at Rios's hands.

In front of his bunker, the rifle fire suddenly increased fourfold. Wilson and Goodman were pinned down. The airmen buried themselves in the protective sand. At a trio of locations, four parachutists rushed forward and hacked at the fence. Afraid of hitting their comrades, the parachutists' gunfire from the woods momentarily slackened. Goodman risked a quick look at the fence line.

"We're in trouble here, Rios!"

Rios continued to fire his machine gun at the large group of Russians advancing on the right. "We're in trouble over here, too."

"They've got us pinned down. They're about to break through the fence. We can't hold them any longer."

"Stay down," Rios said. "But throw every grenade we've got at the ones at the fence."

Wilson and Goodman grabbed the last three grenades. They pulled the pins and, without exposing themselves to the enemy's rifles, tossed each in the direction their mind's eye said they would find the parachutists. In rapid succession, three explosions rocked the wire.

Goodman took a second quick peek. On the other side of the fence, the tattered remains of a dozen misshapen bodies were strewn about on the cold ground. "Jesus, we got them all."

On the western end of the base, the Russians broke free. They rushed onto the flight line and runways. The Americans fell back on all sides. A second building burst into flames. Others soon followed. Wave after wave of black smoke rose once again. The parachutists tore through the small groups of defenders around three reinforced bunkers where fighter aircraft were stored. The aircraft inside the bunkers were quickly destroyed.

Another Spangdahlem was taking shape.

Unchecked, hundreds of determined parachutists moved forward. On foot or in combat vehicles, the confident blue berets surged forth. The Ramstein commander was nearly out of options.

He'd little left with which to stop the merciless Russians from eliminating his air base.

Many of the aircraft out of Lakenheath had arrived too late to take part in the battle for control of the skies. As most of the MiGs disappeared back into Eastern Europe, the frustrated Americans circled over Germany itching for a fight. The last thing the recently arriving F-16 pilots would've ever imagined was attacking one of their own air bases.

That, however, was exactly what they were about to do.

The Ramstein commander, certain of impending defeat, watched as his forces failed to stave off the Russians. He'd reached the point of conceding and ordering a retreat to protect the housing area when word came from the control tower that twelve Lakenheath F-16s had been attracted by the growing pillars of smoke. The F-16s were overhead. The pilots thought the damage below had been caused by an enemy air attack. They were asking for any targeting information the control tower could provide.

The base commander seized the unexpected opportunity.

"Send word for everyone to get away from the runways and flight line," the general said. "Give them five minutes, then order the F-16s to attack anything they find in the open. Tell them to use everything they've got. Hold back nothing. We can fix holes in the runways, but we can't do anything if Ramstein's destroyed."

The word went out. The base's airmen scrambled to find deep holes in which to crawl. The triumphant parachutists came forward to finish off an opponent who appeared to be in complete retreat. The regiment's combat vehicles roared triumphantly onto the runways. Wherever the base commander looked, he saw BMDs and Russian soldiers.

There were gaping holes all up and down the eastern fence. The Russians were pouring through.

On the distant fence line, there was no way to warn the handful of Americans who remained in the fight about the impending attack.

"Give me another ammunition container!" Rios shouted over the gunfire.

Goodman looked down at his feet. Three empty .50-caliber containers lay at the bottom of the bunker. Goodman kicked the containers aside, searching for ammunition.

"There isn't any more!"

"Oh shit!" Wilson yelled. "Here they come from the left."

Two dozen parachutists had breached the wire and were running toward the bunker.

Rios stopped firing. He checked his final ammunition container. He had ten rounds left. Goodman's ammunition clip ran out. He reached into his parka pocket for another. His pocket was empty. Wilson inserted his last ammunition clip and fired at the force hurrying toward them on the left.

"What're we going to do? I'm out of ammunition," Goodman said.

"What about grenades?"

"All gone!"

Rios had no answers. He aimed his machine gun at the parachutists on the right. In three short bursts, he fired his last ten rounds. Four Russians fell.

The group on the left neared the bunker. On the right, the enemy Rios had decimated was fifty yards away. Wilson fired the final rounds from his ammunition clip. Two more Russians, covered in blood, dropped to their knees in the heavy snows.

The Americans' ammunition was gone. There was nothing more the trio could do. The airmen stared death in the face and braced for the end.

Wingtip to wingtip, the F-16s roared over the trees. The instant they hit the fence, they opened fire with their 20mm cannons. At the end of the runway, Rios, Goodman, and Wilson frantically dove for cover. Powerfully striking shells smashed into the frozen ground all around them. The fighters passed so near that Rios could feel the intense heat from their engines.

Round after round rushed toward the exposed parachutists. Caught in the open, the Russians went down. The 20mm shells tore huge holes in the blue berets' bodies. One at a time, or in large, tangled clumps, the attackers succumbed. Their guns blazing, the F-16s ripped across the base at incredible speed. On their first pass, forty Russian vehicles were torn apart. Two hundred parachutists died. Twice that number were severely wounded.

When the F-16s reached the western fence, they circled for another run. The Russians raced in every direction to escape the growing slaughter. Those caught on the vast open runways had no chance. Those on the flight line ran for the protection of the beckoning buildings. Inside the hangars and offices, airmen waited with their rifles at the ready and their fingers on the triggers. They knew the vaunted enemy would soon arrive.

The few parachutists who reached the sheltering structures didn't fare well. Each was torn to shreds in a hail of gunfire.

While the F-16s prepared for their second run, Rios cautiously poked his head out of the bunker. On both sides of the sand, vast numbers of parachutists lay dead or dying. Not one of the attackers had been spared.

A handful of Russians were still in the woods. They took off running, desperately searching for deep cover.

The F-16s started their second pass. This time they'd come in high to allow for the use of their bombs. All over the base, in vehicles or on foot, the remaining Russians scattered in every direction. A handful of shoulder-mounted air-defense weapons appeared. While they raced back toward Ramstein, three F-16 radars told their pilots they'd been targeted. The trio pulled out of line. Two of the three would deftly avoid the air-defense missiles. The third wasn't so lucky. He'd fall from the skies in a ball of flames and smash into the heavy woods on the southern end of the base.

The remaining F-16s came on. Wherever they found a cluster of vehicles, a bomb fell with devastating accuracy. Close to two hundred vehicles had rammed through the gate an hour earlier. There were now sixty. And their numbers were quickly dwindling. The F-16s made run after run. The final blow came when two A-10s appeared over the eastern trees after missions at the front lines. Any fleeting hope the Russians had of somehow snatching victory from their impending defeat disappeared with the Warthogs' entrance into the one-sided affair. There was sufficient ammunition remaining in both planes' noses to mop up what was left of the vanquished Russians. Along with the F-16s, they wiped the parachute regiment from the face of the earth.

When it was over, not a single Russian vehicle had made it through the holocaust. Eleven F-16s would arrive home in Lakenheath in time for lunch. The A-10s landed to a heroes' welcome. But the most gratifying welcome for the Warthog pilots occurred an hour later, when they arrived home to find their families safe.

All of the base's dependents had survived without a scratch.

The maintenance crews set about repairing the runways. The bomb craters would soon be filled and patched. The runways would be ready for use before the sun set.

Airmen went to work removing the destroyed Russian vehicles. Others started collecting the dead and wounded from both sides. A thousand airmen had perished. Only a few handfuls of the proud Russian parachute regiment's soldiers were still alive. The Americans had lost forty aircraft. A dozen buildings were aflame.

The air police combed the woods outside the eastern fence for the last of the enemy. When they completed the body count around Rios's bunker, the kills from .50-caliber machine-gun fire totaled thirty-three.

As a reward for their efforts, Rios and his two surviving partners were given four more .50-caliber ammunition containers, a dozen hand grenades, and a generous supply of M-4 ammunition clips.

Only Ramstein, Rhein-Main, and a single German fighter base in the far north had survived the Russian knife thrust into the Allies' hearts. Even with their severe losses, however, the Americans knew that with their superior planes and pilots, they could still lay claim to the German skies. If they could improve their ability to communicate with the British and American air bases in England and figure out a way to overcome the destruction of the AWACS' ground stations, they'd be back in the air war. The American air forces were crippled, but they weren't dead yet.

Not by a long shot.

When the smoke cleared on that January morning, the Americans were still holding on.

CHAPTER 34

January 29—12:07 p.m.
NCO Housing Area, United States European Command
    Headquarters
Patch Barracks, Stuttgart

After word came that George had arrived in England safely, Kathy took the time for a lengthy cry. With few tears left, she readied a suitcase for herself and Christopher. A diaper bag for the baby completed the task. The packing had been a relief. The activity temporarily took her mind off the absence of her husband.

Mrs. Williams came over from across the hall to sit with Kathy for a while. As an Army wife of twenty-four years, Clara Williams knew all about painful good-byes. There'd been a tour in Korea and multiple ones to Iraq and Afghanistan. Each separation had been as bad as the last, not knowing if she'd ever again see her husband.

After a short visit, Clara excused herself. She had three boys of her own to ready for the evacuation. And as much as she knew Kathy needed her, her own family's needs had to come first.

Alone once more, Kathy put the baby down for a nap. She wandered into the bedroom she'd shared with George. Kathy lowered the shades and lay down upon the bed at a few minutes past ten. In a short while, she lapsed into a fitful sleep.

By 11:00 a.m., it was painfully obvious to the Patriot regimental commander that they'd been had. The surviving batteries all reported that the enemy fighters knew right where to find them. The nine remaining batteries had to move and move soon or face certain annihilation. If there were going to be any Patriots left by the end of the day, they had to change locations.

The small door at the rear of the Engagement Control Station flew open. Shading their eyes, Fowler, Morgan, and Paul turned toward the offensive sunlight. The battery commander was standing in the doorway.

"Regiment wants us to shut it down and move right now," Captain Allen said. "They're convinced our position's been compromised. We need to roll out of here as quickly as we can."

"We'll start deactivating the system immediately, sir," Morgan said.

Forty minutes later, the air-defense battery rolled out of the parking lot. They headed for their next firing position—the eastern edge of Stuttgart International Airport. For the next hour and a half, there would be no Patriot to protect United States European Command Headquarters.

It couldn't be helped.

The moment the Patriot battery left, two gentlemen in a nondescript black car parked down the street rushed to their safe house. The message went out—"The target's undefended; undertake the attack now."

Ten minutes later, fifty MiGs, their strong wings and distended bellies loaded for a ground attack, rose from their base in the Czech Republic. The huge formation rushed west.

Another fifty fighters headed for a blocking position north of Stuttgart. The second group would protect their comrades from any attempt by American aircraft to break through and spoil the attack. With Spangdahlem destroyed and Ramstein's runways unusable, the Russians had little need to worry.

Kathy O'Neill awoke with a start. The baby's crying, her sleep-starved brain told her. But it wasn't the baby.

From the top of a building two hundred yards away, the air-raid siren wailed. Its obnoxious sound shattered the noontime silence. Along with the frightful siren, there came an incessant pounding at the front door.

"Kathy! Kathy O'Neill, are you in there?" Clara Williams yelled through the door. "It's an air raid, honey. We've got to get downstairs right away!"

Kathy leaped from the bed and raced into Christopher's room. The toddler was sitting in his crib. He was playing with his toes and occasionally stopping to pummel his favorite teddy bear by beating it against the crib's railing. Kathy grabbed her child and raced into the living room. Christopher clutched his bear. Without slowing down, she scooped up the diaper bag and threw open the door.

"Thank God, honey," Clara said. "I didn't know what had happened to you. The air-raid siren's been going off for the past five minutes. We'd better hurry down to the basement. All the others are already there."

With a firm hold on Christopher, Kathy followed Clara down the stairs. Her bare feet scarcely touched the cold steps as she rushed from the second-floor landing toward the dank basement.

In the four-story stairwell, there were eight women and fifteen children. Six women and eleven children had taken shelter in one of the basement's storage areas. Clara led Kathy and Christopher to the small laundry room across the hall. The Williams's boys, ages seventeen, fourteen, and ten, huddled together beneath woolen blankets inside the musty room.

"You boys give this sweet lady and her baby one of those blankets," Clara said. Her oldest son shyly got up and did what he'd been told. "Kathy, why don't you take Christopher and get up next to that big pillar by the third dryer. That looks like as good a spot as any."

A wide-eyed Kathy complied. Clutching Christopher to her, she crouched on the damp floor underneath the blanket.

For ten minutes, absolutely nothing happened. The unerring siren continued its incessant wail. All over the base, women and children hid deep within windowless basements. There was nothing any of them could do but wait and hope.

Colonel Cossette put the phone down and looked at Lieutenant Templeton.

"Lieutenant, get me the backup team at Hillingdon."

Outside, the siren's warning went on.

"Hillingdon, Hillingdon, this is DISA," Templeton said into the microphone.

From the outskirts of London the call was answered. "Go ahead, DISA, this is Hillingdon."

"Hillingdon, we need to speak to our backup team."

"Roger, DISA, they're sitting right here."

A new voice came over the speaker. "Senior Master Sergeant Doyle."

The colonel took the microphone. "Denny, this is Colonel Cossette."

"Yes, sir, Colonel."

"Are you guys all set to take over for us?"

"We sure are, Colonel. Sergeant O'Neill and I are ready whenever you need us."

"Denny, we need you to take over right now."

Doyle looked over at O'Neill. From the stunned looks on both their faces, each knew he wasn't mistaken about what he'd just heard.

"Why? What's up, Colonel?" Doyle said, trying to act as nonchalant as possible.

"Denny, I just got off the phone with General Oliver. A large group of MiGs has broken through our defenses. They'll be here in ten minutes. European Command Headquarters is being turned over to the backup team in England. You guys are to take control of the Defense Information System and run it from Hillingdon."

Doyle looked at O'Neill. There was terror in George's eyes.

"Yes, sir, we understand," Doyle said.

O'Neill motioned for Denny to give him the microphone.

"Sir, this is Sergeant O'Neill. Do you know whether the dependents have been evacuated?"

The colonel knew the answer. He suspected, however, that the truth wouldn't be an appropriate response. No use worrying these guys unnecessarily; they were going to have more than enough to concern themselves with in the coming days.

"O'Neill, I don't know for sure whether they're completely gone. But they've been evacuating dependents since early this morning."

The colonel knew the real truth was that two planeloads of women and children were all that had departed. All the NCOs' families were still in the housing area.

"Sir, could you do me a favor and check to see if my wife and child have left?"

"Sure, O'Neill, we'll take care of it for you. But with all that's going on right now, it might take awhile."

"Okay, thanks, Colonel."

The air-defense soldiers anxiously waited on the perimeter. They were acutely aware of how inadequate they were going to be in protecting the small base. They wouldn't be able to stop fifty of the enemy's best fighter aircraft. The soldiers didn't even have fifty Stinger missiles with which to stop them. Even if every engagement was successful, there were going to be MiGs left. And the Stinger gunners knew there was no way every engagement was going to succeed. No way at all.

The defensive mission rested in the hands of two "Avenger" pedestal-mounted Stinger teams and four air defenders with shoulder-mounted Stingers from the 82nd Airborne Division.

An Avenger Humvee, its gunner sitting in a Plexiglas compartment on the rear of the vehicle, waited to protect the mile-long northern fence. In the identical pods on the gunner's left and right sat a total of eight missiles. Next to the Humvee's driver, eight replacement Stingers lay on the floor of the passenger compartment. To cover the close-in dead space, an antiaircraft machine gun was mounted alongside the left pod.

The second Avenger team protected the shorter eastern fence.

Four soldiers stood in the blowing snows to defend the western and southern approaches to the base. Their shoulder-mounted Stingers were at the ready. At the feet of each of them lay four replacement missiles.

Unlike the sophisticated Patriot, the little heat-seeking Stingers could be deceived and defeated. The Russians had years to practice such techniques after the CIA armed the Afghan rebels with Stinger missiles during the mid-1980s war.

As soon as the pilots determined that Stingers were the only things waiting to challenge their attack, they were bound to take evasive actions. The Russians would then identify and eliminate the air-defense positions. When the Stingers were no more, the MiGs would destroy the base.

Even with the Russian pilots' training, the Stingers were bound to score some victories. There was little doubt there were pilots presently soaring through the heavens who'd never again see the sunrise. Yet any way the Americans added it up, there were forty-eight Stinger missiles and fifty MiGs.

The defenders had no chance. And they knew it.

CHAPTER 35

In basements all over the base, the women and children prayed. The siren continued its plaintive wail.

The first six fighters came in high, using the midday sun to their advantage. From thirty thousand feet, they began a teeth-rattling dive at their target—the base's communication tower.

Using his infrared sight, the Avenger gunner protecting the eastern fence targeted the lead Su-35 attack aircraft. Second by second, the fighter formation rushed toward its objective. The Avenger gunner tracked the first fighter all the way. The air-defense system's laser range finder homed in on the plummeting plane. A high-pitched tone sounded in the gunner's ears. The system had locked onto the fighter. The missile was ready to fire.

The fighter plunged through the ten-thousand-foot level. The Avenger gunner squeezed the trigger on his control stick. A Stinger leaped from its tube on the left pod. It raced into the heavens. The Su-35 instantly warned its pilot that he was under attack. In the cockpit, the pilot's radar screamed that certain death was headed for his aircraft. There was no time to spare. He had to act and act now to have any chance of survival. The Russian broke off his dive. He banked sharply to the left and roared back toward the east. The force of his severe evasive actions plastered him against the seat. To live, he had to control his aircraft. And his wits.

The fighter bobbed and weaved, dove and soared. Yet no matter what the pilot tried, it was no use. He couldn't shake the five-foot-long missile. The mindless Stinger matched him move for move. Unless something drastic happened, in seconds the life-ending contest would be over. The Avenger's two-man crew watched the missile's vapor trail as it closed with the fleeing plane. The intense heat from the aircraft's engines beckoned to the steadfast Stinger. The deadly little missile flew into the right engine's exhaust. With a mighty roar of protest, the fighter exploded in the eastern sky.

As the first fighter died, two more of the attackers were in trouble. The Avenger gunner on the northern fence tracked another of the planes in the flight while it rushed toward the ground. The tone wailed in his ears. Another enemy aircraft was ready for the kill. The Avenger fired. While the missile arched skyward in search of the heat it craved, the Su-35 did everything it could to save its pilot's life. But once again, a lethal missile matched a speeding fighter's every move. And a second pilot met his end in the low skies over Stuttgart.

From the southern fence, a soldier with a shoulder-mounted Stinger locked onto the trailing aircraft. He steadied the missile launcher with his left arm. With the missile's tone screaming that the target had been acquired, he fired. Another radar told its pilot that his life was nearly over. The Russian ran. The plane strained to its absolute limits to evade the determined missile. Still it was no use. A third explosion shook the heavens.

While his partner covered him, the shoulder-mounted Stinger gunner laid his expended missile tube in the snow. He removed the grip stock and handles. He quickly attached them to a second missile. By the time he was finished, the communication tower and the buildings on both sides of it were gone.

The Stinger gunners had eliminated half the attackers. There hadn't been enough time, however, for the scant group of air defenders to get them all. The Avenger on the eastern fence made a desperate attempt to engage another of the fighters. But he failed miserably.

With the planes plunging at supersonic speed, the Avenger gunner hurried to acquire a second target. He'd neither the time nor the patience to wait for the firing tone. He aimed at the leading fighter, pulled the trigger, and hoped for the best.

Fired before it was ready, a Stinger leaped from the right pod. It locked onto the nearest heat source—an electrical transformer on a utility pole just outside the fence. The missile raced for the pole. The transformer exploded.

The three surviving fighters released their bombs. The first's bombs were a little short. They hit the roof of the office building twenty yards east of the tower. With an earthshaking roar, the four-story building was ripped apart.

The second group was just a little long. The prolonged string of bombs struck the single-story communication control center a few feet west of the tower. When the deadly munitions were through and the smoke had cleared, there was nothing left of the building. The bombs killed the eight soldiers inside and destroyed all of the base's communication equipment. Black plumes reached into the bright noonday. With the communication center eliminated, hitting the tower became a moot point. Nevertheless, the third fighter's cluster was perfect. One after the other, the bombs fell with absolute precision onto the high tower. The structure disappeared in a thundering explosion. All that was left of the huge tower was an unrecognizable mass of smoldering metal lying in the bottom of a huge crater.

Inside the basement two hundred yards south of the savage assault, the ground trembled and shook with each striking bomb. Every window in the apartment building shattered at the same instant. The women and children screamed in terror. Kathy held Christopher to her with all her might. The sounds of the offensive siren suddenly ended. The bare lightbulb hanging from the laundry room ceiling went out, plunging them into darkness.

"DISA Hillingdon, this is Donnersberg."

"Go ahead, Donnersberg," O'Neill said.

"DISA, we've lost all contact with Stuttgart."

George hesitated, the significance of Donnersberg's pronouncement slowly sinking in. He took a moment to collect his thoughts. "To all communication facilities in Europe," he said. "The DISA detachment at Hillingdon is officially taking control of the Defense Information System."

O'Neill slumped into his chair. He prayed that at this moment, Kathy and Christopher were on a homeward-bound flight somewhere over the Atlantic.

High above the battle, the raid commander watched the Su-35s being chased and killed by the determined Stingers. After several months of air combat in the recent war for the liberation of Eastern Europe, three missiles were more than enough to confirm the extent of the American air defenses.

"Raid pilots," he said. "Our enemy has only Stingers guarding the target. Take appropriate evasive action and commence the next attack."

A second group of Su-35s roared out of the heavens. They screamed toward the ground. Their target was the jumbled cluster of office buildings in the center of the base that comprised the majority of the American European Command Headquarters main complex. Three MiG-29s accompanied the attackers. The MiGs were along to identify and eliminate the American air defenses. They were waiting for the Stingers to fire again, giving away their positions. When they reached the edge of the Stingers' five-mile range, all nine aircraft began dropping lengthy strings of white-hot flares. The intense heat from the flares confused the little missiles. Try as they might, the Stinger gunners couldn't get a lock on any of the fighters.

In the Avengers, the gunners stayed with their targets. They prayed for the firing tone to squeal. The four soldiers with Stingers resting on their shoulders did the same.

When they neared the ground, the Su-35s dropped their ordnance onto the command center. The instant they did, each intentionally stopped emitting flares. The sweet tones went off in the Stinger gunners' ears. At nearly the same instant, six missiles leaped into the sky. The fighters completed their bombing runs and raced upward at incredible speed. The moment their systems told them they'd been fired upon, the pilots released another long line of flares. All they needed to do was fool the American missiles a final time, and they'd be home free.

The lead plane was engaged by a pair of Stingers. The Su-35's flares quickly deceived the first of the heat-seeking killers. The missile went after one of the falling flares. It followed the false image as it dropped toward the snows. But the second Stinger never took the bait. It headed straight for the fighter with unwavering determination. The chess match of pilot and missile was on once again. And as before, an unrelenting missile matched the fighter's every move. Another deafening fireball appeared in the skies over the beleaguered base.

The next plane in the formation never had a chance. Its last-second attempt to confuse the Stingers on its tail was unsuccessful. Both missiles closed with the fighter's engines. A few thousand feet above the destroyed command buildings, the plane exploded beneath the striking missiles. Smoldering pieces of the defeated aircraft tumbled to earth.

The last two Stingers met with mixed results. The Stinger chasing the third Su-35 came within a few hundred yards of the plane. The kill was at hand. At the last possible instant, however, the missile decided that one of the fighter's flares was the real target. The Stinger veered off course and chased the descending decoy.

The final Stinger wasn't fooled. Straight as an arrow it ran for the fourth plane. In his cockpit, the pilot watched his radar as he counted down the last seconds of his life. The Stinger caught up with its prey. Another shower of burning fragments sprinkled forth from the heavens.

The formation's trailing Su-35s hadn't been engaged by the small force of air defenders. With smiles on their faces, the pair flew off toward the east and headed for home. They'd lived to fight another day.

The firing of the Stingers was what the MiG-29s had been waiting to see. The fighters spotted the source of the launches from the north and west. Two MiGs rushed to engage the Avenger on the northern fence. The third Russian aircraft headed west.

The shoulder-mounted Stinger gunners on the western side of the base had laid their weapons down. They were busily removing the handle and grip stock from their empty tubes. Trimming the treetops, the MiG roared toward the kneeling soldiers. The pilot squeezed the trigger on his fighter's 30mm cannon. The shells pirouetted across the frigid white ground. The rounds raced straight for the Americans. The defenseless soldiers had just enough time to look up, and no time at all to react to the fierce cannon fire. The shells ripped into them. Both soldiers tumbled into the snows. Their twisted corpses lay on the bloody ground next to their replacement Stingers.

At the same moment, the northern Avenger was attacked by the other MiG-29s. The fighters were too low and too close for the Americans to launch a Stinger. The Avenger gunner did the only thing he could. He opened fire with his 12.7mm antiaircraft machine gun. Two strafing 30mm cannons versus a single stationary machine gun would never be an equal match. The Russian firepower was far too great for the Avenger crew to match. Nevertheless, the Americans were determined to give it everything they had.

The brief battle was extremely intense. And quite final. When it was over, the Avenger and its crew had been forever silenced.

A dozen MiGs leaped from their perch high above the beleaguered base. They dove to join in on the attack on the overmatched Stinger teams. The final Avenger and the two soldiers on the southern fence stood their ground and waited. They wouldn't go down without a fight. The Avenger acquired a diving MiG-29. The tone screamed, urging the American to fire. A missile arched skyward. The match of man and missile was under way once more.

The MiG pilot, as skillful as any in the Soviet Air Force, used every trick he knew. He had to fool the heat-seeking missile. Strings of flares poured from his plane. The Stinger came on. The pilot dove toward the ground to hide himself in the ground clutter and confuse the missile. Yet the Stinger was right with him. While he roared away, he skimmed the tops of the German houses just outside the fences. Still the killer kept closing. In the end, it was no use. The Stinger wouldn't relent. The pilot reluctantly accepted his fate. He realized there would be no reprieve. The MiG exploded a mile north of the base.

The Avenger picked up a second target. A missile rocketed from its right-hand pod. It curved upward at tremendous speed. Another pilot and missile dueled in the smoldering skies above Stuttgart. And another pilot lost.

The leading MiGs pounced upon the Avenger. The last thing they wanted was to give the Americans another chance to steal a life. The fighters raced toward the Humvee. Gunfire poured from the MiGs' cannons. The Avenger fought back with all it had. But it wasn't nearly enough. The Avenger was ripped apart in a hail of cannon fire.

On the southern fence, the Stinger gunners both picked up firing tones. They fired at the final pair of aircraft in the lengthy column attacking the Avenger. The missiles raced toward their targets. It wouldn't be long before flaming pieces of defeated airplanes would litter the ground once more.

The instant they fired their Stingers, the soldiers scooped up their replacement missiles and ran for the dense woods. They were only fifty yards from the beckoning safety of the broad trees. But weighed down by the Stingers, it was slow going in the deep snows. Russian fighters roared in to eliminate the final pair of air defenders. The Americans just beat the first of the firing MiGs to the tree line. The soldiers disappeared into the woods. The fighters strafed the forest again and again, determined to finish off the Stinger gunners. Protected by the thick evergreens, the Americans somehow survived the tenacious Russian attack. The burgundy berets knelt in the snows and plotted their revenge.

For the next half hour, the pair would pop out of the woods unexpectedly. Each time they would be at a different location. Each time they would fire one of their final five Stingers. Four of the five would destroy a MiG. In the end, however, they would prove to be nothing more than a minor annoyance. A handful of missiles weren't nearly enough to deter the unwavering Russians from their task. They'd come to destroy the enemy headquarters, and they weren't going to be denied. No matter what the Americans did, the MiGs wouldn't leave until their mission was completed.

When the last Stinger had been fired, the Russians had a field day. With nothing left to challenge the attack, their bombing passes were routine and methodical. This was as easy as any practice run. One by one, the buildings of the American base disappeared in a hail of bombs and rockets. Near the western fence, the DISA building was one of the last to fall. By the time the Russians got around to destroying it, not a soul remained in the building. Colonel Cossette and the men and women under his command had all escaped into the woods.

Others on the base weren't so fortunate.

While he raced across the midday sky, the Su-35 pilot fired a long stream of rockets from the pods beneath his plane's wings. With blinding speed, a dozen deadly rockets rushed for their target on the frozen ground below. But the pilot had released his ordnance a fraction of a second late. As they were intended to do, the first few rockets pierced General Oliver's operations center. The southern end of the lengthy building erupted. All inside were killed.

Moments later, it collapsed. One tremendous explosion after another shook the basement of the apartment building on the other side of the narrow street. Those hidden within its sheltering walls had only the briefest of moments to scream.

The remainder of the rockets ripped across the frozen ground that separated the demolished office building and the aging apartment. The constricted cobblestone street between them was torn apart in a thunderous storm of incredible violence. Each striking rocket came closer and closer to the defenseless women and children cowering belowground a short distance away. And the line of lethal rockets kept coming. They reached out to seize the apartment building.

The Su-35's final three rockets smashed into Christopher's room on the building's second floor. The child's crib was vaporized.

The four-story building disintegrated. Tons of shattered mortar and steel, furniture and fixtures, came down upon itself. It pressed in on those waiting below. The immense weight of the falling building caved in the basement ceiling. The ancient pillar Kathy and Christopher were hiding behind buckled. While her world crumbled around her, Kathy bent forward in a desperate attempt to shield her terrified son. The huge pillar shuddered, unable to support the massive burden being placed upon it. It broke in two. The broad beam collapsed. Its ponderous weight crashed down upon Kathy's tiny form. The colossal blow shoved her to the floor. She fought with all her might to hold on to her child. But her frantic efforts were for naught. Christopher was knocked from her grasp. Kathy was slammed to the cold concrete by the oppressive mountain of defeated steel and cement. She was buried beneath thirty feet of suffocating rubble.

The last thing she remembered was the sweet taste of blood in her mouth and the anguished screams of her child.

And then there was nothing.

CHAPTER 36

January 29—12:24 p.m.
1st Platoon, Alpha Company, 2nd Battalion, 69th Armor,
   3rd Heavy Brigade Combat Team, 3rd Infantry Division
At the Crossroads of Highway 19 and Autobahn A7

Tim Richardson stood in the open commander's hatch of his M-1A2 tank. A tanker's helmet covered his auburn hair. On his left in the turret, Clark Vincent rubbed his tired eyes as he stood behind his machine gun. The hurried nighttime journey south from Wurzburg had exhausted them all. Each was watching as a combat engineer used a bulldozer to dig the third of the tank platoon's fighting positions. The other two M-1s were already in their holes on Richardson's left and right. Both tanks' crews were busily making their final defensive preparations.

The fifteen thousand men of the 3rd Infantry Division were going to be the last organized line of the American defense. Sixty miles behind them lay the sprawling cities of southern and central Germany, and the Rhine River itself. The majority of the divisions' 332 Abrams tanks, supported by a similar number of Bradleys and untold smaller combat vehicles, were being placed in defensive positions nearly one hundred miles long.

The real struggle for Germany had begun in the past few hours. Twenty miles east of Autobahn A7, two German armored divisions and the American 1st Armor had made contact with the enemy's lead units. A tank battle of monumental importance had begun.

Six German armored divisions were to the north. The combined British and Canadian division was with them. Four of the German divisions were embroiled in a fierce assault to break through the Russians' tenuous defenses on the East German border. For the moment, the Russian line appeared to be quite thin. The Germans had seen an opportunity to retake East Germany before it was too late and were racing to capitalize upon it.

One hundred and twenty miles to the southwest, the nine thousand men of the American 11th Armored Cavalry and 6th Cavalry were waiting east of Munich to block the enemy's advance into the city of nearly two million.

That was all there was.

Twelve hours into the war, there were thirty Russian divisions in East Germany. Another twenty were crossing into the northern portion of the country. In the south, things were even worse. Fifty Russian divisions were inside Germany and rolling west. Thirty more were making their way across the border.

Eleven NATO armored divisions and the two American cavalry regiments were rushing into battle against 150 Russian divisions. The final elements of the 82nd Airborne were three hours away from arriving in Germany. The 24th Infantry's last units were just now boarding planes in Georgia. Both divisions had planned on joining the 3rd Infantry to strengthen the Americans' defenses. But because of the Russians' airborne assault, those orders had been changed.

For the Germans, British, and Americans, the situation in the initial hours of the conflict appeared quite grim. In this war, there were going to be ten attacking divisions for every one defending. The odds were staggering. Yet they weren't hopeless. On the technology-dominated battlefield, the advantage would go to the defenders. With the West's superior weapons, the attacker was going to suffer severe losses of men and equipment while attempting to root the Allies from their fortified positions.

The combat engineer indicated that the hole was ready. Richardson spoke into his headset.

"All right, Jamie, drop her in nice and slow."

Specialist Tony Warrick stood on the ground, guiding the M-1.

Private First Class Jamie Pierson drove the seventy-two-ton tank forward. He eased it into the sloped hole the bulldozer had created. Using a smaller bulldozer, another combat engineer pushed three large logs in front of Richardson's Abrams. To complete the job, the bulldozer piled dirt and snow on top of the logs. When their efforts were completed, only the tank's turret was visible.

Their task at an end, the engineers hurried off to prepare the platoon's secondary position. Five miles west on Highway 19, three new holes would soon be dug.

Lieutenant Mallory and Staff Sergeant Greene walked up to Richardson's tank.

"Richardson," Mallory said, "let's take a look around while we've still got a little time."

"Okay, sir."

Richardson climbed out of his tank. To evaluate their fighting position, the tank commanders headed into the snow-filled valley. They stopped a few hundred yards down the modest slope. They turned and looked back at the hillside.

"What do you think, sir?" Greene asked.

"I like what I see."

"Me, too," Greene said. "From here, you can't even tell we're there. We're definitely going to get a clean shot at Comrade before he knows what hit him."

The trio of tanks lay hidden on the crest of a small hill. They were on the edge of a patch of dense woods, a mile west of where the only major east–west highway in the area intersected Autobahn A7. To advance, the enemy would have to come down one of the two roadways. When they did, they'd head straight into the crosshairs of the waiting M-1s. What made the location even better was that while the woods protecting the Abrams were thick, the trees behind the platoon were fairly thin.

"What I like best," Richardson said, "is that when the time comes to run, it'll be easy to retract from our holes and escape through the woods in either of two directions."

"There you go again, Tim," Greene said, "always running from something. First it's irate *Frauleins* you've promised to marry in Wurzburg. Now it's Comrade in . . . um . . . aw . . . Where the hell are we anyway?"

Mallory looked around. "Somewhere in Germany, I think."

"Thanks, sir, that's a lot of help."

"Well, wherever we are, we've been out in the open long enough," the lieutenant said. "Let's get back up the hill before some Russian helicopter jockey decides to use us to test out his machine guns."

Richardson scanned the cloudless sky. "I'm with you, Lieutenant."

They climbed through the waist-deep drifts to the top of the hill and clambered back into their Abrams tanks. While the afternoon wore on, there was little more for the tankers to do. Richardson spent the time watching the snarl of automobiles on the intersecting highways below. Frantic German refugees covered every inch of both roadways for as far as the eye could see. Over the noise of the tangled traffic, the twelve soldiers could hear the rumbling thunder of the intense battles raging in the east. The frightful sounds went on without end.

Early in the afternoon, a steady succession of Predator drones began appearing overhead. Each carried two Hellfire missiles. Each was heading east in search of prey.

A few minutes later, a flight of six Apache helicopters appeared out of nowhere. The tank killers screamed overhead. They passed a few feet above the treetops. In their haste to become a part of the historic contest, the helicopters roared through the scenic valley at speeds approaching 180 miles per hour. In less than a minute, they disappeared into the eastern trees. Richardson watched them go. A smile came to his face. The helicopters' obvious hurry to join in the fighting amused him. The young tanker was in no rush whatsoever to become a part of the death and destruction being wrought a scant handful of hills away.

There was no need to hasten things. He knew the platoon's time would come soon enough.

The Apaches hovered one hundred yards apart. Hidden in a blanket of fir and beech, they prepared to unleash their missiles. Twelve unsuspecting tanks scurried through a trackless field toward the attack he-licopters. With their rotors spinning, the deadly spiders waited in the treetops. They needed to ensure that all the flies were ensnared in their web before they struck. The T-80s continued ever farther into the Americans' trap.

"All right, Warrior Flight, let's get 'em," the flight leader said into his headset. "I'll take the middle one and the one right behind him. The rest of you take the two nearest your position."

The Apaches struck. The calamitous conflict's thunder roared once more.

In a little more than a hurried breath, six Russian tanks were burning in a field that had yielded a bountiful harvest of red cabbage and beets five months earlier. The lethal black spiders had popped up in perfect unison. Each had fired a single Hellfire missile, guided it to the target, and faded back into the protective trees. Six tanks were nothing more than twisted, burning wreckage in the middle of the snowbound field. The assault had been so quick and so destructive that only two of the surviving tank crews had determined its source.

While the pair of T-80s blindly fired their antiaircraft machine guns into the treetops, each of the Apaches slid fifty yards to the right. The helicopters reappeared. They fired a second missile. The final six tanks fell prey to Hellfires.

In fifteen seconds, a company of T-80s had vanished from the battlefield.

"All right, Warrior Flight, let's move out."

None of the Apaches had suffered a single scratch. They disappeared over the evergreens. Skimming the highest branches, they moved to spin their web once again. The next group of unsuspecting flies would soon be along.

It was combat like nothing the soldiers of the Second World War had experienced on these same bloodstained fields. It wasn't even a form of battle they'd have recognized. With both sides' remarkable weapons of mass destruction, the only defense was to provide no massed targets.

As the winter sun peaked high on the first day and slowly continued its inexorable movement toward the western horizon, neither side could dare gather too many soldiers or pieces of equipment together. Any Russian attempt to do so would result in a swift and fatal response by B-2 and B-52 bombers or the Army's Multiple Launch Rocket Systems.

Gone forever were the days when immense armies would slug it out in the mud to determine the outcome of a war. As it was, by massing huge amounts of armor at the border, the Russians had risked it all in the previous night's attack. They'd taken a calculated gamble. They'd been forced to endure such a risk for the first eight hours of the war in order to gain a large enough area in Germany within which to operate. To General Yovanovich's relief, his gamble had worked. He'd rolled the dice. And the dice had so far come up sevens. Had the Russians' surprise not succeeded and the Americans been waiting, the result would have been certain annihilation.

This war would be fought by no group larger than battalion size—and even then, only rarely. It would be a war of company against company, platoon against platoon, squad against squad, and soldier against soldier.

It was a form of warfare at which the Americans excelled—and with which the Russian soldier was ill prepared to deal. The resourceful American private made up his own battle plan as he went. If the general's orders didn't work, or he found himself faced with an unanticipated situation, the American simply changed things on the spot. He'd then go about accomplishing the task he'd been assigned. The creative, freethinking American was in his element.

His opponent had no such ability. The Russian soldier was given an order, and he obeyed it without question. Throughout the coming days, when cut off from his unit or faced with unusual circumstances, the Russian would continue to follow the last order he'd been given. Many times it was a useless order two or three days old. A rigid, unthinking society had produced a rigid, unthinking soldier. That soldier was being called upon to fight a thinking man's war.

The individual advantage was strongly with the Americans. The question still to be answered, however, was whether that tactical advantage would be enough to overcome the daunting ten-to-one odds the Americans faced.

The all-powerful tank of sixty years ago had become an ordinary weapon of the battlefield. The Russian attack involved fifty thousand tanks. The defenders had only four thousand with which to meet them. Yet there was still a chance of an American victory. In this world of extraordinary technology, the tank was a valuable weapon. It was, however, no longer king. Its place in the pecking order of the battlefield fell somewhere in the middle. The tank remained a strong destroyer. Nevertheless, the things that could destroy it were now many.

Despite their setbacks in the initial twelve hours of the war, America didn't find itself holding an empty hand. For in its arsenal of cards to play on the killing fields of Germany, it held four aces. America had four weapons so deadly that, without help, the Russian armor was powerless to defeat.

The Apache Attack Helicopter was one of the greatest killers of armor in the world. Still, it was not America's only ace. For there were three weapons in the American arsenal as strong or stronger.

CHAPTER 37

January 29—2:30 p.m.
1st Platoon, Alpha Company, 2nd Battalion, 69th Armor,
   3rd Heavy Brigade Combat Team, 3rd Infantry Division
At the Crossroads of Highway 19 and Autobahn A7

Thirty minutes after the drones and Apaches crossed Richardson's position, two strange creatures passed so low over the evergreens that the snow from the highest branches tumbled down upon the hidden tanks. The small aircraft had been scouring the woods for quite some time, and they were low on fuel. But they decided to make one more run at the Russians while the runways at Ramstein were being repaired. They hurried forward, cautiously picking their way through the trees until they spotted their feast.

The A-10s slammed into a platoon of BMPs. The BMPs never had a chance. From a mile away, the first Warthog pilot made his run. The other stood back to protect him. In a two-second burst, the A-10's seven-barrel cannon fired one hundred armor-piercing rounds into the personnel carriers. The pilot hurried forward. He dropped two five-hundred-pound bombs on the crippled BMPs. The Warthog's lethal ordnance ripped the enemy apart.

When the first ended his run, the second came forward. He wanted to make sure they'd completed the job. Like a pair of relentless hyenas finishing off a wounded quarry, the A-10s went about the task of disemboweling the BMPs. It was over in a few baneful seconds. Inside the mangled armored personnel carriers, forty soldiers were dead.

The Warthog was undisputedly the ugliest ace in the American armor-killing arsenal. Its ugly name and ugly disposition matched it perfectly. Incredibly slow, it was scarcely more than a flying cannon. It was invulnerable to the 12.7mm antiaircraft machine guns the Russian tanks and BMPs carried. The A-10 pilots simply ignored the efforts of the armored vehicles to defend themselves and blew the enemy straight into the next world.

One of the Americans' favorite tricks was to combine the Apaches and Warthogs into a pack of ruthless killers. The strength of both predators could then be played in harmony to destroy whatever strayed into their path. Working in unison, these hyenas and jackals were the scourge of the German forest. Watching for the enemy to show any weakness, they'd attack without mercy to drag their victim down and rip him to pieces. All over southern Germany, these packs of wild dogs were picking the Russian armored bones clean.

Nevertheless, like everything on the battlefield the Warthog was vulnerable. If a MiG found this slow mover, he could kill him with relative ease. And as had happened in the skies over Ramstein and Spangdahlem, Russian air-defense missiles were quite capable of knocking the little Warthog out of the sky forever.

For that reason, the Warthogs' trip home to Ramstein would be made at something less than one hundred feet above the ground. The aircraft would never be in a straight, stable position for more than four seconds at a time.

Or else the nasty little hunter would all too soon find himself the quarry.

Two hundred miles north, another colossal battle had commenced. Rather than being content to defend the German soil still free from the stain of the Slavic invader, four German divisions were attacking the Russians with everything they had. It was an all-out effort to recapture the eastern portion of the country.

The noose had been placed around the East German neck, but it hadn't yet been tightened. The Russians' hold on the East German border was paper-thin. Using everything they had, the German armored divisions rammed into the defenders. The Russian line collapsed in the first hour. By two, it was a rout. A pair of German divisions raced fifty miles into East Germany. They were halfway to Berlin. Another division recaptured Leipzig. The final one wreaked havoc in the far north, freeing Rostock and moving on.

The Russians waited. At just the right moment, they came up in force from the area around the town of Selb. They swarmed in behind the Germans. Ten armored divisions sprung the trap closed. The Germans were cut off. Twenty Russian divisions raced from their hiding place in far eastern Germany. They hit the Germans head-on. The slaughter of half the German army had begun.

By midnight, the four German divisions would be no more. And East Germany would be firmly within Russian hands.

The fast-arriving sunset was only an hour away. Frustrated by his inability to break through the 1st Armor Division's spirited defenses, a Russian brigade commander made a fatal mistake. He brought his three thousand men together to smash the American line. A lazily circling reconnaissance drone spotted the Russian's error.

Richardson watched four Multiple Launch Rocket Systems on modified Bradley chassis tearing down Highway 19. One of the greatest aces of the American armor killers stopped in the open area between the hidden tanks and the crowded Autobahn. A pair of the huge rocket launchers was quickly positioned on a knoll a half mile below the tanks. The other launchers were placed in a wide field a hundred yards west of the Autobahn. Two shoulder-mounted Stinger gunners readied themselves to protect the rocket systems. Each three-man rocket-launcher crew prepared to open fire.

The MLRS platoon leader verified the coordinates for the attack. The launcher commanders inputted the firing data into their computers. All four signaled their readiness.

"Fire!" the lieutenant screamed.

They released unspeakable brutality upon an unseen enemy nearly twenty miles away. In a single minute, each launcher fired twelve 227mm rockets toward the massed Russian brigade. Inside each rocket were 518 antipersonnel and antitank submunitions that would be released once they were over the target area. Each submunition was capable of tearing a three-inch hole in the top of a tank or BMP. Once inside the armored vehicle, the little bombs would fragment to kill everyone aboard.

One hundred tanks and an equal number of BMPs waited in a narrow ravine for the brigade commander to give the order to crush the overextended American lines. From out of nowhere, more than eight thousand armor-piercing bomblets poured down upon their heads. The munitions ripped into the thin tops of the armored vehicles.

In sixty seconds, one the Soviet Union's finest brigades disappeared in a firestorm of unbelievable savagery. Not a single soldier survived the grisly massacre. The corpses of the three thousand, and their burned-out vehicles, would stand forever as a monument to the new world's warfare.

The Multiple Launch Rocket Systems' crews started to reload. They'd be ready to fire again, or to move on to a new location, in three minutes. While the attackers prepared to release fearsome death and destruction once more, they were instantly transformed from aggressor to victim.

A Russian spotter located the source of the rocket firing. He called in a squadron of attack helicopters. Six Mi-24 "Hind-Gs" roared across the American lines. It took them just over a minute to cover the distance to the rocket launchers. The American crews were still in the process of reloading. They were caught in the open by the Hinds' sudden appearance. At the last possible instant, their Stinger team spotted the Hinds as they roared out of the low trees on the eastern side of the autobahn. A Stinger gunner locked onto the lead helicopter. He waited for the sweet tone. The second it sounded, he fired. The helicopter exploded into a thousand flaming pieces one hundred feet above the autobahn filled with terrified German civilians. Death rained down upon the fleeing maze of cars. Scores of German vehicles were soon ablaze.

The other Hinds opened fire with rockets, missiles, and machine guns. On the open ground, the Americans had no chance of escape. The two rocket-laden launcher systems on the snowy knoll below Richardson's position exploded with incredible force. The monstrous blasts shook the hilltop to its very foundation. A mammoth fireball reached high into the heavens.

The second Stinger gunner fired. Only a few feet above the autobahn, the Hind on the far right blew up in midair. The Stinger gunners desperately tried to reload.

A Hind opened fire on the exposed soldiers kneeling on the snowy ground. One of the air defenders went down in a twisted heap.

Hidden on the hilltop, the tank platoon watched the one-sided battle.

"Tim, we can't just sit here and watch these guys get slaughtered!" Warrick screamed. "We gotta help them!"

"They're out of range of my antiaircraft machine gun," Richardson said.

"Well, they're not out of range of our main gun. I'm certain we can nail a few of those bastards and help those guys out. I'm going to start targeting the one hovering on the far left, even if you haven't given me an order to do so."

"Tony, go ahead and target him if you want. I'll even give you a hand with the coordinates. But you're wasting your time. We're not going to fire unless the lieutenant tells us to. And you and I both know that Lieutenant Mallory's never going to issue such an order. We're here to defend this crossroads, and we can't do that if we're dead. If we pick a fight with a handful of Hinds, when they're through with us, there'll be nothing left on this hilltop but three smoldering tanks."

"But we've got to do something."

"There's nothing we can do. All we can do is pray the Hinds don't spot us. Because if they do, they'll do to us what they're doing to them."

Another of the swarming Hinds' machine guns ripped into the last Stinger gunner. He dropped motionless into the snows. The Hinds went after the final pair of American rocket launchers. Missiles tore from pods beneath the helicopters' stubby wings. In a desperate attempt to survive, the launcher crews ran up the hill. They were fifty yards from their launchers when the missiles hit. The launchers exploded with such overpowering violence that even at such a distance, the soldiers were killed instantly.

Like an ancient farmer's scythe cutting the pliant winter wheat, flaming metal and erupting munitions cut a swath thirty yards wide in the civilian cars on the jammed autobahn. The carnage on the roadway was inconceivable. And quite final. Death and suffering were everywhere Richardson surveyed.

The victorious helicopters raced off to the east. In the three tanks, the crews breathed a collective sigh of relief.

The defeated Russian brigade was quickly replaced by another. One whose commander wasn't nearly as foolish as his predecessor.

The Americans had nothing with which to replace the demolished Multiple Launch Rocket Systems.

Throughout the long afternoon, the intense pressure on the Allies' line was unyielding. Russian losses were tremendous. Yet for each Russian soldier lost, for each Russian tank destroyed, one moved forward to take its place. And another moved forward to take the place of the one that had just moved forward. And another moved forward to take that one's place.

The replacement process for those poor souls who'd never again in this lifetime fight for Comrade Cheninko went on almost without end.

Unfortunately, the Americans had no such luxury. For every American soldier lost, for every ravaged American tank, the line grew a little weaker. There'd be no one to take their places. The beleaguered American defenses were dangerously thin. Still, all along their lines, the 1st Armor Division held fast.

The first twelve hours of the battle for Germany had belonged to the Russians. But at noon, the tide had changed. The last three hours had been owned by the stalwart Americans. By midafternoon on the first day, the Russians weren't one foot closer to the Rhine River than they'd been at midday. With the sun settling in the west, both sides prepared to battle throughout the bitterly cold, sixteen-hour night that would follow.

The Americans were in a desperate situation. It was, however, a desperation tinged with the smallest blush of hope.

And so far, the Americans hadn't been forced to use their trump card.

Their final ace had yet to be played.

CHAPTER 38

S lumped over his machine gun, Arturo Rios fell asleep at a little after two. As he did, the temperature reached its highest point of the day—twenty-eight degrees. Neither Goodman nor Wilson tried to keep him from sleeping.

The exhausted Rios had been unconscious for about an hour when a strong hand grasped his shoulder and vigorously shook it.

"Airman . . . hey, Airman, wake up. They tell me after all the Russians you killed this morning, you're in need of a bit of relief."

The hand continued to shake him. Rios slowly opened his eyes. Standing over him were three grinning soldiers with burgundy berets in their pockets. Rios could see the square patch on each soldier's left shoulder with the AA on it, and the word AIRBORNE above the patch.

With Spangdahlem gone, the last American fighter base inside Germany had to be held at all cost. A battalion from the 82nd Airborne had arrived. With them were two companies of Bradleys from the 24th Infantry along with two platoons with eight M-1 tanks. The airborne soldiers and their cohorts had been headed east to reinforce the 3rd Infantry's lines, but they'd been recalled. With refugees clogging every inch of roadway, it had taken the battalion over five hours to cover the sixty miles to Ramstein. The burgundy berets had driven through Ramstein's front gate at two thirty. They were there to ensure that the beleaguered airmen could maintain their fragile hold on the base. Minus one thousand of their countrymen and all of their armored cars and antitank missiles, there was no way Ramstein's survivors could withstand a second determined Russian attack on their own.

Goodman and Wilson sat waiting in an idling Humvee.

"Come on, Rios," Goodman said. "The 82nd Airborne's going to relieve us for a while. Let's grab some food and get a little sleep while we've got the chance."

"Yeah," Wilson said. "Let's go find out if the Russians got the mess hall."

In a fog, Rios staggered over to the Humvee. The weary airman, numb in body, mind, and spirit, crawled into the backseat. Hot food and a soft bed were far more than he'd dreamed he'd ever see again. At least in this lifetime.

The Humvee headed toward the smoldering flight line. After hours of battling the intense fires that raged all over the base, the firefighting crews were letting the final ones burn themselves out.

Wilson leaped from the Humvee the moment they reached the mess hall. "Let's go. I don't care what they've got on the menu—I'm having two of everything."

"Man, look at that," Goodman said. He pointed to the bullet holes and burn marks on all the buildings in the area.

Rios stared at the smoking rubble down the street. A few hours earlier, a huge, four-story building had stood on the spot. "Goodman, our barracks is gone!"

"Christ, all our stuff was in there," Goodman said. "What are we gonna do now?"

"This place sure got hit hard," Wilson said. "How many planes did the driver tell you we lost?"

"I think he said thirty or forty on the ground and another sixty in this morning's air battle," Goodman said.

They threw open the mess-hall doors and entered. Inside the warm building, Rios stripped off his tattered gloves and parka. For the first time, he got a good look at the nasty burns on his forearms. The sudden warmth of the mess hall caused his frozen hands to ache. The heat began bringing each swollen finger back to life. Fourteen hours in the bitter weather, and the intense battle with the parachutists, had taken a severe toll on the young airman.

Wilson sauntered up to the chow line. With his M-4 slung over his shoulder, he looked every bit the savvy combat veteran. He surveyed the long row of steaming food.

"Give me a little of whatever you got. Then give me a whole lot more."

While they ate, Wilson jabbered on about anything and everything. Goodman enjoyed the comfort of a full belly and the relief of being alive. He often pushed his ill-fitting glasses up on his nose, and occasionally added something to the conversation.

The significance of what he'd done this morning was slowly sinking into Rios's muddled mind. He heard little of the conversation and said even less.

When the feast was over, Goodman looked up at the mess sergeant. "Hey, Sarge, our barracks burned down. Where can we find a place to sleep?"

"Hell, there are so many dead, all you have to do is go to any barracks and climb into whatever bunk you want. No one's going to care."

Wilson and Goodman picked up their M-4s. The trio wandered over to the nearest barracks. With the exception of a few soundly sleeping airmen, the building was deserted. Each picked out an inviting bunk. They pulled off their parkas and stripped off their boots. All three lay down on a soft mattress. In minutes, Rios was fast asleep.

At the same moment the 24th Infantry's Bradleys and tanks, and the 82nd Airborne's Humvees, drove through Ramstein's main gate, five hundred miles east, the final regiment of the 103rd Parachute Division entered their transports. The cargo planes were soon heading down the Ukrainian base's runways. In two hundred aircraft, twenty-four hundred men and four hundred combat vehicles headed into the late-afternoon sky. Their target was the American air base at Ramstein. Two MiGs flew on every transport's wingtips to protect them from the enemy's planes and air defenses.

The regiment's soldiers had sat on their parachutes all day, eagerly waiting to join in the fight. Word had arrived in midafternoon. Ramstein still stood. The highest-priority target had been severely damaged. But it hadn't been destroyed. The regiment's orders were clear—eliminate the American air base at all cost. While they hooked up their static lines and prepared to jump, the parachutists were convinced they wouldn't fail. All traces of the enemy base would be wiped from the face of the earth by the time an early moon rose into the night sky.

The regimental commander was completely unaware that the Americans had diverted a battalion of their best soldiers to protect the embattled fighter base.

While the parachutists flew across Germany, the American air forces were licking their deep wounds. Ramstein's runways were still out. Nearly half the Patriot air-defense systems were nothing more than unrecognizable wreckage littering the scarred snows. This time, there was little organized resistance to challenge the Russian transports. A few fighters out of Lakenheath met the incoming threat. The escorting MiGs chased the F-35s off with minimal losses. A handful of air-defense missiles reached up from the surviving Patriots to snatch the plodding transports from the heavens. Yet for most of the regiment, the American defenses turned out to be little more than a minor irritant. Twenty-two hundred parachutists survived the perilous journey through the enemy skies. With dusk fast approaching, the final regiment's parachutes cascaded down upon the broad fields of western Germany.

For the most part, the drop went well. The regiment's losses were minimal. Over two thousand attackers rose from their drop zone northwest of the base. They hurried to their vehicles. In another hour, darkness would be full upon them. The time had come to wrap their powerful coils around Ramstein and swallow their vulnerable victim whole. Within minutes of the first parachutist's feet touching the snows, the regiment moved toward the southeast with single-minded focus.

An air policeman rushed into the barracks. "Wake up! Wake up!" he yelled. "Another Russian unit just parachuted in. They'll be here in a few minutes. Grab your rifles and return to your defensive positions."

"Rios!" Wilson said. "Wake up! The Russians are about to attack again!"

Rios was more asleep than awake. The half-light of the onrushing night confused him. "What time is it?"

"Almost four."

"How long was I asleep?"

"I don't know. About twenty minutes, I guess. Who cares? The Russians have returned. They're getting ready to attack. We've been ordered back to the fence."

With rifle in hand, Goodman walked up to Rios's bunk. "Come on, Rios, let's go. The Humvee's waiting."

Rios reluctantly raised himself to a sitting position. He swung his feet over the side of the bed. The dazed airman reached down and slowly started putting on his boots.

"Come on, Rios, hurry it up!" Goodman said.

Wilson and Goodman ran down the hallway and out the door.

The wind whistled through the Humvee while they raced toward the eastern fence.

"Russians parachuted in northwest of here this time," their air-police driver said. "The base commander says that after all the planes they destroyed this morning, we can't afford any more losses. The 82nd Airborne's going to head out and hit them as far away from here as they can."

"What about us?" Goodman asked.

"You guys are going back to the same spot on the fence line. We've rebuilt all the bunkers along the eastern fence. We're sending out more airmen to man them. There should be four replacements waiting at your bunker when you get there."

And there were. The four were standing by the bunker as the Humvee neared. The moment they spotted the Humvee approaching, the burgundy berets who'd relieved them earlier raced off in their vehicle to join their battalion.

The parachutists were seven miles from the base and moving fast. Four A-10s churned down the first of the hastily patched runways. They took to the air. The Warthogs were intent on slowing the Russians long enough for the 82nd to form up and attack. For the moment, they would keep a handful of the 24th Infantry's Bradleys in reserve to protect the base against any enemy force that was lucky enough to breach the savage American assault.

The Russian regiment was exceptionally powerful. But the confident Americans were building a force that was more than a match for their opponent. This would be another Kaiserslautern. The Americans were comfortable that they'd win. And win decisively. Their goal was to crush the Russians as many miles from the base as they possibly could. After this morning's attack, Ramstein couldn't afford to suffer any additional harm.

It was all a matter of time. A race to see if the American battalion could intercept their counterparts soon enough to spare the base from further damage.

The four new airmen huddled near the main bunker.

"All right, you guys," Rios said, "one grenade could get you all. Two of you grab your rifles and take that bunker over there."

Two airmen ran to the bunker on the left.

"You two, down there."

The airmen raced to the right.

"Home at last," Wilson said.

His cheeks were flush from the sting of the crisp winter air. As the sun started to fade, the temperature was steadily plummeting. It was going to be a viciously cold night. But Wilson wasn't going to let the enemy or the weather change his outlook. His belly was full. And as long as that was the case, a few more Russians coming to kill them weren't going to spoil his mood.

"Aw, shut up, Wilson," Goodman said.

Arturo Rios reluctantly slid into his sandbagged world. He settled in behind the all-too-familiar machine gun. His desperate need for sleep clung to the corners of his weary eyes and tugged at his tortured brain. One thing he knew for certain: if he had to kill thirty-three more Russians to get a good night's sleep, he was going to do so.

CHAPTER 39

January 29—4:10 p.m.
On the Eastern Fence
Ramstein Air Base

The self-assured parachutists raced toward Ramstein. They were certain a great victory would soon be theirs. There'd be no feint this time. The regiment would concentrate its strike at a single point—the northern gate. They'd hit it with an immense blow so intense that the battered air base couldn't possibly withstand. To do so, the oncoming column was closely bunched.

The Warthogs rushed out to greet them.

At the same moment the initial 82nd Airborne company roared out the northern gate, the thunder and lightning of the A-10s struck the Russian column. The 24th Infantry's armor was right behind. At top speed, nearly thirty Bradleys and the eight M-1 Abrams tanks joined the Humvees as they sped across the windswept landscape toward the enemy. With the open ground in front of them, the Americans could clearly see the A-10s' assault five miles away.

As cannon shells poured from the Warthogs' noses, the leading BMDs burst into flames. New trails of suffocating smoke wafted into the hazy skies near Ramstein.

Another bloody battle for the battered air base had begun.

On the A-10 flight's first fierce pass, fourteen pieces of Russian armor fell. Eighty-three parachutists perished in a few fleeting seconds. In response, the Russians hurled malice into the skies at the little killer aircraft. The third Warthog in the formation spiraled out of control beneath the mortal blow of a striking air-defense missile. Its flaming fuselage plunged toward the unforgiving ground.

Another airborne company hurried out the northern gate. With their Humvees spewing snow, they hastened toward the steadily expanding battle. The Russians came on. The smoldering American air base was in sight. The A-10s attacked again. Lethal ordnance poured down upon the steadfast parachutists. And still more air-defense missiles were sent into the darkening heavens to greet the stubborn Warthogs. A horrific end reached up to claim a second A-10 pilot.

The final two companies of burgundy-bereted soldiers rushed out the western gate in their Humvees. The battalion's plan was to ensnare the parachute regiment between the two formations. Once within the Americans' mighty grasp, the slaughter would commence. To the last man, the enemy would be systematically destroyed.

The Bradleys and M-1s pinched in toward the parachutists' column. They would hit the enemy head-on. Eighty Humvees were right with them. The American trap was about to be sprung.

The Russians spotted the overwhelming force heading toward them across the frozen landscape. The regimental commander had no idea from where the enemy had come. But he instantly recognized that he would likely be outgunned by the daunting American weapons. The enemy armor, with so many Humvees in support, would decimate his regiment. In minutes, they'd all be dead if he didn't do something. Even as his men struggled to fend off the persistent A-10s' attacks, he issued new orders to them.

He picked up the microphone in his command BMD. "M-1s, Bradleys, and Humvees approaching from Ramstein's northern and western gates. Implement alternative plan C. Say again—implement alternative plan C."

The parachutists instantly responded to his directive. One hundred and fifty vehicles spread out across the open ground. In a wide, straight line, they surged forward. They'd make a suicide attack on the Americans to tie them up. Behind the attacking line, the remaining vehicles split. Nearly one hundred turned south. An identical force swung to the east. Both groups sprinted across the white fields at breakneck speed. Six miles away lay the protection of the heavy woods on the far ends of the sprawling air base. As the identical columns raced for safety, every two miles, five Russian vehicles turned back toward the enemy to protect their comrades' escape. The regiment's absolute precision was a thing of beauty to behold. They realized they were in deep trouble. But they also knew they could still win the battle if the fleeing columns could outflank the Americans and reach the thick forests surrounding the far sides of their objective. Once into the trees, the parachutists would wait for nightfall. In an hour, the world around them would turn pitch-black. They'd then assault the eastern and southern fences on foot.

Rather than destroying the air base with brute force, they'd become saboteurs. They'd arrived at Ramstein as ruthless bullies. Now, they'd changed into thieves in the night. Stealth, not power, would win the day for the Russians. Despite their tenuous position, their mission wasn't yet lost.

The Americans raced toward the screening line of armored vehicles. The widely spaced Russians came straight for them. None of the onrushing parachutists could be allowed to penetrate their defenses and gain access to the base. Behind the oncoming line, the Americans could see the other columns escaping in both directions. Even so, the burgundy berets had no other choice. They'd first have to deal with the immediate threat provided by the approaching attackers. Only then could they turn their attention toward the significant groups racing east and south.

The regiment's strongest elements, the fierce BMDs, were in the attacking force. The two opposing lines roared forward. Second by second, the deadly foes approached each other until less than a quarter mile remained between them. The Russians suddenly stopped. Each BMD began discharging its five infantrymen to support their attack.

"They're preparing to fire their missiles and main guns," the American battalion commander said. "Halt, release your TOWs, then charge the sons a bitches. Don't let a single one escape."

The M-1s, Bradleys, and Humvees screamed to a stop. Despite the clear threat, the Russians ignored the combat vehicles directly in front of them. Instead, they aimed at the weaker side armor on the Bradleys to their north and south. Missiles flew across the snows in both directions. The Bradleys' and Humvees' TOWs, and the BMDs' Bastions, spun through the rapidly closing darkness. Bushmaster cannon fire, M-1 cannon shells, and searching Russian armaments carried their lethal warheads through the frost-tinged twilight. Machine guns spewed death in every direction. Scores of vehicles on both sides exploded at nearly the same instant. The violence overwhelmed them all. It carried to the far corners of the battered base and well beyond. A startled Rios turned toward the earth-shattering sound. He watched as countless new fires grabbed at the blackening heavens.

The pair of A-10s swung in behind the enemy. They tore at the rear of the Russian line. The monstrous M-1s fired cannon shell after cannon shell. They churned toward the enemy. Both their online TOWs fired, the surviving Bradleys lunged forward, determined to eliminate the direct threat to the air base. The Humvees were right with them, firing their machine guns as they went. There was no time to waste. The Bradleys would reload their TOW firing tubes on the run. They clawed at their foe with their Bushmasters. A life-taking curtain of piercing cannon fire and whizzing bullets ripped through the battlefield and tore into the BMDs' thin armor. It felled the Russian soldiers on the merciless ground in countless numbers. The parachutists futilely tried to answer back. But it was no use. The BMDs crumpled beneath the powerful American assault. The Russian line faltered.

In five minutes of sheer terror, 150 attacking vehicles were reduced by two-thirds. The remaining fifty fought on. It wouldn't be long before the entire parachutists' line was annihilated. The American battalion commander began preparing to hunt down the enemy columns disappearing in the east and south.

The fleeing Russians were three miles nearer to the woods than they'd been five minutes earlier.

After seven minutes of battle, only eleven of the attacking parachutists' vehicles survived. Still, the eleven continued to fight. Their refusal to surrender bought further seconds of precious time for their comrades.

The beckoning woods were a mile closer.

By the eighth minute of carnage, the final eleven were chewed to pieces by the powerful Americans. Not a single one was spared. Not a soul survived. A multitude of Russian combat vehicles lay crushed and burning in the melting snows of western Germany. A thousand parachutists were dead or dying.

Nor were American losses insignificant. The attack had destroyed thirty-four Humvees, eleven Bradleys, and two M-1s. The American death toll neared two hundred. Among them was the trio of smiling soldiers who'd awakened Rios an hour earlier.

There was no time for either celebration or mourning. The American companies split. They raced after the escaping enemy. The small Russian vehicles were quick and had a significant head start. The point elements of both groups were nearing the southern and eastern woods.

The Warthogs headed toward the southern column to cut off the enemy. Two miles away, a small band of parachutists waited to protect their escaping brothers. Air-defense weapons nestled on a half dozen shoulders. The A-10s opened fire. Russian missiles leaped into the air to seek and destroy. The awkward little aircraft had no chance of evading such a concentrated attack. The pilots knew their lives were over. Even so, both Americans frantically clawed at their canopy releases in a desperate attempt to escape their fates. Each hoped against hope that he could somehow free himself from his ammunition-laden tomb before it was too late. But it was no use. The ground-to-air missiles were much too near and far too fast.

Both Warthogs were struck by multiple missiles. Silhouetted by the fading wisps of an orange-tinged sun, burning pieces of the defeated aircraft plummeted toward the earth. The Warthogs' dead pilots were firmly strapped into their fiery cockpits.

In the south and east, the Americans reached the initial line of screening vehicles. They released an immense barrage of machine-gun fire against the Russians' blue-bereted defenders. On each side of the base, the 82nd Airborne blew right through the parachute regiment's thin defensive line. Forty proud Russians perished in a handful of fluttering heartbeats.

And in the south, another Bradley went down.

Rios watched the Russians racing east. The enemy vehicles were almost to their goal. The security of the trees was right in front of the frenetic invaders. Well behind the blue berets, the 82nd Airborne was now in sight as they destroyed the first group of parachutists and hurried forward.

A dire chase was on. Yet despite their best efforts, the Americans were going to be too late.

In the south and east, the parachutists' leading elements raced up to their objective. Two hundred Russians abandoned their vehicles at the edges of the twisted evergreens and ran toward the trees. They vanished into the heavy forest outside Ramstein's fences.

Still more were on the way. With each passing minute, another fifty escaped into the timber. Four miles from them, the burgundy berets rushed toward the woods. Two more lines of covering vehicles waited on both sides of the base to slow them down. The Americans would first have to deal with these before they could address the problems created by the strong enemy force immersing itself in the nearly impenetrable woods.

"Lock and Load!" Rios yelled. "Lock and load!" He didn't know what was happening outside the fences. But he was certain of one thing. A battle that had been taking place miles from his position was reaching out for him.

With dusk taking a firm hold on the lingering remains of the fading day, the 82nd slammed into the second wave of enemy defenders at both ends of the base. As they did, in the distance, more parachutists ran into the heavy thickets and disappeared.

The second line was effortlessly shoved aside and left to die in the crimson fields outside Ramstein. Forty more Russian lives had ended. Another handful of Americans was also gone, never again to fight on the battlefields of the great war.

The American battalion pressed on. A last line waited to slow their advance. The parachutists knew they had no chance. In the four minutes it took for the Americans to reach the enduring group of defenders, an additional three hundred of the enemy found their way into the snow-covered branches in the east and south. And countless others were drawing near.

The Russian's final line in the east fired first. They hoped to catch the Americans by surprise and slow them just a little more. But their desperate volley had little effect on the unrelenting Humvees coming straight for them. Overmatched and outgunned, eighty Russians braced to die. Lethal curtains of machine-gun fire rained down from the onrushing burgundy berets. Within seconds of each other, the Americans brushed aside the razed resistance and hurried on. Even more unspeakable deaths had been added to the tally.

The final obstacles in their path surmounted, the Americans raced toward the waiting trees. But now they faced the most difficult task of all: how to eliminate the vast enemy force that had slipped into the sheltering branches.

With the sacrifices of their dead countrymen, nearly one thousand parachutists had successfully reached the forest's bosom. On each side of Ramstein, the final fifty to enter the woods ran thirty yards into the evergreens and stopped. With a preciseness born of years of practice, they spread out to protect their compatriots. Machine-gun nests sprang up in a half dozen locations. Antitank missiles were raised onto strong shoulders. Mortar teams hurriedly prepared their emplacements.

The remainder of the regiment's forces moved even farther into the shadowy timber. Without hesitation, they headed straight for the fences.

The Americans charged across the open ground toward the woods.

They had to catch the Russians before they reached the deep foliage. Their valiant efforts, however, would be without reward.

The 82nd Airborne roared up to the trees just as the last of their elusive prey melted into the fearful twilight.

The Americans hesitated at the forest's edge, unsure of what their next move should be. From out of the woods on the eastern end, a pair of shoulder-mounted missiles ripped through the heavy branches. Two Humvees burst into flames. Russian machine-gun fire spewed forth. The burgundy berets fell back, dragging their dead and wounded with them. The night's oppressive blanket was quickly closing in around them. The bloodied Americans, the disjointed battle concluded, were in disarray. They needed to regroup and catch their breath. They needed to organize and plan. One thing was for certain. Digging one thousand immensely skilled parachutists out of the thick woods wasn't going to be easy.

Within the dense forest, thirty Russian snipers crept through the gathering darkness. Their brethren moved forward through the fading shadows to protect them. They could see their objective.

The chain link was just ahead.

Their single-shot sniper rifles could kill from a mile away. When they reached the trees just outside the fence, their targets were a scant fifty meters from them. There was no way the snipers would miss.

The long black barrel of a sniper's rifle peeked out from the tree line in front of Rios's bunker. The marksman took careful aim at an airman inside the sandbags. The back of the American's head was dead center in the crosshairs of the sniper's sights.

Within the bunker, Wilson was a changed man now that his stomach was full. Despite all that was happening, he continued to regale Goodman and Rios with a steady stream of stupid jokes.

"He's the one with the clean bowling shirt," Wilson said. He started to laugh at his own bad joke. Inside his parka, his sated belly jiggled.

Goodman had first heard the tired joke when he was nine. And he hadn't thought it all that funny then.

"Rios, what do ya think? Do I have to wait for the Russians, or can I shoot him myself?" Goodman asked.

Only the faintest traces of daylight remained. The dejected Rios knew it was going to be another endless night behind his deadly machine gun. This time, however, he realized he wouldn't have to endure the long hours alone.

"Yeah, Goodman," Rios said, "go ahead and shoot. It's obvious he's not going to shut up until somebody kills him."

The sniper squeezed the trigger on his rifle.

CHAPTER 40

January 30—12:17 a.m.
NCO Housing Area, United States European Command
    Headquarters
Patch Barracks, Stuttgart

In her vivid dream, Kathy was very cold. She could hear Christopher calling for her in the darkness. But she couldn't move to help him. She couldn't move at all.

Suddenly, she realized it wasn't a dream.

An icy shiver soared down her spine. Terror gripped her. The surreal nightmare of twelve hours earlier rushed into Kathy's anguished mind. She began to understand, even as she refused to accept, the helplessness of her situation. She'd no idea how long she'd been there. Buried facedown beneath tons of suffocating rubble, she was unable to move in the slightest. The crushing weight of the shattered building pressed in upon her. It threatened to squeeze the last bits of fleeting air from her tortured lungs.

Her entire body was wracked with pain. Her right leg was mangled. Twisted and distorted, it screamed out to her. She shivered again, cold and clammy. Beads of sweat formed on her upper lip and fell upon the cold floor.

She could hear her child whimpering. He was only inches from her. Still, despite everything she tried, she couldn't reach him.

"Christopher, Mommy's here, baby."

Her voice was no more than a passing whisper. That was all her battered body would allow. She couldn't tell if he'd heard her. Despite the abject suffering it caused, she tried again to comfort him.

"It's okay, baby. Mommy's right here."

But it wasn't okay. Kathy O'Neill was trapped in a nightmare. A nightmare from which, no matter how hard she tried, she couldn't awaken.

Sergeant Major Harold Williams clawed at the huge pile of rubble. A mountain of worthless refuse was all that was left of the place Williams had called home. With six others, the sergeant major worked like a soul possessed. Alongside the giant of a man were a young soldier, three NCOs' wives, and a boy and girl in their midteens. All seven had been lucky enough to have survived the Russian attack.

While he battled to reach the bottom of the bombed-out building, Williams thanked the good fortune that found him at the time of the air assault in an office a handful of yards from the safety of the woods. He also cursed the fates that placed his wife and children in an apartment near the center of the base. An apartment building that no longer stood.

A frigid full moon in a caustically cold midnight sky was the only light the small group had to aid their frantic efforts. They had no tools to help them lift the weight of the world from those trapped below. They had no idea whether those beneath the ground were living or dead. They knew there was little hope of additional help arriving to assist them in their formidable task. Throughout the base, there were far too many rubble piles and not nearly enough survivors to fight them.

The Russian pilots hadn't purposely hit nonmilitary targets. In the cramped quarters of the small base, however, such events were bound to happen. The NCO housing area had been much too near a number of strategic buildings. There had been significant losses.

Fourteen of the thirty-one apartment buildings had fallen. In the officers' housing area nearest the command center, half the apartments were gone. The forfeiture of so many innocent lives was regrettable. Nevertheless, each side knew that in this war, the deaths of millions of noncombatants were inevitable.

Throughout the day and into the fearful night, Williams worked on without rest. There would be no respite until he knew what fate waited for him below. For nearly twelve hours he'd stopped for nothing. He'd relentlessly driven his small band toward a single goal. Find the living— or, if need be, the dead—waiting for them at the bottom of this mountain of debris. With unspoken resolve, Williams and his crew fought every ounce of steel and concrete, every bathtub and bed frame. After more than eleven hours of superhuman effort, the twenty-five-foot pile above the ground had been cut by half.

Inch by painful inch, the sergeant major fought the most important battle of his life.

Twenty feet above her as she lay in absolute darkness, the rescuers provided no hope to Kathy O'Neill. It would be nine endless hours, and the twelve feet closer it would bring them to her, for Kathy to hear the first faint sounds of salvation.

Nine hours of listening to her child cry out for her. Nine excruciating hours of believing the horror would never end.

George O'Neill's eyes flew open wide. Lying in a strange bed, without his loving wife's warmth next to him, his rest was without solace. He hadn't slept in two days. Even so, he couldn't force himself to surrender to the sleep for which his body begged. His mind wouldn't allow it. He glanced at his watch. He'd lain there for forty-five minutes this time. Forty-five minutes in the twilight between consciousness and sleep was all his tortured psyche would permit. It was fifteen minutes more than his mind had granted him the first time he attempted to rest before being dragged back into reality.

His mind raced. Where were his wife and child? What had happened to them? At this moment, they could be on a flight between Philadelphia and Minneapolis, warm, and secure, and almost home. Or they could be dead. Dead at the hands of the Russian air attack that had cut off all communication between the American headquarters and the outside world. Dead. His beautiful wife's body distorted by the cruel fate the Russian fighters spit from the sky. Dead. His tiny son lying blue and breathless in the frigid snows. Like the sergeant major who'd been his next-door neighbor, George would never find peace until he knew.

He climbed out of bed. He dragged himself back into his uniform. Beneath the haze of an eerie English streetlamp, he wandered through the mist toward the communication building. It would be a temporary distraction at best. But until he knew where his family was, work was the only peace George O'Neill would find.

And there was more than enough of that for him to do.

Before the coming day's sun would set, he'd be meeting the arriving DISA communication engineers at Mildenhall.

The time was growing near for him to counter yet another of General Yovanovich's moves.

As the night wore on, a frightening fog, cold and clammy, enveloped the incongruous landscape. The sergeant major and his meager crew scarcely noticed. They worked throughout the bitter hours without the slightest pause. The possibility of halting, even for the briefest of moments, never entered their thoughts. Their labored breaths hung over them in warm, moist clouds. They were bruised and battered from head to toe. The small groups' hands were bloody and torn. Their gloves were little more than tattered shreds of soiled cloth. With each new task, with every daunting obstacle, their bodies screamed for mercy. Still, they refused to stop.

"Sergeant Major," the teenage girl said, "we need your help over here."

"All right, Laurie. Let us finish moving this slab, and we'll be right there."

"Roy, get your back under it," Williams said. "Ryan, help me pry it out."

The soldier did as he was told. The sergeant major and teenage boy moved in. They shoved three hundred pounds of concrete off the pile and pushed it into the parking lot.

They stumbled over to where Laurie and her mother were working. Their all-consuming weariness was evident in every stilted movement.

"Okay, Laurie, let's see what you've got."

Kathy O'Neill lay throughout the infinite night, drifting in and out of consciousness. At nine in the morning, she awoke with a start. Her tortured mind told her that it had heard a sound. Muffled voices, it begged her to believe. The sounds of people working. She was confused and disoriented.

Untold questions raced through her. How long had she been unconscious this time? How long had she been entombed in mortar and cement? Had she imagined the sounds? Wishful thinking? Her mind playing tricks on her? Was it just another dream? Another cruel nightmare?

She had no answers.

Christopher was still. Asleep.

She held her breath and listened. From ground level, there came a faint noise. It was followed shortly thereafter by another. She was certain she'd heard them. She listened again, straining in the darkness with every ounce of strength she could muster for additional confirmation of what her perplexed intellect was pleading with her to believe.

Ten . . . twenty . . . thirty interminable seconds passed. It was a thousand eternities to the trapped young woman as she waited in her man-made crypt for further signs of deliverance to resound from above.

Silence greeted her. Not a single sound reached her ears.

She listened again, hoping against hope. With each tick of the clock, she prayed for confirmation that help was on the way. Yet it was no use. Silence was all that entered her black world. There was nothing there.

Darkness and despair closed in around her, overwhelming her waning hopes. Crushing waves of depression washed over Kathy. Panic possessed her and tore at her constricted throat. Anguish filled every corner of her crippled soul. She was buried alive. Buried alive, with no means of escape and little chance of rescue.

"Please, God, you've already taken one child from me. Please, God, save my baby, somehow save my child . . . Please, God, please be merciful and let me die soon."

The sergeant major hurled a huge slab of cement. It crashed on the growing jumble of debris in the apartment parking area. Kathy clearly heard it. There could be no mistake this time. There was no question that the sound was real. Further comforting noises soon followed.

She could hear them. She could hear them working. She could hear salvation reaching into this bottomless pit to save her and her child.

Now she knew.

They were coming for her.

"Hold on just a little more, Christopher," she whispered to her sleeping child. "They'll be here to get us real soon."

Once again, mankind was rising to the occasion.

A spoiled sixteen-year-old girl who'd berated her parents a day earlier for some minor transgression worked around the clock with a fury born of understanding beyond her years.

A teenage boy who only cared about his video games and his music struggled against the fates with a steadfast determination that defied explanation.

A woman who felt deprived because the single American television channel had out-of-date programming battled the elements with unbelievable power.

All over the defeated base, small groups toiled against impossible odds to aid their fellow man.

The human spirit fought on.

CHAPTER 41

Bonnie Lloyd was handed a piece of paper from off camera. She glanced down and began reading.

"We've just received this breaking news from Berlin. The Russians have hanged Manfred Fromisch. I repeat, after a trial conducted by the Russian high command, Manfred Fromisch, leader of the German neo-Nazi party, has been hanged. For the latest on this story, we take you to Berlin and our correspondent Stewart Turner."

The picture switched to the handsome face with which in the past twenty-four hours all of America had become quite familiar. Turner was standing in his usual broadcast position on the blustery roof of the Berlin Sheraton.

"Thank you, Bonnie. As you can see behind me, sunrise has taken hold here in Berlin. This historic city is awakening to its second morning under Russian rule. A half hour ago, an officer of the Russian Information Ministry came to my room here in the Sheraton. He handed me a note and the video our audience is about to see. I'd first like to warn our viewers that some of the scenes depicted in the video are rather graphic. They might wish to consider whether children should be allowed to view them. The note stated that what you're about to see happened at approximately four o'clock this morning Berlin time. That would be a little less than five hours ago. Stan," Turner said to his cameraman, "go ahead and roll it."

An inferior-quality video clip started running. The voice of the narrator was accented, but not heavily so. The scene was some sort of dingy courtroom. A panel of three stern-looking judges in Russian military uniforms could be seen. The picture slowly panned the courtroom. It stopped to show the face of a badly beaten figure. Manfred Fromisch, stooped and handcuffed, stood in front of the judges. There was no mistaking the fear on Fromisch's face.

"To the American and German people. In a trial before the Berlin Military Tribunal, the German provocateur, Manfred Fromisch, was tried for his crimes against humanity. In the same spirit as the Nuremberg trials held after World War II, the criminal was found guilty and sentenced to pay for his crimes by the immediate forfeiture of his life."

The video switched to a predawn scene of the Brandenburg Gate. Two dozen powerful spotlights illuminated the German monument. A silent gathering of what appeared to be ordinary Germans stood at the foot of a newly constructed gallows. Many of those in the crowd had been part of the forced labor involved in its construction. It would have been far easier to hang Fromisch from the nearest lamppost at the moment of his capture, but Cheninko wouldn't hear of it. He wanted a grand spectacle. He wanted the world to understand in no uncertain terms what would happen to those who dared to challenge him.

With great ceremony, Fromisch was led up the gallows' unpainted steps. A Russian officer stood the neo-Nazi leader in front of the waiting noose. A black hood was placed over Fromisch's head. The noose was positioned around his neck. The rope was tightened. The officer moved to the front of the platform and read a short statement in German and again in Russian.

A drumroll began. The officer grasped a wooden lever. He paused for dramatic effect. The lever was wrenched backward. A trapdoor beneath Fromisch's feet flew open. For an instant, the neo-Nazi leader's diminutive body jerked and twisted in the night air. Then he moved no more.

The crowd could be seen flinching and looking away. On cue, they gave a meager cheer. The picture remained focused on the grisly gallows as the voice returned.

"People of Germany and America. Manfred Fromisch is dead. This is the justice all tyrants will receive from the peace-loving peoples of the world. Soon, all who chose to follow his twisted path will receive their just rewards. There is no longer any reason to fear the reviled neo-Nazi spewers of hatred and poison. Germany is free! Stop the senseless slaughter of the German people. We beseech you to throw down your arms and send the Americans, oppressors of your country for over eighty years, home. Tell your leaders you will no longer tolerate the war and misery they and their imperialistic American and British conspirators have brought upon your homeland."

The video ended. The screen went blank.

Lloyd's face reappeared. Somberly she said, "We'll be right back after these messages."

The picture of the clashing American and Russian flags with the words THE BATTLE FOR GERMANY beneath them appeared on the screen. The theme music for the war blared.

The image on the screen changed to a woman wooing her love with the latest expensive perfume.

CHAPTER 42

In a misty, dream-shrouded ballroom, Robert danced with Linda. He was in his dress blues. She wore a flowing white wedding gown with a lengthy train. From the edges of the dance floor, an indistinguishable group of family and friends looked on with approval. It was a traditional wedding waltz. But Robert Jensen had no idea how to perform the simple box steps of the ritual dance. So he moved his feet to the music, hoping not to be too obvious in his ineptitude. More than anything, he attempted to allow his lovely bride of thirty minutes her time in the spotlight. Linda had talked of little else during the three months of their engagement. While they danced, he looked into her loving eyes.

"Linda . . . Linda . . ."

"Sarge . . . Sarge . . . Sergeant Jensen," Ramirez said. In the austere hospital bed next to his platoon sergeant's, Ramirez propped himself up with his good arm. "Are you awake? Sarge? Lieutenant Morse! Lieutenant Morse, down here!"

A woman in floral scrubs came running down the gray hall.

"What? Who's there? Where am I?" Jensen said. His voice was hoarse and distorted.

"Sarge, it's me, Ramirez. We're in the hospital in Wurzburg."

"Why can't I see?" He struggled to sit up and nearly tumbled over the hospital bed's railing.

Elizabeth Morse reached out her hand and grasped his shoulder.

She eased him back onto his pillow. "Easy there, Sergeant. You're going to tear out your stitches and IV if you're not careful."

"Who are you?"

"First Lieutenant Elizabeth Morse. I'm the charge nurse for this wing." Her throaty voice was full of power and sexuality.

"Why can't I see?"

"Your eyes are covered with bandages from your operation."

"Operation? What operation?"

"Try not to talk too much, Sergeant. Your condition's quite serious. You were operated on a little over twenty-four hours ago for a bullet wound to the foot, another in the leg, and a severe head wound. I need you to lie there quietly for me. Will you do that?"

"Yeah, I guess so." His confused mind wasn't sure if any of this was real or just part of his dream.

"Is there anything more I can do for you, Sergeant?" There was true concern in her voice.

"My leg and foot really hurt." That was unquestionably real.

"Okay. I'll find the doctor and have a stronger painkiller prescribed. If he has the time, I'll try to get him to stop by and talk with you for a moment. Watch him for me, Ramirez."

"Yes, ma'am, you can count on me."

The enticing smell of a light, sweet perfume and a strong antiseptic disappeared.

"Ramirez, where's everybody else?"

"Everybody else?"

"The rest of the guys."

"I don't know, Sarge. I guess they're all dead."

"The entire platoon?"

"I think so. But I really don't know for sure. Except for you and me, though, I'm pretty certain everyone's dead."

"What happened?"

"What do you mean, what happened? How can you not remember what happened? Don't you remember the apple orchard?"

"The apple orchard?" Jensen said.

"Yeah, the apple orchard. The Russian tanks and all that snow. Don't you remember?"

Oh, God, the apple orchard! Every moment of yesterday's horror came flooding back to the bandaged man. Each haunting face of the defeated platoon leaped into his battered brain. The taunting images dangled before him in his sightless world.

"How'd I get here?" Jensen asked, trying to shake the faces.

"That's also a long story. Let's just say Steele saved your life. I guess I had something to do with it, too."

Footsteps echoed through the open room of beds filled with the wounded. Jensen could hear the sounds of suffering all around. The smell of death was everywhere. It was an overpowering sensation he recognized all too well.

"Sergeant Jensen, I'm Dr. Wehner. How are you feeling?"

Jensen could smell the same oddly alluring combination of perfume and antiseptic. The sweet-sounding nurse had to be standing with the doctor.

"I've been better."

"Well, you're lucky to be alive. From what I've heard, if it weren't for the actions of Private Ramirez, you wouldn't be. As it was, when the medevac brought you in, we didn't know if we were going to be able to save you. It was touch-and-go there for quite a while. You're obviously a difficult man to kill, Sergeant."

"I guess that's true, sir."

"Lieutenant Morse tells me you're experiencing some discomfort."

"Yes, sir. My leg's hurting me a lot."

"Well, after the trauma you've suffered, that's quite understandable. I'll prescribe some morphine for the next couple of days. After that, we should be able to switch you to a codeine painkiller. Lieutenant Morse will be back to administer it in a couple of minutes. I'll have her set up a morphine drip after she gives you the shot so you can control the dosage yourself whenever you feel you need something for the pain. Until she gets back, you do the best you can to rest."

"Yes, sir."

The doctor turned to Ramirez. "How's your shoulder? Those bandages too tight?"

"No, sir. I'm doing okay. Inside a warm building, getting three hot meals a day, and not having to make my own bed—what more can a guy ask?"

"Private Ramirez seems to be doing just fine, Doctor," Lieutenant Morse said. "In fact, I sometimes think he might be doing just a little too fine if you know what I mean."

Ramirez grinned in response to her comments.

Dr. Wehner looked at Jensen once again. "Sergeant, if you need anything, tell Lieutenant Morse or Private Ramirez," he said. "He's already pretty much taken over running this ward anyway. I'll check in on you later if I get a chance."

"Doctor, one more thing," Jensen said.

"Yes, Sergeant."

"When will these bandages come off so I can see again?"

"The bandages will come off in a few days." The doctor hesitated. It was clear he was struggling to formulate the proper response. "Until then, we won't know if you'll ever see again. The shrapnel hit you just above the temple. The damage to that area of your head was quite extensive. Until the bandages are removed, we won't be able to tell what long-term damage your eyes might have suffered. For now, you just try to rest."

While his mind struggled to cope with what he'd been told, Jensen listened to the doctor's footsteps disappearing down the hallway.

"I'll be right back to give you the painkiller, Sergeant," Morse said. "Just take it easy while I'm gone."

A second set of footsteps disappeared down the hall. The enticing smell went with them.

"Hey, Sarge! You know what?"

"What's that Ramirez?"

"I know you can't see them, but there's a purple heart and a silver star pinned to your pillow."

"What?" He'd only half heard what Ramirez had said.

"Yeah! This three-star general was here yesterday afternoon. After I told him how you figured out how to wipe out all those Russian tanks and kept the platoon alive for as long as you did, he gave you a silver star right on the spot."

"That's great, Ramirez." There wasn't the slightest hint of enthusiasm in Jensen's voice.

"You know what else that general told me?"

"No. What?"

"He said when all this is over and done with, they're going to put you in for the Medal of Honor. He told me that normally the act of heroism has to be witnessed by two people, and they only had me. But in your case, my story matched with reports they'd received about what was happening up at the border. So he had this captain take my statement. The captain said he's pretty sure you're going to get it."

"That's nice, Ramirez." But it didn't really matter one way or another to the wounded platoon sergeant. At this moment, he would have eagerly traded all the medals in the world for any of the men of his platoon.

Accompanied by her footsteps, the sweet smell returned.

"Okay, Sergeant, I'm going to give you a shot of morphine. This is going to sting a little."

He could feel her cold hands on his hip. A pinprick rushed to his brain. It was nothing more than a minor annoyance compared to the pain he was in.

"That should do it," Morse said. "In a few minutes, the morphine will take hold. It'll relieve your pain and put you back to sleep. I'll be around in a while to set up your morphine drip and show you how to use it."

The footsteps headed down the hallway once again.

When the footsteps were gone, Ramirez said, "Sarge, guess what."

"What is it now, Ramirez?"

"I'm in love."

"Again?"

"I mean it this time, Sarge."

"A real looker, huh, Ramirez?"

"Face like an angel, Sarge. Face like an angel. Long dark hair and big brown eyes. And, Sarge, I don't care how much she tries to hide it, there's a body under that nurse's uniform that just won't quit."

"Well, she sure smells nice. Maybe someday if I'm real lucky, I'll get to see the face that matches the sweet smell. By the way, Ramirez, why the hell are you in here?"

"Well, Sarge, let's just say I took a bullet for a friend and leave it at that for now."

As he returned to the land where his pain was relegated to his dreams, Jensen wondered what Ramirez had meant by his odd response. It wasn't long before the powerful drug took hold. Jensen drifted deep into the world within his mind. Once again, he was dancing with his beautiful bride. Her flowing dress swirled behind her. Linda's captivating smile radiated throughout the corners of the glistening room.

This time, however, the faces of the people standing on the edges of the dance floor were no longer indistinguishable.

The faces of the onlookers were those of the dead soldiers of 2nd Platoon.

CHAPTER 43

As darkness had fallen upon Ramstein on the previous evening, the immediate response to the dire threat created by the deadly parachutists was to hammer them with an immense strike by B-2 bombers or a relentless assault by napalm-loaded fighter aircraft. Either approach was one that would have destroyed the vast majority of the fanatical killers within the foreboding woods' sheltering branches. Within minutes, however, it became clear that neither action was one the Americans would want to undertake.

The risk from both was far too great.

With the base's fences so near the masking trees, even the slightest miscalculation by a single B-2 during the nighttime assault and rather than dropping its massive load of essence-devouring bombs on the Russians, it would strike Ramstein instead. Such an error was one with the potential to severely damage the critical runways. With the huge bomb craters the errant strike would create, it would take incalculable hours, possibly days, to repair the extensive damage. The B-2's mistake would have accomplished the parachutists' mission for them. Ramstein would be out of the war for an indefinite period by the Americans' own hands.

Burning down every tree in the profuse forest with napalm strikes was certainly tempting. But creating a raging forest fire on the eastern and southern edges of the air base, especially with the prevailing winds,

was a far greater peril than anyone wished to face. Watching the endlessly cascading embers sailing toward the base's structures was something none of them wanted to see. And the horror of being unable to
stop the torrent of falling flames tumbling into the base ammunition-
storage dump was beyond reason. They needed to find another far-less-
hazardous way.

This was an action requiring a surgeon's scalpel, not a butcher's
cleaver. And there were numerous alternative methods available to the
defenders to eliminate the perilous menace to the base's continuing
existence without accidentally destroying Ramstein in the process.

Precision, not brutality, was what was required.

The circumstances called for helicopters, drones, mortars, and
Bradleys.

Within minutes of the Russians escape into the woods, the Americans
undertook a powerful response. First, six Apaches appeared like aveng-
ing angels over the forest. Without warning, the helicopters dove at the
snowy evergreens. Rios watched their guns blazing in the early-evening
darkness. The tortured shrieks of the wounded and dying were carried
to him on the crisp night air. Deep within the dark forest, Russian blood
flowed down the broad trunks of the ancient trees.

The Russians responded with venom of their own. They added their
own brand of poison to the witches' brew. Antiaircraft missiles soared
up through the branches. The missiles screamed through the forest's
canopy. An exploding Apache fell from the low heavens in thirty flaming pieces.

The Apaches sought to revenge their squadron's loss. The killers
from above brought perdition's fires down upon the treetops. Rockets
ripped through the thick evergreens. Five 30mm chain guns rained
unspeakable savagery upon the ground below. The Russians clawed
deeper into their holes, digging for the earth's frail protection. Like a
heavy spring sap, the crushed remains of the parachutists' tattered
bodies oozed onto the forest floor. The forest's snows turned bright red.
Suffering and carnage were everywhere.

The angel of death looked down through the darkness and smiled a broad, satisfied smile.

Twelve Black Hawk helicopters, supported by half as many furiously buzzing drones, swooped in to relieve their brothers. The Black Hawks' machine guns kept the pressure on. Once again, missiles and rockets rained down. The less-well-armored Black Hawks were an easier prey for the enemy hiding in the trees. In the first ten minutes of this new battle between ground and air, three whirling rotor blades stopped in midflight when struck by a hail of gunfire. When they were hit, the crippled Black Hawks slowly spun out of control. They plunged into the waiting evergreens. Spinning helplessly toward the unforgiving ground, the Black Hawk crews watched their lives coming to an end. The exploding helicopters filled the wicked night with mayhem once more. The Black Hawks pulled back.

The drones continued their relentless pressure.

The 82nd Airborne's mortar teams raced to set up their firing tubes on the runways. A mortar barrage of fearsome intensity came down around the Russians' heads. The exploding mortar rounds cut deep swaths through the trees. The majestic timbers were splintered by the fierce assault. The parachutists answered back. Using the long range of their sniper rifles, the Russians responded by picking off the soldiers of the mortar teams one by one. The surviving burgundy berets grabbed their equipment and withdrew. The helicopters returned to take their place.

The Apaches struck once more. Scores of rockets roared from beneath the attackers' bellies. Shimmering fireworks thundered as the soul-stealing armaments struck the trees. The lethal munitions fought their way through the heavy foliage, reaching for the mortal flesh hiding on the frozen ground below.

With each new clash, the fence line would be illuminated by glittering flashes of fire and light. Like a sudden summer storm, the thundering bursts distorted the winter world, turning it surreal and misshaping its images. The menacing lightning bolts caused the dead Wilson to appear to be trying to speak. Wilson's spectral grin, flashing over and over again in the darkness, haunted Rios and Goodman.

"Wilson, leave me alone!" Rios screamed.

But Wilson continued to grin and talk with every fearsome burst.

Death reached up to pluck a second spinning blackbird from the star-filled heavens. Another Apache went down.

The Bradleys rolled onto the runways. The fighting vehicles' crews unleashed a curtain of cannon fire with their Bushmasters. The parachutists cut holes in the fences in a number of locations and futilely attempted to answer back with their shoulder-mounted antitank missiles. The killing went on without letup. The night reached its middle, and a suffocating fog rolled in upon the gruesome darkness. The casualties on both sides grew with every passing minute. During the countless hours, the suffering never ceased.

Finally, the sun rose on a new day. As it continued its midmorning journey, the morose shroud of frigid gray refused to relinquish its strangstranglehold upon the mangled forest. It was apparent that Ramstein would remain covered in a heavy fog for many hours to come.

Half of the one thousand parachutists who had reached the safety of the woods as darkness fell had failed to see the morning. The night's sixteen hours of killing were finally at their end. A day filled with anguish was about to begin.

The smothering fog had swallowed the world around them. In the middle of a fierce battle involving thousands of men, the two airmen in the isolated bunker were all alone.

Hidden deep within the sand, Rios indiscriminately fired his machine gun into the mist-shrouded forest. The Russians answered back with wild gunfire of their own. Every now and then, mortal screams shattered the sinister morning as combatants on both sides were felled by a perverse death's random whims.

The only parts of Rios's body that were visible were his hands and forearms. With his tattered gloves, he gripped the powerful gun. There was no need to expose himself further to the enemy. The fog had grown so thick in the past few hours that he could not make out the ghostly fence fifty feet away. There was no possibility of seeing the parachutists lurking in the trees beyond even if he tried. During the unrelenting hours, Rios had learned a painful lesson from the Russian snipers and their lethal night scopes. While he watched his countrymen die around him, he'd discovered that an exposed American was a dead American.

"Goodman, the Russian rifle fire's picking up again. I sure could use some help up here."

Near the rear of the bunker, the luckless Goodman grappled with a badly bleeding left thigh. The wound was the result of a parachutist's haphazard handiwork. He looked up at Rios and spoke through clenched teeth.

"Let me try to get this bleeding stopped first. The bullet hole in the back of my leg's so damn big that no matter what I do, I can't seem to slow it down."

Next to Goodman, Wilson's body lay where it had been tossed by a sniper's bullet seventeen hours earlier. The back of Wilson's head was gone. The dead airman was faceup in the pink snow. Beneath what remained of his splintered skull, the pool of blood and brain cells was frozen solid. The silly grin on Wilson's face was also frozen in place. The grin would be there for all eternity.

The grin haunted Rios and Goodman throughout the long night. The annoying smile on the purplish lips mocked them. It was as if the smirking Wilson knew something in death that they could not know. It was almost as if Wilson were urging them to come join him in his ghoulish discovery. The eerie grin had enticed Rios, beseeching him to unmask Wilson's unearthly secret. More than once during the terror of a horrific night of continual angst, Rios had believed it might be better to get it over with once and for all. A quick death from a sniper's bullet just might be the ticket.

He'd fought those beckoning impulses often during the darkest moments. It would've been so simple. All he had to do was leap to his feet. In a matter of seconds, his misery would end. He'd receive the sleep for which his body screamed. A long, satisfying sleep. A sleep to last forever.

On more than one occasion, he'd come close to giving in to his tortured mind's persistent prodding. Yet in the end, his innate need to survive hadn't allowed him to take that final step into oblivion.

"Goodman, I'm almost out of ammunition."

Goodman dragged himself through the dirty snow toward the front of the bunker.

"Use my M-4 if you have to. I've still got two clips left." The grimacing Goodman dug into his parka pockets and pulled out the ammunition clips. "Here."

Seventeen hours they'd been pinned down by the Russians. Unlike the maniacal enemy Rios had battled on the previous day, the group he clashed with during the eternal night had been exceptionally patient. They'd spent the dark hours picking off the sixty airmen protecting the eastern fence. By 10:00 a.m. on a winter morning thick with a suffocating blanket of morbid gray, only eight of the airmen on the fence line had survived unharmed.

The fog had hampered the Americans' efforts. Three times during the night, small groups of Russians had found openings in the air base's defenses. They slipped through unnoticed and headed for the aircraft hangars. Deeper inside the base, the M-1s, Bradleys, and Humvees waited. Each time, the armored vehicles' sophisticated thermal sights located the invaders. On all three occasions, the 24th Infantry soldiers, supported by the burgundy berets, stopped the Russians before any serious harm could be done.

A fourth close call had occurred at a little before five. Nine parachutists crept through the fence and got to within a few hundred yards of the ammunition-storage area. The parachutists were preparing to fire rockets into the huge mountain of ordnance when two airborne soldiers in a Humvee spotted them. An expertly placed burst from the Humvee's machine gun dropped six of the Russians. A second quick squeeze of the trigger eliminated the rest. Ten more seconds, and the eastern half of Ramstein would have disappeared in a crushing explosion.

Even if they'd accomplished nothing more, the presence of the parachutists and their lethal antiaircraft missiles at the end of the runways had caused Ramstein's planes to remain on the ground. The fighter aircraft had sat throughout the night in their deeply bunkered worlds. The pilots' inability to take to the skies had been acutely felt by the frontline soldiers in desperate need of air support.

With Ramstein out of the fray, the task of wrestling the Russians for control of the heavens had fallen upon Lakenheath and Mildenhall. Using their superior weapons, the American pilots from across the English Channel had succeeded in claiming tenuous ownership of the moonlit skies.

Reinforced by a number of stateside squadrons and supported by the Royal Air Force, the American fighters had done a magnificent job of crossing the narrow seas and holding on to the night. During the long hours of air combat, the star-strewn skies had been dominated by the outnumbered defenders. The talented American pilots had forced back threat after threat from the dogged MiGs.

Still, the besieged ground forces would have no chance of surviving the coming day without the continuing dominance of their air forces. If they were going to avoid a quick defeat, the Allies had to rule the skies.

As the sun edged higher on the second full day of the war, the Americans knew they'd have to improve their fragile hold upon the heavens. To do so, the Russians had to be cleaned out of the woods around Ramstein. With the parachutists eliminated, Ramstein's powerful air assets would be able to race into battle once more. With Ramstein back in the war, the Americans would be in an excellent position to maintain some control of the skies throughout the second day.

Without Ramstein, all was lost.

With Ramstein out of the war, another massive Russian air assault similar to the one on the previous morning would undoubtedly succeed in gaining permanent control of the air war.

For the moment, the Americans were in no position to stop such a determined attack. Ramstein's fighters had to rejoin the struggle. And they had to do it soon. While the sun continued its frosty rise, eradicating the staunch parachutists hidden deep within the twilight of the sinister woods had become an imperative.

It would be no easy task. With seventeen hours to prepare for the American attack, the Russians were well dug in. Their positions were strongly fortified. And despite the untold agony they'd experienced, the surviving parachutists were as resolute as they'd been yesterday afternoon. The Russians weren't yet ready to concede defeat. In fact, they believed quite the opposite. Despite the sobering reality of their situation, the parachutists remained convinced that a miraculous victory would somehow be theirs. Ramstein would fall. They were certain of it. They'd gone through a hellish night of endless cruelty at the hands of the fierce American assaults. Yet despite everything the Americans tried, the parachutists were still there, ready and waiting. And as lethal as ever.

As the long hours passed, the 82nd Airborne had waited for the sunrise. Entering the forest in total darkness to battle such an elite enemy was beyond consideration. The Americans were certainly their equals. But during the horrid night, they'd have to battle from afar and wait for the new day before daring to approach the killing ground.

The situation in the skies over Germany was growing desperate. The Americans had to get Ramstein's fighters back into the war. They couldn't wait any longer. The time had come to enter the ominous woods. The burgundy berets would use the thick fog to conceal their presence. In small groups, the airborne soldiers started silently slipping into the trees on both sides of the base. In fifteen minutes, nearly a thousand Americans had infiltrated the tattered forest. Five hundred talented assassins waited in the mist to greet them.

One company of American paratroopers and the surviving M-1s and Bradleys were left in reserve inside Ramstein.

Both sides had spent thousands of hours preparing for the hand-to-hand combat that was moments away from erupting in the frightening forest. This time the dying was going to be up close and personal.

In twos and threes, American apparitions warily crept into the malignant evergreens. Step by stolen step, they drew ever deeper into the shadowy woods. The enemy bided his time. Behind fallen logs, in fog-infested glades, in the trunk of the next tree, the Russians watched and waited. The Americans continued on.

Without warning, a burst of gunfire rattled through the branches, echoing from limb to limb as it shattered the morning's fleeting calm. Two shots rang out in return. A scream filled the forest on the far left. Another mortal cry could be heard in the distance. A soldier's death rattle was devoured by the gray world. Two spectral figures sprang into lethal combat. Their long knives glistened. Further battle to the left. A struggle on the right. The forest was suddenly full of life. And death.

The Russians had the element of surprise. The Americans had the superior numbers. In the beginning, surprise was winning. Two Americans fell for every Russian loss. The pitched battle wore on, reaching the twenty-minute point. And as the Russian positions were identified and engaged, superior numbers steadily turned the tide toward the burgundy berets. Blood flowed like a raging river. The fight, man on man, went on without pause.

After forty minutes of nonstop killing, it was painfully obvious to the Russians that their position was hopeless. Three-fourths of the parachutists who had slipped into the forest as yesterday's sun fell were dead. The survivors were outnumbered three to one. The final 250 knew if they stayed where they were, they'd soon be joining their mortally wounded comrades. And Ramstein would still be standing.

A new plan was hastily drawn. It was conceived at the height of the fierce struggle in the fog-filled forest. It would be little more than suicide, but it was the only option left. Leaving a small force behind in the woods to hold off the Americans, the parachutists would make an all-out assault at the fence lines. If they could catch the Americans unprepared, they might be able to break through the wire and breach the enemy's defenses. All it would take was one swift missile into the air base's mountain of high explosives to avenge their comrades' deaths and their own impending ones.

If they could get near enough to the ammunition-storage area, their efforts and the efforts of their fallen friends would not have been wasted.

Five minutes inside the fence was all they'd need to be in a position for a shot at the storage depot.

Surprise would be everything.

In the forest's gray world, the Russians disengaged. The parachutists slipped away. Handfuls remained behind to occupy the Americans. Using the frozen fog to shield them, the Russians stealthily moved toward the southern and eastern fences. The burgundy berets noticed a marked decrease in the struggle. But for the moment, they didn't understand the reason for the abrupt change in the battle's intensity. After an hour of unrelenting killing, the 82nd Airborne's soldiers presumed the vast majority of the Russians had been eliminated. The Americans believed the battle was nearly over. They cautiously continued to search the shadows deep within the solemn forest for further signs of the enemy.

The Russians' main force was quite near the fence. The snipers inside the tree line intensified their fire, pinning down the handful of surviving Americans on the other side of the wire. The desperate mission was poised to commence.

"Man, I can't get this bleeding stopped," Goodman said. Pain was etched on his features.

Preoccupied with his own injuries, Goodman hadn't been listening to the gruesome fight to the death that floated on the thick haze out of the tortured trees. But Rios had heard the dying quite clearly.

The sounds of battle, the quick bursts of gunfire, and the cries of anguish had been carried to him on the heavy layers of gray. For the past ten minutes, the sounds had been growing increasingly quiet. Like the American airborne soldiers, the embattled airman suspected the second struggle for Ramstein would soon be at its end.

It would be. But not for the reasons the exhausted airman suspected.

"Hang in there," Rios said. "The battle's almost over in the woods. The snipers are making one last attempt to find us before the 82nd Airborne finds them. After that, we'll be home free. There's hardly any fighting going on. I'll bet the medics will be able to get out here to get you in the next fifteen minutes."

Goodman stared at the glistening blood covering every inch of his pant leg. "I don't know if I'll last that long."

"Sure you will. Just tighten that tourniquet real good and hold on. I'm certain help will be here soon."

Yet as Rios cautiously peeked over the wall of sand at the devouring world around him, he wasn't certain of anything. He couldn't see more than a few feet. And he wasn't at all sure what was happening. The airman slid back into the bunker. He sat staring at nothing in particular, wondering what to do next. He thought about firing a few rounds into the woods from Goodman's M-4. He decided, however, to wait a little longer before reminding the snipers he was still here, ready to take their lives should they make a mistake.

Much to his surprise, the world around him was about to turn upside down.

CHAPTER 44

A dozen satchel charges were tossed from the trees.

Without warning, the chain link exploded. Gaping holes appeared everywhere. In the confusion, scores of parachutists rushed through the eastern fence before anyone could react to what had happened. A similar group burst through the southern wire.

The largest force, nearing one hundred in number, broke through in the center of the shattered eastern wall. They appeared out of nowhere. They ran toward Rios's bunker.

Caught by surprise, the two hundred American airborne soldiers inside the base moved to counterattack. But in the heavy fog, the bewildered Americans had no idea what had just transpired. The Bradleys and M-1s were picking up movement everywhere.

Rios leaped to his feet. Fifty gray ghosts were headed straight for him.

"Jesus! Goodman, get up here quick! The Russians have broken through the fence."

Rios grabbed Goodman's M-4. He fired at the attackers. It didn't even slow the parachutists down. The Russians ran in every direction. They raced past the bunker. Running at full speed, a parachutist hurled his body into the sandbags. The bunker collapsed. It fell in on the still-firing Rios. The airman was pinned beneath the heavy layers of sand. He struggled to free himself from the trap. But it was too late. The parachutist was on him in a flash.

Arturo Rios stared into the angry features of the man who was going to take his life. The remorseless Russian, five years older and fifty pounds heavier, stared back at him. The menacing parachutist's long knife glistened as he raised it to plunge deep into Rios's heart.

The six-inch blade flashed as the Russian struck. At the last possible instant, the desperate airman freed his left arm just enough to partially deflect the powerful blow. The knife missed its target by the narrowest of margins. It sliced into Rios's shoulder. The steel dug deep into the struggling airman's flesh. The blade sank to its hilt. It tore a huge gash just below his collarbone.

Rios screamed in pain. His face was distorted with anguish. His arm went limp against his side. The Russian ripped the knife from his victim. He prepared to stab a second time to finish the kill. This time there'd be no escape. The American wouldn't survive. The parachutist raised the knife over his head. Its silver blade flashed once more in the suffocating mist. Rios was trapped by the sand and pinned by his heavier opponent. He lay helpless. Death was full in his eyes. The Russian's arm swung downward.

Goodman wrenched Wilson's M-4 from the grinning corpse's hands. He fired a long burst from five feet away. The rounds caught the attacker square in the face. He was dead before what little remained of his head hit the ground.

Two parachutists turned toward the sound of the firing. They spotted the American standing at the rear of the demolished bunker. Both opened up with their machine pistols.

Bullets riddled Goodman's body. He crumpled to the ground. Within seconds of killing the Russian assassin, Goodman followed him into the next realm.

Hidden by the sand, Rios lay unmoving. The parachutists were in a hurry to reach their objective. There was no time to waste. In their haste, the severely wounded airman was overlooked.

It was a race to see if Ramstein would remain in the war. The Russians had caught the Americans off guard. The parachutists ran at full speed toward the ammunition depot. It would be a half-mile run through deep snows before they'd be in a position to fire their final four antitank missiles into the base's armaments. The Russians were superbly conditioned. But exhausted by the relentless events of the eternal night and weighed down by their equipment, they would need five minutes to arrive at a point where they could release their missiles with any hope of success.

The parachutists were on foot. Their enemy was in fast-moving vehicles. Even so, the American response was slow and disjointed. They hadn't anticipated such a bold move. And with the poor visibility, the Americans were still uncertain of what had actually occurred. One thing was definite, something was happening, and they needed to figure out what it was as quickly as they could. The 82nd Airborne battalion commander had been busy with the reports coming in from the caustic battle in the woods. He refocused his attention on the new threat. The confusing information from his armored forces about what their thermal sights were seeing wasn't helping.

"Send a half dozen scout vehicles to the fences to find out what the hell's going on," the battalion commander ordered.

Six Humvees rushed away. In each Humvee, a pair of Americans roared into the clouds and disappeared. Small groups of Russians raced in every direction to confuse the Americans and mask their true intentions. All six Humvees quickly came under fire from these roving bands of raiders. The confusion inside the fence continued. Each scout team reported that they'd made contact with the enemy. The Russians appeared to be everywhere. How many there actually were, and from exactly where they'd come, no one knew. More importantly, what they were attempting to accomplish was still undetermined.

It was the teams in the two Humvees on the far left who were the first to figure out the parachutists' true intentions. They spotted a significant Russian force carrying satchel charges and missiles running toward the ammunition depot.

The sergeant in the Humvee second from the far left keyed his headset. "Sir, they're after the ammunition-storage area!"

"That's right, Colonel!" the corporal in the final Humvee said.

"There's no doubt about it! Must be about a hundred of them headed that way."

The battalion commander trusted completely in the judgment of his scouts. "Roger," he said. "We're on our way."

Both Humvees circled even farther to the left. They were determined to cut the Russians off and hold them at bay until help arrived. The parachutists could hear the Humvees racing ahead of them. But they were just as handicapped by the fog as the Americans while playing their deadly game of hide-and-seek. They knew the Humvees were out there somewhere. Nevertheless, in the dense fog, they couldn't determine where.

Three hundred yards closer to the depot, both Humvees were waiting in the dull gray. When the first running Russian appeared through the haze, the Humvees opened fire with their machine guns. A handful of parachutists went down. The rest fell back. Using the fog to protect them, they dropped to the ground fifty yards from the Americans. The Humvees continued to fire, pinning the Russians' noses in the snow.

Given time, the parachutists would've sent men to the left and right to encircle the Americans. But they had no time. Time belonged to their enemy. Every second they delayed was one more second American reinforcements had to arrive. The Russians could hear the armored vehicles and Humvees roaring across the wide base in their direction. They couldn't wait. They had to destroy the American soldiers who stood in their way. Ninety machine pistols opened fire.

A Humvee's crew went down. Their machine gun was forever silenced. The other Americans remained in the fight. The Russians scrambled to their feet. Firing as they ran, they charged straight for the sound of the American machine gun. The corporal and his driver fought back with everything they had. One after another, more of the Russians appeared through the fog. Each crumpled to the ground when hit by the steady stream of machine-gun bullets and rifle fire. Even so, the parachutists didn't waver. They continued their feverish charge toward the spitting guns.

From out of the gray a hand grenade landed five feet from the Humvee. The grenade exploded. The Americans fired no more. Seventy-five parachutists had survived. They raced past the dead soldiers sprawled across the battered vehicles.

The Russians were in the clear once more. In another minute, they'd be in a position to fire their missiles. They ran through the masking world toward the ammunition depot.

In large numbers, the quicker Humvees raced ahead of the Bradleys and M-1s. They swept through the ground-hugging fog in their desperate search for the Russians. Behind the Humvees, an overpowering force of venomous armor roared across the runways. The Americans hurried toward the sounds of the battle the destroyed scout teams had been waging. With the world gone quiet once again, the burgundy berets scoured the swirling mist for the enemy.

By now, the battalion commander was certain of what the Russians were up to. The parachutists were making a suicide attack on the ammunition-storage area. After what his men had gone through, there was no way he was going to let the parachutists snatch victory from the jaws of their impending defeat. He had to protect the ammunition depot at all cost. Three M-1s were ordered to change course and head for a blocking position in front of the bomb-storage area.

The trio of tanks peeled off. They rushed toward their objective. The remainder of the battalion continued to search for their elusive prey. The Russians had to be out there somewhere and not too far away.

They were.

Four parachutists knelt on the cold ground. They'd penetrated far enough into the base to have reached a point where they could try firing a missile into the storage area's front gate. They shoved their night-vision equipment over their faces, hoping it would somehow help them penetrate the heavy fog. It didn't help much. From this distance, they were really guessing. It was going to be a long, difficult shot. Yet if any of the four succeeded, eighteen hours of watching their comrades die would've been worth it. Ramstein would be leveled in a mighty blast. American Air Force Headquarters would be destroyed. The American munitions would be gone. The great air base would be out of the war. Russia's victory would be assured.

The kneeling parachutists waited. It had been a difficult run across the snows. Each had a single missile. If they were going to have any chance, they'd have to bring their labored breathing under control. For thirty seconds, they waited for their heavy panting to subside. It seemed like an hour. All around, their fellow parachutists fanned out to protect them.

The time had come. Their breathing and their nerves were finally calm enough to attempt the desperate volley. Each raised his missile to his shoulder. They could just make out in their sights what they were certain was the depot's opening.

Suddenly, the opening disappeared. Something had moved in front of the depot's entrance. Each parachutist recognized that his shot was gone. Three M-1s had materialized from nowhere. They were sitting side by side one hundred yards from the depot's gate. The huge tanks had formed an impenetrable barrier that only a miracle could breach. There was no way to fire a missile into the American munitions. For an instant, the parachutists thought about firing anyway. Destroying an M-1 would at least let the parachutists go to their graves with a moral victory. There was no chance, however, that their small missiles could defeat any of the three monsters' heavy frontal plating and destroy an American armored vehicle. The gunners dropped the weapons from their shoulders and hung their heads.

In the fog, the lead Humvee's team was right on top of the Russians before they spotted them. The Americans roared forward. The Humvee's machine gun blazed. Burst after burst ripped into the exposed parachutists. The Russians responded with their automatic weapons. Three more Humvees leaped into action. They jumped into the middle of the fray. More were right behind. The Russians fell back. They'd been caught in the open. The nearest fence was a half mile away. There would be no chance of escape. They knew they'd pay for their failure with their lives.

The parachutists did the only thing they could. They fought and died on the bloody ground of Ramstein. At the very least, they were determined to drag a few more Americans into the netherworld with them. They'd been close to victory. In the end, however, the parachutists' defeat was complete. In a one-sided battle, all seventy-five went down beneath the power of the swarming Americans.

The depot had survived. Its immense supply of bombs and missiles would continue to be carried to the flight line. The bellies and wings of the American fighter aircraft would be filled with death and destruction over and again in the days to come.

Throughout the base, the handfuls of surviving parachutists were soon identified, isolated, and destroyed. With a vengeance, the Americans swooped down upon the remaining pockets of resistance. They swiftly eliminated the last of their airborne adversaries.

The process of cleaning up the battlefield began. Wounded parachutists were shown no mercy. The revenge-minded Americans killed them on the spot. Far too many of their friends lay dead in the fields and woods surrounding Ramstein for them to show any compassion to their ruthless opponent.

It was all over. The Americans had won. Ramstein was back in their control. The parachutists had been swept clean from the evergreen forest and the runways of the immense base. The time had come to sweep the German skies clean.

Squadrons of virulent fighters rose from Ramstein's runways. They burst through the fog and headed into the late-morning sky. Flight after flight roared east to vanquish the enemy.

It was now almost a certainty. With Ramstein back in the war, the skies on the second day would belong to the Americans.

In another hour, the air police would discover the lone surviving airman in the collapsed bunker near the middle of the eastern fence. Rios was plucked from the sand. The critically wounded airman was rushed to the base hospital.

Inside the chaotic hospital, Arturo Rios lay unmoving while medics applied sutures and dressings to his mauled shoulder. The young airman knew he'd survived to fight another day. That thought, however, gave him little comfort. He'd witnessed far too much death and come much too near his own to ever again be the same. He'd straddled the line that separates the living from the dead, and he was no longer sure on which side of the line he truly belonged.

Stoically, he stared at the ceiling while they attended to his wound. The light in his dark eyes no longer burned.

In many ways, he envied Wilson and Goodman.

CHAPTER 45

Sergeant Major Harold Williams lifted a crushed and twisted bed frame. He passed it up to those at ground level. Twenty feet away, the teenage boy dug in another section of the shattered building. The two were well into the bombed-out basement. All morning long, they'd been painfully raising cement and furniture over their heads and handing it to those above.

For the past twenty-four hours, the exhausted fifteen-year-old had worked on without thinking. With every inch of his tortured body pleading with him to stop, he continued his demented digging. For each member of the determined group, it had become an all-encompassing fixation. Using only their bare hands, they were going to defeat the tons of mortar and concrete to reach into hell and rescue those trapped below.

If they could find anyone alive.

The boy peered into the twisted rubble. A curious expression spread across his face. For a better view, he knelt and pressed his nose against a small opening next to a crumbling cement slab. He looked up at the sergeant major with a start.

"Hey, Sergeant Major! I think I see something down there!"

"What is it, Ryan?" Williams answered.

The boy stuck his face into the opening once again. He turned back to the sergeant major. "It's a baby! And he's alive!"

Williams rushed through the jumbled refuse toward the boy's position. "Are you certain?"

"Yeah. I can see him moving."

The rescue party scrambled into the hole. The weariness of twenty-four hours of mind-numbing toil was swept away in an instant. Harold Williams was the first to arrive. He knelt and looked into the opening next to the top of one of the laundry room's dryers. Three feet below, he could see the small child.

"Christopher! Christopher!"

The baby moved in response to Williams's words.

"It's okay, little one; lie still. We'll have you out of there in no time."

While he stared into the hole, the sergeant major saw something else. He looked up at the group of rescuers.

"There's an outstretched hand a few inches from the baby."

"Is it moving?" one of the women asked.

"No," Williams said. "Mrs. Reed, why don't you and Laurie go see if you can find those medics who were around here a few hours ago. I think Christopher's going to need them real soon."

The woman and her daughter hurriedly climbed to ground level. Each set out in a different direction in search of the medics.

While they walked through what remained of the housing area, the news spread like a raging forest fire. A tiny survivor had been found at the bottom of the pit where Building 2417 had stood.

The sergeant major and the teenage boy started working at eliminating the three feet of debris separating them from their prize. After a full day of backbreaking effort, the valiant rescuers' reward was within their grasp.

Williams lifted the dazed handful of a child from the depths of the depravity. He handed him to the taller of the waiting medics. A crowd of forty had gathered at the edge of the pit. As the little one was carried out, the cheer from the exhausted onlookers was meager but genuine.

The medic placed Christopher in a thick woolen blanket. He handed the blanket to Mrs. Reed. She held the confused child as lovingly as if he were her own. The medic started examining the filthy toddler.

"His heartbeat's really strong," the medic said. "But he's got to be badly dehydrated. How long's it been since the attack?"

"Twenty-six hours," someone in the crowd volunteered.

"We need to check him real close for shock and exposure," the other medic said.

"Let's get him into the ambulance and get an IV in him," the first medic said. "Then why don't you look him over real good while I climb back down into the basement to see if there's any chance the person they spotted next to where the baby was found is still alive."

The seven rescuers watched as the whimpering child was taken to the ambulance. Each felt a soaring roller coaster of emotions rush through them at incalculable speed. Their pride spewed forth. It swelled in their chests and burst into their battered brains. For the rest of their existence, they'd know they'd saved a life. But at the same time, they also understood that more than twenty others, dead or alive, were still buried beneath the unyielding jumble of the demolished building.

Their herculean task had a long way to go.

By the time the medic returned to the abyss, the sergeant major and the teenage boy had uncovered the area around the outstretched arm. The rest of Kathy's body remained securely encased in its tomb of suffocating wreckage. The rescuers were unable to see anything in the devastation beyond the exposed limb.

"It's got to be Kathy," Williams said.

"You know who it is, Sergeant Major?" the boy asked.

"Yeah, it's got to be Christopher's mother, Kathy O'Neill. She and her husband lived across the hall from us on the second floor."

The medic took his stethoscope and held it on Kathy's bluish forearm. He listened for a second and pulled it away. He quickly placed it back on the outstretched arm. This time he listened for what seemed an eternity.

"My God," the medic said, "I've got a pulse. It's weak, but I'm certain I heard it. Whoever's under there is alive."

Harold Williams struggled with the medic's startling news. The wonderful possibilities created by the medic's surprising revelation were unmistakable. If Kathy's alive, there's hope for the rest. If Kathy's alive, his family could be, too. There was one thing the sergeant major realized with resounding clarity. Dead or alive, he wouldn't allow himself a minute's rest until he'd accounted for everyone buried in this unspeakable place.

"Are you sure?" the sergeant major asked.

"Yeah, I'm sure. Listen for yourself."

He handed Williams the stethoscope. The medic helped him place the instrument on Kathy's arm. The sergeant major held his breath and listened.

There it was. The heartbeat was weak but definitely present. A wide grin spread across Williams's dirt-streaked face.

"What are we waiting for! There's another one down here to save!"

"We'd better hurry, Sergeant Major," the medic said. "It doesn't sound like she can last much longer."

The word spread through the crowd like a lightning bolt. Another one down there to save. There were eighty eager hands grasping at the edge of the hole, each wanting to be a part of the miraculous rescue. It was, however, still the sergeant major's show.

He surveyed the task in front of them.

"We've got to get this beam off her first."

After many hours of laborious practice, the boy had become an expert at judging the effort involved in clearing the next rubble pile.

"Probably take a dozen of us to get something that big out of here and up to ground level."

The sergeant major turned to the crowd. "Carefully, very carefully, I need twelve people to climb down and help us clear this beam away. Then I need another group at the edge of the pit to lift it out of here once we get it up to you."

A dozen people, women and teenagers mostly, climbed into the hole.

"Careful," Williams said, "careful where you walk. There may be other survivors down here." The hope in his voice was genuine.

The group set about the onerous task. They had to hurry. But one mistake could be fatal. They warily freed the rubble from around the ancient beam. Then, with the sergeant major as their anchor, the group put their backs into it. Ever so slowly, the giant monolith rose from the grave. The end nearest Kathy's arm was raised a few feet into the air. The sergeant major slipped beneath the twelve-hundred-pound slab. With his broad back in place, he guaranteed that no matter what it took, the beam would never be allowed to return to the pile.

Others rushed into the space the sergeant major had created. The slab was torturously lifted from the ground. With all their might, the group succeeded in propping the imposing pillar against the side of the hole. From there it was easy. Above them, twenty-five sets of hands clawed for a firm grip on the monolith. The massive beam was dragged up to ground level and pushed aside. The last impediment to Kathy's rescue had disappeared.

"Great job! Great job!" Williams said.

Their task completed, the twelve climbed back out of the basement.

The medic and the teenage boy went to work clearing the area above Kathy's arm. The sergeant major went after where he expected Kathy's legs to be.

In ten minutes, the job was completed.

"Jesus!" the sergeant major said. "Get over here quick."

One look at Kathy's leg and the medic knew what they faced. The leg was severely twisted. A razor-sharp piece of jagged bone was sticking through the skin just below her right knee.

"Man," the medic said, "that's the worst-looking compound fracture I've ever seen."

The boy had just finished uncovering Kathy's head.

"You'd better take a look at this, too."

The medic examined the area where Kathy's head had suffered the greatest blow from the falling beam.

"Looks like a possible skull fracture," the medic said.

The coagulated blood in Kathy's once-beautiful hair was thick and matted.

"Nasty gash to the back of her head. Going to take a lot of stitches to sew that up. I need a stretcher and some splints down here right away!" the medic yelled to those at ground level.

"Is she gonna make it?" the boy asked.

"I don't know. She's in pretty bad shape, and she's obviously lost a lot of blood. There's the stretcher. Can you get it for me? I want to look her over real close before we try to move her."

"Sure," the boy said. He picked his way through the rubble to the side of the hole. The stretcher was passed down.

The medic began a further examination, checking her arms and left leg. Next came the torso.

"Oh, no."

"What?" the sergeant major said. He barely recognized the unconscious rag doll of a person lying on the cold cement. This couldn't possibly be the pretty young woman so full of life he'd last seen just yesterday morning.

"I think her back's broken," the medic said.

"Are you sure?"

"No, I'm not. I won't be until we get her out of here and up to the ambulance, where I can get a better look at what we face. Tell Bill to get an IV and a backboard down here as soon as he can!"

Moments later, Laurie scrambled into the pit with a backboard, IV, and a long needle.

"Stay here, Laurie," Williams said. "It'll probably take four of us to maneuver the backboard through this maze once we get her on it. Do you think you can handle the job?"

The girl stared at Kathy's twisted form. She nodded yes.

"First the IV," the medic said. "After that, I'll need to immobilize her leg before we try to do anything else. We don't dare turn her over. Once I get her leg ready, we'll strap the backboard on her as she lies. If her back's broken, we can't move her until she's securely strapped onto the board. One mistake, and we could paralyze her for life."

The medic gripped the IV bag in his teeth. He bent down and found himself an inviting vein. He jabbed the needle into her arm. Satisfied with the IV's placement, he taped it in place.

"Laurie, come over here and hold the IV while I immobilize her leg," the medic said.

The girl took the IV from the medic.

"Hold it up high enough that it doesn't get tangled and stop flowing."

"Okay."

The medic started working on the fracture. Where the sharp piece of splintered bone had pierced the skin, it protruded two inches outside the leg.

The medic placed a slat on each side of the shattered leg.

"Sergeant Major, I'll need you to give me a hand with this."

"What do you want me to do?"

"Hold the splints in place while I wrap them."

It didn't take long to complete the job. "That'll have to do," the medic said. "I think it'll stay together until we can get her to the field hospital. Now comes the fun part."

"What do we do next?"

"We've got to strap the backboard on her tightly. Once that's done, we'll lift her straight up, turn her over, and carry her out. If all goes well, we won't kill her in the process. Sergeant Major, you and Ryan get on the other side. I'll thread the straps under her. You'll have to reach beneath her body and pull them through."

The medic picked up the backboard. He covered Kathy with it. Satisfied with the board's positioning, he knelt and inched the first strap beneath her legs.

"Put your hand under her legs real careful there, Ryan, and pull the strap through."

The boy reached under Kathy's legs and located the strap. "I've got it."

"Pull it through and strap it as tight as you can to the board."

The boy pulled the strap up and buckled it in place. "All done."

Three additional straps were threaded beneath her torso. When the task was finished, the medic checked everything one final time.

"Okay, we seem to be all set. Everyone get a corner. We'll need to turn her over before we do anything else. Try to lift her as evenly as you can."

The four took their positions.

"Ready?" the medic asked.

His companions indicated they were.

"Okay, on three . . . one . . . two . . . three!"

They lifted the backboard straight up. The straps were as snug as they could possibly be under the circumstances. Still, Kathy's pummeled body pressed against them as she was lifted into the air.

Searing pain ripped through her. Consciousness leaped into her tortured soul. Screams of anguish crushed the quiet afternoon.

Three sets of concerned eyes looked into the medic's.

"It's okay," he said. "Let's get her turned over. Once that's done, we'll get the pressure off her, and she'll be a lot more comfortable. Flip her over, real easy."

They turned her right side up. Kathy screamed again. The pain was too much to bear. She passed out once more.

"All right," the medic said, "let's get her out of here and into the ambulance."

"Kathy . . . Kathy O'Neill," the sergeant major said. His voice was sweet and comforting.

Kathy's mind told her she knew that voice.

The gentle voice entered the darkness of her terrifying world once again. "Kathy . . . Kathy, can you hear me?"

"Wha . . . what?" she said. Her response was less than a whisper. And she couldn't yet find the strength to open her eyes.

"It's me, Kathy, Harold Williams from next door. You remember, don't you?"

"Yes, I remember. Where am I?"

"You're in an ambulance. We just brought you up from the basement. You know, Kathy, the basement."

The basement! Her eyes flew open wide. She fought to lift her head. Unspeakable pain raced at her from every part of her body.

"Easy, Kathy," he said. "Everything's going to be all right."

"I can't move. Why can't I move?"

"You've been immobilized by the medics. You're badly hurt. Try to lie still."

"My baby! Where's my baby!" She screamed at the top of her lungs, but it left her parched throat as little more than an anguished gasp.

"He's right here, Kathy," Williams said. "He's fine. A little dehydrated, and very dirty. And he's really quite angry. But he doesn't have a scratch on him."

A weak smile formed on Kathy's tortured lips.

"Kathy, I need your help. You and Christopher are the only ones we've found so far. I know it's difficult, but you've got to concentrate for me. Where was everyone else when the building collapsed?"

He could tell she didn't understand.

He tried again.

"Kathy, where were my wife and boys when the building fell?"

There was still no sign of recognition in Kathy's eyes.

"Kathy, where's Clara?"

"Clara? Clara's right here next to me in the laundry room."

"Where are the others, Kathy?"

"Others?"

"Yes, Kathy. Where are the other women and children in the basement?"

"The others are in the storage room across the hall. They're hiding from the Russian planes."

Williams could hardly contain his excitement. He had what he needed now. He knew where to dig. The sergeant major pulled up a filthy sleeve and checked his watch. There were nearly two hours of daylight left. He couldn't free them all by then. Still, two hours would be more than enough to clear the remaining wreckage from the laundry room.

By sundown, he'd know his family's fate. By midnight, he'd have reached all the women and children.

"Kathy, I've got to get back and help the others dig. You lie still. As soon as the medics have finished examining you, they're taking you and Christopher over to the mobile hospital they've set up at the airfield. Good luck, honey."

He gently patted her hand.

And with that, he was gone.

Just before midnight, the sergeant major pulled the last tiny body from the debris. He took the child to the edge of the hole and handed her up to the waiting arms.

The dead child, a girl of five, was carried over and placed in the snow with the others. Twenty-one bodies, all in a row, lay in the shimmering moonlight.

For the seven deliverers, thirty-six hours of soul-devouring effort were finally over. Their horrific journey had reached its end.

After the rescue of Kathy and Christopher, they'd located no more survivors in what remained of Building 2417.

The sergeant major wandered back to the spot in the laundry room where he'd discovered the bodies of his wife and sons. The hulking figure dropped onto the cold cement. He started to sob uncontrollably. Tears flowed from his unseeing eyes. His sorrow ran in torrents down his dirt-streaked face.

The rescue had been a triumph for the spirit of man.

Harold Williams had saved two lives. In a few weeks, the sergeant major would come to realize that he'd always have this small victory to carry him through the rest of a long, lonely life.

CHAPTER 46

January 30—3:47 p.m.
1st Platoon, Alpha Company, 2nd Battalion, 69th Armor,
   3rd Heavy Brigade Combat Team, 3rd Infantry Division
At the Crossroads of Highway 19 and Autobahn A7

The leading Russian tank turned west off the long-ago-deserted north–south autobahn. The T-72 started up the narrow highway. In the gunner's position of Richardson's M1 Abrams, Anthony Warrick watched his main gun's laser range finder lock in the T-72's coordinates. The enemy was less than a mile away. The armored column was taking its time as it waited for a handful of stragglers to catch up. In the enveloping dusk of late afternoon, Richardson and his crew prepared to open fire. They sat waiting for the order to come from the platoon's command tank.

In the command tank, Lieutenant Mallory called out over the radio to 2nd Battalion headquarters. "Echo-Yankee-One, this is Sierra-Kilo-One-One."

"This is Echo-Yankee-One. Go ahead, Sierra-Kilo-One-One."

"Echo-Yankee-One, we're in contact with an enemy formation of a dozen heavy tanks, supported by what appears to be a company of infantry in BMPs. This force is presently leaving Autobahn A7 and turning west onto Highway 19. In the distance, we can see another armored column of equal size heading down the autobahn toward our position. Request immediate air support. Say again, request immediate air support."

"Sierra-Kilo-One-One, wait one."

The three-tank platoon waited as the radio operator conferred with the battalion commander.

"Sierra-Kilo-One-One, be advised, we've nothing available at this time. Eliminate as much of the first column as you can, then withdraw to your secondary fighting position."

"Roger, Echo-Yankee-One. We copy. Attack enemy and withdraw to secondary position. Will do."

The Americans still controlled the skies over most of the battle zone. Yet with the tremendous losses of the past thirty-six hours, there were no longer enough Apaches, Warthogs, or Multiple Launch Rocket Systems to assist many of the ground forces. In the coming days, the men of the 3rd Infantry Division were going to often find themselves on their own.

"Well, you heard the man," Mallory said into the radio. "Looks like we're alone on this one. Greene, Richardson, prepare to fire on the enemy column."

"Roger," Greene said.

"Will do, Lieutenant," Richardson said. "Preparing to fire."

"Richardson, Warrick's still got the leader. My team will take the second one. Greene, you're on the third."

The T-72s continued to plod up the hill toward the hidden Americans.

"Tony, did you get that?" Richardson said into the intercom. "We're still on the lead tank."

"Roger, I've got him locked in. I'll fire as soon as the lieutenant gives the word."

Mallory was back on the radio. "If the BMPs dismount infantry to support the tanks, tank commanders open fire with your machine guns immediately. Try to keep the infantry as far away from our position as you possibly can. Let's hit them real hard, then get out of here fast. Get off two or three good shots at the tanks. We'll then retract from our holes and head for our secondary fighting position."

"I'm all for that, Lieutenant," Richardson said. "Lead tank ready to be engaged whenever you give the word. Will fire two or three rounds and get the hell out of here."

"Which escape route are we going to take through the trees?" Greene asked.

"We'll go directly west," Mallory said, "unless it's blocked. If we get separated, form up at the secondary position. Does everyone have the map coordinates?"

"We've got them okay," Greene said.

"No problem, Lieutenant," Richardson said. "Retreating's something I'll be able to handle just fine."

A typical Richardson comment. The kind the platoon had long ago come to expect from its junior sergeant. They were seconds away from their first combat. Even so, inside the three tanks, the soldiers let out a nervous laugh.

The re-formed Russian column picked up speed. Led by the tanks, they moved up the highway. From the snowy hilltop, the M-1s had an excellent angle with which to attack the entire line of T-72s. From their vantage point, they could unleash a clean shot at any of the twelve tanks.

Warrick had his hand on the firing mechanism. Sweat ran down the Americans' faces. The cramped space inside the tanks was smothering and oppressive. The soldiers' breathing was short and labored. Richardson, Mallory, and Greene waited to open fire. Each would remotely fire his .50-caliber commander's machine gun from inside the fully secured tank.

The lieutenant bit his lip and waited. The Russians closed to within five hundred yards. At this distance, the sophisticated firing systems of the M-1s wouldn't miss.

Mallory screamed into the radio, "Open fire!"

Warrick fired his Abrams's 120mm main gun. The moment the huge shell leaped from the cannon's barrel, a giant "whoosh!" could be heard for miles around. Two more "whooshes!" quickly followed as Mallory's and Greene's tanks fired.

Three shells raced across the quarter-mile distance that separated attacker and prey. Warrick's lethal warhead smashed into the lead T-72's eight inches of armor plating. The shell blew right through the thick armor. The Russian tank erupted in roaring flames. Red-hot pieces of metal flew in every direction. The mighty explosion reverberated throughout the once-peaceful valley. Two more shattering explosions were right on its heels. They filled the fading day with riotous sound. Fire enveloped the destroyed tanks.

"I got the bastard!" Warrick screamed. "Did you see that son of a bitch go up? I got him! I got him good!"

Richardson was feeling the same battle-induced euphoria. He knew, however, he had to keep his head if his crew was going to live to see the onrushing sunset. He tried to sound composed and workmanlike.

"Tony, calm down. Calm down. Start targeting another tank, or else some Russian gunner's going to be saying the same thing about us in a few seconds. Get that big sucker trying to pull out of line about three tanks back of the burning ones."

"Roger," Warrick said. "Targeting tank pulling out of line."

In the rear of the command compartment, Clark Vincent withdrew the first of the forty-one replacement shells from behind the thick metal panel that separated the lethal ordnance from the crew. He shoved the eighty-pound shell into the main gun's firing chamber. That task completed, he closed the munitions panel, protecting the tank crew from the possibility of their own exploding shells entering the crew compartment should the tank be hit by an enemy round. Although only six weeks removed from the completion of his training at Fort Knox, Kentucky, the tank's new loader handled his tasks with relative ease.

In seconds, the main gun was ready to fire again.

The remaining Russian tanks fanned out on the snowy ground below the Americans. They'd yet to locate the exact origin of the attack by the well-hidden defenders. A trio of T-72s started blindly firing their machine guns toward the knoll. BMPs rushed forward to support the tanks. They screamed to a stop. Infantrymen spewed forth from the rear of a dozen armored personnel carriers.

"Tank commanders, open fire!" Mallory yelled.

Richardson squeezed the trigger on his machine gun. A line of tracer fire rushed straight for a squad of seven exposed infantrymen running forward on the open ground in front of the hill. The infantry continued to struggle through the deep snows toward the small crest. Two of the running figures were hurled backward by the force of the striking bullets. Their comrades dove headlong into the snows. But there was nowhere for them to hide on the trackless hill.

Warrick fired the tank's main gun. Another "whoosh!" filled the valley. Still unable to pinpoint the precise location of the attack, the Russian tank had been attempting to move toward the hilltop. The M-1's shell bore down upon the T-72. Another funeral pyre of roaring flames and billowing smoke filled the valley as a fourth tank died.

A second squad of foot soldiers charged up the middle of the slope. Mallory's and Greene's machine guns went after them. Six of the Russians were struck by the American fire. They crumpled to the ground. The seventh, a panicked private of eighteen, took one look around and turned to run back down the incline. Three bullets smashed into his back and shoved him into the pink snows. The soldier's body slid down the hillside.

The other American tanks fired their cannons in quick succession. Two additional T-72s wilted beneath the Abrams's insurmountable main gun.

The Russians finally located the origin of the attack. They began returning the Americans' fire. A T-72's cannon shell burst at the base of the logs and dirt in front of Richardson's tank. Inside the M-1, the fiercely echoing sound of the exploding shell resounded throughout its metal hull.

"Man, that was close! Everybody all right?"

"Yup," Vincent said as he loaded another round.

"I'm okay," Jamie Pierson said from his position in the driver's compartment at the front of the tank.

"Fine here, too," Warrick answered.

"Tony, get another good shot at one of those bastards. Then let's get ready to get the hell out of here."

"Roger. I'm already targeting. A few more seconds and we'll be all set."

Another squad of infantry rushed forward. They threw themselves into the snow. One of the Russians got to his knees. He aimed his shoulder-mounted rocket at the American position. His squad attempted to cover him.

It was a difficult angle. The soldier was firing uphill at well-protected targets. There was no margin for error. With death swirling around him, he had to hit the turret of one of the tanks if he was going to have any chance of penetrating an M-1's stout armor and killing the Americans inside. The missile roared off his shoulder. It was a blur as it catapulted up the short incline. The anxious shot went just a little high. The rocket whistled over the three tanks. It smashed into a huge evergreen a short way up the rise. The tree's trunk was severed. It fell forward. With a thunderous thud, the evergreen's broad branches slammed across the turrets of the American tanks.

"Christ, what was that?" Warrick asked.

"Never mind! Just fire that damn gun so we can get out of here."

The firing of the rocket attracted the attention of the American tanks. Three converging lines of machine-gun fire waltzed across the snows. The tank commanders closed in on the exposed Russians.

The beleaguered infantry leaped to their feet and ran from the hill. The machine guns cut them down before any of the squad had traveled more than a handful of retreating steps.

Another Russian tank fired its cannon at the Americans. Two BMPs followed with Spandrel missiles. Tumultuous explosions tore through the crest of the hill. The earth beneath the tank platoon shuddered and yawed. But inside their strongly fortified worlds, the Americans were unharmed.

Richardson's machine gun continued to spit death at those trapped below.

"Whoosh!" filled the valley once more as Warrick fired a third mighty round. A T-72 exploded a fraction of a second later.

"I got a third one!" Warrick screamed.

Vincent moved forward with another of the heavy rounds.

"Jamie, get ready to move out as fast as you can when the lieutenant gives the word," Richardson directed his driver.

But no word came from the command tank. And the BMPs continued to unload their foot soldiers. Scores of white-clad figures moved toward the snowbound crest.

Warrick quickly joined in on the slaughter of the Russian infantry, firing the machine gun next to the tank's huge cannon toward the onrushing soldiers. Four American machine guns were now firing at the struggling Russians. Unspeakable carnage was spreading unimpeded to every corner of the snowy slope.

"Enough is enough, come on, Lieutenant," Richardson said, "fire a final round already and give the order to move."

"Whoosh!" went the cannon on Greene's tank.

With a lightning machine-gun burst, Richardson cut down a solitary soldier crawling forward with a missile tube. Another widow would wail in the streets of Moscow.

"Whoosh!" went the cannon on the platoon leader's Abrams.

An eighth and ninth enemy tank were added to the ferocious fires.

"Let's get out of here!" Mallory said into the radio.

"I'm with you, Lieutenant," Richardson said.

"Richardson, back out and go. We'll cover you."

"Roger," Richardson said. "Jamie, you heard the man. Let's go!"

While the other tanks continued to fire their machine guns, Richardson's compelling giant backed out of its hole. The tank turned and ran. As the M-1 wheeled about to head down the back side of the hill, Richardson cranked the turret around to protect Greene's and Mallory's escape. Unlike the inferior Russian tanks, which could only engage their opponent while standing still, with its fully coordinated fire-control system, Richardson's M-1 was capable of accurately firing and hitting any target even while moving at full speed.

"Tony, get your cannon and machine gun ready. Nail anything stupid enough to come over the crest of that hill after us."

Richardson spoke into the radio. "Okay, Lieutenant, we're clear and on our way. While we run, we'll protect your retreat the best we can."

"Okay, Greene, you're next," Mallory said.

"Roger, Lieutenant."

A second tank eased out of its hole to begin its escape to the next protective burrow. Five miles west on Highway 19, the platoon's secondary firing position was waiting. Greene's tank performed the same maneuvers Richardson's had. It disappeared over the slope on the western side. Another Spandrel missile slammed into the logs and dirt at the crest of the hill.

"Okay, Lieutenant, we're all set for you to come out," Greene said.

In seconds, the lieutenant's tank also vanished from the battlefield. In all, the deadly encounter had lasted slightly less than two minutes.

Nine Russian tanks and sixty enemy infantry were no more.

With Greene protecting the lieutenant, Richardson cranked his turret around to face forward. The M-1s weaved their way through the thinner trees on the western side of the hill. They headed for the twisting highway, hidden in a magnificent forest of august fir.

"Jamie, go ahead and get onto the road."

Pierson adjusted the motorcycle-like handlebars to move the menacing tank onto the asphalt. As he did, Richardson popped open the tank's commander hatch. He cautiously poked his head out. To his left, Vincent did the same. The young soldier settled in behind the loader's machine gun.

The brisk afternoon air rushing by the fleeing tank brought tears to Richardson's eyes and stung his boyish features. While he peered down the winding roadway, the fleeting strands of the day's disappearing sunlight danced on the deep forest's floor.

Mallory was on the radio once again. "Echo-Yankee-One, this is Sierra-Kilo-One-One."

"Roger, Sierra-Kilo-One-One. Go ahead," the voice at battalion headquarters said.

"Echo-Yankee-One, have destroyed nine tanks without sustaining a single casualty. We're presently moving toward our secondary fighting position."

"Roger, Sierra-Kilo-One-One, we copy. Be advised, enemy helicopter activity in your sector has been extremely heavy in the past hour. Be prepared to repulse a possible air attack."

"Thanks for the warning, Echo-Yankee-One. Estimate arrival at secondary position in fifteen minutes. Will contact for further instructions then."

The second Russian armored column was fast approaching Highway 19. They would soon take up the chase.

Like so many before them, the American tank platoon moved farther west.

It was a war of unyielding intensity. It was a war like none that had come before.

As the day's sunset neared, the toll on both sides was obscene. American deaths were approaching one thousand per hour. Fifteen Americans were dying every minute in the reddening fields of Germany. By the end of the second day, American losses would be greater than in three years of fighting in Korea. By the end of the third, American casualties would reach beyond those in ten nightmarish years in Vietnam.

German military losses were twice that number.

Russian deaths were five times as great as that of the Americans. Around the clock, without respite, five thousand Russians were dying each hour.

Still, they kept coming.

The real suffering, however, was occurring among the civilian population. The estimates at the end of the second day ran as high as one million German dead. Another three million were injured. In a country as small and heavily populated as this one, such casualties were inevitable.

They died in droves when caught between the combatants. They were slaughtered by the unspeakable death reaching down for them from the sky. And from the unpredictable death coming at them from the ground. To add to the ever-mounting misery, they were killed in untold thousands by Comrade Cheninko's summary executions and firing squads.

Twenty miles east of Richardson's position, the initial armored battle of the new war had ended a few hours earlier. It'd been a truly historic struggle. For twenty-four unrelenting hours, the vastly outnumbered Allies made a valiant stand. But the inevitable finally happened. The razor-thin German and American line in the southern half of the country collapsed late on the morning of the war's second full day.

Two German divisions and the American 1st Armor Division had withstood hour after hour of immense pressure throughout the first day and the endless night that followed. Wave after wave of attackers smashed into the defenders' fragile defenses. Yet the Allies didn't give an inch. One of the fiercest artillery barrages in history crushed their bodies and sapped their spirits. Still, they held on.

Late on the previous evening, the Russians overwhelmed the nine thousand American cavalry soldiers protecting Munich. The city was eerily peaceful and quiet. The Russians chose to surround, but bypass, the sprawling metropolis to avoid the time-consuming, house-to-house battle taking Munich would entail. There'd be ample time for such later.

The Russians were prepared to fight a five-day war. The clock was steadily ticking. The precious hours in General Yovanovich's plan were rushing past. Stalemated by the resolute Americans, Yovanovich turned to the only answer he could find. He upped the ante. He introduced nerve gas to the battlefields of the great war. The unspeakable horror of chemical weapons became a crucial part of the battle for control of Germany.

It had begun at three in the morning. After sixteen hours of nonstop killing, the embattled Americans inexplicably found the fields in front of them quiet and deserted. The surprising silence was fearfully deafening to the exhausted men of the 1st Armor Division. A war of unbelievable ferocity had given way to absolute peace. For an hour, not a shot was fired. The Americans futilely searched the killing ground for an enemy who had somehow vanished into the darkness and couldn't be found.

At 4:00 a.m. the image-wracking stillness suddenly was broken. Hundreds of obscene Russian helicopters appeared in the misty night sky. A few feet off the ground, they roared along the front lines. From their stubby wingtips certain death spewed forth for those unprepared to deal with it. On a swath of earth 150 miles long and 12 miles wide, they dropped life-ending liquid from the black winter skies. Colorless, odorless droplets rained down upon an unforgiving world.

For seventy years, the Americans had anticipated the use of such tactics. They were thoroughly prepared for such an eventuality. The poison gas would have little effect on the Bradley and M-1 crews, secure within their armored vehicles' fully integrated chemical defenses.

For the exhausted infantry soldier on the ground, however, the nerve gas was a far different story. The Russians caught him at the lowest physical and mental point of the night.

He had nine seconds to get his gas mask on or face a certain, horrible end. He had ninety additional seconds to clothe himself in his chemical suit and booties or suffer the consequences.

Each soldier had practiced for this moment hundreds of times. The steps were imprinted on his brain. Ripping open his gas-mask pouch. Removing the horrid mask. Placing the grotesque object over his face by inserting his chin first. Pulling the straps over the back of his head and tightening them. Clearing the mask by blowing out. Verifying the mask was properly positioned and the seal was tight. Giving himself an atropine injection by slamming the thick tube with its long needle into the fleshy part of his thigh.

He'd done the drill over and over. He could do it in his sleep. Nine seconds was all he had to put on his mask. Timed again and again, he'd practiced and practiced the task for untold hours past. No time for panic. Nine seconds.

Twenty percent of the American soldiers died.

With no protection whatsoever, one hundred percent of the German civilians caught by the spraying helicopters' lewd nozzles were killed. Within seconds of the droplets being released, their bodies began to twitch and flail uncontrollably until, after a few torturous ticks of the clock, their nerves mercifully twitched no more. A quick, violent death was their reward.

The poisonous gas falling to the earth was an indiscriminate killer.

The murderer refused to distinguish between man and woman, adult and child, evil and innocent. On this night, they were all treated alike by the perverse death that poured from the heavens.

With the introduction of chemical warfare to the killing fields, the Russians forever changed the rules. They greatly escalated the stakes. Man's world would never again be the same.

An hour later, the Russians were back in force. They relentlessly attacked the 80 percent who hadn't panicked under the life-ending pressures of the deadly gas. Both sides fought on in full chemical clothing.

They could fight in the cumbersome gear. They'd practiced many times. They could eat and drink in their protective world. They could curse and swear, talk on the radio, and relieve any bodily function. They'd practiced.

They could bleed and die in their protective suits.

Even with 20 percent casualties, the staggered Americans didn't falter. The Russians furiously pounded the brittle line, expecting to breach it at any moment. But as the gray winter sunrise pierced the darkness, the battered 1st Armor was where it had been at sundown on the previous day.

The Russians shook their heads in disbelief and attacked once more. The pitiless slaughter of both countries' daunting young men went on without reprieve. It would continue to do so, unabated, until the Americans finally acquiesced.

For six interminable hours after the grisly nerve-gas attack, the fighting continued. The defenders, their force growing thinner with each passing minute, tenaciously held on to their positions. Without the briefest pause, they resisted one withering assault after another.

The clock continued its unerring movement across the sordid morning with no end to the tumultuous struggle in sight.

This time, when their stalwart adversary did not yield, it was the increasingly frustrated Cheninko's patience that was challenged beyond its limits. And his turn to up the ante ever further.

A stunned Yovanovich initially resisted. His concerns with what he'd been commanded to do at so early a point in the war were great. But his rousing pleas for the manic dictator to reconsider his decision fell upon deaf ears. In the end, he was powerless to withstand the edict he'd been given. His orders were to break the Americans at any cost. Cheninko was going to crush the Germans in five days, no matter what it took. He directed Yovanovich to use the one thing he knew would forever end the 1st Armor Division's valiant efforts.

At a handful of minutes past ten on that horrid morning, the Russians struck.

The first of the tactical nuclear weapons fell upon a company of Americans deeply entrenched on a rustic German hillside. In rapid succession, five more detonated at critical locations in the American defenses.

The small nuclear armaments had been specifically developed by both sides for use in battlefield situations.

Within a mile of where the nuclear devices were unleashed, nothing survived the onslaught. Anyone caught in the target area of the overwhelming slaughter died instantly from the irrepressible heat of the initial explosion. They simply disappeared. Not a trace of them would remain.

For twice that distance, the nuclear detonations' mighty blast toppled everything in its path. The fearsome winds created by each frenetic burst consumed untold numbers more on that unspeakable morning.

But in one way, the Americans had been fortunate. At the time of the attack, the day's breezes were light. Once the holocaustic heat and furious burst passed, the faltering winds kept the final lethal element of the detonations from dispersing over a widely spaced area. For most of the survivors, the level of radiation poisoning they received was minimal.

Shortly before noon, the battered Allied line crumpled. In thirty minutes, it irretrievably collapsed.

The 1st Armor retreated. The scattered remnants of the proud division made their way through the 3rd Infantry's lines.

The cautious American optimism of the previous twenty-four hours now faced the glum reality of a new day. The Americans began to undeniably understand that there was little hope of their holding on for the two weeks it would take to change the face of the war.

Without extreme measures, the defenders were going to find themselves with their backs to the Rhine in the next seventy-two hours.

If they could hold out that long.

The result was there for all to see. The desperateness of the defender's situation had finally settled in.

The Russians came on. Within a few hours of the 1st Armor's defeat, the debate over the need for drastic action was undertaken. America had played three of her aces against the unwavering Slavic invader without achieving success. At sundown on the second day, the American leadership started seriously considering using its final ace.

CHAPTER 47

January 30—4:04 p.m.
1st Platoon, Alpha Company, 2nd Battalion, 69th Armor,
   3rd Heavy Brigade Combat Team, 3rd Infantry Division
Three Miles West of the Crossroads of Highway 19 and
   Autobahn A7

Hidden in the thick forest's protective cover, Richardson anxiously gripped the handles on the tank's antiaircraft machine gun as he pointed it toward the treetops.

Four Russian Hind-F Attack Helicopters slowly circled the roadway, scouring the deep underbrush for the American tanks. The platoon was in serious trouble. If they tried to run, the helicopters would find and destroy them. If they remained hidden, the Russian armored column coming up from behind would catch the M-1s in the open and kill them on the ground. There was no time to waste. They needed a miracle. And they needed it now.

"Echo-Yankee-One, this is Sierra-Kilo-One-One," Lieutenant Mallory said. "Echo-Yankee-One, this is Sierra-Kilo-One-One."

Fifteen miles to the northwest, battalion headquarters answered. "Roger, Sierra-Kilo-One-One. This is Echo-Yankee-One."

"Echo-Yankee-One, we're halted approximately halfway to our secondary position. Four Hinds are circling overhead. They're obviously looking for us. As of yet, they haven't located our hiding place in the deep woods covering the highway. But I don't believe our luck will hold much longer. We need immediate assistance."

"Roger, Sierra-Kilo-One-One. Wait one, I'll see what I can do."

Richardson fearfully scanned the low heavens, watching for the deadly helicopters. Thirty seconds passed. It felt like thirty hours for the twelve Americans trapped in the tanks.

The voice at battalion returned. "Sierra-Kilo-One-One, be advised, we've located two F-35s in your neighborhood who tell us they're itching for a fight. They say they'd be more than happy to kill a few helicopters for you if you so desire. Hang tight, the F-35s are on the way. Their estimated arrival at your position is forty-five seconds."

"Roger, Echo-Yankee-One. That's welcome news. Let's hope we can remain undetected that long. Tell the jet jockeys we'll greatly appreciate any assistance they can provide."

"Understood. Keep your heads down and hold on, Sierra-Kilo-One-One."

Overhead in the growing darkness, the helicopters slowly continued to poke and prod at the forest's canopy as the fleeting seconds passed, searching for the enemy they were certain they'd find if they just turned over the right rock. One of the flying tank killers explored a promising thicket. Richardson watched a set of spinning rotor blades appear over his hiding place. The helicopter couldn't be more than three hundred feet above him.

The Hind spotted its prey. They were right below. Three American tanks were sitting in the deepest shadows of the twilight forest. The Russian pilot radioed his companions.

"M-1s located beneath my position. Stand off and prepare to attack with antitank missiles."

The helicopters slid a short distance south. They prepared to rain thunder and lightning down upon the tanks. Each was in place, ready to fire multiple launches of Spiral missiles into the tree line. There'd be no escape for the Americans. Another second or two, and the flight leader would give the order to fire.

Suddenly, the helicopters' systems screamed that they were being targeted by an engagement radar. The helicopters frantically searched heaven and earth for the source of the threat to their survival.

From seven miles away, a Sidewinder missile leaped from the wing-tip of both F-35s. Two helicopters were seconds away from their total destruction if they didn't do something and do it fast. Both Hinds dove for the treetops, with the Sidewinders in hot pursuit.

At twenty miles per minute, the F-35s sprinted toward the remaining targets. A second pair of Sidewinders tore from their roosts beneath the American fighters. They hurtled toward their victims. The destruction of the tanks was long forgotten. The final pair of helicopters turned and ran for their lives.

The heat from the Hinds' engines beckoned to the Sidewinders. Like a moth to a flame, the missiles couldn't resist the siren song of the heat-producing helicopters. The missiles ran true. The helicopters were racing away at nearly two hundred miles per hour. Yet they appeared to be standing still as the Sidewinders rushed at them at ten times their top speed. The helicopters bobbed and weaved. They dove and climbed in an attempt to shake the attackers. Even so, the missiles were unperturbed. They matched their fleeing victim's every move.

The missiles craved the heat. They needed the heat.

In seconds, the Sidewinders closed with their targets. Each rammed its lethal nose into the rear of its prey. Four explosions rocked the eastern skyline. Pieces of burning metal fell in twisted clumps into the woods a half mile east of the hiding tanks.

The immediate threat to the platoon was no more. The F-35 stealth fighters roared low over the trees. They dipped their wings in victory. In less than a minute, the fighters were nothing more than fading specks in the darkening sky.

"Okay, Richardson," Mallory said, "let's get the hell out of here while we still can." The relief in the platoon leader's voice was vividly evident.

"You heard the man, Jamie. Let's get going."

Richardson's tank pushed through the gnarled thicket and back onto the winding roadway. The other two tanks were close behind. Westward, ever westward, the platoon ran.

Westward, ever westward, the Americans retreated.

———

Five minutes later, the platoon arrived at the place for which they'd been searching. Richardson's tank reached the edge of a wide glade with a deep, swift brook running through it.

"Richardson," the lieutenant said, "our secondary position should be up ahead somewhere on the left. It's supposed to be inside the trees on the other side of this meadow. We'll cover you while you cross the open ground."

"Roger, Lieutenant, we're on our way. Keep a good eye on the skies for us, guys. We're going to be kind of vulnerable out here."

"Come on, Tim," Greene said. "After what we just went through, you should be used to it by now. Find those holes the engineers left so we can all get out of the open."

The lead tank entered the somber clearing. The charred remains of four cars and a Humvee were scattered about the night-tinged meadow. The five vehicles had been attacked late on the previous day by a MiG-29. Each had stopped smoldering hours earlier. The ravaged metal was cool to the touch. Inside the destroyed vehicles, Richardson could see the blackened skeletons of those who'd died while attempting to cross the same ground he was entering. A child's doll, singed and gutted, lay in the snows covering the dead winter grasses near the closest car.

The tank hurried across the three-hundred-yard clearing. As it neared the trees on the far side, Richardson spotted a likely location for the platoon's new fighting positions.

"I think I see the holes, Lieutenant," Richardson said. "Fifty yards away, right between the second and third trees on the left side of the road."

"That sounds about right," Mallory said. "You need to check it out fast. We've got to find those holes and dig in before it gets too dark and we're unable to locate them."

"Or, worse yet, before the Russians find us," Greene said.

"Jamie," Richardson said, "ease her into the trees just far enough that she won't be easy to spot from the air. Then bring her to a stop."

The tank continued to move forward.

"Okay, right here's good." The M-1 came to a halt. "I'm pretty certain the spot we're looking for is in that area over to our left. I'll need to get down on the ground to check it out. Tony, you and Vincent watch real close for the bad guys. Don't let anything happen to my tank while I'm gone."

"Don't worry, Tim. I'll protect your spoiled child real good while you're out playing in the woods," Warrick replied.

Richardson spoke into the radio. "Lieutenant, I'm dismounting to take a look around."

"Roger. But make it quick. We're in trouble if we stay out here much longer."

"Okay, Lieutenant, I'm on my way."

Richardson lifted himself from the commander's hatch. He made his way across the tank. Leaping into the snows, he quickly moved through the maze of evergreens toward the location where he believed he'd find the platoon's next ambush position.

There they were, just as he suspected. In front of him were three tank holes, protected by heavy logs and mounds of dirt. He took a look around. This was certainly not as good a position as the first had been. The ground was flat, so they'd lose many of the advantages the hill had given them in the earlier battle. And there was only a single escape route through the trees. Still, as he'd learned a few minutes earlier, any fortified position was going to be a vast improvement over fighting on the open ground.

Richardson ran back through the deepening shadows. The rapidly closing night was pressing in on them from all sides. He scrambled onto his tank and disappeared into the commander's compartment.

"Okay, Lieutenant, we're in business. The holes are right where I thought. They're waiting for us fifty yards to the left of my position."

"Sounds good. Cover us, we're coming across."

"Roger, Lieutenant, bring 'em on in."

"Okay, Greene, you're up. Take her straight across the meadow and drop her into her hole. We'll start over as soon as you're safely into the trees on the other side."

"We're on our way."

A second cautious tank headed through the wide glen. They rushed by the grisly reminders of how fragile the soldiers' lives truly were. The M-1 hurried for the protection of the trees on the far side. In thirty seconds, Greene's tank passed Richardson's. It disappeared into the thick forest.

"Okay, Lieutenant," Richardson said, "ready whenever you are."

"Roger. We're coming over."

The final Abrams edged across the open meadow. Richardson watched the lieutenant's tank pass his position and disappear into the trees. He scanned the darkening skies for any sign of the enemy. So far, their tenuous luck was holding.

Greene stood on the cold ground in the shadows of the forest. He directed his driver's efforts as he slid seventy-two tons into the hole on the left. Lieutenant Mallory waited in the open commander's hatch of the second tank.

Greene's broad tank dropped into its hole. One down, two to go. The lieutenant leaped to the snows. He guided his driver as the second tank eased into its lair on the far right. Mallory clambered back into his tank.

"Okay, Richardson, we're all set, bring it on in."

"Roger, Lieutenant, we're on our way."

Under Jamie Pierson's skillful control of the handlebars, the final tank dropped into the middle den a short while later.

"Echo-Yankee-One, this is Sierra-Kilo-One-One," the lieutenant said into the radio.

"Roger, Sierra-Kilo-One-One."

"Echo-Yankee-One, have arrived intact and are emplaced in our secondary position. We're waiting to repulse a strong ground assault by a second Russian column. Anticipate enemy arrival at our location in the next half hour. We'll notify when contact is made."

"Roger, Sierra-Kilo-One-One. Rifle platoons from Delta Company will be linking up with you on your left and right shortly. Good luck."

The battalion radio operator knew the three tanks were going to need it.

CHAPTER 48

Fifteen minutes after the withdrawing tank platoon settled into its holes, George O'Neill was waiting on the tarmac at Mildenhall Air Base as a deafening C-17 cargo plane slowed to a stop. The moment the rear ramp lowered, he walked around the side of the plane to wait for the DISA civilian engineers to exit.

As soon as all twenty-four engineers cleared the plane, the C-17's loadmaster began pushing the first pallet down the ramp. Two Air Force cargo trucks and a large ten-ton tractor waited a short distance away. The lead truck would soon be taking the satellite ground-station equipment nestled on the initial pallet to Hillingdon. The minute the pallet was free of the plane, the supporting ground crew began moving it into position to load onto the transport truck. A fuel truck nestled up next to the plane, and the refueling process quickly began.

An air policeman waited nearby in his Humvee. Three of the engineers would ride with him as he escorted the precious cargo the seventy miles to the vital communication center in northwest London. Once there, the engineers would install the satellite equipment next to the communication center and begin making the necessary cabling connections to bring the ground station to life.

Denny Doyle had spent most of the day coordinating with EUCOM to determine what new and previously existing circuits would be placed on the satellite system. Under Doyle's direction, Hillingdon's communication controllers would then begin loading the highest-priority command and control users.

As the loadmaster returned to the plane for the next piece of critical equipment, O'Neill walked over to the miserable-looking group of civilians. After twenty-four hectic hours preparing and eight hours crammed into the C-17 for the trip from Dover, Delaware, none of the sleep-deprived team felt particularly spry. And each knew there was a great deal more for them to do before the next day's sun would appear.

"Which of you is Randy Carson?" George asked as he searched the huddled group for DISA's senior electronics engineer.

A nondescript individual in his late forties stepped forward and reached out a hand.

"You must be George," Carson said. "Glad to finally put a face to the voice I've been talking with incessantly for what feels like days."

O'Neill watched the ground station being loaded onto the truck. "I see you really were successful in locating the satellite equipment and delivering on your promise."

"Yeah, it was a bit of a challenge. These things aren't something you find sitting on the shelf in the electronics department at your local Walmart. But I was able to get my hands on two—one for Hillingdon and a second system for Donnersberg. As I told you on the phone, the only problem is both systems are rather old and small. The capacity on each will be limited to thirty-six circuits."

"With as much trouble as our command and control's in," O'Neill said, "thirty-six additional circuits at Hillingdon and another thirty-six at Donnersberg will really help. Although I sure wish we could figure out some way to establish a microwave link directly from Donnersberg to Hillingdon. Right now, just about everything from Germany to England depends on Feldberg. With the progress the Russian armor's made today, Feldberg will likely be overrun in two or three days at the very most. Donnersberg's in a much better position. It's situated fifty miles deeper into Germany, securely on the western side of the Rhine. If we have a choice, it would be a far more ideal spot than Feldberg to center our communications."

"When we've finished installing all of this, why don't you and I take a look at that," Carson said. "Who knows, if we can accomplish what we've pulled off in the last day and a half, maybe we can pull another rabbit out of our hat. Anything's possible with a pound of creativity and an ounce of luck."

The loadmaster began pushing a second pallet down the ramp. O'Neill saw it the moment it left the plane.

"Oh my God! They got to Dover in time," he said.

"Yep, two AWACS ground stations. One for Mildenhall, and a second one for my team headed to Germany to install at Donnersberg. The ground stations arrived in Delaware less than two hours before we were scheduled to depart. If you thought finding existing satellite terminals to bring over here was difficult, you should have seen these. It's not like there's normally a big demand for them. The manufacturer in California typically builds a new one at the military's request every few years or so. It's a tiny part of their business. Most of their AWACS work comes from providing spare parts when a ground station somewhere in the world needs repair. Luckily, they had enough parts on hand to build one of the two systems we brought on the plane. The other, they had to manufacturer from scratch. But as you can see, less than thirty-six hours after the Russians destroyed both AWACS ground stations, they were able to build new ones and get 'em all the way from California to England. As soon as we unload the communication van and the parts for Mildenhall's new microwave tower, we'll get to work installing the first one. The sooner my team's at work, the better we'll all feel."

"Mildenhall's destroyed communication center is less than a half mile from here. It'll take no time at all to get over there and get to work."

"How bad a shape is the original site in?" Carson asked.

"The damage is total. When I got here a few hours ago, it was nothing but a pile of scrap. I spent most of the day helping the site's airmen lucky enough to not be on duty when it exploded clear away the wreckage in preparation for your arrival. They were nearly finished when I started for the flight line. You should have no problem placing the van in the exact location the demolished building was. And I don't see any issues in erecting the new microwave tower where the old one previously stood."

"Were you able to recover anything at all from the site?"

"From what I saw, some of the underground cabling that fed into the communication center might still be okay. If it's even partially usable, that might save us a few hours in getting Mildenhall's communications fully online. Is the plan we last talked about for Donnersberg, Hillingdon, and Mildenhall still in effect?"

Just then the loadmaster appeared from the plane with a third pallet. This one contained the pieces needed for Mildenhall's new microwave tower and two brand-new microwave dishes. At the same moment, the last tie-down strap for the satellite equipment bound for Hillingdon was secured. Three of the engineers headed for the air policeman's Humvee. They, and the truck, were soon departing the flight line. O'Neill and Carson paused in their conversation to watch the loadmaster's efforts and the engineers and equipment pull away.

"Nothing's changed from what we talked about," Carson said. "As you saw, three of my guys will handle Hillingdon. Six will get back on the C-17 and fly to Ramstein with the satellite and AWACS ground station. MPs will be waiting to escort them and their equipment to Donnersberg. We figure they should get there by nine or ten tonight. The remaining fifteen of us will stay here to reconstruct Mildenhall."

"How long do you estimate it's going to take to get everything in place?"

"Even doing all this in the dark, the Hillingdon satellite should be ready by midnight. Depending on what problems we encounter, Mildenhall should be back online by about 4:00 a.m. at the very latest. Donnersberg should have both a working satellite and an AWACS ground-station terminal before tomorrow's sun rises."

The ten-ton tractor eased up to the C-17's ramp to remove the final piece of equipment. The fifty-foot-long communication van was soon attached and ready to go.

Before they left for the brief drive to the demolished site, George had one more task to complete. He walked over to his Humvee, removed a pile of items from it, and returned to where the remaining engineers were gathered.

"Randy," he said, "which of your folks are getting back on the plane and heading for Donnersberg? I need to meet with them for a few minutes before they go."

The six were soon gathered around O'Neill. He began passing out the gas-mask pouches, atropine, and chemical protective clothing to the perplexed engineers.

"Each of you is going to need these while working in Germany. The Russians unleashed a massive nerve-gas attack against the 1st Armor Division early this morning. We've no idea if, or when, the Russians will do it again, but the stuff is absolutely lethal. If you're unprepared, there's no possibility of surviving. If there's a chemical attack, you must get your gas mask on immediately, give yourself an injection, and get into the protective gear as fast as you can. Before you get back on that plane, let me give you a quick lesson on how to use this stuff."

O'Neill took a few minutes to go over the procedures and have the engineers practice the steps necessary to protect themselves. He did the best he could in the brief time he had. They were certainly no experts at defending against chemical weapons, but if they didn't panic, there was a decent chance most of them would survive.

Shortly thereafter, the C-17 carrying the satellite system, the AWACS ground station, and the six engineers started out onto the runway to depart for Germany. As they did, the small convoy with the van and the other AWACS ground station headed the short distance across Mildenhall to where the communication center had stood.

The hours had passed quickly, but the job was nearly completed. Just a few minutes more, and both Mildenhall's communications and the new AWACS ground station would be fully operational.

Inside the pristine van, O'Neill stood in the center of the impressive communication control station, admiring what he saw. Randy Carson stood next to him. Both in front of and behind them, all fifty feet was crammed with the latest technology. There was no doubt the van would be more than capable of handling all of Mildenhall's needs. Just a final, precise adjustment of the microwave dishes, and the communication link between Mildenhall and Hillingdon would be restored.

"Randy, this van is incredible. I'd no idea anything like this existed in mobile form. Where did you say you got it?"

"FEMA. They have over three dozen of them at their regional headquarters around the country. They use them to handle communication needs in a national emergency, like major hurricanes, earthquakes, and things like that. This is just the basic model. They've got others far more sophisticated than this. But we knew this one would easily handle all of Mildenhall's needs, so we only asked for what we needed. Some of them are set up to act as communication nodes, with over three hundred channels that can handle an entire network of smaller communication centers spread over a wide area. The big vans are over eighty feet long. They have multiple transmitters and receivers and enough supporting equipment to handle an entire region of the country's needs should it come to that. FEMA can handle the biggest cities and the smallest towns all in one interconnected network. It's not all that different an idea than our worldwide Defense Information System. The only significant difference is that while our network is in fixed locations in friendly countries around the world, FEMA's is designed to be far more flexible."

O'Neill's quick mind instantly seized upon what he'd just been told. Given his knowledge of the American military communication system in Europe, the potential implications of what Randy Carson had said were unmistakable.

"Do you think there's any chance you could get your hands on a couple of the fancy ones and a number of the smaller units if I asked you to?"

"Why? What have you got in mind, George?"

"I'm not certain just yet. It might turn out to be nothing but a dead end. And I'm not sure the higher-ups would be interested in it even if we can make it work. But it's something we should take a look at. I know your team's exhausted, but do you think you could still get some fairly advanced, highly technical work out of them for a few hours more? What I'm planning on us examining is going to keep them from seeing a bed anytime soon."

George O'Neill's next surprising move had appeared.

It would be one for which General Yovanovich could not have prepared.

CHAPTER 49

Sixth Floor, East Surgical Wing
Wurzburg Army Hospital

"Sarge!" Ramirez said. "Sarge, wake up. We've got to get out of here!"

Jensen's mind struggled to escape its drug-induced, early-morning sleep.

"What is it, Ramirez?"

"We've got to get out of here. The 3rd Infantry's units in front of Wurzburg have collapsed. The Russians have broken through. They're moving on the city. They'll be here in a little more than an hour. The hospital's being evacuated to Landstuhl."

Jensen, the sterile bandages tight around his eyes, could hear the commotion all around him. The hospital staff was frantically trying to save the lives of those placed in their care.

"Which one's next?" a male voice at the end of the hall said.

"Specialist Johnson. Third bed on the left," Lieutenant Morse replied. "Be careful with him. He was operated on just a few hours ago, and his stitches could easily come out."

"Yes, ma'am."

Jensen's muddled brain started to focus. There were scurrying feet in every direction. Urgency was in all the voices. The anxious sounds mixed with the ever-present groans of the injured soldiers in the open ward.

Ramirez crawled from his bed. He struggled beneath the cumbersome bandages covering his right shoulder and upper arm.

"Lieutenant Morse, what can I do to help? I've still got one good arm."

"Can you get yourself dressed? It's quite cold outside."

"Yes, ma'am, I can do that."

"When you're ready, let me know. There's lots to do and no time to do any of it."

Robert Jensen lay listening to the turmoil. The air in the room was tense and electric. Fear floated on the moist morning.

"What about Sergeant Jensen?" Elizabeth Morse asked Dr. Wehner. "Medevac or ambulance?"

"He probably should be put on a medevac, but we've only got three left. Put him in an ambulance, but make sure it's one where a doctor or nurse will be riding."

"All right, Doctor, I'll place him in one of the leading ambulances. What about Sergeant Larimer and Private Sill?"

There was hesitation in Captain Wehner's voice. "They're both too critical to move. Neither would survive the medevac ride. We're going to have to leave them here. They're putting the fifty unmovable cases on the third floor. A doctor and two medics have volunteered to stay with them."

"Which doctor's staying?"

His response was almost nonchalant. "I am, Beth."

She knew what his volunteering would mean. Widespread execution of American prisoners was common knowledge. But they couldn't just abandon the most severe cases. Someone had to stay with the wounded being left behind. There was nothing remaining for either to say. Wehner hurried off to move the critical patients to the third floor.

Morse motioned to the orderlies. "Over here. This one's next. Make sure you put him in one of the lead ambulances."

"Yes, ma'am."

"All right, Sergeant," a male voice said, "we're going to slide you out of bed and onto a stretcher. Just relax; we'll take care of the rest. Will you do that for us?"

"What choice do I have?" Jensen said.

Four experienced hands went to work. In a half minute, the orderlies were carrying Jensen's bouncing stretcher onto a creaking elevator.

Outside, the orderlies placed the canvas stretcher on the frigid ground. They turned and rushed back into the hospital for another human load. The severe cold was quite a shock to the platoon sergeant's system. After two days in the warmth of the hospital, he'd almost forgotten how it felt to be shivering in the damp German snows. Still, in a way, it was a welcome relief to be out of the aging building. He was temporarily free from the omnipresent smell of suffering and death.

The morning's first rays, and their fragile warmth, were three hours away. A late moon shone down upon the sightless sergeant. Around him, the sounds of frenzied activity were everywhere. The medical convoy's drivers, and a military-police detachment, were working feverishly to load their countrymen into the olive-green ambulances with huge red crosses blazoned on their tops and sides.

A fierce Russian artillery bombardment sounded in the distance. With each exploding shell, the Americans redoubled their efforts.

"Load this one into the third ambulance."

Strong hands once again gripped the ends of his stretcher. Robert Jensen was effortlessly lifted from the snows.

"Watch his IVs," the voice at his feet said.

"I've got them. Go ahead and load him."

"Where do you want him?"

"Put him on the bottom row on the left side."

The stretcher slid into place in the rear of the ambulance. Jensen could hear the anguished moans of the wounded soldier in the position inches above his head. The cavalry sergeant lay in the darkness for what seemed a long time. One by one, the six spaces in the ambulance were filled. And they waited still longer while the massive convoy continued to load its precious cargo.

At last, the time had come to make their hurried escape. The drivers and escorts rushed to their vehicles.

Ramirez poked his head inside the rear of the ambulance. "Hey, Sarge!" he said. "We're about ready to roll. Man, are you lucky. Lieutenant Morse is going to be riding back here with you guys. I sure wish

I were going to be back here with you, too. Don't worry about me, though. I'm gonna be right up front with the driver."

"Okay, Ramirez. I'll rest easy knowing you're up there to protect us." The hint of sarcasm in his sergeant's voice was lost on the young soldier.

The ambulance started. The motor softly rocked the wounded soldiers. All around, the convoy's vehicles came to life. The lengthy line of stretchers and stethoscopes began to move. An MP detachment was generously dispersed throughout the column. Stinger teams rode at its front and rear.

The Russians were thirty minutes from the eastern outskirts of the city.

Captain Wehner was far too busy to take the time to say good-bye. As the vehicles pulled away, a quick glance out a dingy window was all the doctor could afford.

Two hundred ambulances, a handful of trucks filled with medical supplies, and two dozen Humvees headed down the hospital's icy cobblestone driveway. The endlessly stretching convoy eased its way onto the narrow street that would lead it to the nearest autobahn.

The relative safety of the sprawling Army hospital complex at Landstuhl waited 135 miles away.

Fear-tinged chaos instantly engulfed the convoy on the teeming streets of the panicked German city of over one hundred thousand. The Americans were quickly swallowed up by the limitless masses of German refugees intent on escaping the marauding Russians.

This wasn't going to be an easy task.

The convoy ran into problem after problem as it pressed its way through the terrified sea of humanity. With skilled MPs at its head, the medical formation fought forward through the jammed roadways. The entrance to the autobahn was only a mile from the hospital. But the Americans would consume ten precious minutes covering this first difficult distance.

The Russians were drawing ever nearer to the city.

The scene that greeted them at the westerly-reaching autobahn was no better than what they'd experienced on the city's ancient pavement. For as far as the eye could see, cars stretched to the horizon. On both sides of the divided highway, refugees crammed every inch of its eight lanes. All were headed west. The tidal wave of German civilians was desperately attempting to cover the sixty miles of asphalt that would take them to the outskirts of Frankfurt.

The American convoy wasn't going to be traveling nearly so far on this roadway. They only needed to cover the first ten miles to reach their initial objective, a second wide autobahn running southwest to Heidelberg.

After a seventy-mile run to Heidelberg, the convoy would cross a section of the Rhine River being held by the 82nd Airborne. They'd head for Kaiserslautern, fifty miles farther west. Passing Ramstein on the way, a handful of miles beyond Kaiserslautern, they'd finally reach their destination.

But they had to complete this ten-mile stretch of torturous highway first. All roads west, big and small, were filled far beyond capacity, with millions of frantic civilians running for safety in front of the unstoppable Russian juggernaut. Countless numbers of haphazardly abandoned vehicles further hampered their desperate efforts. Scores of wrecks blocked the way to freedom. Frightened, desperate people were absolutely everywhere. The Los Angeles freeway system at its worst had nothing on the gridlock the Americans found.

The journey was being further hindered by the night's oppressive darkness. In the first hour, the medical convoy covered less than ten miles. Even that wouldn't have been possible if the MPs hadn't been so forceful in their actions to clear a path for their wounded countrymen.

After fighting forward for an hour, the leading edge of the American column reached the western end of Wurzburg. A half mile away was the turnoff for Heidelberg. In five minutes, the widely dispersed American ambulances would turn southwest. The traffic on the Heidelberg autobahn was extremely heavy. Yet it was nothing compared to what they'd so far endured. It wouldn't be long before their pace would dramatically increase. The Russians were closing fast. Still, it appeared the medical convoy was going to escape.

The inviting road to Heidelberg was just ahead.

It was at this point in their perilous journey, with the promise of the less crowded roadway to the southwest right in front of them, that disaster struck.

From the black eastern horizon, the specter of twenty-five Havoc Attack Helicopters appeared. The Havocs, the most advanced helicopters in the Russian arsenal, rushed forward with their stubby wingtips nearly touching.

The threat to the American convoy was immediate and unmistakable.

"Emergency! Emergency!" the MP lieutenant in charge of the convoy yelled into his radio handset. "This is the Wurzburg medical convoy. We're trapped on the Frankfurt autobahn approximately one-half mile east of the Heidelberg cutoff. A large number of Russian helicopters are approaching. If you can hear my voice, we need help. Say again. A half mile east of the Heidelberg cutoff. The Wurzburg medical convoy needs help from any source."

The lieutenant waited for a response. His pleas were met with nothing but static on the radio.

At the rear of the column, the Stinger teams sprang into action. Four shoulder-mounted gunners leaped from their vehicles. Each began targeting the enemy. In their Humvees, the two Avenger teams swung around to face the onrushing threat. For the moment, the Stinger teams at the front of the sprawling formation were too far away to be of any help.

The Americans held their fire and prayed. They waited to see if the Russians would respect the red crosses of the medical convoy.

In the early-morning darkness, the helicopter pilots spotted a stretching military column in the crush of German automobiles on the roadway ahead. Without hesitation, the Russians dove toward the wide highway.

From the twenty-five attackers, a massive assault of rockets and missiles rained down upon the frozen autobahn. The night sky shimmered and flashed as death streaked toward the icebound pavement. Near the rear of the convoy, a quarter-mile stretch of roadway suddenly erupted beneath the frightful power of the immense barrage. Lethal pieces of flaming metal and huge chunks of rock-hard asphalt leaped high into the air. Within the attack corridor, the horror that befell the crammed throngs was unspeakable. The death toll instantly reached into the thousands.

Eight ambulances burst into flames. In each, nine American lives were lost without anyone within them ever realizing what had occurred.

An Avenger succumbed to the powerful Russian assault. Behind the air defenders, two MP Humvees also were gone.

At the same instant, 450 German cars exploded. Their gas tanks were eager receptacles for the explosive charges pouring down upon them. Hades itself couldn't have provided a more terrifying scene. A raging inferno three hundred feet high enveloped the quarter-mile stretch of highway. The lucky ones died instantly. The unfortunate souls who somehow survived the death swirling all around them found themselves trapped in the searing fires. Flaming figures, their clothing and flesh burning, raced from the conflagration.

The Americans answered back. Five Stingers leaped into the air. The little missiles raced toward the attackers. At the close range of the swarming helicopters, the missiles found their targets in seconds. Silhouetted in the darkness, five exploding Havocs fell from the black heavens.

Three dropped harmlessly into the open fields on the southern side of the autobahn. Two of the burning helicopters fell upon the jumble of cars below. A mile behind the convoy, a smaller inferno erupted beneath the pair of exploding Havocs.

The shoulder-mounted Stinger gunners rushed to remove the grip stocks and handles from their expended missile tubes. They started furiously preparing a replacement Stinger. With seven missiles waiting in his pods, the Avenger gunner targeted another of the enemy.

The surviving Havocs swooped in. They fired a second tremendous volley of rockets and missiles. Two miles ahead of the original attack, another gruesome portion of the autobahn fell beneath the sword. A dozen ambulances and hundreds of cars were engulfed by the firestorm that leaped from the unmerciful skies. A thousand more souls were added to the rolls by the night-shattering assault.

Thunderous explosions rocked the column. A few hundred yards in front of the location of the second attack, Robert Jensen could feel the hellish flames of the fearsome barrage.

The Avenger fired once more. A helicopter went down. The gunner quickly targeted a third soaring Havoc and released another missile. A heat-seeking Stinger leaped from the Avenger's left pod. It reached out at supersonic speed to seize its quarry. Scattered pieces of the defeated Russian flamed to earth.

Two Stinger gunners were ready to fire again. Standing side by side, each waited for the tone to sound. The sweet tones went off. Death reached into the starlit skies to snatch a pair of Havocs. Another pair of attackers tumbled from the heavens.

The Avenger had another helicopter in its sights. The final pair of Stinger gunners rose to their feet.

The Russians fled into the eastern sky. Three Stingers leaped high to give chase. The heartless little killers would catch their prey just prior to reaching each small missile's five-mile limit. A trio of retreating Havocs exploded. The thirteen survivors disappeared into the black night.

With the immediate threat gone, the stunned Americans attempted to regroup.

There was nothing anyone could do for those caught beneath the Russian assault. Two long stretches of white-hot, flaming pavement were a horrifying no-man's-land. Those trapped within couldn't be saved.

Many would undertake their somber journey across the river Styx on this sordid morning.

The MPs and medics stared in disbelieving silence at the grisly nightmare unfolding all around them. They were experts at handling emergencies. But they'd never before faced anything approaching this.

The panic that gripped the German refugees was absolute. Many of the shocked survivors left their expensive automobiles and ran into the open fields on both sides of the roadway. In a futile attempt to escape, others mindlessly slammed their cars into those blocking their path.

The eighty-three-year relationship between the Germans and their American conquerors always had been a somewhat uneasy one. Like an arranged marriage, the two sides had been involved in over eight decades of an extended love-hate relationship.

At this moment, the deep-seated resentment many Germans held for the Americans boiled over. The shocked German survivors stared at the thousands of dead and dying on the fiery autobahn. Fear and anger overwhelmed them. They needed an outlet for their pent-up rage. They needed to strike out at something.

The hospital convoy was right in front of them.

CHAPTER 50

January 31—6:45 a.m.
Wurzburg Hospital Convoy
A Half Mile from the Heidelberg Turnoff

The Americans sat in the center of the confused queue of terrified souls. A badly burned German woman kneeling in the snows cradled the charred remains of her only child. The grief-stricken woman shrieked for blood. Out of her mind over the loss of her three-year-old son, she screamed for death for the Americans.

In a flash, the Germans turned on the medical formation. At the front of the convoy, ten angry people became twenty. In a few heartbeats, twenty became one hundred. Men, women, and children as young as ten joined the ballooning crowd. One hundred grew to one thousand. A large group of cajoling skinheads pushed their way to the head of the swirling mass of furious souls. Intent on revenge, the incensed mob closed in on the Americans. There was menace in their eyes and rage in their hearts. They needed to lash out to vent their insatiable frustrations in any way they could.

Six MPs and the four soldiers of the forward Stinger teams waited to stop the surging throng. The Germans came on. The defenders fired a warning volley into the air from their M-4s. The mob hesitated for the slightest of moments. But the perverse brown shirts weren't going to back down. They burst forward. From thirty yards away, the Germans hurled sticks and stones. The ever-burgeoning crowd rushed the beleaguered Americans. In the cab of the third ambulance, Ramirez watched as the infuriated Germans raced toward the MPs.

The autobahn's roaring fires had cut off the remainder of the MP detachment. For the moment, the ten soldiers at its head were alone in their defense of the lead elements of the convoy.

The Americans hesitated, not anticipating the incalculable fury of the wrathful riot. The soldiers fell back a few steps. The lead ambulance was scarcely ten yards behind them. There was nowhere left to go. The Americans were out of options. They lowered their M-4s, and when the lieutenant gave the order, they fired. Twenty Germans dropped on the frigid asphalt.

The crazed mob stopped dead in its tracks. Fifty stones whistled through the air. Four soldiers were felled by the stinging stones. Streams of blood ran down the MPs' faces.

The Germans saw their opening. The rabid gathering, growing larger by the second, charged the dazed Americans. The soldiers staggered backward a few stumbling steps. They squeezed the triggers on their M-4s a second time. A dozen more in the melee went down. The throng slowed, but propelled by its sheer numbers, it refused to stop. The soldiers fired a final burst from point-blank range. The dead dropped around them once again.

The lethal swarm was right on top of the Americans. They closed in from all sides. Hundreds more joined in on the attack. The seething rabble wanted blood. There was nothing more the MPs could do. They tried to fight back, but it was no use. The defenders disappeared as the weight of the surging multitude washed over them. All ten went down beneath the frenzied crush of rampaging people.

The Germans started savagely beating the fallen Americans. In less than a minute, three of the MPs were stomped to death by the jack-booted brown shirts. In five minutes of sheer terror, each of the Americans lost his life. There were satisfied smiles on the killers' faces as the thugs surveyed their handiwork.

Nevertheless, the horde's uncontrollable lust was far from sated. Their boundless fury had yet to be appeased. The vexed crowd needed much more of the twisted gratification they'd just experienced. They turned to lash out again. In their path waited the lead ambulance. Inside its cab, the driver and his partner saw the irate masses rushing for them. Too late, the medics reacted. The soldiers grabbed the M-4s propped between them in the seat. But the neo-Nazis were soon upon them. A dozen rocks smashed the ambulance's windshield. Inside the cab, the pair dove for cover. Angry hands clawed at the door handles. The doors flew open wide. The insane throng dragged the screaming Americans from the truck. They threw them upon the cold, hard ground. A swirl of feet, fists, and stones smashed the defenseless soldiers.

It was quickly over. Every bone in the medics' bodies had been broken. At the head of the column, the number of American dead had grown to twelve.

Still, after three days of watching a million of their countrymen die, it wasn't nearly enough. The ambulance, with its white American star, was theirs for the taking. The crowd rushed forward on both sides and began furiously rocking the vehicle. Inside, the doctor and his injured patients tumbled into the narrow aisle. Stitches and tubes were ripped from those who'd fallen in battle while attempting to protect German soil.

With a mighty shove, the ambulance fell onto its side. It slid into the wide ditch on the edge of the autobahn. Two of the wounded soldiers were dead before the wild-eyed attackers ripped open the doors.

The skinhead-led legion dragged the Americans from the rear of the ambulance. Once more, they vented their hysterical rage. Even the dead soldiers were pulled from the vehicle and assaulted. The mangled bodies of the doctor and his patients were tossed into the snows like broken rag dolls.

The crowd turned toward the second ambulance. Thirty yards behind the first, the Americans in the cab had witnessed what had happened to their friends. They were standing on the roadway with their rifles at the ready. The pair of medical technicians had never fired a shot in anger in their lives. But they weren't going to let that get in their way. The moment the ravaging host turned toward their ambulance, they opened fire. The pair fired over and again as the intemperate rabble raced across the pavement toward them. A dozen or more dropped beneath the medics' gunfire. The mob faltered, but its immense weight pushed it forward once more.

The Americans continued to fire. The number of bodies in front of their ambulance grew. Both soldiers' ammunition clips held thirty rounds. Each ran dry at nearly the same moment. The inexperienced medics clawed at their pistol belts for a replacement.

The debased surge, led by those with years of pent-up anger in their sadistic souls, was soon upon them. The soldiers went down beneath the onrushing crowd. They were dead in seconds. The sound of their cracking skulls could be heard over the insanity of the mob. From the cab of the next ambulance, Ramirez watched the mounting horror in disbelief. The wretched host, their rage continuing to boil, rushed to destroy those within the rear of the second ambulance.

Another ambulance was tossed onto its side. Bloodstained hands reached into the rear compartment. Seven more bodies were soon strewn about on the bitter highway.

Still, the vengeance-filled swarm hadn't had enough.

They turned toward the third ambulance.

Seven MPs had extricated themselves from the fiery column. They were running at full speed toward the unholy scene. In another two minutes, they'd be in a position to help their countrymen.

Ramirez looked over at the ambulance driver. The terrified soldier sat frozen in fear.

"Get out there and stop them!"

The soldier stared at Ramirez, incomprehension spreading across his frightened face.

"Dammit! The least you can do is get out there and go down like a man."

With his good arm, Ramirez grabbed the soldier's rifle. He shoved it toward the driver. The driver reached out to take the weapon. But he'd hesitated a fraction of a second too long before mustering the courage to act. As the tips of his fingers touched the M-4's plastic stock, the driver's door flew open. Blood-soiled hands tore the screaming soldier from his seat. The mob was on him in an instant. It wouldn't be long before his screaming would stop.

Another group moved toward the passenger door. Ramirez was waiting. The door was ripped open. The determined soldier stared into a pair of evil eyes set deep within a shaved German skull.

Cradling the driver's rifle under his left arm, Ramirez calmly blew the skinhead's face off with a single shot. The nearly headless body fell back into the crowd. Ramirez sprayed a quick, three-shot burst. Two more neo-Nazis fell. The mob hesitated.

A smaller group of ill-destined deviants was at the rear of the ambulance. The wide door swung open. Elizabeth Morse had no way of protecting her charges. And each was too seriously injured to be of any help to her. Nevertheless, she boldly stood blocking the entrance to the rear compartment of ambulance number three.

Two shaved-headed Germans in their early twenties reached in. They snatched the pretty nurse from the rear of the ambulance. She let out a terrifying scream. The pair dragged her away from the vehicle. They threw her onto the bleak asphalt and tore at her clothing. Before they killed her, they'd every intention of raping the appealing, dark-haired American. She fought back with everything she had, struggling to keep the vile creatures from her.

Her screams attracted the chaotic mob's attention. The malevolent ones, blood dripping from their hands and feet, turned toward the new drama unfolding a few feet away. For the moment, the injured soldiers inside the doorway were forgotten.

Morse's scrubs were gone. The tattered cloth had been ripped from her frame. Even so, while she lay on the freezing roadway clad in only her undergarments, she continued to vigorously resist her antagonists' efforts. The beautiful nurse was determined to go down fighting. A swift kick to the head from a sturdy German boot silenced her struggle. She lay alive but unmoving on the harsh ground. The final shreds of clothing were savagely torn from her body.

The first of the grinning attackers pulled his filthy pants down around his knees. He dropped to the ground to mount the fallen figure.

Without warning, a single shot rang out. The skinhead fell on top of the unconscious lieutenant. The back of his head was gone. In a flash, his partner fell dead next to him, the victim of a second ringing shot.

The defiling crowd instinctively parted. It was just long enough for the stone-faced American to force his way through. Ramirez kicked the dead rapist's body from Elizabeth Morse. With the rifle menacingly raised under his left arm, he stood over the unconscious figure. The brown shirts closed in from three sides. The battle-tested Ramirez took his time. Firing a single shot only when necessary, he held the threatening tangle at bay for a full forty-five seconds. One by one, bodies dropped around him. By the time he was finished, ten corpses would lie at Ramirez's feet.

The seven MPs were nearly there.

The fallen lieutenant stirred. Ramirez's undoing. Her movement distracted him for the briefest of moments.

"Stay still, don't move," he said.

He glanced at her struggling form. When he did, the clustering attackers saw their chance. From every direction, they pounced upon the wounded soldier. Ramirez tried to respond. He fired two belated rounds. But it was too late. The deadly rifle was ripped from his hands. He vanished beneath the crushing mountain of inhumanity.

On the side of the roadway one hundred yards away, the MPs knelt on the hard ground. As one, they opened fire on the huge melee of marauding figures near the rear of the third ambulance. From this distance, they wouldn't miss. At the edges of the horde, the Germans dropped in clumps. Flowing blood was everywhere. The death toll quickly mounted. The mob staggered back. They scattered to the four winds from the concentrated gunfire. The MPs continued to shoot into the fleeing crowd. The soldiers stopped to reload. An irrational force of four hundred seized the opportunity. They re-formed and charged across the pavement directly for the MPs.

The Americans opened fire again.

The running Germans fell beneath the persistent gunfire. Even so, their uncontrollable passion for ruinous revenge propelled them forward. Undeterred by the death around them, the neo-Nazis raced screaming across the pavement toward the MPs. Three hundred raging animals closed to within fifty yards of the firing soldiers. One hundred more lay dead, or dying, behind them. The Americans continued to fire. Two people were falling for every yard of ground covered. But still, the mob came on. At the present rate, two hundred Germans would reach the seven Americans in the next ten seconds. The MPs knew they were in serious trouble.

More chattering rifles suddenly joined in on the slaughter. On the MP's left, the four medical technicians from the cabs of the fourth and fifth ambulances were shooting into the sprinting crowd. The defenders had the frenetic assembly in a crossfire.

From the sheer weight of the killing, the attack ground to a halt. Thirty yards from both groups of Americans, the Germans stopped in the middle of the roadway. The sergeant in charge of the MPs signaled for his men to cease firing. The ambulance drivers responded in kind. They waited while the disheveled audience milled about on the cold pavement. With their rifles at the ready, the Americans prepared to fire again if the Germans should charge once more.

Those in the mob hesitated, unsure of what their next move should be. At its edges, many started slipping away. Still, its central core of crazed killers remained intact.

It was the Russians who'd end the calamitous circus once and for all. From low in the east, the thirteen surviving Havocs returned. At the rear of the convoy, the Stinger teams were waiting. The Americans fired first, hoping to stop the helicopters before they could loosen their lethal munitions. Five missiles ripped through the cold morning. The targeted helicopters raced away. All five, prepared this time to counter the swift Stingers, released strings of flares. Three helicopters would ultimately be successful in fooling the little killers. A trio of Stingers would uselessly attack falling flares. The other missiles continued straight and steady. A pair of deadly Havocs exploded in midair.

The Avenger gunner targeted his next victim. The four Stinger teams scrambled to prepare a new missile. The final eight helicopters roared forward, intent on destroying the air-defense teams.

The Havocs opened fire on the rear of the column. A barrage of rockets and missiles, smaller than the initial attack but still quite deadly, reached down for the ground below. Two hundred yards of highway erupted in a blazing fireball. Hundreds more, American and German alike, joined the dead on the scorched autobahn.

In one quick strike, the Stingers were gone. Every last one had been consumed in the all-encompassing flames.

With the American air defenses eliminated, the eleven surviving attack helicopters would be free to rampage up and down the highway. At the front of the column, the disorganized Germans broke and ran in stark terror.

The defenseless Americans braced for a fiery death to pour down upon their heads. There was little chance any of them would survive. Yet to their surprise, the pitiless helicopters unexpectedly turned and raced east. Hot on their vapor trails were the Sparrow missiles of three Lakenheath F-16s. The dead MP lieutenant's pleas had finally been answered.

The savage hunters were on the run. With a gleam in their eyes, the American pilots chased the slower-flying enemy. The F-16s fired their missiles and cannons again and again.

One by one, they tracked their overmatched prey. In less than five minutes, all eleven Havocs lay burning on the outskirts of Wurzburg. And the F-16 pilots were on their way back to England.

At the rear of the third ambulance, the naked lieutenant sat on the frigid ground cradling the lifeless private's crushed body. While she clutched Ramirez to her, huge tears fell upon his unseeing face. He'd given his life to save hers.

He wouldn't have had it any other way.

For the moment, the threat from the Russians was over. The threat from the civilians also appeared to have dissipated. The Americans picked themselves up and re-formed the column as best they could. All around, the doctors and nurses found themselves faced with hundreds upon hundreds of injured and dying Germans. After what had transpired, the Americans chose to turn their backs and walk away. They'd leave the Germans to their fates—and the Russians.

With the enemy close behind, there was no time to adequately care for their own dead. The Americans took their fallen brothers and sisters and laid their remains in straight rows in a snow-covered field at the edge of the roadway. Ramirez was among them.

The remainder of the trip would be slow going. It would take the convoy nine hours to cover the remaining 125 miles to the final-standing American Army hospital. In the rear of the now-leading ambulance, for the entire journey, Elizabeth Morse's tears never stopped.

Inside his mask of white cloth, the battle-hardened sergeant in the bottom left stretcher cried along with her.

CHAPTER 51

January 31—10:00 a.m.
Defense Information Systems Agency
Hillingdon

As the battered medical convoy continued its ill-fated journey, five hundred miles north George O'Neill and Randy Carson were ready to unveil their ingenious plan. When they'd finished explaining their idea, Colonel Hoerner, Major Siebman, and Master Sergeant Doyle looked at the pair in complete disbelief.

"So, George," Denny Doyle said, "you're telling us in the middle of a war you can completely rebuild in a day and a half the Defense Information System it took decades to complete?"

"Not the whole thing, Denny, just the small part west of the Rhine. I figured there was no point of even looking at anything in Germany east of there. By the time we'd get the system in place on that side of the river, it'll likely be in Russian hands."

The skeptical expressions on the three faces hadn't changed.

"I thought George was crazy, too, when he first told me about this idea," Carson said. "But the more my engineers looked at it, and the more we talked about bringing over additional FEMA vans, the more it began to make sense."

"With Donnersberg as our central location," O'Neill said, "and the large site we have at Pirmasens as our secondary hub, we can completely restore our command and control west of the river. In fact, there's nothing but our own ingenuity to limit us. We can even keep some vans in reserve to add locations to the system wherever the generals tell us they want a new one. And if our engineering calculations are correct and we can get a functioning microwave system directly from Hillingdon to Donnersberg, we'll not only be able to tie western Germany together but also connect it directly with England and the States. That will overcome the limits of the smaller-capacity satellites Randy's team was able to install last night. We'll have a fully integrated network. Once we get the system in place, as long as we can keep the Russians from blowing up most of the sites, there's going to be no problem letting the generals maintain precise control of every element of our defense. If this works like we think it will, we'll almost be to the point where, should he choose to do so, the President could talk to any second lieutenant on the battlefield."

"Are you sure you can make this work, Sergeant O'Neill?" Colonel Hoerner asked.

"Yes, sir. With Randy's engineers and the FEMA vans, if we can get our hands on them, this will work. His crew already gave us back a fully functioning AWACS system and a couple of very welcome satellite terminals this morning; why not give them a chance to do significantly more? I'm not sure EUCOM's even interested at this point, but if we decide to make a final stand at the Rhine, this will give us a far greater chance of succeeding."

"All right, Sergeant O'Neill," the obviously reluctant Colonel Hoerner said. "I'll make the call to EUCOM and see if we can arrange a meeting."

At Upper Heyford, shortly after noon, Staff Sergeant George O'Neill stood in a spacious conference room with Randy Carson at his side. Twelve colonels, a couple of admirals, and four generals sat at a lengthy table. Other officers, from each of the services, sat along the crowded walls. With the way the war was going, each wore a haggard face.

It was quite clear to everyone, from the lowest private to the highest levels of command, that unless something dramatic happened in the next few days, the Russians were going to swiftly conquer Germany and prevail in the egregious struggle.

Even a week earlier, O'Neill could never have imagined his country in such a desperate situation.

He understood the war wasn't going well, and he was generally aware of the major events as they occurred. Still, even in the position he held, his conceptual understanding of the overall American plan was, naturally, quite limited.

He'd no idea if any of those present would be even vaguely interested in his concept or exactly how it would fit into the big picture, if it fit at all. But he'd come this far, and there would be no turning back.

O'Neill taped the map of the existing European Defense Information System on the wall and began going over the critical elements of where the system presently stood and where it had the potential to be if DISA was given the go-ahead to install the new network.

For twenty minutes he spoke without a single question being raised, an event exceedingly rare with so many senior officers present. From the moment he'd begun talking, each could see there was a great deal of potential in what was being presented. And each one's frustration with his inability to control the frightful conflict made him a more-than-willing listener.

Like nearly everyone in the twenty-first century, the ability to communicate with anyone they wished, whenever they wished, was something they'd all long ago taken for granted. That is until they'd lost the ability to actually do so.

Twenty minutes was ample time for O'Neill to go over the major elements of the plan. Finally, Colonel Morrison, now EUCOM's acting head of operations after General Oliver's death during the Russian raid on Patch Barracks, asked a question. It would be the first of many from those at the table. O'Neill understood that the continual stream of questions, one right after another, was a good sign. Clearly, those present were extremely curious about what they were being told.

"What you've just explained is certainly interesting. Do you really think you can pull this off, Sergeant O'Neill?" Morrison said.

"Well, sir, nothing this complex is ever one hundred percent certain. There's always the possibility of something completely unexpected happening, and there are bound to be some glitches along the way. But if you decide to do this, Mr. Carson and I are confident that what we have just gone over with you will succeed."

"So, if we ask the President to commit to this plan, what should we tell him is our greatest concern?"

"That the Russians destroy Donnersberg, sir. I would recommend before we even consider implementing this approach we make sure we can defend the site from both air and ground attacks. It sure would be nice to put at least a company of infantry and a significant number of Stingers on the mountaintop to defend it. And if by some chance you happen to have a Patriot Missile System lying around that you aren't using, that would make things even better."

O'Neill had included the final comment more to break the tension than anything else. He was quite surprised by the answer he received.

"Actually, Sergeant, it's funny you mentioned that. Right before you came in, we were talking about what to do with the Patriot Missile System at Rhein-Main we hadn't been able to use because nearly all of its soldiers had been killed during the Russian airborne attack a couple of days ago. We've been gathering surviving soldiers from the Patriots that have been destroyed and were planning on sending them to Rhein-Main to retrieve the system. We just hadn't figured out where we needed it most. Donnersberg sounds like a perfect place to send it."

It was now one of the generals' turn to inquire. "You're going to need qualified soldiers to operate the new communication sites you're proposing. Where do you plan to get them?"

"In the same way you're going to man the Patriot system, sir," O'Neill said. "We'll be cutting it close, but we're going to take people from the existing Air Force and Army sites, especially those presently east of the Rhine. We'll send those we free up to handle the new locations."

The general asked a second question. "You said protecting Donnersberg is the most critical part of your plan. What do you consider second most important?"

"Without a doubt it's timing, sir," O'Neill said. "We need to get the sites in place and the command and control system ready for your use at the exact moment you need to use it. If we're even a few hours late, and we can't support our forces defending the Rhine in the manner we've promised, it could cost thousands of lives and ultimately lead to our failure."

"Do you think you'll be able to get the system in place in time, Sergeant?"

"Again, sir, there are lots of variables. We'll need a day and a half once we're told to begin the project. So the sooner we get the go-ahead and can lay our hands on the FEMA vans, the better. And the sooner all the major units identify their command and control needs in defending everything west of the river, the more efficiently all this will go. Our circuit engineers in Virginia will use that time to design each individual circuit to meet the exact demands of every user."

It was now an Air Force general's turn to ask the question he'd been dying to ask.

"Sergeant, you said you can place elements of the system wherever we need them, even where nothing presently exists. Am I hearing you correctly? Thirty-six hours from now, we could have fully functioning communication centers for an entire air base should we elect to reopen any of those we closed during our phasedown in Europe?"

"Absolutely, sir."

"At Sembach?"

"Yes."

"At Hahn, Zweibrucken, and Bitburg?"

"Yes, sir. We can do all that. We have the potential to support as many fighter air bases as you'd like to create. Just be aware that the faster we know what you're exact needs are, the easier this will be. After we have the central network in place at Donnersberg and Pirmasens, we can begin connecting the smaller vans at the outlying locations. You just tell us where you need them, what you need, and when you need it, and we'll take it from there."

The questioning continued for nearly an hour.

When all had been asked and answered, Colonel Morrison turned to Colonel Hoerner.

"What your team's presented today is extremely interesting. Let us talk among ourselves before we go any further. But I think I can tell you with some degree of certainty that we'll be passing your idea on to the Pentagon quite soon."

General Yovanovich's plan for the conquest of Germany had been a good one. For the moment, it was very much on schedule. It appeared to all the world that the Russians would seize every inch of German soil in the five days he'd predicted.

He'd surprised the ill-prepared Allies with the fierce winter attack. His deception had worked. He'd hammered their command and control, even if he'd come up short on his promise to completely destroy it. For the most part, his sabotage had succeeded. Now the Russians' overwhelming power was in the forefront as they continued to push the reeling Allies back.

But his plan had a potentially fatal flaw, one the dashing general had no ability to recognize. He hadn't accounted for George O'Neill. Or the untold numbers just like him in the American military. He'd failed to identify them and the potential influence they'd have on the war because no one even close to them existed in the rigid, top-down Russian military. No sergeant would have ever had the opportunity O'Neill was given to present such a complex plan to his generals.

As the war continued on its furious journey, the shy sergeant had provided the Americans an opening they could potentially exploit.

The only question remaining was whether or not they'd be bold enough to seize it.

CHAPTER 52

T he expression on Bonnie Lloyd's face never changed as she read from the TelePrompTer. "Repeating our top story this hour. The American aircraft carrier *George Washington* has been sunk. For more on this story, we take you to WNN's Pentagon correspondent, Patricia Moore."

The picture switched to another of the well-known WNN faces standing in her customary position in the foyer of the Pentagon.

"Thanks, Bonnie. Pentagon sources officially announced a few minutes ago that the aircraft carrier *George Washington* was sunk this morning four hundred miles west of the Azores. From what we've gathered, the attack occurred approximately three hours ago as the ship was on the way from its home base in Norfolk, Virginia, to support the American air forces in Germany."

The screen split to show both women's faces. "Patricia, have any details been released on what caused the sinking?" Lloyd asked.

"So far, Pentagon officials have provided little concrete information. We do know the *George Washington* was being supported by a screening force of destroyers and cruisers. WNN has been told unofficially that Russian submarines apparently slipped through the escort squadron and fired up to nine torpedoes. The carrier was struck multiple times."

"Has the Pentagon given out any casualty figures from the loss of the ship?"

"My sources tell me, Bonnie, that the *George Washington* was carrying nearly six thousand men and women. Rumors are saying most of the torpedoes hit the ship within seconds of each other. There was extensive damage. The giant ship sank ten minutes after the surprise attack. While exact figures aren't available, it appears the escorts were able to rescue approximately eight hundred sailors from the dying aircraft carrier. Apparently, the winter seas were quite stormy, and in addition to those killed on board, hundreds of sailors drowned before help could reach them."

"So," Bonnie Lloyd said, "what you're saying is that the number of dead from the sinking of the *George Washington* is approximately fifty-two hundred?"

"That would be about right, Bonnie."

"What effect will the loss of the *George Washington* have on the war? Has the Pentagon said anything about that?"

"Naturally, the Pentagon's declined to answer such questions. We do believe, however, from what we've been told about the general location of our other naval fleets at the beginning of the war, that no other carriers are in a position to come to the aid of the NATO forces for at least another week. That, of course, is purely speculation on the press corps' part. It's not something that has been, or is likely to be, confirmed by the military."

"Thank you, Patricia."

The screen returned to a single image of Bonnie Lloyd sitting at the anchor desk.

"Repeating this hour's top story. The American aircraft carrier *George Washington* has been sunk four hundred miles west of the Azores. Loss of life is put at over five thousand. We'll have more on this story as further details become available. After these messages, we'll be back with more late-breaking reports from our correspondents Jim Haney in London and Russell Reese in Frankfurt."

The image on the screen switched to the picture of the American and Soviet flags clashing, with the words THE BATTLE FOR GERMANY running across the bottom of the screen. The war's theme music blared.

In a few seconds, the picture changed to a sleepy man in striped pajamas staring into a mirror while holding a bottle of mouthwash.

CHAPTER 53

The medics lifted Kathy's stretcher from the ambulance. They carried it toward the rear of the C-17 medevac plane. The early-evening winds kicked up. They blew the blustery night's first hint of bitterness at the helpless figure wrapped in woolen blankets. The quick winds scattered the low-lying clouds. They revealed a haunting moon, a yellow hue distorting its glow. A handful of twinkling stars were etched on the horizon.

The medical evacuation plane's jet engines were already running. The C-17 sat on the exact spot her husband's plane had waited to take on its load of passengers sixty hours earlier. A nurse held Christopher's hand as the child struggled to walk next to his mother. His stubby legs fought to keep up with the stretcher. Christopher stumbled and fell in the patchy gray snows at the edge of the runway. Tears flowed from his eyes. A wail of protest filled the air. The nurse scooped him up, and, none the worse for wear, the toddler entered the aircraft behind his mother's stretcher.

The medics moved down the left aisle, past the rows of partially filled positions. They stopped near the front of the plane. The airmen carefully transferred Kathy onto one of the medevac's permanent positions. The tubes and bottles that accompanied the C-17's latest passenger were attached to the specially designed fuselage. After a quick check of their efforts, the medics returned to the cold to retrieve their next patient.

The nurse took the reluctant child to one of the passenger seats at the front of the aircraft. She buckled him in. While they waited for the medevac to fill, Christopher turned toward Kathy. Never once did he look away from his mother. The love in his eyes overwhelmed her. Through her pain, a smile filled Kathy's battered face. Tears of relief soon followed. Huge teardrops flowed. The knowledge that she and her child were taking a giant step out of the nightmare overwhelmed her.

For twenty minutes, ambulances unloaded their human cargo onto the flying hospital. Every stretcher position was filled. Behind them, thousands more, both injured and healthy, waited on the numbing ground for their turn to come.

The rear ramp closed. As the aircraft taxied onto the runway, the nurses and medics made final preparations for the long flight home. Over the suffering around her, Kathy could hear the sound of the revving engines.

The C-17 with the red crosses on its fuselage hurtled down the runway and took to the skies. In eight hours, the medevac would arrive in Dover, Delaware.

At the same moment, one hundred miles north at Rhein-Main, another aircraft was preparing to leave the ground. The aging 767 with the giant eagle on its tail and the words EARLY EAGLE AIRLINES beneath the ferocious bird of prey waited for the final handful of passengers to make their way across the tarmac.

In the pilot's chair, Evan Cooper surveyed the damage on the ground below. The burned remains of the fierce battle two days earlier were evident everywhere he looked.

The war continued to be a financial godsend for Cooper. A broad grin was plastered on his features while he waited for the boarding process to be completed. From his previous combat experiences, however, he understood that war was nothing to be celebrated. And such knowledge tempered his euphoria. Still, he knew that if he could keep the old plane flying for three more days, his financial problems would be over. Three more days of flights to Germany, and he'd be in a position to ask the court to terminate his bankruptcy. Early Eagle Airlines would be his once more. For the first time in a long time, he, not the lawyers, would be deciding how to run his one-plane airline.

Thirty minutes of daydreaming was all it took from touchdown to turnaround. The loading of passengers and luggage, fuel and food, was quickly completed. With 289 women and children and a crew of eight, the dark silhouette of the 767 rushed down the runway. The plane struggled into the western sky.

As the passenger aircraft started its steep ascent, a mile west of the base a Russian parachutist waited with his shoulder-mounted surface-to-air missile at the ready. The Russian private had been cut off from his unit for two days. He'd remained hidden for all that time, waiting for guidance to somehow find him. It had not. Finally, just after sunset of the second day, he suspected the time had come for him to take some kind of action.

He'd no practice at thinking on his own. With no one to tell him what to do, he decided to use his missile to shoot down the next plane to take off from, or attempt to land at, the American base. A few minutes later, the 767 roared down the icy runway.

The blue beret took his time. In the darkness, he couldn't make out the eagle on the aircraft's tail. As the plane strained to reach the heavens, the parachutist fired. He'd no idea what he'd fired at, or what cargo it carried. It really didn't matter much to him.

Evan Cooper spotted the bright flash of the missile as it streaked across the sky. He knew his fate was forever sealed. He'd no chance of saving his passengers or his aircraft. Yet he wasn't willing to concede the inevitable. He dove the cumbersome plane for the western horizon. It was a hopeless attempt to evade the death that was growing quite near. In the passenger compartment, the steep dive tore loose everything that wasn't firmly tied down.

Nevertheless, it was all for naught. Cooper watched helplessly as the missile quickly closed. A fiery explosion filled the western sky as the missile hit the right wing's engine and destroyed it. The wing was severed, followed moments later by the ignition of the aircraft's fuel. The vivid explosion momentarily illuminated the ever-darkening evening. Pieces of flaming wreckage tumbled to the ground. Not a soul survived.

The Russian soldier melted back into the deep woods to wait for someone with further orders to find him.

The next day, a German mob found him instead.

George O'Neill, Kathy and Christopher always in the forefront of his anguished mind, asked Colonel Hoerner the same question he'd asked six times today and seventeen times overall. "Any further word on our families, sir?"

"Not yet, O'Neill. We haven't heard anything more definite out of Patch Barracks. The damage from the Russian raid was apparently quite extensive. And there were a number of casualties. They told me as of this moment, most of the dependents who survived the attack have been evacuated. But that's all I know for sure."

At two on a European morning, seven in the evening in Delaware, the medevac touched down on American soil. The ambulances were waiting. The first pair of soldiers taken from the plane were placed in a black hearse. They were driven to a makeshift morgue at the air base's recreation center. The eight-hour plane ride had been too much for the critically wounded soldiers.

Kathy and Christopher were among the last to leave the plane. They were placed in an ambulance and driven to the base gymnasium. In the past three days, the gymnasium had been converted into an overflow center for the base hospital.

Fifteen minutes later, the medevac returned to the runway and headed east for its next load of wounded Americans.

Inside the gymnasium, the scene was beyond tumultuous. The overburdened medical staff was doing its best to deal with the tidal wave of injured patients arriving every few minutes at this first stateside stopover. Kathy lay on a stretcher beneath a basketball hoop at the far end of the cavernous gymnasium. Christopher sat wailing at her feet. Hundreds of others were haphazardly strewn about on the wooden floor. In the confusion, she lay unattended for nearly an hour.

At last, one of the doctors, a balding reservist from Tampa with a thriving surgical practice, approached. He looked down at his clipboard.

"Mrs. O'Neill?"

Christopher continued to scream at the top of his lungs.

"Yes."

"I'm Dr. Zamora. Sorry for the delay. But as you can see, things are a bit hectic. I've looked over your chart. Normally, with injuries as extensive as yours, we'd send you straight to the nearest military medical facility. Unfortunately, with the tremendous number of wounded arriving from Europe, every military hospital in the United States is filled to the brim."

Even the sweet-spirited Kathy was at the end of her rope. Through her pain she said, "What then, Doctor, do you suggest we do?"

"Well, most of the civilian hospitals on the East Coast are also jammed beyond their limits with injured military personnel. For the past two days, many corporations have been donating their private jets to take patients to hospitals near their homes. So what we've been doing, when the case is not life-threatening, is letting the patient pick what hospital they want to go to. Once we have that information, we've been working out a way to get the patient there. Even though your injuries are quite serious, I believe it would be all right to send you on to a civilian hospital immediately. What I'm here to ask you is, where would you like to go?"

It took Kathy a moment to comprehend the full meaning of what the doctor was saying. Suddenly, a wide smile spread across her face.

"Home! I want to go home."

"Where would that be?"

"McMichael, Minnesota."

"Do they have a hospital there?"

"Yes, there's a small one."

"Okay, let me see if they're capable of providing you with adequate care. Then, if they're willing to take you, I'll get someone to start working on getting you there. But before I do any of that, the first thing I'm going to do is find someone to take care of your child."

A few minutes later, a grandmotherly Red Cross worker arrived. She scooped up the screaming Christopher and disappeared. By the time the doctor would return to Kathy, the now-happy Christopher would've eaten every sticky bite of two cherry Popsicles and been an active participant in countless rousing choruses of "Itsy Bitsy Spider."

Without her child, Kathy lay on the crammed floor in the middle of a sea of suffering. A half hour later, Dr. Zamora walked up with a grin on his face.

"Mrs. O'Neill, I've spoken with the doctor in charge of the hospital in McMichael. I relayed your status and condition to him. He says they're adequately equipped to handle your case, and are more than willing to accept you as a patient. But the really good news is that 3M's corporate jet will be arriving here in a couple of hours to pick up two neurological cases for the Mayo Clinic. There appears to be room on the 3M jet to send the two of you along with them. As we speak, the doctor in McMichael is arranging to have an ambulance waiting in Rochester, Minnesota, to take you the rest of the way. You and your child are going home. If all goes well, you should be arriving by sunrise tomorrow."

Her pain momentarily left her. A smile, so wide that it devoured her, spread across her bandaged features.

Kathy O'Neill was going home. Nevertheless, there were still going to be more long hours to wait, and a final takeoff and landing to make. Aware that she was actually headed home, each passing minute was incredibly slow. But finally, she and Christopher were on their way.

It was just after sunrise when the Learjet eased up to a private terminal at the Rochester Airport. The plane's engines stopped, and the door opened. Kathy and Christopher waited while the two critical patients were removed. Then it was their turn.

Kathy's stretcher was taken from the plane. A huge crowd was waiting. It appeared half the people in her small hometown had made the trip to greet her. From all around, the excitement of the moment fell upon them. Her mother smothered the grandson she'd never seen with hugs and kisses, toys and tears. The bewildered child wailed at the top of his lungs.

They loaded Kathy into a final ambulance for the five-hour drive. The procession headed through the breaking winter morning. Ten miles from the North Dakota border sat her home. The little farming community had been the only place she'd ever known until George O'Neill entered her life. While they drove, ten-foot walls of snow blocked Kathy's view of the Minnesota countryside she so adored. Many times during this final ride, she looked over at her beaming mother holding her sleeping grandson, and tears filled Kathy's eyes.

Finally, it was over. The ambulance entered the small town Kathy dearly loved. It eased to a stop in front of the fifteen-bed community hospital. For the next five months, this would be Kathy's home.

As they wheeled her in, a peace she'd never before known passed over her. Waves of joy swept her away. Uncontrollable tears flowed for hours on a drab Minnesota morning. Three days ago, a Russian MiG had buried her and her child in an unspeakable place. She'd been certain there'd be no reprieve from her man-made tomb. Now, in what seemed to be little more than a heartbeat, she found herself home. Kathy was back in the place she'd loved for all her life. A place full of wonderful memories. A place where she felt safe and secure.

Things were going to be all right. Her adoring husband was in London. He was five hundred miles from the fighting. And she and Christopher were home. She was far away from the horrors of the war that had nearly stolen her life.

Kathy's long ride home was over.

As she entered the hospital, she'd no idea that while she was on her way home, her husband had received a huge role in the next phase of America's effort to overcome Russia's aggression.

CHAPTER 54

Five hours after George O'Neill made his presentation to the EUCOM staff, the Secretary of Defense and Chairman of the Joint Chiefs walked into the Oval Office. With them was the Secretary of Homeland Security. While none of them was smiling, the deathly pall each face had carried throughout the previous days was gone.

The President, however, who had refused to take the decisive action these same advisors had recommended prior to the onset of the Russian invasion of Germany, showed the immense strain of the war's wretched hours in his every tortured thought, stilted action, and hesitant movement.

The moment the three were seated, the Secretary of Defense looked at the President and said, "Mr. President, we're going to win this war. And we're going to win it sooner rather than later."

The supremely confident statement was the exact opposite of what he and General Larsen had been telling the President since the moment the war began. It took the country's leader by utter surprise. His answer was almost disbelieving and even a bit terse.

"What? How? For the past three days, you stated with absolute certainty that we'd no chance of holding on long enough for our forces to get there in time to change things. You were quite clear there was no viable way to stop the Russians from destroying Germany."

"We've been telling you that, Mr. President," General Larsen said, "because of our inability to control the battlefield. It made no sense to do anything but fight a delaying action in Germany and not risk the loss of additional troops or equipment in a disjointed defense when we could save those forces for a counterassault. We felt the appropriate action was to buy time to get our divisions onto ships, sail them to England, and in a few weeks, when we'd assembled an overwhelming force, launch a D-day-style attack to annihilate the bastards. But we were wrong. A few hours ago, that assessment was turned upside down. With your permission, we wish to seriously consider taking a far-more-aggressive approach to the war. Our intent is to win this thing by taking bold steps rather than waiting any longer. It's a risk, but we believe it's a risk worth taking."

"Why the sudden change?" the President asked.

"Because," the Secretary of Defense replied, "we've identified a way to completely reestablish our command and control. At least the part of it west of the Rhine. And that opens up a wide range of avenues for us to consider."

"With all of the damage the Russians did to our infrastructure in Europe, how in the world are you going to restore command and control?"

"Assuming you will allow us to borrow FEMA's emergency communication vans, we can rebuild our entire command and control structure in the next two days. With a fully operational AWACS and our command and control restored, we've got a real chance here. You're going to be remembered as the President who snatched a miraculous victory from what was by all appearances a hapless rout."

The President, like so many who'd held the office before him, had an acute sense of history. He was more than willing to consider any option that would keep him from being portrayed as the first American President to lose a major war in Europe and his presidency from being labeled an abject failure.

They knew that statement would get the President's attention.

"With the potential to control the conduct of the war," General Larsen added, "we began looking at a number of options. But we don't want to waste your time, Mr. President. There's no reason to talk any further about our plan unless we know we're going to have the FEMA vans to work with."

"That's why we brought the Secretary of Homeland Security with us," the Secretary of Defense said. "FEMA, and their communication vans, belong to him."

The three of them turned to the Secretary of Homeland Security.

"Robert," the President said, "does Homeland Security have any objection to loaning the vans to our military?"

"Sir, with the way the war's gone, our only concern would be that, horror upon horror, this conflict escalates even further and before anyone can stop it results in total nuclear war. Should we face such an unimaginable situation, we won't have the vans available as we attempt to care for our surviving citizens and begin picking up the pieces."

"And you think having a handful of communication vans will make the slightest bit of difference if the entire country's been destroyed?"

"No, Mr. President, we don't. That's why, at the military's request, I've already ordered the FEMA regional offices to begin preparing the vans for transport to Dover Air Base as soon as you give the order. We can have the first few onto Air Force cargo planes in a matter of hours."

"Okay, that's settled. Homeland Security says the FEMA vans are available. Now tell me, General Larsen, why should I direct them to hand them over to the military? I'm certainly not willing to do so until I know a great deal more than I know right now. Explain this idea of yours."

"Mr. President, first understand that our plan has many moving pieces, and we're still working out the exact details. We only learned of the likelihood of restoring our command and control a few hours ago. Everyone at the Pentagon, from the highest levels to the lowest private, is on this, and it's coming together well enough for us to want to present it to you. Essentially, here's what we have in mind. Our forces east of the Rhine will fight a delaying action for as long as they possibly can. When we can no longer hold the eastern side, we'll blow every bridge across its wide waters. That alone will buy us valuable time while the

Russians bring forward enough equipment to build bridges, cross the river, and attempt to overwhelm us. As the Russians are constructing them, we'll use the AWACS' capabilities to pinpoint the enemy's actions and guide our response. It will tell us with exacting detail when and where to send our B-2 bombers and fighter aircraft to destroy each bridge before it reaches the western side. That will buy us even more time."

"Do you have a contingency in place should Cheninko attack the AWACS ground terminals again and we lose the precise coordination you anticipate?"

"We don't believe that's even a concern, sir. We've got more than three dozen air police guarding the ground station at Mildenhall and have cordoned off the entire area around the communication center. And the 82nd Airborne has provided one of its best companies to protect Donnersberg. We doubt the Russians have any clue we've moved so quickly to overcome the damage they did to the ground stations. And even if they do, they've no idea where we've placed the one in Germany. It'll likely be days before they figure out that the AWACS is fully operational. By then, it will be far too late for them to do anything about it."

"Okay, so far, so good. Tell me more."

"With the command and control we'll have established, we'll make our initial stand at the Rhine."

"I don't understand. Who'll make their stand? If nearly all of our forces are fighting a delaying action in the east, there'll be few units left to provide such a defense once the Russians find a way to cross the river."

"That's where our idea gets interesting, Mr. President," General Larsen replied. "We think you're really going to like this. Two days from now, we're planning on having two brigades from the 1st Cavalry Division dug into strongly fortified positions at or near the Rhine, ready to repel the enemy. Eleven thousand of our best soldiers along with more than two hundred M-1s, an equal number of Bradley Fighting Vehicles, and scores of attack helicopters will be waiting for the Russians. In those same two days, we'll also have built up a force of over three hundred additional F-15s and F-16s that we're going to place at Sembach, Zweibrucken, Bitburg, and Hahn. All four former air bases are still in good shape. The Germans turned each into a regional airport after we gave them back. They're well maintained and will be more than adequate for our needs. Their runways are just waiting for us to arrive. A few of the fighter aircraft will be from active-duty wings presently on the way from the West Coast. Most we'll get from National Guard and Reserve units. After the loss of the *George Washington*, we'll desperately need the newly arriving fighters' support."

"The 1st Cavalry's final brigade and the 3rd Armored Cavalry Regiment will join the defenders two days later," the Secretary of Defense added. "In all, four days from when you give us the go-ahead, we'll have twenty thousand soldiers with nearly 450 M-1s and an equal number of Bradleys waiting for the Russian advance. With arguably our strongest division in place and four additional air bases from which to mount counterattacks, we'll have established vigorous defensive positions in the western part of Germany. We believe such a force will be strong enough to hold off the Russians for ten days, maybe more."

"That sounds quite encouraging, Mr. Secretary, but I've still no idea how you think you can possibly get that many soldiers and armored vehicles to Germany in such a short time. And if you actually succeed in doing so, how in the world is one additional division going to keep the Russians at bay for that long? We've seen what happened to the 1st Armor and what's presently happening to the 3rd Infantry. Why do you think the 1st Cavalry will fare any better?"

"Because, prior to sending them to the Rhine, we're going to unleash 'The Final Ace' to cut the enemy down to size," the Secretary of Defense said.

Both could see from his expression that what they'd just told the President was not something he wanted to hear.

"Mr. President," General Larsen said, "we need to face facts. We're out of options. And out of time. I can understand your reluctance, but whether we like it or not, we've no choice. The Russians have forced this upon us. We can't win now, and won't win in a few weeks when we attempt a full-scale invasion without it. The enemy's just too strong. To have any chance at all, we must implement the plan as soon as we possibly can. The only alternative is to minimize our losses by withdrawing our forces and conceding total domination over Europe to Cheninko."

"I understand, General, but there are significant political implications that need to be considered before taking such a drastic action. What if your assessments are wrong, and it doesn't stem the tide? What if it fails to cripple the enemy? Think of what the result will be. We'll have made things far worse, then end up losing the war anyway."

"Mr. President, we're not going to lose," the Secretary of Defense said. "We have a great deal of faith in the 1st Cavalry Division. We really believe we can make this work. Let us tell you more about what we have in mind before you even consider making a decision."

When the President didn't respond, the Secretary of Defense continued.

"After we've got the 1st Cavalry in place and the air bases established, we're going to do this all over again. While the 1st Cavalry holds the Russians, we're going to use the same approach to bring our second-most-powerful division, the 4th Infantry, with all their tanks and Bradleys, from Colorado to western Germany. And we'll also send over the last three hundred of our fighter aircraft. We anticipate having them all in place well before the ten days end. What remains of the enemy might be able to defeat a single division, but after what they'll have gone through, we don't believe the Russians will be capable of vanquishing both the 1st Cavalry and 4th Infantry. At the very worst, after using 'The Final Ace' and putting two of our most powerful divisions on the ground, we'll have them stalemated. Once we have both divisions in place, we'll further analyze the situation. If we see an opening, we might decide to attack the Russians then and there. Or we might delay such an action just a little longer. The 2nd Marine Division's ships departed Charleston this morning. The 10th Mountain will leave Bayonne by sunrise tomorrow. And the 101st Airborne will sail from Norfolk in the next forty-eight hours. After we've cut the enemy down to size and the

1st Cavalry and 4th Infantry hammer them for ten days, we believe we can make a successful landing of the three arriving divisions in northern Germany. We'll then bring the transport ships back here as quickly as we can to pick up the 1st Infantry and as many National Guard units as we can squeeze onto them. Either way, it won't be too much longer before there's not a single Russian soldier, alive anyway, in Germany."

"But I still don't see how you expect to get the 1st Cavalry and 4th Infantry over there in time to make all this happen. I thought you told me you didn't believe we had the logistical ability to get a force that size to the battlefield in time to make a difference. Why the sudden change?"

"Well, Mr. President," the Secretary of State said, "let's just say we've gotten creative."

"How?"

"We're going to have FedEx and UPS deliver a number of 'packages,' intended for Comrade Cheninko and his friends."

"And the major airlines are going to arrive with thousands of well-armed 'tourists' for us," General Larsen added.

Wry smiles appeared on the faces of both the Secretary of Defense and the Chairman of the Joint Chiefs.

"Okay, now I'm either thoroughly confused or completely curious," the President said. "What are you two talking about?"

"Mr. President," General Larsen said, "once we realized how adroitly we could control such a powerful force after we got it into the field, it became a matter of figuring out how to get that many units to the war zone in the brief time we have. You're correct in assuming our logistical abilities to move so many units so quickly weren't there. So we began looking at alternatives to reaching our goal."

"The biggest problem," the Secretary of Defense said, "was figuring how to get more than two hundred seventy-two-ton M-1s to Germany that quickly. The only aircraft we have with the capability to transport such an immense payload are our C-5s and C-17s."

"If we push each C-5 to its load limits," General Larsen added, "and the tanks carry no shells or ammunition with them, we can transport two M-1s in each plane. Each C-17 can transport a single tank. At

428 **WALT GRAGG**

twenty-five tons, we can get three Bradleys to Germany in one C-17. But again, that's only if they carry no ammunition. Counting our Reserve and National Guard air units, we have just over one hundred C-5s and a little more than double that in non-medevac C-17s."

"It's going to be tight, Mr. President," the Secretary of Defense added. "But we believe if we focus all of those aircraft on this mission we can get the communication vans, all the Abrams and Bradleys, plus the larger items needed to support our forces and to run the four air bases to Germany onto the C-5s and C-17s. But that's all we'll be able to do with our huge cargo planes."

"There's a downside, of course," General Larsen said. "If we commit all of our C-5s and C-17s to this, it will mean they'll not be available to aid our units presently fighting in Germany. And getting just the tanks and Bradleys over there without anyone to support them and no ammunition makes no sense at all. So we realized we needed to start thinking way out of the box. We had to figure out how to get all the supporting elements in place at the same time we moved the M-1s and Bradleys."

"Obviously, from what you've told me, you came up with an answer," the President said.

"When one of my staff muttered something like, 'How can we deliver the necessary elements to the battlefield in the short time we have?' the answer came to all of us at once," General Larsen said. "Who's famous for making thousands and thousands of daily on-time deliveries?"

"So we called the CEOs of FedEx and UPS a couple of hours ago," the Secretary of Defense said. "We told them that under the War Powers Act, we had the right to seize their planes if forced to do so. We also told them if they voluntarily provided every cargo aircraft they had capable of reaching Europe, we'd make sure Congress rewarded them handsomely once this is over."

"How did they respond?" the President asked.

"Well, they weren't too happy about filling their cargo planes with bombs and missiles rather than belated birthday presents for Grandma, but both complied. Each began grounding their 767s, 777s, and any other aircraft that could do the job. They're unloading them now and getting them ready. They're even going to send their expert loadmasters with the planes to ensure the right aircraft carries the right cargo, so we can maximize absolutely everything we send over."

"If we use UPS and FedEx, will that be enough? Can we get the job done?"

"We're talking about well over four hundred additional aircraft, Mr. President. Aircraft with the ability to routinely handle large items and heavy loads. Take the rotors and wheels off an Apache, and you can fit a number of them quite nicely, plus a whole lot more, into a FedEx or UPS plane. We believe that part of our plan will be more than adequate to make things work. But there was still a missing piece. We can get the tanks over there and all the equipment needed to support two brigades, but that still left us needing to get our soldiers in place. So I made a few more calls. Gave the major airlines the same War Powers speech and briefly explained their assistance could change the conduct of this war."

"How did they react?"

"Actually, most seemed okay with it. With no one buying tickets to fly to Europe at the moment, they'd been forced to cancel hundreds of flights. Their long-haul planes are just sitting on tarmacs around the country. They weren't too happy about putting their crews at so great a risk by sending them into the middle of a war. But they were thrilled Military Airlift Command could put the planes to good use and would be providing some nice paychecks in doing so."

"So the pieces are in place, Mr. President."

"Maybe so, but it doesn't sound like it'll be easy. Are you sure you can pull this off?"

"The most difficult thing is the timing, sir," General Larsen said. "We've got to make sure things are where they need to be when they need to be there. It makes no sense to have an F-16 arrive at Zweibrucken if no one's waiting with jet fuel and armaments. So the ground crews need to be in place before the fighters arrive. The same is true for our ground forces. A tank appearing on the battlefield without cannon shells or machine-gun bullets isn't going to be a big threat to the enemy. So everything needs to line up. It's those millions of little details that we're working on."

"One of the concepts we've come up with," the Secretary of Defense said, "is sending over self-contained flying convoys with a number of different aircraft traveling together. Each convoy, when unloaded, will have everything our soldiers must have to head directly to their defensive positions. Maybe something like six C-5s carrying tanks, a passenger 767 landing right behind them with an entire company of infantry to support the armor, some Apache and Black Hawk crews, and a few mortar teams. Seconds later, a number of FedEx or UPS planes will land carrying Humvees, helicopters, cannon shells, missiles, bullets, food, water, and whatever else is needed to support that unit for ten days. The moment the soldiers get off their plane, they and the airbase support personnel will quickly unload all of them and start getting everything ready. Within the hour, they'll move into battle. As the soldiers leave, the refueled flying convoy will be loaded with as many dependents as we can cram onto each plane and return home. We've still got thousands and thousands over there who need to be removed from harm's way just as rapidly as we can. When the convoy arrives back here, we'll give the pilots eight hours to sleep while we reload the aircraft with the final 1st Cavalry Brigade and the entire 3rd Armored Cavalry Regiment. Then we'll head for Germany once more to repeat the process. In four days, we'll have twenty thousand fresh soldiers, with all of their equipment, waiting in the German woods for the Russians. Once that task is completed, we'll have the aircraft fly to Colorado and begin the same process with the 4th Infantry."

"Naturally, there'll be lots of logistical issues to deal with along the way," General Larsen added. "For example, we'll need to stop most of the flying convoys at Dover, McGuire, or Charleston Air Bases on the East Coast to refuel them before they cross the Atlantic. And we'll have to refuel our fighter aircraft and some of the planes while on the transatlantic flight. So we'll have to fully coordinate our huge fleet of KC-135 tanker aircraft to do midair refueling while additional tankers fly on to the new air bases to make sure we've ample fuel when the fighters arrive. As you no doubt recognize, the clock is our biggest enemy. There are a myriad of things to do and little time to do any of it if we're going to get the 1st Cavalry on those planes in time."

"Where's the 1st Cavalry now?"

"We've stopped them and the 3rd Armored Cavalry Regiment halfway between Fort Hood and Galveston, where they were planning on loading onto their cargo ships to head across the Atlantic. They're approximately fifty miles southeast of Austin. We're planning on turning them around and having them head back to the Austin airport to meet the cargo aircraft that will transport them and their equipment to the reestablished air bases in Germany."

"Why Austin?"

"A number of reasons, Mr. President. First, it's the closest major airport to the division's present position. It's located in the southeast corner of town, away from most of the city, so we won't have much hassle with traffic or other concerns in moving hundreds and hundreds of military vehicles to the airport. The airport's located at one of our deactivated B-52 bases. When we shut it down some years past, the city purchased it and converted it for their use. It has some of the longest runways in the country. It can handle any plane we've got. And while it only has twenty-five passenger gates, because it was once an air base it has lots and lots of room in every direction to handle the controlled confusion headed its way. We'll begin shutting it down to commercial traffic and preparing it for what's to come in the next few hours."

"When will you begin actually implementing your plan?" the President asked.

"We'll start the communication vans over as soon as you give us the okay, Mr. President," General Larsen answered. "They're the first thing we'll need to get into place. We're going to wait, however, before beginning to send the 1st Cavalry to Germany until we're certain we've made significant progress on setting up the command and control system. We'll also need time to thoroughly assess the damage we inflict with 'The Final Ace.' We may require up to twenty-four hours to determine whether we've succeeded in creating an equal enough playing field for it to make sense risking our best division. During that time, we'll gather all the aircraft from every source. Most we'll send to Austin to begin loading our soldiers and their equipment. Others will be dispatched around the country to pick up the airmen needed to reestablish the four air bases. During that time, we'll also get Dover, McGuire, and Charleston ready to receive the endless streams of refueling aircraft headed their way and prepare the KC-135s to support our Atlantic crossings."

"So the skeleton of the plan's ready, Mr. President," the Secretary of Defense said. "We know such a monumental effort's going to be total chaos. But we believe it'll be organized chaos. We're determined to handle every problem smoothly and efficiently as it arises. We're convinced we can get the entire 1st Cavalry and 4th Infantry Divisions along with six hundred fighter aircraft to Germany in the next ten days. What we need is you to give us the go-ahead. Once you do, our path to victory will have taken its first big step."

"If I give you the okay, when do you plan to use 'The Final Ace'?"

"We'll need a few hours to get everything ready, Mr. President," General Larsen said. "So probably late this afternoon here, middle of the night in Germany."

"All right," the President said reluctantly, "you have my authority to do so."

The Americans' daring plan was about to begin. Whether it would turn out to be a truly viable one depended greatly on whether their desperate forces inside Germany could delay the Russians long enough to get everything in place.

CHAPTER 55

January 31—11:27 p.m.
1st Platoon, Alpha Company, 2nd Battalion, 69th Armor,
    3rd Heavy Brigade Combat Team, 3rd Infantry Division
On the Edge of a Meadow, Six Miles West of Autobahn A7

Jamie Pierson screamed into the intercom. "Tony! Get that big bastard that's right on top of us! If you don't, we're all dead!"

"Relax, Jamie, I've got him all the way."

Warrick fired the M-1's main gun at a T-72 charging across the meadow straight for them. The Russian tank exploded, further illuminating the nightmarish battle. In the three hundred yards of open ground in front of the Americans, the scorched hulls of more than two dozen tanks lay smoldering in the snows. Nine ravaged BMPs sat silently at their countrymen's sides. The persistent fires of the frantic struggle also illuminated the bloated bodies of hundreds of dead Russian infantry. Many of the lifeless forms had been lying on the ground for nearly thirty hours. Mangled enemy corpses were absolutely everywhere the eye surveyed.

On Richardson's left, the skeletal remains of the demolished American tank sat in its fighting hole. Staff Sergeant Greene's charred body, unsuccessful in its desperate attempt to escape, was sprawled half-in, half-out the commander's hatch. Twenty-four hours earlier, a BMP's Spandrel missile had penetrated the tank's exposed turret. It had destroyed the M-1 and ended the lives of those inside.

On Richardson's right, Lieutenant Mallory's tank was still ablaze three hours after its destruction by a Russian attack helicopter. The Abrams burned on throughout the frightful night.

To Richardson's rear, there was little organized resistance. For the past three hours, only the quartet of soldiers in the platoon's final M-1 had stopped the Russians from breaking through for a nearly unfettered dash to Heidelberg and, beyond that, the Rhine. Richardson hadn't heard a single shot fired in at least that long from either of the 3rd Infantry platoons stretching out to his left and right. He'd no idea if the American soldiers were all dead or if the survivors had decided they'd no choice but to disengage and withdraw. Either way, his hard-pressed crew was on their own as they struggled to hold the critical highway.

Behind the remnants of the 3rd Infantry, there remained three armored brigades. All three had arrived in Germany in the past four days. With the tanks and weapons they'd drawn from the Kaiserslautern depot, a five-thousand-man brigade from the 24th Infantry Division waited in front of Frankfurt. A second brigade from the same division braced for battle a few miles east of Stuttgart. The American brigade was preparing to meet the ten Russian divisions that had smashed the Allied forces in the southern portion of the country. The final brigade from the 24th was spread across a hundred-mile front between the two cities. The lightly armed 82nd Airborne continued to hold the critical assets to the rear and, wherever possible, plug the 24th Infantry's lines.

Twenty thousand readied themselves to meet a force seventy times their number. The American soldiers waiting in the steadily melting snows of Germany knew they faced an impossible task. Not one had the vaguest inkling that if they could hold on for just a few days, more help would be on the way. For all they knew, they were all alone.

"Tony, how many rounds do you have left?" Richardson asked.

"Nothing for my machine gun," Warrick said. He glanced at Vincent.

The tank's loader answered without being asked. "About fifteen shells for the main gun."

Fifteen rounds out of the forty-two they'd left Wurzburg with three days earlier.

In the forward portion of the tank, directly beneath the main gun,

Jamie Pierson peered out through the periscope in front of his driver's chair. "Aw, shit, there's another infantry squad trying to flank us. Tim, you can't let them find a place to ford that stream and get around behind us."

Inside the fully buttoned-up tank, Richardson stared at the killing grounds of the broad meadow. He'd been watching the Russian squad as it desperately searched for a place to cross the icy currents. His voice was detached and strangely matter-of-fact. "I know, I know. Relax. I've had them the whole way. Just wanted to wait for a little better shot. If it'll make the three of you feel better, I'll kill them right now."

After the destruction of the platoon's other tanks, his crew had noticed how oddly Richardson was acting. It was almost as if their tank's commander had accepted the inevitable and given up hope.

With the loss of the lieutenant's tank, Richardson had come to realize that his own death was grinningly waiting for him on the dark night. His jealousy of Pierson and Warrick had spewed forth and seized his fragile soul. The members of his crew had a strong, supportive family back home. Families who'd grieve greatly at their demise. But the young tank commander had no one. He'd never known his father. And he hadn't spoken to his alcoholic mother in eight years. Not since she, in a drunken rage, had kicked him out at the age of fifteen.

There was no one else.

Richardson knew there'd be no one to mourn his passing.

He whirled the machine gun to the right. For the past ten minutes, the Russian infantry had been working its way through the thick trees along the edge of the wide meadow. The squad had just begun moving across a small clearing near the swiftly flowing stream. Without warning, the tank commander's machine gun pounded away at the exposed soldiers. Richardson aimed at the pair of Russians carrying antitank missiles. Four of the eight soldiers fell beneath the withering gunfire of the sudden attack. The antitank missiles dropped into the open meadow, along with the soldiers who'd carried them.

The remaining infantrymen dove into the trees. They returned the tank's fire with their rifles. Each shot at the Abrams while waiting for one of the others to run into the glade to retrieve the antitank weapons. None was as yet so stupid, or so brave. The rifle bullets bounced harmlessly off the foot-thick armor plating on the front of the M-1. Richardson laughed at the feeble efforts. In his deeply protective world, no bullet was going to reach him. The infantry soldiers were wasting their time.

Unlike Richardson, Warrick and Pierson hadn't given up hope.

"Tim, we've got to get out of here," Warrick said. "If we don't make a run for it soon, we've got no chance."

"Yeah, Tony, I know. But battalion ordered us to hold this position no matter what."

"I understand, but that was two hours ago. Why don't you talk to them again?"

Richardson rubbed his tired eyes. None of the M-1's crew had slept more than scant minutes in the past three days. And they hadn't closed their eyes for a single moment in more than a day and a half.

"All right, all right, let me see what I can do." He spoke into the radio. "Echo-Yankee-One, this is Sierra-Kilo-One-Two."

"Roger, Sierra-Kilo-One-Two. Go ahead."

"Echo-Yankee-One, we're greatly outnumbered. Our position has become untenable. Request we be allowed to retract and retreat."

"Understood, Sierra-Kilo-One-Two. Wait one."

Richardson fired at the first of the infantrymen foolhardy enough to attempt to retrieve the missiles. The Russian dropped like a stone at the edge of the glen. He fell into the wide brook. As the soldier's blood was added to the stream, its swirling, frigid waters turned an ever-deepening shade of red.

The battalion radio operator returned. "Sierra-Kilo-One-Two, be advised, we need you to remain in place a little longer. The battalion's going to conduct an organized retreat in approximately thirty minutes. Until then, you must hold Highway 19. If the Russians break through your position, the entire battalion's going to be trapped."

Not that there was much of a battalion left. After thirty hours of ruthless battle, eleven of forty-five tanks fought on. Only five of the unit's Bradleys were still in the fray.

"Roger, Echo-Yankee-One. But you need to understand, we're in severe distress. It's highly unlikely we can hold out that long. We're running out of machine-gun ammunition, and the enemy's advances are growing bolder by the second. We're going to be dead in the next ten minutes if required to remain in our present position."

"Okay, Sierra-Kilo-One-Two, let me see what I can do."

A BMP moved to the tree line on the far side of the meadow. The armored vehicle opened its rear door to discharge its infantry. Warrick started targeting the personnel carrier.

The soldiers inside the Abrams held their breath and waited. They knew their lives were going to end quite soon if the battalion commander insisted on their holding this impossible defensive position.

"Whoosh!" The mighty sound reverberated throughout the frightening night as Warrick fired at the BMP. The BMP erupted in roaring fires reaching into the highest treetops. The Americans watched two dreadful figures emerge from the rear of the defeated personnel carrier. Each was fully engulfed in flames. The fiery forms staggered into the snows and fell. Three hundred yards away, the Americans couldn't hear the anguished screams of the blazing humans.

Just to remind the survivors of the infantry squad that he hadn't forgotten about them, Richardson fired a quick burst in their direction.

There was nothing but silence over the radio. The tension in the tank's confined spaces grew heavy.

Warrick's patience was spent. "Where the hell's battalion?" he said.

"Relax," Richardson said, "it's probably time for their coffee break."

No one was in any mood to laugh.

The radio suddenly crackled to life. "Sierra-Kilo-One-Two, Six," the radio operator said, using the slang for the battalion commander, "says you're to hold your position at all costs. If you don't, the battalion's retreat will be cut off."

"Roger, we understand. Hold at all cost."

"Hang in there, Sierra-Kilo-One-Two. Six just released his last two Apaches to assist you. They're on the way. They should be there in three minutes."

"Roger. Hanging in there."

A roller coaster of emotions roared through Richardson. As the fearsome Russian assault had gone on minute after minute, hour after hour, he'd watched his friends die on his left and right. For the past few hours, he'd grown to accept his own impending end. At this point, he saw no reason to let his hopes get too high. The lone American tank was in an extremely dire position. But with the promised Apaches soon to be overhead, there was a growing chance the Abrams's crew might actually live to see the sunrise. For the first time since Lieutenant Mallory's death, Richardson allowed the slimmest glimmer of hope to enter his anguished mind.

It would be the longest three minutes in any of their young lives. Within seconds of the battalion's message, three T-72s moved to the edge of the trees on the eastern end of the meadow.

Behind the tanks, five BMPs slithered to a stop. Each began discharging its infantry.

"Tony, get ready! Looks like they're going to rush us again."

One of the surviving Russian soldiers on the right chose that moment to race forward and wrestle an antitank missile from the clenched hands of his dead comrade. Richardson's attention was focused on the armored force building on the other side of the glen. The infantryman's movements went unnoticed. The soldier dove into the snows. He grabbed the missile, raised it to his shoulder, and fired.

The missile slammed into the logs in front of the M-1. A powerful explosion ripped at the protective fortification at the base of the Abrams. The thunder of the detonating ordnance echoed throughout the tank.

The Russians instantly recognized the unexpected opportunity. All three tanks fired. Around the Americans, the world erupted as the T-72s' massive shells slammed home. The earth heaved and sighed beneath them. It threatened to swallow the beleaguered defenders whole. The forest behind them was ripped and shredded. Inside the Abrams, horrific sounds tore at their eardrums. The tankers screamed until every last ounce of air was expelled from their lungs. Deep within its earthen womb, the American tank somehow survived the intense assault.

With Richardson's crew pinned down, the T-72s roared out of the trees. They rushed forward to destroy the rattled Americans. Behind the steel giants, thirty-five soldiers raced across the snows. Having disgorged their infantrymen, the BMPs entered the meadow fifty yards behind the tanks.

"Everybody all right?" Richardson asked.

"Yeah," was the response from the driver's compartment.

"I guess so," Warrick said.

"I'm okay," Vincent added.

Richardson peered at the meadow. The Russians were speeding across the bloody ground.

"Oh, shit! Tony, they're right on top of us!"

Richardson opened fire on the charging infantry. Death's leering face entered the morose scene once again. His machine gun cut down one after another of the running foot soldiers.

His senses partially restored, Warrick took aim at the middle T-72 as it rumbled across the open ground. At this close range, the M-1 wouldn't miss.

Warrick fired at the gray tank coming at him from two hundred yards away. "Whoosh!" the M-1's main gun screamed. The T-72's turret was sheared off by the powerful blow. The tank exploded. The Russian crew's death was immediate. And appalling.

Vincent hurried to load another round.

Richardson's machine gun continued to chatter away. Its power fell upon the enemy soldiers, filling the hideous midnight battle with further suffering.

Two BMPs found a clear lane. They fired Spandrel missiles at the American fortification. One went just high, barely missing the top of the tank. It ripped into the dense forest behind the M-1. The other hit the dirt mound scarcely two feet below the tank's turret. The missile brought all the horrors of hell down upon the floundering tankers. Once more, the earth around them shook and trembled. Sounding thunder reverberated throughout the enclosed space. The Americans inside the tank instinctively dove for cover.

The missile tore at the thinner layer of logs and dirt at the top of the embankment. High explosives clawed at the heavy armor on the front of the M-1. The plating held fast. It resisted the near miss and protected the embattled crew. Large metal fragments from the exploding missile reached out for the American tank. The fragments tore at the Abrams's turret. Still, the daunting armor didn't yield. Had they been in one of the inferior Russian tanks, they'd all be dead by now.

The missile's fierce impact knocked the tanker's helmet from Richardson's head. The helmetless figure was slammed against the sophisticated equipment in the commander's station. A three-inch gash opened in the center of his forehead. Blood gushed from the new wound. It washed down his nose and tore at the sides of his face. Dazed and disoriented, he struggled to gather his wits. Through unfocused eyes, he fought to regain control of his fragile world. He sensed the overpowering presence of death reaching out to crush him. The grappling sergeant swiped his sleeve across his battered face. Thick red ran down his jacket.

Richardson blinked rapidly, desperately trying to clear his vision. Through the red haze, he peered toward the killing ground. His machine gun, which served the dual purpose of defending against ground forces and acting as the tank's primary antiaircraft gun, had been destroyed. Shredded pieces of the gun hung from the tank's turret.

"Shit! My gun is gone."

He glanced to the left. The loader's machine gun had also been destroyed.

"Vincent's gun's gone, too!"

"What about the main gun?" Warrick asked. "Can you see if it's damaged?"

Richardson blinked again and again. "It looks okay from here. I can't tell for sure." The T-72s and BMPs were bearing down on their position. "We don't have any choice. We're going to be dead if we don't do something. Damaged or not, fire the damn thing."

Warrick targeted the tank on the right. The T-72 was barely a hundred yards away and closing fast. The Americans knew that if they fired a damaged main gun, the shell would blow up inside the tank. Finding its path blocked, the projectile would explode in the firing chamber. The tank's crew would be hideously killed. It was quite possible that in the coming moments, the tankers were going to suffer a horrendous end from their own weapon. But at this point, they were out of options. In seconds, they'd be dead at their own hands or the hands of the Russians. It no longer mattered. If the main gun was damaged, they'd never know what hit them. Warrick swung the massive cannon toward the T-72. His mind went numb.

"Tony, don't think about it, just fire," Richardson said. "Might as well go down fighting."

Warrick fired the cannon.

The shell tore from the undamaged barrel and roared toward the enemy. In a fraction of a second, the T-72 was engulfed in a raging inferno. Four foot soldiers had been using the mauled tank to shield them from Richardson's machine-gun fire. The infantry were torn into a thousand pieces by the razor-sharp shards of molten metal that leaped from the defeated tank.

Warrick's machine gun was out of ammunition. And both supporting machine guns had been destroyed. They still had a dozen cannon shells for the main gun. So they could continue to battle the opposing armor. But nothing remained in their arsenal with which to stop the infantry.

The game was nearly over.

Vincent slammed another eighty pounds of horror into the firing chamber.

The final Russian tank stopped at close range and prepared to fire. The T-72's gunner had them in his sights. With the American machine guns silenced, two infantrymen knelt in the middle of the open field. They brought their antitank weapons up to their shoulders and took careful aim. A BMP's Spandrel missile had the Abrams in its crosshairs. Helplessly, Richardson watched.

Tony Warrick swung the turret toward the remaining T-72. But the Russian had beaten him to the draw. Long before he could target the tank, he knew the enemy would fire.

It was too late to climb out and run. Ripe for revenge, scores of eager rifles would cut them down before any of their feet reached solid ground. They were trapped. Their lives were over.

Despite his rising panic, Warrick rapidly prepared to fire at the T-72. Maybe the Russian would somehow miss.

Richardson didn't have any such luxury. With nothing to do but watch through blurry eyes, he braced for the end.

The Russian tank suddenly erupted. Caught in the open, it had been sliced in two by an Apache's Hellfire missile. The tank's ruptured workings spewed forth upon the frozen ground. The second Apache fired. A hail of rockets ripped into the BMPs. Three of the armored vehicles were chewed to pieces by the lethal fusillade. The BMPs' smoking hulls moved no more. The remaining pair of Russian personnel carriers hurriedly backed toward the protection of the woods. A Hellfire pounced upon the slower of the duo and devoured it. The second was fifty yards from the safety of the trees when a barrage of rockets fell upon it.

In a handful of flittering heartbeats, the Russian armor had been destroyed. The lethal Apaches' chain guns started thundering mayhem upon the exposed infantry. In abject terror, the soldiers ran toward the evergreens. But the safety of the forest was much too far away. And none would escape the determined assault. In less than a minute, the slaughter was complete. The dead and dying were everywhere.

Three T-72s, five BMPs, and thirty-five foot soldiers had entered the meadow intent on destroying the last American tank. Not one had lived to tell about it.

The Apaches dropped into the trees to wait for anyone insane enough to enter the caustic glen. For twenty solemn minutes, Richardson's crew sat in their ravaged hole, viewing the unholy scene in the meadow.

The radio suddenly came to life. The tension in the battalion radio operator's voice was unmistakable. "This is Echo-Yankee-One. Urgent. To all units. Everyone except Sierra-Kilo-One-Two is to fall back immediately. Head for Highway 19. Once there, each crew is to make it on their own the fifty miles to Heilbronn. The battalion will re-form on the eastern end of that city. The artillery's moved forward. They're preparing to fire. The planes are in the air. Get as far away from the front lines as you can. 'The Final Ace' has been called for forty-five minutes from now. Repeat. Get away from the front lines immediately. Countdown for 'The Final Ace' has begun."

"Echo-Yankee-One, this is Sierra-Kilo-One-Two," Richardson said. "What about us?"

"Sierra-Kilo-One-Two, you're to hold your position for ten minutes to allow the battalion to escape. Ten minutes, no more. Then get the hell out of there as fast as you can. Do you copy?"

"Roger, Echo-Yankee-One. We'll try to hold on here. But be advised, all of our machine guns are out of commission. Only our main gun's working."

The radio operator conferred with the battalion commander. "Sierra-Kilo-One-Two, the Apaches will stay with you for the next ten minutes."

"Roger, understood. With the Apaches in support, we'll attempt to hold on here for the next ten minutes, then retreat to Heilbronn."

"Roger, Sierra-Kilo-One-Two. We'll see you there."

From the small trails and thick woods for ten miles north and south of Highway 19, the ragged vestiges of the battered battalion scurried for an entrance onto the narrow highway. Retreating behind Richardson's protective screen, each entered the winding road west.

Forty-five minutes from now, as part of their plan to stop the Russians and save Germany, the Americans were going to unleash their immense arsenal of tactical nuclear weapons. Without consulting with their German allies, the Americans were implementing a plan they'd developed nearly seventy years earlier at the direction of President John F. Kennedy.

For over six decades, the Americans had understood their only real chance of winning a ground war in Europe would be by escalating the conflict with the explosion of hundreds of small tactical nuclear devices. This was going to be America's final grasp at changing the tide in a war they hadn't been ready to fight.

Two days earlier, the Russians had severely increased the stakes by introducing nerve gas and a handful of nuclear weapons onto the perverse fields. Now it was the Americans turn to up the ante. They'd play the only card they had left if they were going to win the grievous conflict. They'd play their final ace. In forty-five minutes, the fires of an unspeakable hell man's imagination was unwilling to address would rain down upon central Germany. The Americans were going to explode score after score of nuclear devices over an area one hundred miles long and twenty miles wide.

In forty-five minutes, two hundred thousand Russian soldiers were going to be consumed in a nuclear holocaust. Another two hundred thousand would find themselves piteously begging for death from the effects of the radiation poisoning seeping through their skin.

To have any chance of saving Germany, America was going to be forced to destroy it.

With the menacing Apaches lurking in the trees, Richardson's tank crew waited to repel any further attackers. But none came. The Russians weren't going to risk any additional charges into the meadow until their own air support arrived to deal with the deadly Apaches.

One by one, six hundred seconds torturously ticked past. Richardson kept a bloody eye on the cracked crystal of his watch. It slowly slid toward the moment when the final American tank would be allowed to retreat.

The instant the ten minutes were up, Richardson's crew sprang into action. The last thing they wanted was to die beneath the destructive power of their own nuclear weapons. The tank crawled from the hole it had been sitting in for the past thirty hours. Jamie turned the Abrams and carefully picked his way through the evergreens until they reached the beckoning highway. Back on the slender ribbon of asphalt, the M-1 rushed west. It trailed far behind its fleeing comrades. As the last tank disappeared, the Apaches pirouetted and roared away.

There were thirty-five minutes before America would play its final card.

CHAPTER 56

February 1—12:25 a.m.
1st Platoon, Alpha Company, 2nd Battalion, 69th Armor,
   3rd Heavy Brigade Combat Team, 3rd Infantry Division
On the Road to Heilbronn

The moment they were away, Richardson and Vincent popped their hatches and poked their heads out. Normally, the tankers would have settled in behind their machine guns and prepared to repulse any enemy infantry they might encounter. With both of their machine guns destroyed, however, neither loader nor tank commander could do anything but stare at the road ahead and pray that no Russians had yet infiltrated the highway to the west. As the tank rolled forward, the oppressive night's brutal cold stabbed at Richardson's gaping head wound. The cold was helping to slow the flow of blood. But even so, every few seconds the tank commander would take his sleeve and swipe at his eyes in a futile attempt to improve his vision. Until they were well away from the danger area, there would be no time to stop and tend to the wound.

Deep within the sheltering trees, the highway unpredictably twisted and turned. In the driver's seat, Jamie Pierson fought the unfamiliar pavement and the onerous night. The tank's broad tracks churned through the sinister forest. He understood that their lives depended upon getting as far away from the target area as they possibly could in the small amount of time remaining. Nevertheless, despite everything Pierson tried, he couldn't maintain a speed above twenty miles per hour under these conditions.

They hadn't traveled three miles when they stumbled upon the first group of Americans. Four soldiers had been hiding in a dense thicket near the roadway. They recognized the shape of the American tank. At the last possible moment, they rushed onto the asphalt. Pierson slammed on the brakes. The Abrams screeched to a halt inches from the group.

"Jesus!" Jamie screamed.

Even in the darkness, Richardson could make out the triangular shape of the 1st Armor Division patch on the soldiers' left shoulders. He could also see that only two of the four had weapons.

"Christ, you guys have a death wish or something?" Richardson said. "Do you have any idea how close you just came to being roadkill? I've seen what happens when an M-1 runs over someone. It's not a pretty sight."

"Sorry, man," one of the soldiers said. "We've been wandering around behind enemy lines for the past two days. When we saw you were Americans, we had to take the chance. We all figured it was better to get run over by an American tank than to stand in front of a Russian firing squad."

"Look, I understand. But I'm not sure my driver will. You guys scared the crap out of him."

It was apparent the ragtag group had been through a great deal.

"We're the last tank out," Richardson said. "And 'The Final Ace' has been called for this sector in less than half an hour. So we don't exactly have time to stop and chat. Why don't you guys pile on and let's get the hell out of here while we still can."

For the first time in two days, an exhausted smile appeared on the four filthy faces. Without another word, the soldiers scrambled onto the M-1's wide hull. The tank lurched forward and headed west once more.

There were twenty-five minutes until the horrors of the nuclear attack.

In another winding mile, three more ghostly figures raced from the woods. They were added to the tank's growing list of anxious hitchhikers.

And seven minutes later, a group of six appeared from the darkness. Thirteen battle-weary soldiers clung to the broad tank while it rolled forward on the confining thread of asphalt. The top of the Abrams, in front of and behind Richardson, was rapidly filling.

Richardson's crew wasn't alone. All along the highway, the remnants of the battalion were scooping up loads of stragglers and rushing with them toward the west.

Fifteen fleeting minutes remained until the mass nuclear detonations. The fresh-faced tank commander knew they were still too close to the target area. But they'd ample time to avoid hell's unforgiving fires. Even at this plodding pace, he was certain they'd add at least five additional miles to their flight before the first mushroom cloud erupted in the depraved night sky behind them.

High overhead, a circling F-35 spotted movement deep within the forest's cover. The pilot's instructions were to protect the retreating Americans from any Russian units giving chase. He'd been told his countrymen would be well clear of this area by now.

The F-35 had previously expended two missiles on an unsuspecting pair of MiG-29s. Its pilot decided to make his air-to-ground attack on the enemy vehicle with his armor-piercing, four-barrel Gatling gun. The fighter entered a teeth-rattling dive. The aircraft rushed straight toward the shadowy movement on the black highway below. As the Lightning II swooped in over the treetops, its cannon started to blaze. A long burst of gunfire spewed forth from beneath the F-35.

With the exception of its driver, those on and in the Abrams had just relaxed for the first time in days. Despite his psyche-crushing weariness, his pounding headache, and the blood running down his face, Richardson's mouth actually held a hint of a smile while he attempted to carry on an animated conversation over the noise of the fleeing tank's engine.

The first deadly rounds struck the roadway twenty yards in front of them. The shells chewed deep holes in the frigid pavement. The ordnance danced its way down the highway. In a flash, Jamie drove the M-1 headlong into the onrushing line of 25mm shells.

Four soldiers on the front of the tank were ripped apart by the murderous hailstorm that thundered from the merciless heavens. Each screamed mortally when struck. The injured Americans tumbled from the moving tank. Two dropped from the right side of the Abrams. They fell into the dense woods. The first was dead before he hit the unyielding ground. His severely injured partner was barely breathing but still alive.

Another of the wounded fell to the left. He landed on the rough asphalt. The tank's spinning treads passed within inches of his head. The final soldier pitched forward. He plunged to the ground in front of the M-1. The right tread caught its helpless victim, crushing him beneath its tons of rolling metal.

All around him, Richardson could hear the terrified screams of the wounded and dying as the ricocheting shells ripped into the M-1's thinner upper armor. In the middle of the maelstrom, the tank's commander survived the onslaught without a scratch.

The other members of his crew, however, weren't so fortunate. Waves of lead knifed through the top of the tank. The shells sliced into the driver's and gunner's areas. A red-hot round smashed into Tony Warrick's upper leg. It ripped a huge hole in the specialist's thigh. Warrick shrieked in agony. He grabbed at his injured leg. Blood spurted from the gaping wound. A sea of red quickly spread across the interior of the tank.

Clark Vincent was hit in the center of his chest. The young private died instantly.

Another round tore at the Abrams's driver. The shell crushed Jamie Pierson's right arm just below the elbow. He also howled in pain. Pierson instinctively released the tank's handlebars and clutched at his injured arm. Seventy-two tons of out-of-control metal veered toward the trees on the left side of the roadway.

The havoc completed on the front of the tank, the cannon fire continued its brutal death march across the M-1. The striking shells slammed into two of the five soldiers riding on the engine compartment. They were thrown from the rear of the Abrams. The mortally wounded soldiers dropped onto the pavement near the edge of the woods.

As the fighter screamed overhead, Richardson recognized the distinctive silhouette of the F-35.

"Shit! It's one of ours!" He grabbed at the radio. "Echo-Yankee-One! Echo-Yankee-One! This is Sierra-Kilo-One-Two. We're under attack by an F-35. Say again. We are under attack by an F-35. Get him off us! Get him off us, now!"

"Roger, Sierra-Kilo-One-Two. I'm on it."

The Abrams plowed off the roadway. It plunged into the snowy forest. The careening tank ripped its way unabated through fifty yards of an old growth of evergreen and beech. It toppled everything in its path. Fighting his mind-numbing injuries, Jamie wrestled with the bucking tank. The M-1 ground to a halt deep within the pristine forest. The seven hitchhiking soldiers who'd survived the air attack had been tossed like fall leaves onto the forest floor. At the conclusion of their roller-coaster ride, they lay scattered from one end of the tank-gouged trail to the other.

The F-35 turned to make a second run. The pilot roared over the trees, intent on finishing the task. With a thumb on the hair trigger, he soared a few hundred feet above the asphalt ribbon. But try as he might, he couldn't locate the target. His victim wasn't where it was supposed to be on the constricted roadway. The F-35 flew off a short distance. It turned for another run. Again the fighter hurtled down the highway, trimming the highest branches of the mighty forest in search of prey. Still no luck. Whatever the pilot had attacked in the darkness had somehow disappeared. Given enough time, however, he knew he would find and destroy.

The aircraft's radio leaped to life. "Victor-Seven! Victor-Seven! Break it off! Break it off! You're attacking friendly forces! Break off your engagement immediately!"

The stunned pilot banked sharply to the left. He raced back toward the west. Inside the cockpit, a burgeoning cloud of the pilot's worst nightmares was coming true. He'd attacked his countrymen. He'd killed American soldiers.

On the ground, Richardson was left to pick up the shattered pieces of the pilot's efforts. And he'd little time left. There were ten precious minutes before America would unleash its nuclear arsenal.

The moment the tank ground to a halt, Richardson leaped from the Abrams. He jumped to the forest floor. Inside the gunner's area, Tony was yelling his head off. Jamie was little better. Clark Vincent was silent and still, his lifeless body slumping against the side of the loader's hatch.

If any of them was going to live, Richardson had to get things under control and get the M-1 out of there. The seven soldiers who'd survived the attack were strewn about on the frozen, rock-hard ground. They were slowly picking themselves up. One had broken his arm. Another had badly twisted a knee. Richardson had five healthy soldiers with whom to work.

He motioned to the two who'd fallen closest to the highway and yelled, "Get back down the road and see if any of those hit by cannon fire are still alive."

The soldiers signaled their understanding. They hurried onto the pavement. The pair started jogging up the center of the highway.

He looked toward two uninjured Americans getting to their feet twenty yards away. "You and you, help those guys." He pointed to the pair of soldiers injured by the fall. "Get them onto the tank as fast as you can. We've got to get out of here." He turned to the soldier closest to him. "I need you to give me a hand with my crew."

Richardson and the soldier climbed onto the battered Abrams. They pulled the still-screaming Warrick from the compartment. The moment they lifted him onto the top of the tank, they could see his injury was extremely serious. Warrick's shredded pant leg was soaked in thick blood.

"We're got to get the bleeding stopped," Richardson said. "Apply a tourniquet and dressing to his leg as fast as you can. I'll get my driver out."

"I'll take care of it, Sarge." The soldier ripped off his belt to use as a tourniquet and pulled a dressing from a pouch on his pistol belt. He went to work on the injured tank gunner.

Richardson moved forward to the driver's compartment. He had to get Pierson out of there.

Jamie had stopped yelling. But the instant the tank commander placed his arms beneath Pierson's to lift him up, the young soldier wailed once more. Ignoring Jamie's pleas, Richardson dragged him out and laid him next to Warrick. With the help of their companions, the soldiers with the broken arm and the twisted knee hobbled up to the M-1.

Richardson quickly examined Jamie's wound. He looked down at the arriving survivors. "Help those two onto the back of the tank. Then I need one of you up front to take care of my driver. We're getting the hell out of here as soon as I check the engine."

The tank commander leaped into the snows. He rushed to the rear of the tank. A half dozen bullet holes were visible in the armor covering the engine compartment. But the M-1's powerful engine sounded none the worse for wear. There was no time to worry about it now. Richardson was back in front. He scrambled into the bloodstained driver's chair. Jamie was in no condition to handle the beast. It would rest upon Richardson's thoroughly exhausted shoulders to save their lives.

It had been four years since Richardson had worked his way up from driver to gunner, and from there to tank commander. His skills were a little rusty. Yet in his day, he'd prided himself on being the best driver in his battalion.

The injured were spread front and rear across the tank. Richardson started guiding the Abrams out of the woods, picking his way toward the highway.

When he reached the twisting pavement, the pair he'd sent in search of survivors was waiting with a critically wounded soldier. They carefully handed the soldier up. The others stretched him out next to Warrick and Pierson.

"Hurry up, get on board," Richardson said.

"There's another wounded guy back down the road about a hundred yards or so," the shorter of the pair said. "Wait a minute, we'll go back and get him."

"How badly is he hurt?"

"Real bad. He took a round to the chest. He's barely breathing."

"Will he survive a three-hour ride on the top of this tank?"

"Probably not. With the way he's struggling right now, he doesn't look like he'll last anywhere close to that long."

"Leave him," Richardson said.

The soldiers looked at each other in disbelief.

"But, Sarge . . ."

"If you want to see the sun come up tomorrow, leave him and climb onto this tank now!"

They reluctantly dragged themselves onto the bullet-scarred metal hull. Their unhappiness with Richardson's decision was plainly evident. But the order the struggling sergeant had given was just as distasteful to him. Nevertheless, he was doing what he had to do. If he waited while the pair retrieved the hopelessly injured soldier, none of them would see the morning.

There was less than five minutes until the horrific holocaust began.

Richardson had no more time to concern himself with the wounded. He'd leave that task to the others. The M-1 roared onto the roadway. They had to hurry if they wanted to live.

He knew they were far enough away from the target areas to survive the nuclear detonations. That wasn't his concern. Of the three elements of the approaching nightmare, he was certain they'd live through the first. The immense heat from the twenty-megaton blasts wasn't going to consume them. At their impact points, the exploding nuclear fireballs were going to be as hot as the center of the sun. But the range of these small tactical devices would be limited. Only those unfortunate souls who found themselves within a half mile, a mile at most, from the middle of one of the countless detonations would die instantly from the searing heat of the imploding atom.

The second stage of the nuclear storm was a far-more-serious problem for the Americans. An instant after each explosion, a blast wave of unbelievable intensity would rush out for many miles in every direction. Like Thor's mighty hammer, the hot winds would roar from the center of the detonations at incredible speed. The voracious winds would devour everything in their path for great distances. The strongest houses within a mile or two of the explosions would disappear in the nuclear assault. Entire forests would topple for three or four miles beyond that. An uncontrollable firestorm of insatiable intensity would sweep through the toppled trees. In the next hour, it was possible the fleeing soldiers would find themselves enveloped in a raging inferno of such magnitude that nothing could possibly escape.

Yet even that wasn't Richardson's greatest concern. For with each tick of the clock, the Americans were distancing themselves from the second lethal element of the nuclear blast.

It was the third phase of the impending attack the tank commander truly feared.

While the tank careened around another unpredictable corner, Richardson's primary worry was receiving a heavy dose of radiation poisoning.

Fallout. Even the name struck terror in the tank commander's heart.

Although, as they moved farther away from the target areas, he suspected they were going to find themselves distant enough to endure the initial intense fallout levels from the concurrent explosions in the east. After the initial blast wave and its accompanying radiation reached them, the heavens would still once more. With the night calm, a quick-acting, lethal dose of radiation was probably not their fate.

The question still to be answered, however, was what level of radiation they'd receive. If the amounts were significant, their end would be rapid. Flu-like symptoms, followed by hair loss, bleeding, open sores, and finally death within a few days. The results would be irreversible. Not one of them would be alive a month from now.

Richardson ripped the monster around a sharp curve deep within the black night's all-enveloping mantle. The snowy asphalt continued to pass beneath the tank's spinning treads. Their lives rested in the steady hands locked onto the M-1's steering controls.

The Abrams raced west. They needed to get as far away as they possibly could. Just a little farther. A few minutes more. Another mile might make all the difference. All the difference in the world. Just a little additional time was the only thing Richardson wanted.

But time had run out.

Behind them, the eastern sky turned brighter than the brightest day. One after another, frightening explosions crushed the deplorable night. In great numbers, billowing mushroom clouds shattered the darkness.

"Tell everyone to avoid looking directly at them," Richardson said to the nearest soldier, reminding him of their training.

Temporary, even permanent, blindness awaited anyone failing to heed that lesson. For as far away as seventy miles distant, those observers unaware of the effects the fireballs in the night sky were having would be blinded for days to come.

Despite the debased events happening all around them, Richardson knew he couldn't panic. While he urged the tank forward, the Abrams commander began counting. The all-powerful blast wave, down to a modest fifty miles an hour by the time it reached their location, passed the speeding tank in just over forty seconds. They were somewhere between five and eight miles from the center of the nearest explosion. The hair on Richardson's arms stood straight up. Run. Run as fast as you can. The next hour's fallout would determine if they lived or died.

For thirty minutes, remorseless mushroom clouds appeared at regular intervals on the horizon.

From high-flying fighters and bombers, from nuclear-tipped artillery shells and missiles, the unspeakable death, the death that had been poised on man's lips for the past eighty-three years, spewed forth. They'd whispered about it. They'd prayed it would never happen. But their efforts to stop it had been of no use. They'd unleashed the power of the fearful atom upon their fellow man, and the results would be forever irreversible.

To stop the Russians, the Americans would explode every tactical nuclear weapon they had. In all, the barrage would number more than two hundred. When it was over, a wide swath of central Germany would become an uninhabitable no-man's-land.

Beneath the exploding twenty-kiloton nuclear devices and the one-kiloton neutron bombs, the most unspeakable cruelties occurred. Those caught by the airbursts simply disappeared.

Vaporized by the atom's power, they vanished into the universe's nothingness.

Those a little farther away had their skin burned from their bodies. Their lungs ruptured and bled. The intense fallout at such a close range would shortly end these tortured souls' abject suffering.

Those unprotected and close to the detonations died within the first hours from the destructive doses of heat, blast, and radiation.

Others a little farther away or a little more protected would survive for a few more days. By the time it was over, however, they'd be horribly ill and begging for the end to come.

More distant, still others were caught by the power of the blast. Crushed by its irresistible winds or buried alive, they'd never be rescued from the fallen forests and shattered houses of the killing zone. Thousands more were trapped within the raging fires that swiftly ensued. They were engulfed by its ferocious flames and quickly devoured.

Like the nerve gas that had preceded it, the nuclear storm falling upon Germany killed indiscriminately. It cared nothing about age, gender, race, creed, religion, or nationality. The young and the old, the virtuous and the evil, the rich and the poor, all died within the unforgiving attack. Over a million, Russian and German alike, were gone before the long-term effects of the radiation's poisoning fell upon the earth's frail creatures.

On the fringes of the nuclear circle, those receiving a small dose of radiation would survive for years to come before the effects of the man-made cancers would finally cut them down.

Into which category the soldiers clinging to Richardson's tank were going to fall would remain, for the moment, unresolved.

The last M-1 would arrive in Heilbronn three hours later minus a wounded soldier who'd failed to survive the tyrannical journey. Having lost significant amounts of blood, Tony Warrick's breathing was labored and unsteady. Jamie Pierson was in shock.

Still, under Richardson's leadership, most of his battle-scarred passengers had survived to see the coming day. Whether the radiation their pliant skins had absorbed would allow them to live much longer was anybody's guess.

Richardson waited in the driver's seat while the others were carried away. Far behind the final soldier to leave the battered tank, perdition's fires continued to burn.

There was no doubt they'd staggered the Russians. But the question that remained was whether it had been enough to allow the Americans to go forward with their daring attempt to emerge victorious.

CHAPTER 57

General Yovanovich and his second-in-command, Colonel Antonin Zulin, handed their pistols to the guards outside the Premier's office. No one except Cheninko's personal bodyguards would ever be allowed inside the magnificent room while armed.

Yovanovich grabbed the weighty door handle, took a deep breath, and entered. The shorter Zulin was right behind. Cheninko waited behind his desk. Having been awakened at this early hour with the horrendous news of the American tactical nuclear attack, the Russian leader was in a particularly foul state.

They were barely inside when Cheninko, the anxiousness quite evident in his voice, asked, "How bad is it?"

"The reports are still coming in, Comrade Premier," Yovanovich said.

"That doesn't answer my question, Yovanovich. How bad is it?"

"It was a massive assault. From what we've gathered, hundreds of thousands are dead—or will be in the coming days from radiation poisoning." He paused for Cheninko to respond. When the Premier said nothing, he continued. "This was certainly no surprise. The Americans had warned us for decades that this would be their response should we ever invade Germany."

"Yes, General, you were quite clear such an eventuality could occur. What I want to know, however, is even with our losses, is our army still strong enough to finish the destruction of Germany?"

Yovanovich's finely honed body visibly drooped. The immense effort needed to prepare for and conduct this war had taken him to the edge of both physical and mental collapse. The futility of recent events overwhelmed him, and he was ready for the crushing nightmare to end.

"There's nothing more to accomplish, Comrade Cheninko. We've already destroyed the Germans. We've already won. There's no need to continue. Fromisch and his followers are dead. The vast majority of Germany's in ruins. It will take decades for them to rebuild. They're no threat to us. Now is the perfect moment to put an end to the madness before it's completely beyond control. At this point, any significant escalation from either side and hundreds of millions, Russian and American alike, will be dead. All that is left if the conflict goes much further is total nuclear war. Our cities will be nothing more than smoking ashes beneath blowing mushroom clouds. And for what purpose?"

Cheninko, however, was unmoved by his general's pleas. "We'll stop, Yovanovich, when I decide we stop. Now answer my question. Is our army sufficient to complete the total destruction of Germany?"

Unaware of the Americans' ingenious plan to counter the Russians in the coming days, Yovanovich answered. "Yes, despite what has occurred in the past few hours, our force remains powerful enough to finish the task. The enemy has little left inside Germany with which to resist."

"Then we shall not cease until every meter of Germany is conquered."

"Comrade Premier, I beg you to reconsider. Your decision makes little sense. Continuing the slaughter adds nothing to our triumph. Our finest young men are gone. Why add one more widow to the rolls of the grieving? We must end this. We must stop before it's too late."

Cheninko's absolute rule called for absolute obedience. Few had ever questioned his decisions in even the slightest. Those who did quickly discovered what the consequences were for such a rash decision. The late hour, and the shock of the American attack, made Cheninko's quick temper show. He was ready to erupt.

"Are you questioning me, Yovanovich?"

"Comrade Premier, what does it matter what we do at this point? We won't be able to change history. In three months, possibly less, Germany will be back in American hands."

"What?"

"We can conquer, but we no longer have the capability to hold what we've gained. Even without the American nuclear attack, our losses have been far greater than anticipated. The Americans, while defeated, mounted an exceptionally aggressive defense. No Russian division would ever have been able to stand up to such an unrelenting assault the way the Americans did. They took a huge toll on our forces. With our casualties, we're still able to take Germany, but we'll never be able to keep it."

"If I so decree, Yovanovich, we'll hold Germany no matter what the cost. I'll see to that."

"Comrade Premier, we must be realistic. Force of will, while important, will never be enough. The Americans are no doubt going to seek their revenge. And with the losses we've sustained, we'll never be able to resist so powerful an enemy. Their soldiers are probably loading on their ships this very moment. If necessary, to defeat us they'll bring everyone they have to the battlefield. Their anger will know no bounds. Our forces may be able to defeat the first division they send. With luck, we might withstand the second. But the third won't be stopped. When those that follow join them, they'll quickly annihilate our men and push us out of Germany forever. And you shouldn't be surprised when they refuse to stop at the German border. We committed our entire army to this battle. We have no meaningful reserves. There will be little to dissuade them from rolling across Eastern Europe. Unless we act swiftly to appease them, their tanks will be rumbling down Moscow's streets by spring's first blooms."

"Appease them? Appease the Americans? I'd never consider anything of the sort. When I ordered you to prepare for this war, why didn't you tell me of the possibility of such events?"

"Because you never asked, Comrade Premier. You ordered my staff to prepare a plan for the destruction of Germany. We did as you directed. Germany is nothing more than a festering boil."

Cheninko considered what he'd heard. Deep within him, he sensed the truth in Yovanovich's words. His mind, however, was unwilling to accept such a blunt assessment. His ego, and the depravity that comes with absolute power, would never let him back down.

"Commence further attacks immediately. Hold nothing back. Strike with everything we've got."

Yovanovich's frustration with such a senseless pronouncement knew no bounds. If he hadn't been so weary, or so completely exasperated by the outlandish edict, he'd have never uttered what he did.

"And what if I decide not to carry out such an order?"

Cheninko exploded. "Yovanovich, men have visited my courtyard for far less! Unless you wish to join them, you'll carry out my directive without the slightest hesitation. I'll accept nothing but complete compliance as your answer."

There was no mistaking Cheninko's not-so-veiled threat. The Premier's office looked down upon a wide courtyard. At the courtyard's far end, the sorrowful wall was littered with bullet holes and streaked with red. Some of the mortal stains had been there for the six years he'd controlled Russia. Some of the blood was quite fresh. Untold scores of luckless souls had met their fates in front of the grim wall's firing squads. A visit there was always a final one.

Cheninko would stand at his open window, perverse pleasure on his face as he watched those he'd personally selected for execution reach the final moments of their pitiful lives.

Colonel Zulin knew this battle of wills wouldn't end well if he didn't step in. He would be risking his own life, but he had to protect his commander. "Comrade Premier, won't you at least let us finish the damage assessments before we begin the assaults anew?"

"No. My orders are clear. The war will continue. Initiate the attacks at once. Keep the pressure on until every German has felt my wrath."

Zulin could see the anger in Yovanovich's eyes. To keep his superior from being marched into the courtyard in the coming minutes, he jumped in a second time, "It will be done, Comrade Premier."

He grabbed Yovanovich's arm and began moving his recalcitrant superior toward the doorway. The displeasure on the general's face was quite evident. He did nothing to mask his animosity.

The door soon closed behind them.

It wasn't until the pair was a great distance from the Kremlin's walls that either said a word. Always aware of prying eyes and unfriendly ears, they spoke in hushed tones. It was clear Yovanovich's anguish was unabated.

"I laid the truth in front of him, and he spit it back in my face," he said. "Thousands and thousands more are going to die just to satisfy the grotesque ego of one man."

"Yes, Comrade General," Zulin said, "but you did what you could. You should be proud. Few are brave enough to tell him such things."

"There's nothing to be proud of in failure, Zulin. I should have stood up to him."

"And forfeited your life, Comrade General? What purpose would that have served?"

"Even so, before this goes much further, confronting him is an action I may have no choice but to hazard. One thing's certain. At some point the madness must stop. No matter how severe the risks I'm forced to endure, this is going to end."

There was little doubt what the Director of Operations was saying. Both understood that drastic measures might soon have to be undertaken if they were going to keep the world from being destroyed in total nuclear war, with hundreds of millions dying.

"You know your staff is completely loyal to you. Each would gladly give up his life in your service."

"I know. But we are fewer than one hundred, and the Kremlin guards are more than three times our number."

"True, Comrade General. But that may not be the insurmountable obstacle you believe it to be. The commander of the guards is a good friend. We go back many years. A week ago, after far too much to drink, he confided a deep secret to me."

"What would that be?"

"The Kremlin guards despise that fat, old bastard as much as we do. My friend was quite concerned his men wouldn't be willing to mount much of a defense should a threat to Cheninko appear. So if we decide to act, our chances, despite the odds, would likely be far greater than you anticipate."

"That's good to know, Zulin. It's certainly something I'll need to give serious thought."

"So what do you wish me to do?"

"Let's play this out a bit further. For now, we'll do what that pompous fool wants. Order the attacks to recommence."

"It will be done, Comrade General."

The war would continue into another day.

CHAPTER 58

Jeffrey Paul listened to his headset as he received a short report from the communication van. Having been briefed by the crew they were replacing, Fowler and Morgan settled into the engagement controllers' chairs. For the next four hours, the cramped space at the front of the small van would be their home.

"Last of the reserve missiles have been loaded onto the launchers," Paul said.

"How many Patriots does that give us?" Fowler asked.

"Twelve total."

"When does regiment anticipate we'll receive some more?"

"They didn't say. There definitely aren't any more in-country. The eight they sent us were all there were. They said replacement Patriot missiles are on the highest priority possible. But so is basically everything else. Rumor has it they loaded a C-5 full of Patriots in El Paso twelve hours ago, and they're due in Germany anytime now."

"That's the same rumor I heard in the mess tent yesterday," Fowler said. "And the day before from a friend of mine at battalion."

"Twelve missiles," Morgan said. "One thing's certain, if the Russians make another determined attack, we're all dead."

"That's for sure," Fowler said.

"What about our Stinger supply?" Morgan asked.

"We're in fairly good shape there," Paul said. "All three gunners have at least one missile. And the 24th Infantry has offered to give us six to eight more. Seems their commanding general likes the fact that you two, and the other engagement teams, keep knocking the bad guys out of the sky every time they try to attack the 24th's troops."

"We've done all right so far," Morgan said.

"What's our present kill total?" Fowler asked.

"In eight shifts in the Engagement Control Station, it's been confirmed that the team of Morgan and Fowler has destroyed thirty-one enemy aircraft," Paul said.

More kills than the other three shifts combined.

"How many Patriot batteries are still in the war?" Morgan asked.

Paul posed the same question to his headset. In the communication van fifty yards away, a voice gave him the answer.

"Delta Battery, with its reconstituted personnel, has left Rhein-Main and is headed across the river to protect a high-priority communication center. They'll be there in a couple of hours. Besides that, there are three still fighting in the north, two German and one American, and us in the south. They're planning on moving the American one across the Rhine later today to protect Ramstein."

"Ask them how far away the last report places the Russian armor," Morgan said.

Paul spoke into the headset once more and waited for the answer to come.

"Lead elements of the 24th Infantry are presently engaging the Russians thirty miles east of downtown Stuttgart."

Enemy tanks were twenty miles from where the Patriot battery sat in a rest area on the autobahn connecting Stuttgart and Munich. Unless something drastic happened, the Russians would reach their location by noon. But the Patriot team wasn't overly concerned with such an eventuality. With so few missiles remaining on their launchers, Fowler and Morgan understood it was death from the sky that posed the greatest threat to their survival.

The radar screens were quiet at this early hour of the morning. Well to the north, a dozen triangles circled over the western one-third of Germany still in Allied hands. The aircraft had been identified as friendlies by the previous shift.

Locked in their electronic world, there was little for the Patriot crew to do. Some shifts were like that. Quiet and uneventful, four hours of staring at the screens would slowly pass.

The somber heavens were calm.

"Paul, why don't you start working on getting those Stingers from the 24th Infantry before they change their minds and withdraw the offer," Morgan said. "I suspect we're going to need them pretty soon."

"Yes, ma'am."

Paul spoke into his headset. A few minutes later, the communication van relayed the news that six Stingers would be on their way to the Patriot battery shortly after sunrise.

For the next twenty minutes, the radar screens remained quiet. Outside, the darkness was cold and eerily still. The damp German winter hung heavy over the Patriot soldiers' small world. Only the distant rumble of the developing battle between the five thousand men of the 1st Brigade of the 24th Infantry Division and the ten Russian divisions they faced disturbed the early-morning silence of the first day of February.

But things were going to change soon. The Patriot team's boredom was about to be unexpectedly shattered.

Without warning, a dozen triangles appeared in the east. At the speed the triangles were moving, they had to be helicopters. Concern leaped onto Morgan's face and filled the corners of her eyes. She began interrogating the triangles.

The Patriot radar reached out and requested the lead helicopter return the proper response. The Patriot's interrogation, friend or foe, was completed in a heartbeat.

Foe.

A hostile symbol appeared next to the first triangle on the screens. Morgan continued to interrogate the formation. One by one, the results were the same. Twenty miles away on the black horizon, a dozen enemy helicopters were headed toward the Patriot battery. The helicopters were already well within range of the Patriot's missiles. Unless stopped, the Russian threat would reach the battery in six minutes.

Fowler looked into Morgan's eyes. Her eyes mirrored his fears.

"What do you want me to do?" he said.

"Paul, alert the Stinger teams to get ready," she said.

"Yes, ma'am."

"Go ahead and target the first five helicopters. But don't give the command to fire until we're certain they're coming for us."

"Roger," Fowler said, "targeting first five helicopters. Command to fire won't be given until directed."

"Paul, tell the Stinger teams it looks like twelve Hinds are headed our way. If the helicopters attack, we'll engage the first five with Patriots. They're to kill the next three . . . more if they can. We'll play it by ear from there. If we're lucky, we just might have a few Patriots left when this thing's over."

She was gambling the Stingers could handle some of the helicopters before the Russians got close enough to get off a good shot at the Engagement Control Station. It was either that or put the battery out of business by using the last of her missiles to destroy the Hinds.

The attackers churned through a raven sky at nearly two hundred miles per hour. Their steadfast course didn't alter in the slightest as the seconds ticked by. There could be little doubt. The Hinds were headed straight for them.

The killers were within fifteen miles.

Morgan waited to give the order to fire. Her mouth and lips were dry. Her pulse was racing.

Suddenly, eighteen rapidly moving triangles leaped onto the screens. They roared west. The new threat was seventy-five miles away and approaching fast. Their course appeared to match that of the first group of attackers. At six times the speed of the helicopters, the MiGs raced toward the Patriot battery. At their present rate, the fighters would arrive at their target in four minutes. The helicopters were going to reach the battery at precisely the same moment. Fowler and Morgan instantly recognized they were in serious trouble.

"Paul!" she said. "Get us some air support down here right now! We need at least a half dozen fighters, more if you can find them."

Without air support, they'd have no chance. Paul spoke into his headset once again. Morgan started interrogating the high-flying formation. Neither she, nor Fowler, needed to look at the screens to know what the results would be. All eighteen were going to come up "foe."

"Disengage from targeting the helicopters," Morgan said. "Direct the system to attack the fighters."

"Roger," Fowler said. "Reprogramming the computer to engage the second formation."

The MiGs were already in range.

"Paul," Morgan said, "tell the Stinger teams there's been a change of plans. They're to engage all the helicopters."

"But, Lieutenant, they've only got five Stingers, and there are twelve helicopters."

"Never mind that, just do it. Then tell the communication van to get in touch with the 24th Infantry. See if any of their Stinger teams are in the neighborhood. Tell them we've got to have help, and we've got to have it now. The helicopters will be here in three minutes."

Both enemy formations continued on their unwavering path toward them. There was no longer any question in either of the American air defenders' minds. They knew the hostile triangles were coming to claim the Patriot battery.

Fowler directed the computer to target the enemy fighters and fire when they were thirty miles away. The flight of eighteen MiGs roared past the fifty-mile point. The helicopters were within eight miles.

"Lieutenant!" Paul said. "Regiment says F-16s are on the way. But there's no way they'll get here in time. "

"What about the 24th?"

Paul spoke into his headset.

"There aren't any Stinger teams close enough to help us," Paul said.

"Order the communication van to wake everybody up as fast as they can. Tell them they've only got a couple of minutes to get into the woods before this place is blown to kingdom come."

"Yes, ma'am."

Fowler and Morgan looked into each other's eyes, hoping to find some reassurance. Both suspected there wasn't going to be any last-minute reprieve this time.

It took only sixty seconds for the first of the MiG-29s to reach the thirty-mile point. A Patriot missile roared from its launch canister. Silhouetted by the darkness, its fiery form ripped into the black heavens. Right behind it, one after another, four more Patriots leaped into the sky.

Fowler glanced at his watch. "We have five confirmed launches at zero-six-forty-two."

"Roger. Confirm five launches at zero-six-forty-two," Morgan said.

"Notifying regiment of five launches," Paul said.

They'd continue playing the game until the bitter end. And Fowler and Morgan were determined to keep fighting until the last possible moment. They'd every intention of taking out as many Russian pilots as they possibly could. For now, with five missiles in the air, all they could do was wait and watch their screens as the Patriots undertook their life-and-death duels in the star-choked German skies. Five Russian pilots were involved in a final hopeless struggle to see the coming sunrise. With the nineteen-foot killers hot on their tails, the MiGs broke from the formation. Using every trick imaginable, they fought to survive.

But the pilots' frantic actions were wasted on the Patriots. With the computer countering the Russians' every move, the missiles rapidly advanced toward their victims. The first flashing tic-tac-toe soon appeared. More were on the way. In rapid succession, the five missiles plucked their soaring prey from the heavens.

The remaining fighters continued on their unrelenting quest to destroy the final Patriot battery in southern Germany. Twenty miles out, the Russians began targeting the air-defense system. The MiGs were sixty seconds away from firing their missiles and ending the Patriot soldiers' lives.

The attack helicopters were six miles from the battery. They skimmed over the treetops, intent on defeating the Americans.

The Stinger gunners stood in the darkness, waiting for the helicopters to come within the five-mile range of their deadly missiles. In another few seconds, a trio of Hinds was going to find out just how lethal the little killers could be.

The target-acquisition officers in the attack helicopters armed their missiles and rockets.

The Americans had seven Patriots left.

At one thousand miles per hour, the MiGs moved in for the kill.

Another Patriot fired, shattering the morning stillness. Seconds later, four more missiles roared skyward to meet the enemy.

Their radars beseeching them to take evasive action, five Russians begged their aircrafts' powerful engines to save their lives. Once more, the mortal chase was under way in the blood-tinged darkness over Germany. It was another heart-searing drama the Patriots would soon win.

Straight and steady, the eight remaining fighters continued with their determined task. The helicopters neared.

"We've got two missiles remaining on the launch platforms," Fowler said.

"Paul, notify regiment that we have two missiles left, and eight MiGs are nearing our position."

"Yes, ma'am." Paul spoke into his headset.

The helicopters were four miles away. The first of the Stinger gunners locked onto a Hind. The little missile leaped from the gunner's shoulder. The Russian crew turned and ran. The Stinger was right on its tail. It wouldn't be much longer before the helicopter would burst into flames. The remaining Stinger teams located the whirling enemy. Death spit forth from American shoulders once again. Two more Hinds were near their end. The Stinger gunners looked up. The surviving Russian helicopters were coming on much too fast. In seconds, they'd be right on

top of them. There wasn't enough time for the Americans to ready replacement missiles. They threw down their empty firing tubes and raced
for the woods. Most of the men and women of the Patriot battery had
already run deep inside its protective cover.

The leading missile in the second group of Patriots eliminated its target. On the screens, another tic-tac-toe flashed. The eight untargeted fighters were six miles out and coming on. Each was ready to fire. In another
three miles, they'd unleash a fierce barrage of air-to-ground missiles.
Fifteen seconds was all that remained before the attack would begin.

A Patriot soared from its launcher in search of prey. In seconds, one
of the oncoming eight would reach its fiery end. There was a single
missile waiting on launcher number four to bring death to a final pilot.
In moments, the computer would order the missile to fire.

Another blinking symbol appeared on the screen. Another MiG
had perished. The time had come for the computer to send the last Patriot skyward. That would be it for the air-defense battery.

In a mighty blast, the lone missile hurtled from its launcher. It
rushed into the skies to seek and destroy.

As it did, air-to-ground missiles leaped from the now-leading fighter's wingtips. The Russian pilot, targeted for destruction by the final
Patriot, wouldn't live long enough to see his missiles reach the ground.

On their screens, Fowler and Morgan saw the incoming Russian
missiles the moment they were fired.

"Get out! Get out, now!" Fowler screamed.

Paul ripped off his headset. He tore at the small door behind him.
Only five seconds remained before the air-to-ground missiles would
reach them. The door flew open. In the darkness, Jeffrey Paul tumbled
onto the frozen asphalt. He scrambled to his feet. On a severely twisted
ankle, he hobbled toward the safety of the beckoning woods.

The passageway through the Engagement Control Station's massive
array of electronic equipment was so narrow that only one person at a
time, turned partially sideways, could successfully navigate their way
through it. Rapidly covering the eight feet to the rear opening was nearly
impossible.

With death rushing to steal them away, Morgan froze in her chair. Fowler grabbed the front of her uniform and attempted to push her toward the door. She stumbled and fell faceup into the middle of the constricted aisle. On her back, she struggled to reach the opening. But it was no use.

Fowler leaped from his chair. His escape was blocked by the fallen lieutenant. He glanced at the radar screen. The missiles were right on top of them.

He knew they had no chance.

In a futile attempt to shield the pretty lieutenant, Fowler dropped to the floor. With his body, he covered hers the best he could.

The effort was entirely symbolic. He realized he wasn't going to be able to save her from dying. Her vivid green eyes stared into his in disbelief. He could see the terror in her beautiful features. It reflected the emotions present in his.

Both knew that in a fraction of a second, their lives would end. There was nothing either of them could do. At the last possible instant, Morgan accepted her fate. The terror suddenly left her.

Her eyes shimmered. A hint of a smile found the corners of her mouth. She reached up and wrapped her arms around him. Fowler looked into her eyes. His smile matched hers.

The Russian missiles, their noses filled with death, headed for the helpless pair. The missiles rammed into the Engagement Control Station. The strength of the impacting ordnance sent shattered pieces of jagged metal and electronics equipment flying in every direction. Locked in a final embrace, Fowler and Morgan disappeared in a blinding flash of light. The minute fragments of their bodies, and of their souls, were tossed to the four winds.

Paul was ten yards from the safety of the shadowy trees. A razor-sharp metal slab raced from the decimated van toward the hobbling figure. The white-hot metal cut him down in midstride. His severed body lay on the asphalt. His freely flowing blood ran down the black surface toward the woods. He'd died so quickly that only the edges of his face showed any signs of recognition.

Missile after missile streamed from the heavens upon the crippled battery.

The MiGs and helicopters feasted for a very long time on the dead carcass of the defeated American air defenses.

The last Patriot battery in southern Germany was no more.

CHAPTER 59

Nearly seven hours after Fowler's and Morgan's deaths, Arturo Rios sat behind the powerful machine gun in his deeply bunkered world. He stared at the ruinous remains of the evergreen forest on the eastern edge of Ramstein. He was back in the same anguished bunker he'd been carried from two days earlier. His terrifying memories of those earlier days had returned, too.

The remnants of the monumental blizzard were all around him. Although they probably wouldn't be for much longer. The afternoon thermometer was reaching into the upper forties. The unmistakable signs of the drab snow's disappearance were everywhere.

The crimson remains of Wilson and Goodman were still visible on the ground at the rear of the bunker. The dead airmen's faces were also there, forever alive in Rios's vivid dreams.

After two full days of good food, clean sheets, and profound sleep, Rios's broken spirit had been partially restored. As he spent his second hour back on the line, his injured shoulder throbbed in the damp winter weather. But more difficult than the pain in his shoulder was the pain from his bitter remembrances of the tired bunker. Those memories were intensely present. The tortured airman knew that no matter how long he lived, they always would be.

They'd promised him he'd only be out there for a twelve-hour shift. Just long enough for the exhausted men on the line to sleep for a little while and enjoy a couple of robust meals. They didn't want to release Rios for such duty. He certainly wasn't in shape for it. Nevertheless, there weren't enough defenders left to guard the distant miles of chain link alone. They needed the hero of the eastern fence to return once more. All they wanted was for him to protect the wire long enough to provide a little relief to his worn countrymen.

It had been a relatively quiet two days for the air base. Fewer and fewer fighter aircraft returned each hour, and the number of planes had grown critically low. The spirits of the base's men were nearly as crushed as Ramstein's air forces. Yet there'd been no further assaults upon them. And for that, everyone was thankful. They'd all seen far too much killing. And, like Rios, each had been permanently scarred by his experiences.

Until midnight, the twenty-year-old airman would be alone with his thoughts and two hundred yards of fence line. His thoughts scared him more than the battered fence ever would.

Just until midnight, they'd promised. No more.

Rios turned to watch two C-17 medevacs taxi to the edge of the runway behind him. One right after the other, the medical aircraft rushed down the runway and headed west. He sat watching them for the longest time as they grew smaller and smaller in the distant sky.

Five minutes behind the C-17s, a commercial airliner rolled to a stop. The Boeing 767 revved its deafening engines, quashing the airman's solitude once more. Rios stared at the huge plane sitting a few feet away as it waited for clearance to depart. A small face in a window seat a third of the way back stared down at him. The smiling child raised a tiny hand and waved. Rios slowly lifted his good arm to return the gesture. But the plane was already heading down the concrete ribbon. The child never saw the lonely airman's response.

Rios's tenuous afternoon droned on.

Two miles away from his sandbagged world, ten thousand women and children were crammed together in a pockmarked building. Each was waiting for their turn to head for home. The Americans were halfway through the fourth complete day of the war. One hundred and thirty thousand dependents remained at Rhein-Main, Ramstein, and a dozen smaller airfields. With the Russians relentlessly closing in, everyone understood there was little time left with which to finish moving the women and children out of harm's way. Rhein-Main, in particular, had grown perilously near the front lines. The base would soon have to be abandoned.

Colonel Zulin approached the Director of Operations.

"Comrade General, our agents in Germany report that within the past hour, a Patriot air-defense battery has begun setting up in front of Ramstein."

"That finalizes our decision, then," Yovanovich said. "I've promised Comrade Cheninko that I'll end this thing as quickly as possible. We cannot allow the enemy to set up their air defenses in front of Ramstein and foil this afternoon's air attack to destroy it. After last night's nuclear assault by the Americans, Premier Cheninko has ordered me to use our intermediate range SS-20 nuclear weapons upon the air base and any other target in Germany if we deem it necessary."

"Comrade General, should I give such an order?"

Yovanovich hesitated. He knew the use of the significantly larger weapon would be escalating the nuclear component of the conflict even further. They were already standing much too close to the edge of a world-devouring whirlwind, and he needed to be exceptionally careful. The planet was staring into an unspeakable abyss from which it would never recover. The launch on Ramstein was something he didn't want to risk. As he stood weighing his options, it was far too clear, however, that for the moment, he had little choice. His plan for dealing with Cheninko wasn't nearly ready. And confronting him at this point would foil his plot.

"Looks like we've no other choice. Order a fire mission for a nuclear attack on Ramstein."

"Yes, Comrade General, it will be done at once. Ramstein will be destroyed before the day fully sets over Germany."

Behind Rios, the sun dropped into the western horizon. He'd miss the fragile warmth it had provided during his first hours back on the line.

The young airman sat on the edge of the runway, alone with his terrifying thoughts. He stared into the splintered trees. The broken pieces of the fearful forest were still red with blood from the grisly battles just days earlier. But after the horror he'd lived through, the trees no longer caused the slightest apprehension for the isolated airman. As the first hints of darkness appeared in the corners of the ravaged forest, Rios laughed out loud. How many years had it been since he sat out here in the darkness afraid of every shadow?

Four days. He couldn't believe it. It had only been four days. Four days, and a thousand lifetimes.

In the western Ukraine, the three-man crew prepared to fire the nuclear missile across the late-afternoon sky. Perched on the long rocket's nose sat a trio of 150-kiloton warheads. All three warheads had been programmed to destroy Ramstein. One would land in the middle of the base, exploding above the control tower. Another would strike the aircraft bunkers on Ramstein's northern tip. The final was targeted to crush the ammunition storage area a half mile from the eastern fence.

The firing sequence began.

"Five . . . four . . . three . . . two . . . one . . ." The rocket's engine ignited. It lifted the huge missile into the heavens.

The shadows were growing quite long. Darkness would soon be upon them. Alone on the fence, Rios could hear the eerie echoes in the trees on the other side of the wire. Echoes of the fearsome combat in the gray fog a few days past. The sounds and voices were clearly there.

"Michael, have you got him?" a soldier dead for two days whispered to his ghostly companion deep within the evergreens.

"Watch it, Smitty!" another mortal voice warned his long-departed friend.

A burst of gunfire from the prior battle chattered in the broken forest.

A voice in Russian screamed an urgent directive Rios couldn't understand.

In the mists of a small glade, a soldier's dying cry was whispered on the winds to the solitary airman sitting in the brown bunker.

In complete fascination, Rios listened to the warfare between the recently dead as they clashed once more for control of their souls. The unearthly sounds didn't concern him in the slightest. In some strange way, the sounds of the struggle, which would be carried on for the rest of time, were reassuring to him.

He'd stared death in the face more than once in the past four days. And death no longer scared him. Rios had looked into Satan's fiery eyes, and the young airman hadn't flinched.

He now knew that only the living could cause him pain, for he had no fear of the dead.

The sounds of the spectral battle in the whispery corners of the shattered woods disappeared. Another plane loaded with dependents was approaching for takeoff.

Rios looked at the faces in the windows and wondered if any of them were bound for Miami. He realized he should have thought of that earlier. Get one of the women to carry a message to his mother and sisters telling them he was all right. He'd do that first thing when they came to relieve him at midnight. He'd find someone to take a message for him. But what would he say? "Dear Mother: How are you? I am fine. Killed fifty Russians this week. One almost killed me. Your loving son, Arturo."

Well, he'd eight more hours out here at the end of the world to figure out what to tell her. Maybe after dark, Goodman and Wilson would help him come up with something.

The airliner's engines wailed. Rios turned to watch. The plane started down the lengthy runway. It wasn't long before the aircraft lifted its struggling wings a few feet into the air. As it did, the 150-kiloton nuclear detonation burst above the control tower. The silver airliner vanished in a mighty flash. Arturo Rios would never see the second and third blasts of fusing atoms that smashed into the air base a fraction of a second later. For the first brilliant flash of light had forever stolen his eyesight.

The massive explosions tore the flesh from Rios's limbs. They ruptured every blood vessel in his lungs. His eardrums burst from the thunder of the imploding atom. Rios was dead a second later when the nuclear blasts' four-hundred-mile-per-hour winds picked him up and impaled him on the fence. The scattered pieces of the ancient forest disappeared forever.

In seconds, Ramstein was nothing more than a smoking crater beneath three rising mushroom clouds. When the tiny atom was through, there'd be nothing left of the once-mighty air base.

There would be no survivors.

Goodman and Wilson were waiting when Rios climbed down from the fence. Wilson had that stupid grin on his face. Goodman handed Rios the machine gun. Without a word, the three of them returned to the bunker to continue battling the ghostly Russians until eternity itself reached its end.

CHAPTER 60

In the early-evening darkness, the battalion's lead tank moved east. Tim Richardson stood in the open commander's hatch. They'd been the last tank in. Now they were going to be the first tank out. His Abrams was battered. And his driver had one good arm. In front of Richardson, Jamie Pierson did his best to steer the monster with his useless right arm wrapped against his side. There was no one else available to handle the M-1.

Inside the turret, Richardson's Abrams had a new gunner. He also had a new loader, whose name Richardson had yet to learn, sitting next to him in the bullet-scarred turret. The two were 1st Armor Division soldiers he'd rescued on the previous evening.

Tony Warrick was barely alive when they'd arrived early in the morning. He hadn't survived a hurried helicopter ride to Landstuhl. He had been pronounced dead upon arrival.

Richardson and Pierson felt his loss deeply.

The 3rd Infantry Division had been re-formed. The division was less than the size of one of its original brigades. The 3rd Brigade was less than one of its battalions. With the arrival late on the previous night of its final tank, the 2nd Battalion of the 3rd Brigade was smaller than company size.

For half a day, they'd been off the front lines. They'd received twelve precious hours of respite while the 24th Infantry held the enemy long enough for their countrymen to lick their gaping wounds. They'd been reorganized, fed a hot meal, and prepared to go forth into battle once more. And for the first time in four days, Richardson and Pierson had actually slept. A five-hour sleep of the dead for the two survivors of the twelve-man tank platoon.

While they slept, hasty repairs were performed on their crippled tank. Any tank, even a badly damaged one, was of too much value to abandon. In the short time they were given, the maintenance crews succeeded in replacing the loader's machine gun. They'd cannibalized a working one from the burned-out shell of an Abrams whose crew hadn't been so fortunate. But Richardson's tank would have to enter battle without the tank commander's antiaircraft machine gun. There hadn't been enough time to install one even if they could have located a functioning replacement. In its belly, the M-1 had seventeen shells for its main gun.

As they rumbled toward the coming battle, the battalion's last eleven tanks and four surviving Bradleys split up. Two tanks and the four Bradleys headed back down Highway 19.

They were moving forward to meet a strong enemy force twenty miles distant and closing fast. The remaining Abrams tanks, including Richardson's, were churning toward where two of central Germany's main autobahns met ten miles east of Heilbronn.

The battalion would wait on the snow-tinged fields in a wide valley of ancient farms and small villages. There they'd engage an enemy force forty times their size. On the open ground, air support would be critical. Unfortunately, the few surviving Apaches were spread much too thin to be counted upon. And with Ramstein only a memory, gone nearly two hours earlier beneath the billowing mushroom clouds, the battalion would be depending upon Lakenheath and Mildenhall for assistance.

There'd been no time to prepare firing holes. The battalion would take up positions on the open ground and await the enemy's appearance. Inside the lead tank, all four soldiers understood they'd seen their last sunset.

Two hours earlier, Pierson and Richardson had sat on a serene riverbank watching the winter sun go down. Both had refused to leave the sacred spot until the final fleeting wisps of its warming rays completely disappeared. Richardson had known for quite some time that there was little chance of their living to tell the tales of the great war. With Warrick's death, Pierson had also come to understand the awful truth. Each knew he would be added to the bloody list of American dead long before the sun would rise again over central Europe. By morning, the tank's crew would be nothing more than four additional names on the ever-growing rolls.

Behind the battalion, there was no organized resistance on this side of the Rhine. When the small group of tanks and Bradleys was gone, in this portion of Germany the Russians were going to be able to roll unimpeded to the banks of the mighty river.

Richardson's struggling Abrams continued moving east.

"Richardson, before we left, did you happen to get any further word on how far away the Russian armor is?" Specialist Haines, his new gunner, asked.

"Nothing more than what they told us at this afternoon's briefing," Richardson said. "They think it'll probably be a few more hours before Comrade's attack begins. But just in case battalion's wrong, keep your eyes open wide and your hand on that trigger."

From Richardson's and Pierson's camouflage uniforms, a shiny silver star dangled at the end of a red, white, and blue ribbon. The medals had been awarded a few hours earlier to the survivors of the brave tank platoon that had held the crucial highway. The division commander promised that Tony Warrick's and Clark Vincent's medals would be presented to their families in an appropriate ceremony in the near future. In a moving speech, the general stated that without their valiant actions, the entire battalion would've been lost. The battalion would've been cut off and destroyed during the previous night's battle if not for the lone tank's willingness to stick it out against overwhelming odds.

After the horrors of the past two days, Richardson was in no mood for speeches. Even if the speeches praised him. They'd done what they had to do. There was nothing more to say.

A week ago, the surviving tankers would've given anything to be awarded a silver star. Now neither of them cared one way or the other.

In thirty minutes, the tattered remnants of the once-powerful battalion arrived at the deserted autobahns. With the Russians drawing near, the broad roadways' final frantic refugees had disappeared in the past half hour. The tanks continued on. Five miles to the east, they reached their objective. The nine M-1s spread themselves across the wide valley. In front of them, Richardson spotted the position he wanted.

"This spot looks as good as any, Jamie. There's an off-ramp just ahead. Let's set up at the top of it. We can use the ramp's incline for protection."

The creaking tank moved up the incline. As it neared the top, Jamie brought it to a halt. Richardson leaped down and guided the M-1 forward. When he was finished, only the Abrams's turret was visible over the crest of the ramp. Richardson viewed his efforts. He liked what he saw. The position was nearly as good as being dug in. Ground forces or armor units were going to have a difficult time killing the M-1.

He knew, however, that helicopters or MiGs were going to be another story entirely. If Russian air forces successfully penetrated the last elements of the battalion without help arriving, Richardson realized with resounding clarity that the one-sided battle would soon be over.

The stoic sergeant climbed back onto the tank. He dropped into his hole and pulled the lid shut behind him. For three hours, they sat in the bloodstained interior of the foul-smelling M-1. Outside, it was a wondrous, star-filled winter night. Alone in their reflections or talking quietly on the intercom, the four of them waited for the enemy to appear. They knew it was only a matter of time.

At shortly after nine, Richardson spotted the first of the Russian armor as it crested a distant hill. The enemy tanks and BMPs were widely spaced. Richardson continued to watch. A steady stream of armored vehicles eased over the hill and moved toward the valley floor. The line appeared to go on forever.

"Echo-Yankee-One, this is Sierra-Kilo-One-Two. Have armor movement on the hillside five miles away."

"Roger, Sierra-Kilo-One-Two. We see them. We've called for fighter support. With any luck, the F-16s should be crossing the English Channel as we speak. Battalion is to open fire when the enemy's within two miles. Six wants to stop them as far away as possible and hold them there until air support arrives. Sierra-Kilo-One-Two, open fire on the lead tank at two miles. Battalion will follow on your cue."

"Roger," Richardson said. "Will engage at two miles."

Nine minutes, no more, and the battle would begin.

"Haines, you heard the man. Target the leader. Fire at two miles. Let's get off as many shots as we can before the Russians figure out where we are."

"I'm already on it," Haines said.

"Let me know if you need my assistance in targeting the column and prioritizing the targets."

"Roger. If I need help, I won't hesitate to ask. But as slow as the Russians are moving, I think I can handle it by myself for now. Why don't you just sit back and enjoy the show. I'll try to make it a good one."

The seconds slowly ticked by. Richardson peered through the tank's night-vision system at the approaching armor. It didn't take long for him to recognize that the tanks cresting the distant hill were older T-64s. Still good tanks but not top-of-the-line. They were certainly no match for the M-1s in a fair fight. The tank commander recognized that the enemy they were going to face in this final battle wasn't going to be a first-line Russian unit. Possibly Regular Army, but definitely not one of the best or most prepared.

As the war neared the end of its fourth day, Richardson had no way of knowing that first-rate Russian armored divisions were few and far between. Almost all of the finest young men Mother Russia had to offer lay dead in the bloody fields of Germany. After four fierce days of fighting, an entire generation was gone.

He knew the M-1s would chew the older tanks to pieces. But nine Abrams tanks against an entire armored division, even a second-rate one, wasn't going to work for long.

"Richardson," Haines said, "another ten seconds and they'll be at the two-mile point. I've locked onto the leader. He'll be dead before he knows what hit him."

"Roger. Engage when ready."

Richardson had nothing to do but wait and watch the battle unfolding in front of him. For the moment, all of the engagement responsibilities rested on the shoulders of his new gunner.

Haines fired. The huge cannon expelled its first round. The Abrams recoiled, shuddering beneath the power of its main gun. On the distant hillside, the leading T-64 erupted in flames. A billowing fireball, an image that had become so much a part of the German countryside in the past four days, soared high into the dark heavens. The battle had begun.

Behind Richardson's tank, eight more fired. Fierce explosions ripped through the overmatched Russian armor. The American guns quickly took their toll.

The defenders bided their time and destroyed their outgunned opponent without suffering a single loss of their own. On the fiery hillside, the Russian division faltered. The enemy armor ground to a halt. For the first ten minutes, the struggle was slow and predictable.

But things were about to change.

For by the fifteen-minute point, the battle had suddenly turned desperate.

This time it was the Russians who'd sprung the trap. Their lure, the older tanks, had worked in bringing the Americans out into the open. By sacrificing their aging armor, they'd identified the M-1s' positions in the valley below.

From the hills, forty attack helicopters roared west. They were also older equipment, Hind-Ds manned by less-than-top-notch crews. Yet they were still quite lethal. And there were far too many of them for the handful of scattered tanks to handle. Like a swarm of raging hornets, the helicopters were quickly upon the American tanks. The first Abrams was gone before the battalion could react.

Without their antiaircraft gun, Richardson's crew was nearly helpless against the buzzing helicopters. But he wasn't going to let that stand in his way. He moved left through the compartment, popped the loader's hatch, and settled in behind its machine gun.

Two flights of F-16s were on the way from Lakenheath. It would be another ten minutes, however, before the first of the fighters would arrive.

With the Americans busily battling the new threat, the Russian armor saw an opening. The T-64s quickly picked up speed. They roared toward the battlefield.

"Richardson, I've still got twelve shells left for the main gun. Do you want me to disengage from the armor and target the Hinds?" Haines asked.

"Negative. Keep firing at the tanks. We need to keep them pinned against that hillside until help arrives. If they reach open ground and are able to spread out, the battalion's finished. We've got to somehow hold the armor where it's at if we're going to have any chance at all. You handle the tanks. I'll use the machine gun to keep the helicopters off us."

Richardson knew it was wishful thinking. A useless gesture, bound to fail. Still, he had little choice.

Without warning, two Apaches suddenly appeared in the sparkling night sky. The sleek forms raced into the center of the soaring Russians. In a version of combat seldom seen before this war, helicopter against helicopter, the desperate struggle continued. The Hind-D pilots were no match for their deftly skilled opponent.

Hellfires roared from beneath the American killers. For three minutes, one right after another, aging Russian rotor blades stopped spinning in midflight. They fell from the frigid skies in regular intervals beneath the Apaches' fierce attack.

But two against forty wouldn't succeed for long. A Russian Swatter missile ripped through the frightful night. An Apache exploded in midair. Seconds later, his partner fell prey to the concentrated Russian fire.

The Apaches were gone as quickly as they'd appeared. Both had been blown forever from the twinkling heavens. And the F-16s were still seven minutes away.

The Russians were ready to put an end to the uneven struggle. They swooped in on the Americans once more. A pair of determined Hinds headed for the lead M-1. As the helicopters neared, Richardson fired long bursts from his machine gun. But the gun's range was far too limited, and its armament much too small, to deal effectively with an airborne attack.

The Hinds were right on top of them. There was nothing Richardson could do but continue to fire and pray for divine intervention.

Within seconds of each other, both helicopters fired Swatter missiles at Richardson's crippled tank. At blinding speed, death raced through the night toward its target. The first missile was a fraction high. It missed the turret by inches. The Swatter smashed into the rear of the crippled American tank. In a blinding flash, its engine was destroyed. The Abrams buckled. Its crew was tossed about like a child's discarded toy. In the rear of the compartment, the tank's new loader lay dying. A raging inferno roared forward from the twisted mass of burning metal at the back of the M-1. The tank's fire-suppression system was overwhelmed by the unholy blaze.

If the Americans didn't do something, in a handful of flittering heartbeats the frantic flames were going to engulf the crew compartment and end their lives.

"Get out!" Richardson screamed. "Haines . . . Jamie . . . save yourselves any way you can!"

Terror stabbed deep within Richardson's heart. He struggled to free himself from the hatch. His crew did the same.

The second missile was right on target. Just as Richardson began to lift himself from the compartment, the missile struck the Abrams dead center. The M-1's turret exploded in a mighty blast. In a fiery pyre, the American tank commander disappeared. A rising ball of death and destruction carried the shattered remains of the disheartened sergeant and his new gunner high into the heavens. In the final instant of his brief life, Richardson was gripped by an overwhelming sense of sadness. His last conscious thought was an undeniable realization that no one would mourn his passing.

And no one ever did.

Sitting in the front section of the defeated M-1, Jamie Pierson was still alive. But he wouldn't be much longer if he couldn't get out of the flaming metal coffin. With the roaring inferno rushing forward to devour him, Jamie stabbed at the driver's hatch release with his good hand. The hatch sprung open. He tumbled out of the destroyed tank. If he was going to live, he had to get away from the tons of exploding metal. As his feet touched the frozen ground, the victorious Hinds spotted him.

Pierson took a first tentative step to run from the burning Abrams. A long burst from a helicopter's machine gun, and the tank's fleeing driver went down.

He was dead before his blood-splattered remains hit the ground.

By the time the F-16s arrived, not a single American tank was still in the fight. The battalion's last survivors had been annihilated. And the Russians, with the F-16s in hot pursuit, were headed toward the Rhine.

Early the next morning, a sparkling sun peeked over the low mountains. Its first shimmering rays shone into the silent valley below. A Russian soldier walked through the hazy battlefield, scavenging. In front of him was the burned-out shell of an American tank. Its hull still showed the slightest hints of the smoldering embers alive within. On the frostbitten ground near the tank, the Russian found a dead American with a bandaged right arm. There were a dozen bullet holes in the enemy soldier's tattered body. The American was faceup. His unseeing eyes were open wide and fixed in a surprised stare. The freckled face, distorted in death, was no older than his own.

The Russian reached down. With his knife, he cut the shiny metal with its pretty red, white, and blue ribbon from the dead American's uniform. He stuck the medal in his pocket and walked away.

CHAPTER 61

A handful of hours after the initial Russian units reached the spanning Rhine, George O'Neill contacted EUCOM to speak with Colonel Morrison. The ongoing installation of the new command and control system was progressing exceptionally well. All but a few of the vans were ready. And those were nearly so. O'Neill could find no reason why everything wouldn't be fully operational when the first stateside units arrived. The plan was set to proceed.

The moment the call ended, an elated Colonel Morrison notified the Pentagon.

Within minutes, final preparations to launch the aircraft convoys carrying the support personnel for each of the four air bases were begun. Within the hour, they would be heading for Germany. An hour later, the leading 1st Cavalry units would board their planes to join them.

Everything was precisely timed.

All the Americans needed to do was keep the Russians from crossing the turbulent waters in significant numbers for a reasonable length of time, and their plan would likely succeed. When the enemy arrived on the western side, the 1st Cavalry would be there to greet them.

The fully functioning AWACS and its crew had every intention of making sure that few, if any, Russians reached the distant shore.

Standing outside the huge communication van, an exhausted George O'Neill rubbed his sleep-starved eyes. The number of hours he'd slept since the war's beginning could be counted on one hand. Even so, the overtaxed sergeant wore a huge smile on his face that wouldn't fade for many glorious days to come.

It had taken endless attempts. Yet finally, his mother-in-law's e-mail found him. The message had been a simple one, but one the relieved American would cherish a thousand times over. Every word was imprinted on his brain. The e-mail read—"Mother and beautiful son safely arrived McMichael. Both awaiting the moment when you will join them."

Because of George's importance to the war, Kathy had insisted her mother say nothing about her injuries or the horrors she and Christopher had experienced. Her mother had complied with that wish.

The plan was in motion. Its fleeting minutes were steadily passing.

At the Austin airport, the steadfast passengers began walking down the ramp at gate number six. Each camouflage-clothed individual had an M-4 slung on their shoulder. The Delta Airlines 767 was waiting.

A half mile away, the C-5 loadmasters made a final check of their cargo—M-1 Abrams tanks. A few hundred yards distant, the UPS and FedEx flight crews did the same. The support the soldiers needed would arrive with them.

The time was almost here.

In minutes, the first aerial convoy carrying a company of 1st Cavalry soldiers and all of the equipment they needed for battle would depart.

Their destination was Bitburg.

They would be there in fourteen hours. Two hours after that, they would reach the Rhine.

CHAPTER 62

Twelve miles from Ramstein, nearly a day after the air base's destruction, Sergeant First Class Robert Jensen balanced on the edge of an uncomfortable hospital bed. A doctor stood over him while carefully removing the thick bandages from the platoon sergeant's eyes.

At the same moment, the ever-growing Russian armor sat poised on the eastern banks of the Rhine River. The Russians were watching the swirling currents on the murky blue water's journey to the sea. Everything on the eastern side of the great river was in the Communists' hands. As they fled, the Americans had successfully demolished all the remaining expanses over the wide, flowing waters. While their combat units enjoyed a brief rest, the Russians were bringing forward the first of the bridging equipment needed to span the river in a dozen places.

On the western banks, widely scattered elements of the 82nd Airborne and 24th Infantry waited to repulse any successful crossings. Until a few hours earlier, they'd believed there was little chance of prevailing against so powerful an enemy. But the news of the soon-arriving 1st Cavalry had buoyed their spirits and strengthened their timber. No matter what it took, they were determined to hold their immense foe until help arrived.

Tremendous numbers of those on the eastern bank were ill and dying from the poisons of the American nuclear attack.

Fifty miles behind the river, the Americans continued their orderly evacuation of their wounded countrymen from the giant Landstuhl hospital complex. They were intent on getting the multitude of patients away from the war zone. For the moment, there appeared to be ample time to accomplish the vast undertaking. With Ramstein a smoking crater and Rhein-Main behind enemy lines, convoy after convoy was driving to Sembach to meet the arriving C-17 medevacs. Without incident, the takeoffs and landings had been going on incessantly.

The last layers of gauze and wrappings were about to be removed from Jensen's eyes.

"All right, Sergeant," the major said. "You may not be able to see once the final bandages come off. If you can't, don't panic. It doesn't mean your condition's permanent. Your eyesight might return over time. Or you might require further operations to regain your vision. It's really too early to tell. So don't be too disappointed if you can't see right away."

It almost didn't matter to the sole survivor of the cavalry platoon. Jensen's voice was strange and detached as he answered. "Yes, sir, I understand."

He could feel the doctor's gentle hands taking the final swatches from his eyes. The moment the bandages were removed, the bright light of midday poured into his black world. He blinked rapidly. After one hundred hours locked in total darkness, his eyes fought against the offensive sunlight. Everything was still quite blurry. Yet one thing was certain, he could definitely see.

His gray eyes were working once again. A statuesque woman in green scrubs was standing behind the doctor. She wore a silver first lieutenant bar on her collar and carried with her the strangely seductive smell of antiseptic and sweet perfume. The look upon her face was a combination of concern and curiosity.

"You must be Lieutenant Morse," Jensen said.

A captivating smile spread across her sweet face. He instantly understood why Ramirez had been so taken with her. The platoon sergeant's heart melted beneath the glow of Elizabeth Morse's infectious smile.

A smile to match hers appeared on his face. His reaction surprised him. He'd never believed he would ever smile again.

"I can see why Ramirez thought he was in love. You're every bit as beautiful as he told me you were."

"Thank you, Sergeant."

Her embarrassment from his flattering words was evident on her reddening cheeks. In a flash, however, her smile disappeared. An overwhelming sadness gripped her at the mention of the determined soldier who'd saved her life.

The doctor examined Jensen's temple and looked into his eyes.

"Well, it appears things are coming along wonderfully. You must be a very quick healer, Sergeant."

"Yes, sir. I've always sort of been, I guess."

"Your leg and foot are still both going to give you problems. They've experienced severe trauma. But if you continue to progress at this pace, you should be up, taking your first tentative steps, in a few weeks."

Jensen's voice returned to its strangely detached tone. "That's good, sir."

The doctor was anxious to be on his overburdened way.

"Is there anything more I can do for you, Sergeant?"

It didn't take long for Robert Jensen to seize upon what he wanted more than anything.

"Sir, if it'd be all right with you, I'd sure like to sit outside in the sun for a while and take in a bit of the day."

The doctor's brow furrowed. "Well, I don't know if you're quite ready for that." The hopeful look in Jensen's eyes caused the major to quickly reconsider. "What do you think, nurse? Do you think our patient could stand the stress of a wheelchair ride?"

"I don't see why not. It's nearly fifty outside, his IVs have all been removed, and the last radiation reading was low enough to allow for at least a few hours of outdoor activity without any long-term effect. From what I heard about him in Wurzburg, Sergeant Jensen deserves whatever he wants. I think the least we can do is give him an hour in the sun."

"Good, then it's agreed. An hour in the sun for Sergeant Jensen is so ordered. And I think there's an exhausted nurse who also deserves her hour in the afternoon sunshine. I suspect we can afford to spare her for a little while. Would you like to take care of our outdoor patient?"

"Doctor, I'd love that."

"What time is the sergeant's convoy leaving for Sembach?"

"Not until five," Elizabeth Morse said. "His flight's scheduled to depart for the States at about seven."

"What about your own flight?"

"I'm on the same one as Sergeant Jensen. We're both a couple of feisty Texans, so they found two spots for us on a medevac to San Antonio."

"Very well. Then go out and enjoy your hour of sunlight. There'll be plenty of time when you get back to get both of you ready to leave."

With a blanket tucked under her arm, Elizabeth Morse pushed the tired wheelchair out the hospital's front entrance. The moment the sun's warmth fell upon him, Jensen's broad smile returned. A light, pleasant breeze tugged at the day's fragile heat. The duo moved quickly to distance themselves from the massive gray hospital complex so full of suffering and misery.

Down the grassy incline on the eastern side of the hospital, the treads of the well-worn wheelchair rolled. An occasional patch of melting snow crunched beneath its spinning wheels.

"How's this?" she asked.

They were three hundred yards from the nearest depressing building and well beyond its growing eastern shadow.

He looked around. "This'll do just fine."

She set the brake on the old chair to keep it from slipping from her grasp. The last thing she needed was her patient roaring down the little incline with her in hot pursuit. Satisfied that the chair would hold, she took the woolen blanket and spread it on the damp ground next to the wounded platoon sergeant. She sat down beside him. Elizabeth Morse slowly removed the scores of pins from her raven hair. The task completed, she shook her head. Flowing black strands, shining in the early-afternoon sunlight, fell down around her.

Jensen smiled at her sitting figure. She returned his smile. Just beneath the surface, both sets of eyes reflected an unmistakable sadness the passage of time would never be able to erase. The pain within them couldn't be masked. Neither tried to hide their suffering. For the first time, he noticed the severe bruises on her face and the deep scratch marks up and down her arms.

The attack by the skinheads had done more than damage her soul.

She stared at the horizon. In the distance, a dozen wafting trails of smoke were visible in the east. She turned and looked at him with a puzzled expression on her face.

"Why?"

"Why what, ma'am?"

"As long as we're by ourselves, please call me Beth, if that's okay with you."

"All right, Beth. Why what?"

She stared again at the distant smoke.

"Why did all this happen?"

The smile left his face. He weighed his answer carefully.

"Beth, before a few days ago, I'd never concerned myself with such things. For twenty-four years, I've done nothing but prepare myself and others to kill their fellow man. That was my job, and I did it the best I could without giving it a second thought. But locked in my own private prison these past four days, I've had lots of time to think. And there's only one conclusion I can reach."

"What's that?"

"That the reason this happened is because man's the lowest form of life on this pitiful planet."

She gave him a surprised look. "What do you mean?"

"What I mean is, man's the only creature on this spinning blue globe that kills for no reason. Only man kills for the sport of it. Only man kills for the perverse pleasure it brings him. No other form of life spends so much time plotting how to murder its own kind. Only man is so despicable and so vile. Look at what we've done here in the past five days. The cruelty and violence of mankind's fragile existence cannot be denied."

Morse paused for a moment as she took in his words. "When will it end?" she asked. She quickly changed her question. "Will it ever end?"

"Yes. It will end."

"When?"

The sorrow of his newfound discovery appeared in his emotionless eyes and filled the corners of his mouth.

"When the last man kills the next-to-last man."

His brutal insight stunned her. She fumbled for a response but was unable to form the words. They each realized there was nothing more for either to say. After what had happened, the truth of Jensen's revelation couldn't be denied. And the strong bond between them needed no further expression. Both stared at the peaceful landscape that surrounded them. Filled with the beauty of winter, the German hills and forests were magnificent and serene. For nearly an hour, they silently lounged in this idyllic world. A warming sun in a cloudless sky shone down upon their backs. A flock of tiny snowbirds joined them. The brown birds danced upon the sunlight, frolicking on the winds and rejoicing in the sun's promise of better days to come.

Only once was their peace broken when a stretching line of ambulances departed for Sembach. Jensen and Morse smiled again as they watched the vehicles pass. In three hours, it would be their turn to board those same ambulances for a final German journey. In five hours, they'd be winging over the Atlantic. By this time tomorrow, Robert Jensen would be in his wife's arms in a San Antonio hospital. He was certain he'd already be frustrated with the antics of his teenage daughters.

After a month's separation, there'd be much catching up to do. He understood his world would never again be whole. For he could never escape the vivid nightmares of the past five days. But with Linda, he'd find his solace. He'd quietly live out his remaining years with the woman he loved. They'd grow old together. And he knew he'd never once speak of the horrors he'd witnessed in the snowbound fields of Germany.

The pair's unspoiled hour in the sun continued to slowly pass. While they basked in its glow, the old sergeant and the pretty nurse were overwhelmed by the simple pleasure of spending time lost in their own thoughts. In some ways, neither had ever felt better than this in their entire life. Neither was more at peace than they were at this instant. Their contentment was complete.

Each knew that no matter how much longer they lived, they'd probably never experience a better moment than this one.

"Don't we need to be heading back soon?" he asked, breaking the long silence.

"Oh, it's just so pleasant out here. If you think you can handle it, let's stay for a few minutes more."

While the Russians waited to cross the Rhine, waves of attack helicopters swooped in over the American-held section of Germany west of the historic river. There remained few effective fighting units in the portion to the rear. Even so, Kaiserslautern and Landstuhl had to be eliminated. There were too many Americans in those areas, and the Russian leadership had no more patience. The fifth day was near its close. And Comrade Cheninko wanted it to end. Completely unaware that the American plan to stymie his every action was unfolding, General Yovanovich reluctantly complied with the brutal dictator's demands.

As they reached the attack corridor, the nozzles on the helicopter's stubby wings began spraying droplets of an odorless, clear liquid upon an unforgiving planet.

Relaxing on the hospital's hillside, Robert Jensen saw the helicopters approaching. He initially didn't react. For a moment, he believed it was another of the endless flights of Black Hawks bringing in American wounded. Too late, his freshly seeing eyes realized their mistake.

The Hinds were drawing near.

He twisted in his wheelchair to look at Morse's beautiful face.

"Run!" he screamed.

She didn't understand what he was trying to tell her. She sat frozen beside him. Confusion spread across her face at his sudden panic.

"Run! Those are Russian helicopters, and they're spraying chemical weapons! Run now! Get inside as fast as you can!"

She leaped up and reached for the wheelchair's handles.

"It's too late. You'll never make it if you try to take me with you."

"No, I can't leave you here."

"Forget about me. It's too far back to the building. You'll never get up the hill fast enough pushing this contraption. Get inside and run as far into the building as you can. Do it now! Run!"

She hesitated, but when she saw the look in his eyes, she turned and started running toward the hospital. Her flowing hair trailed after her as she raced up the gentle slope. While she ran, she looked back at him. He hadn't taken his eyes from her.

The spraying helicopters were right on top of him.

He could feel the droplets falling onto his exposed skin. He knew it would be over soon. Still, he continued to encourage her progress.

Fifty yards from the nearest building, she stumbled and fell. She looked back. There was disappointment in Jensen's eyes. The helicopters were on her in seconds. Their nozzles continued spraying while passing over her and heading toward the hospital complex.

Jensen pitched forward from his chair. He fell upon the damp ground. He lay with his back to her on the wet grasses. Both their bodies began to tremble and twitch uncontrollably.

Inside the hospital, the seeping gases found a further home for its lethal poisons. In another hour, over the Atlantic, most of the medevac flights would turn around and head back to America. They weren't going to be needed. There'd be few survivors remaining to pick up.

In a brief handful of painful seconds, Robert Jensen and Elizabeth Morse twitched no more.

Above him on the small hill, the beautiful lieutenant lay. Her limbs were distorted by the severe convulsions of her sudden death. Her sweet eyes were open wide, staring out but seeing nothing. Her face, turned toward the east, was filled with an overwhelming sadness.

He lay where he'd fallen toward the bottom of the hill, with only the flock of dead snowbirds to keep him company. The old soldier, responsible for the first American victory of the great war, would also see no more.

His face was as calm as a quiet spring morning.

He'd had his final hour in the sun.

CHAPTER 63

February 2—6:00 p.m.
Delta Troop, 1st Battalion, 12th Cavalry Regiment, 3rd
   Brigade Combat Team (Greywolf), 1st Cavalry Division
Bitburg

In the early-evening darkness, the aircraft convoy touched down at the former American air base. With only a few widespread landing lights to guide them, one after another the fifteen planes arrived. The first to land was the Delta Airlines 767 carrying 275 soldiers. Five C-5s, sheltering tanks within their holds, were directly behind. Three FedEx and two UPS cargo planes were next. A C-17 filled with large military trucks followed. The final three in the stretching procession were also C-5s. The minute they were safely down, the landing lights were extinguished.

They were all soon moving onto the tarmac. Before their jet engines stopped, air-base ground personnel swiftly moved to support the massive fleet. As the soldiers deplaned, many joined the airmen in beginning to unload their lethal cargo. Others began assembling and arming their units' weapons. There was frantic but controlled action everywhere. Everyone knew their role.

Fuel trucks were sliding up to the planes and beginning their task. Within minutes, nearly a thousand hands were working as one.

Apaches and Black Hawks were being readied, their rotors and wheels hurriedly attached. In no time at all, a first was armed and moving skyward to support the air police guarding the perimeter.

M-1s with freshly loaded cannon shells, machine-gun cartridges, and full gasoline tanks were roaring to life. Humvees and hand grenades, bandages and bullets, machine guns and mortars, all left the planes. The list was nearly without end.

As each aircraft was emptied, dependents were being led out and loaded onto them without delay. Given what had happened to those waiting at Ramstein yesterday for the chance to return home, not one complained about being crammed onto the unyielding floor of a C-5 for the very long, torturous ride to safety.

As the airmen and soldiers worked, six F-16s landed.

Crews hurriedly went about the process of refueling and arming the fighter aircraft.

Minutes later, a second aerial circus landed at Hahn, with two companies of Bradley Fighting Vehicles.

A quarter hour after that, Zweibrucken received its first soaring fleet.

The process was soon completed at each location.

The tank company, its supporting infantry, mortar teams, and helicopters headed east from Bitburg toward the Rhine.

As they did, the patchwork airborne convoy returned to the runway filled with anxious souls headed for home. In less than two days, these same planes would return anew filled with another critical load.

It was a scene that would be repeated over and over in the coming hours.

The Americans were on the move.

As the newly arriving cavalry soldiers steeled themselves for battle, little could they know that this ill-fated war was going to end much sooner than any of them could ever have imagined.

CHAPTER 64

Valexi Yovanovich stood before Cheninko's desk. A few steps behind the Director of Operations waited the highly talented general's second-in-command, Antonin Zulin. The Russian Premier, his impatience showing, glared at them.

None was aware that fresh American armored forces had been reaching the Rhine for the past few hours. Or that many more were on the way. They'd no idea their every move in the venomous game had been countered by their apt adversary. In many ways, with what Yovanovich had planned on this evening, it really didn't matter.

Cheninko remained ruthlessly certain that on this night he'd have his final revenge on the Germans. He continued to believe that the annihilation of Germany and their domination over it for decades to come was all but assured. Despite what Yovanovich had told him, even if the Americans counterattacked in the coming weeks, Mother Russia would prevail.

"Why hasn't the second wave of bridging equipment arrived at the Rhine, Yovanovich?" There was unmistakable malice in Cheninko's voice. "Are you intentionally delaying the construction of the bridges and the crossing of the river? Because if you are, Comrade General, you'll leave me with just one choice. Your actions can only lead to a place you do not wish to see."

Cheninko looked toward the window where he'd stood witnessing countless executions. There could be no mistaking his meaning.

"Comrade Premier," Yovanovich said, "we thought we'd have little problem breaching the river. With Ramstein destroyed, we hadn't anticipated our enemy's mounting such an aggressive defense. Despite our MiGs' efforts to support them, nearly every attempt we've made to complete the spans and begin our crossings has been met by a brutal aerial assault. And much to our surprise, the handfuls of units that have reached the other side have found determined ground forces waiting for them. It's as if the Americans know exactly what we are doing. The new bridging equipment is on the way. Our combat engineers are, however, facing severe difficulties. There are few remaining roads on our side of the Rhine, and each of those is littered with untold obstacles. Even so, there will be enough equipment at each of the fording points to construct multiple crossings within the next twelve hours. We're going to commit every fighter aircraft we have to making sure we succeed."

George O'Neill's plan to use the fully functioning AWACS ground stations to provide instantaneous data to every level of American forces over the highly functioning command and control system had worked to perfection. The Russians had been thwarted at the Rhine long enough for the Americans to implement their deft actions and eventually emerge victorious. General Yovanovich didn't know how or why, but he had been checkmated.

"Twelve hours, Yovanovich? We won't cross the Rhine for another twelve hours? Such is beyond comprehension. I don't wish to wait even five minutes more before we begin the final stages of our glorious victory. This war is to reach its conclusion now."

"Even with the delays, Comrade Premier, I promise you it will draw to a close shortly. Once the bridges are in place, we'll be able to move multiple divisions to the far bank in no time. We'll then attack with everything we've got. Our actions will be swift and decisive. There'll be scant resistance when we reach the western shore. The remaining Americans are few in number and widely scattered. They'll be not much more than a trifling annoyance. We'll brush them away with relative ease. By this time tomorrow, all of Germany will be in our hands."

"This time tomorrow? You're asking me to wait for another day, Yovanovich? Impossible . . . just impossible. Your five days is up. Do as I order, or the consequences will be exacted swiftly and without mercy. What I want isn't open for further consideration. There'll be no more excuses. We'll finish our conquest directly. This will end well before the sun rises. Am I making myself clear?"

"Quite clear. But how do you propose we accomplish such an unachievable undertaking?"

"Swim our armored vehicles across the Rhine. Attack with everything we've got within the hour. Finish off the Americans. We'll control all of Germany before the day breaks, or you'll bear the burden for your failure."

"But Comrade Premier, the river's quite wide and its icy flows unforgiving. It's the middle of the night in the middle of winter. The frigid waters will swamp our tanks as they struggle against the brutal currents. Our men will stand no chance of surviving such intolerable conditions in total darkness. Their deaths will be agonizingly swift and certain. The bitter elements will devour them. Thousands will die. We'll lose over 60 percent of our attacking force before we reach the far embankments."

"Then send those who are dying of radiation poisoning. They're of no use to us anyway. After they gain a foothold and the chaos lessens, swim the remainder of our units to the western side."

Yovanovich hesitated ever so slightly. The die, however, had been forever cast. There was no other option. He would most certainly not follow such an outrageous command.

There could be no turning back. It was time to put an end to the madness.

"No, Comrade Premier. I'll do no such thing."

For the briefest of moments, Cheninko took in Yovanovich's pronouncement. He looked at his general with utter disbelief. A fraction of a second later, he leaped from his chair. Rage filled every measure of his being. His anger knew no bounds. The Russian dictator's face turned a bright shade of red. His clenched hands visibly trembled. He slammed his fist against the desktop. Not once had anyone said no to him in the past six years. And he'd every intention of making sure it never happened again.

"What did you say, Comrade General?"

Yovanovich stood his ground. "I'll not issue such a contemptible order. I won't needlessly send men to their deaths in the Rhine's foreboding waters."

Cheninko could scarcely contain himself. "Do you understand what you've done?"

"I understand quite well, Comrade Premier. Even so, I'll never give our soldiers such a vile command. I'll not further blacken my soul."

"Then you leave me no choice. Colonel Zulin, go out into the hallway and get my bodyguards. Tell them they're to arrest General Yovanovich and prepare the courtyard for immediate use. Once you finish, you are to communicate my directive for our forward units to begin crossing the Rhine at once. Tell them to send those who are dying first."

"Yes, Comrade Premier."

Zulin turned and headed out the doorway. It closed behind him.

Ten . . . fifteen . . . twenty interminable seconds passed. The powerful Yovanovich could have reached across the desk and easily snapped Cheninko's feckless neck if he'd so wanted. But that wasn't part of the plan.

The door reopened. Colonel Zulin entered with his pistol drawn. Behind him were six soldiers, each with weapons at the ready.

Zulin stopped in the middle of the room. The armed men spread out behind him.

"The men of the firing squad are present, Comrade Premier. I'll conduct the execution personally."

Cheninko looked at the soldiers. "Where are my guards?" He instantly recognized the Director of Operations symbol on the soldiers' uniforms.

"These men have volunteered to carry out the sentence," Zulin said.

A smile came to Cheninko's face. "I thought your men loved you, Yovanovich. But obviously I was mistaken. Here they are, standing with their weapons at the ready, eager to participate in your demise."

"Oh, they're not here for me, Comrade Premier," Yovanovich said after pausing for effect.

This time it was the general who smiled.

It took little more than a fleeting breath for Cheninko to recognize the implications of the fateful pronouncement. The shock on his face was sudden and complete.

"Take him to the courtyard," Zulin said, the loathing in his words quite evident.

He motioned for his men to seize Cheninko. A pair of soldiers hurriedly crossed the room. Strong hands grasped the ruthless dictator and began dragging his struggling form toward the doorway. Another pair moved to take up positions in front of them. The final two settled in behind.

Cheninko, his resistance against those who held him futile, started yelling at the top of his lungs. "Guards! Guards! Stop them. Kill them all."

Yet no one appeared to defend the country's maniacal tyrant.

"Get him ready," Zulin said. "I'll meet you in the courtyard shortly."

The six nodded their understanding.

When they reached the hallway, Cheninko expected to find his bodyguards preparing to counterattack those attempting such a heinous crime. But the guard positions had been abandoned. No one appeared in the empty corridor to challenge Yovanovich's men as they dragged their stunned captive toward the courtyard.

The instant Cheninko left the office, the new Russian leader was born. Valexi Yovanovich settled in behind the Premier's desk. He looked up at Colonel Zulin. "Be quick about it before the Kremlin guards have a change of heart. Once you're finished, you need to return immediately. Issue the order for all of our forces to conduct a unilateral cease-fire. They're only to return fire if fired upon. After that, I want you to prepare a communiqué under my signature for the American President. Inform him that Comrade Cheninko's dead, and I've taken charge of the Russian military and the Russian people. Let him know that if he accepts our terms, the killing is at an end."

"Yes, Comrade Premier," Zulin said. "What is it we wish from the Americans?"

"Our conditions are simple. Join us in the cease-fire at once. Allow us to withdraw without interference and promise not to cross the fences when they reach the eastern edge of Germany. If they're willing to comply with what we ask, this war is over."

"It will be done, Comrade Premier."

"Then take care of our unfinished business in the courtyard, and let's put a stop to this. When they're through with Cheninko, I want our men to scrub the wall clean. There are to be no reminders of the perversions that occurred there during the past six years."

Colonel Zulin came to attention, saluted, and hurriedly left the Premier's office.

Unlike Cheninko before him, Yovanovich took no pleasure in ending a life. Even if it was a life as corrupt as this one. He wouldn't demean himself by standing at the window. Instead, he immediately focused his attention on the myriad problems his country now faced.

Minutes later, the sound of automatic gunfire echoed in the yard below. Yovanovich scarcely paused as the ringing sound sang out.

This would be the last execution the courtyard would ever see.

For over three decades, Valexi Yovanovich would rule his nation. He would make plenty of mistakes along the way. Yet compared to those who'd led Russia before him, his reign would be one filled with enlightenment and hope for his people. He'd seen the corruption of absolute power, and he wouldn't allow its sweet allure to entice him.

Far in the future, he would die a quiet death while sleeping in his bed.

His Deputy Premier, Antonin Zulin, having learned much from the man he followed, would continue to bring peace and prosperity to his country for many years after Yovanovich's passing.

CHAPTER 65

February 9—9:14 a.m.
3rd Platoon, Delta Troop, 1st Battalion, 12th Cavalry
   Regiment, 3rd Brigade Combat Team (Greywolf), 1st
   Cavalry Division
The Rhine River

As agreed, the Americans allowed seven days for the invaders to leave Germany.

The entire 1st Cavalry and most of the arriving 4th Infantry waited on the western side of the Rhine for the cease-fire to end. Even with the truce, the Americans had no idea if they could trust the new Russian Premier to keep his word. With a million of his soldiers inside Germany at the war's end, the Americans had continued with their frenetic pace to bring both divisions to the battlefield.

The moment the time elapsed, an initial 1st Cavalry platoon headed into the heart of Germany. Thousands of their countrymen soon followed.

On the temporary bridges their engineers had constructed, they crossed the Rhine's flowing waters and moved ever deeper into Germany. With devastation and destruction at every turn, it would take the lead elements ten days to reach the eastern border. On the way, they saw incalculable numbers of Russian soldiers. None, however, was still breathing. Whenever they found the body of a fallen American, they'd stop and mark the remains for the graves-registration teams that would follow. It would take some time, but most of America's dead would eventually find their way home.

When they reached the German border with Poland and the Czech Republic, they stopped. The President had decided there would be no more killing. He'd promised that his soldiers would go no farther. It was a promise he'd keep. The Americans would dig in and rebuild their defensive positions. Their first task would be to reconstruct the fences the Russians had destroyed. New guard towers would soon follow. The border's bleak images would stand for decades to come as a vivid admonition of just how far man remained from truly learning the lessons from his five days of abject folly.

The damaged building where Robert Jensen and his platoon had lived during their challenging months at the border was soon repaired and occupied by the 1st Cavalry. The constant vigil that had become a way of life in this starkly somber place would commence once again.

The war was over, but it would take much, much more for the peace to be won.

EPILOGUE

Conceived in the final fleeting moments his parents shared before their crushing separation, George O'Neill Jr. was born on a late-October afternoon as the first brief snowfall of the year sprinkled itself upon the expansive farmland of western Minnesota.

The birth had been an exceptionally difficult one, for his mother's injuries were still quite severe. Giving birth in her condition had been highly dangerous. The doctors had urged her to consider terminating the pregnancy, but Kathy wouldn't hear of it. She'd already lost a daughter and nearly her first son. She couldn't contemplate losing another child.

With unwavering determination, Kathy survived the perilous ordeal. And a healthy child had entered the world. With his arrival, her battered spirit was partially restored.

Her shattered body, however, would never return to anything nearing its prewar state. The doctors had performed the best they could, but with the extensive trauma she'd suffered, they'd only been able to do so much. For the rest of her life, she'd carry deep scars from her fateful German days.

Her children would never know her as anything but stooped and broken. But that mattered little to the resolute young woman. She was alive. She was loved. And for the moment, there was cause to celebrate her new son's appearance.

His father wasn't there for the child's birth. George O'Neill remained more than four thousand miles away from his family and the woman he adored. Kathy hadn't seen him since their hurried, tearful good-bye on the second-floor landing.

Even though his enlistment had ended three months earlier, the Army had involuntarily extended his term of service. He was back at Patch Barracks working eighteen-hour days to help create a new American command and control system. Given ample time and significant resources, he'd build one nearly invulnerable to attacks from any source. With his efforts, such a system was slowly taking form.

He understood that what he was doing was quite important, but without Kathy at his side, his life had little meaning. When the interminable days in Stuttgart would end and his country would allow him to return home was as yet undetermined.

O'Neill would receive not a moment's recognition for his efforts during the war. But he never once cared. In his mind, he'd done nothing but what was asked of him. How the war would have ended without his contributions was something he never gave even a passing thought. Only a small number of people were even aware of the difference he'd made during the horrid conflict.

For the remainder of his life, he'd never speak a single word about it. Not even Kathy would know what he'd accomplished in one of his country's darkest moments.

He missed his family dearly. And Kathy felt each tortured hour without him. Both longed for the moment they'd be one again.

He contacted her whenever he could. Still, he had little time and even less energy to do anything but send an occasional e-mail. Kathy eagerly devoured each sporadic message a hundred times over. All were read again and again, with every new reading bringing her both sorrow and joy.

There were even a few deeply cherished phone calls on those rare occasions when he could find the time.

He was aware she'd been severely wounded but had yet to completely comprehend the magnitude of her injuries.

He knew his son was on the way.

A few hours after little Georgie, as the family would call him, had arrived, his proud father received the welcome news of his birth. The eagerly awaited e-mail made his longing for Kathy almost more than he could bear.

The days were without end for them both.

Kathy's mother put the final touches on the precocious child's first birthday cake. She looked at her handiwork with self-assured satisfaction. No one could deny her ability to create a beautiful cake. She knew it would taste as good as it looked.

She walked into the living room. Her daughter was propped in a chair, watching the boys play.

"Kathy, the weather's going to turn quite bitter in another couple of days. Before it does and winter sets in, why don't we put on the boys' jackets and take them out in the yard?"

"What about Georgie's cake?"

"It can wait for a few minutes more. We'll start his party after we're done outside."

"Okay, Mom."

Her mother began helping her to her feet and slowly moving her toward the doorway.

A warmly bundled Kathy sat in a rocking chair on the comfy farmhouse's front porch. She was enjoying the fleeting warmth of a fading fall sun while she watched her mother play with the boys.

Three-year-old Christopher, his energy boundless, ran to every corner at breakneck speed. His younger brother, his first toddling steps just days old, did his best in a futile attempt to be a part of the game. Their grandmother chased after them, enjoying each moment of her time with the children.

Kathy's mother suddenly stopped, her senses telling her something wasn't quite right. Out of the corner of her eye, she spotted the reason for her sudden alarm. She peered down the lengthy drive leading to the highway, staring intently at a distant figure walking up the farm's dirt road toward them.

Kathy soon noticed her mother's gaze. She stopped rocking, puzzled by her sudden actions. She looked up to see what it was that had attracted her mother's attention.

Someone was coming toward the house. From the person's size and gait, it was obviously a man. He was, however, still too far away for either of them to determine much more. The figure continued unerringly down the stretching path, his progress steady. His features slowly took form.

Both mother and daughter could just make out that his hair was dark. The gangly form appeared to have a duffel bag, or something of the sort, slung over his shoulder. Step by solitary step, he neared.

The seconds passed.

A growing smile slowly crept onto the corners of Kathy's mouth. It soon seized her soul. It had been twenty-one months since she'd last seen her husband. But there could be little doubt. Their wretched time apart was at its end. The celebration they'd soon have would be a glorious one.

For the first time in nearly two years, her pain disappeared.

"George!" she screamed.

At the exact moment of George O'Neill's arrival in Minnesota, on a porch nearly a thousand miles south, Linda Jensen knelt with her daughters. She'd planned on sharing the modest home with her husband for the remainder of their days. But as it had been for far too many who'd found themselves in the grips of this vicious struggle, the fates hadn't been kind.

She silently prayed her husband's sacrifices hadn't been in vain. She pleaded with her God to somehow show the way for mankind to learn the lessons of its five evil days.

She begged Him in His mercy to provide humanity with the compelling wisdom to never again contemplate the need for war.

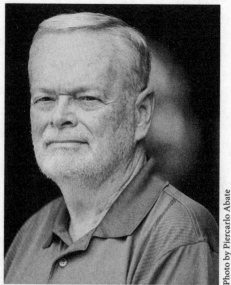

Photo by Piercarlo Abate

Walt Gragg lives in the Austin, Texas, area with his wife, children, and grandchildren. He is a retired attorney. Prior to law school, he spent a number of years in the military. His time with the Army involved many interesting assignments, including three years in the middle of the Cold War at the United States European Command Headquarters in Germany, where the idea for *The Red Line* took shape. In this assignment, he was privy to many of the elements of the actual American plan in place at the time for the conduct of the defense of Germany. While there, he also participated in a number of war games that became the basis for many of the book's events. *The Red Line* is his first novel.

EAST ORANGE PUBLIC LIBRARY

3 2665 0045 6198 3

DISCARD